Fi

Book 2 of The Fallen Arcana

Jared Bennett

Enjoy!

This is a work of fiction. Names, character, places, and events are products of the author's imagination.

Copyright © 2015 Jared Bennett
All rights reserved.

No Part of this book may be reproduced, or stored in a retrieval system, or transmitted in any form or by any means, electronic, mechanical, photocopying, recording or otherwise, without express written permission of the Author.

Amazon and the Amazon logo are trademarks of Amazon.com, Inc., or its affiliates.

ISBN-13: 978-1515232247

ISBN-10:1515232247

Edited by Michael Adams and Shelley's Editing Service, www.facebook.com/pages/Shelleys-Editing-Service/
Cover Art by Cosme Lucero, **www.cosmelucero.com**

I'd like to take a quick moment to thank a few people.

I'd first like to thank my wife, for supporting me in this hobby, even though it hasn't brought much back. She is also responsible for the text work on the cover and for formatting it to fit Amazon's requirements.

My artist, Cosme Lucero, for the custom image he created for this book.

My editors, Shelley's Editing Service and Mike for giving me feedback and fixing the MASSIVE amounts of grammar, spelling and tone errors in the work. (And that one word I used 2987 times)

And I'd like to thank my test readers for reading the various versions of the story and giving me their insight into how they think it went.

And last I'd like thank all of you for sticking with me on this long (longer than I wanted!) journey and I hope you enjoy the second book!

Prologue: Fire's Fall

The light from her torch flickered slightly in the harbor breeze. The nights had grown colder in the past few weeks, lending to a change in the winds. Tonight promised to be the coldest so far.

She pulled her cloak tightly about herself as her escort moved to open the warehouse door for her. It was necessary to meet the Falcree here over the church, there were far too many parishioners still loyal to the Harpies within the halls of Betala and they would be sure to report back to Ezra if she were to meet the Falcree publicly.

She wished she had met with the other tribes before they fell. She regretted not being able to safeguard them as she sought to do with the Falcree now, but they had fallen too quickly for her to act. The Ospa were wiped out in less than a week and the Egla soon after. Ezra's son had made a name for himself by slaughtering them.

"Are you sure you want to go through with this, Ardelle?" Her guard, Mancel asked. "It's not too late to go back, no one has seen us here."

"Krelmer and the Just have already broken the siege, if I can break Barrah's punishment then the Falcree stand a chance against Ezra." His face fell but he nodded in agreement.

It had been weeks since the Just had broken the back of the army arrayed against the Falcree, but the Harpies still assaulted their cousins. Ezra, and the abomination she called a son, attacked any Falcree, Ospa or Egla they could find. The latter two tribes were nearly extinct as it was, theirs were the first to be besieged by the monstrosity that was Drech.

She passed her torch to Mancel as they stepped into the large, dimly lit central chamber of the warehouse. Row upon row of old crates littered the space, but an area near the back of the building had been cleared to act as their council chamber. She had met King Gavyn of the Falcree many times before, but it had always been in an official capacity. To see him here, dressed in his battle attire, was a sight she wasn't likely to forget.

A shining steel breastplate covered his chest down to his waist, though she knew it wouldn't have a back to allow for his great wings. Greaves to match bedecked his legs and even his talons had been covered with steel. Twin blades hung from his hips, a strange sight for one of their race as they preferred the reach a spear or polearm gave them, but in these tight quarters the swords would serve better. His wings were folded back to hang about his body like a thick cloak of feathers. He cut a magnificent figure, especially as the light from her torch reflected from his armor. Had she been anyone else, his chiseled features would have set her heart racing, but she was above such desires. Her mistress needed the Falcree, Ardelle couldn't spare any time fawning over their leader.

"Mistress," Gavyn uttered before dropping into a low bow, far lower than convention dictated. "The sight of you brings me great hope, have you thought on our plight?"

"I have, and I believe I can help," Ardelle drew out a worn scroll from a pocket within her cloak. "Priests and their parishes are protected by their Avatar's guidance under some of the oldest articles ever written. If your people were to swear themselves to the church, I can use Betala's influence to protect you from the curse Barrah has placed on you. Since you are their king, you can speak for them in this matter."

"If I do this, will my people be subject to the church? Am I trading one enslavement for another?" Gavyn asked gravely.

Ardelle had expected this response. "No. As Avatar, I am head of the church, so you swear to me and I induct you as your own branch beholden only to me. The rest of the church has no say in your governance and I have no desire to rule."

Tears welled at the corners of Gavyn's eyes. "It is as they say. You are as wise as you are beautiful."

She forced the blush from her face, "you flatter me sire. We must do this soon, will you need to speak to your people?"

"No, they were all prepared for whatever you had for us. The Just drove the Harpies back, but I fear it may have been too late." He sighed and stared at the ceiling, "if you had told me ten years ago that this would happen, I would have laughed in your face. We've lost all but Oryol, the other cities have all been destroyed or abandoned. Roslayl was taken in a freak storm just last week. We're a dying people."

She led the king through the rituals that would complete the church's protection. It was a complicated spell, but she could see the weight of Barrah's punishment lift from Gavyn's shoulders as it completed. The curse was gone, Barrah no longer controlled their destiny.

Gavyn turned to embrace her, but a blinding light drove them both to the floor. Thunder followed the flash, causing Ardelle to throw her hands over her ears.

"You dare defy me?!" a voice not of this world echoed through the warehouse. Barrah had discovered her. "Betala's bitch seeks to control the Arcana?" The sound of marching broke through the ringing in her ears, "that was your last mistake."

Men in grey cloaks seized her arms and lifted her from the floor. They bound her hands behind her and used some form of magic to prevent her from reaching her gift. Gavyn was largely ignored, though one of them delivered a vicious kick to the Falcree's head when Gavyn attempted to stop them from taking her. Mancel stirred as they neared the door but one of the men grabbed him by the hair and unceremoniously slit his throat.

She tried to call out, but a gag was forced into her mouth.

They dragged her to a carriage and drove her deeper into the city. Krossfarin slept as the minions of Barrah took her to face his judgment.

Falderal

"Charles!" Ardelle shouted to the small man crouched in the ruins of a house. "Get out of there!" She let loose another torrent of flames to distract the swarming demons. Her sword had been useless in their first few encounters, it barely scratched the things that chased them. Even her fire seemed subdued when it collided with their skin. Another burst of flame erupted from her left, black as pitch. She dropped low to avoid it, but her sleeve didn't clear fast enough. The hungry flames licked up her arm but didn't touch the skin beneath her clothes. Betala's gifts still held. Heat wouldn't be a problem, but the black fire wasn't a normal flame. If she didn't stop it, it would start to tear at her magic and pull it away from her.

Charles leapt to action when he saw her plight. With a flourish, he sent a wave of energy into the heart of the flames on her arm and snuffed them out. His sword was back in his hand, but she knew that it would do little good when it came right down to it. He could barely keep from stabbing himself with the weapon when he had tried to use it in their few practice sessions. It seemed to comfort him, so she ignored it.

They had left the cliff nearly a week ago, traveling cross-country to reach the city they were now attempting to flee. They were following the last spell Charles had cast to find his master. It was a cold lead, but they had nothing else to go on.

The small creature, Scritch, left them after about a day afield. A gust of wind carried it far from them and it had never returned. Charles had been shaken by the disappearance, but didn't dwell on it for long. A few silent tears when the creature didn't answer his calls and the occasional look into the horizon were the only indication that he had missed Scritch at all, though she expected he harbored deeper loss. With Aurin gone and now his only other companion missing, she knew his loneliness must be unbearable. She had tried to make him more comfortable, but he kept her at arm's length. She expected that he didn't want to grow close to her and have her leave. He had experienced so much loss in such a short life, she couldn't really fault him.

They had reached Falderal the day before, but decided to camp outside and wait for daybreak before entering. She regretted not waiting a second day. If she had taken the time to study the city, she would have seen the obvious signs of the Demons presence. Thankfully, their Harpy allies hadn't joined the fray. It was a small measure of relief, given that they were facing nearly one hundred of the purple skinned goat-men.

The building that Charles just vacated erupted into a shower of splinters and rubble. Ardelle threw up a column of flames to stop the larger pieces, but she couldn't stop everything. Shrapnel reached her and Charles, causing them to stumble in the presence of their pursuers. She could see the edge of the ruins, but those last fifty strides may as well have been fifty leagues. Without Charles' full magic, they weren't going to break through the lines of demons.

"Charles!" she screamed. "We're trapped!" She stabbed her finger toward the demons that had moved to cut them off.

The color drained from his face. "I'm sorry." After a brief moment, his eyes lit up and he turned toward the south, the only direction not closed to them. "Teleportation!" He shouted, then tore off down the street, leaving her alone.

She dashed after him, sending another burst of fire toward the demons that were barreling through the ruined house. They ran toward the center of the ruins, toward the tallest of the fallen spires. "Charles! That's further into the city, we need to get out!"

"Trust me!" He shouted back to her, speeding up as he crossed the cracked pavement.

Ardelle hadn't known him for long, but from a young man like Charles, 'Trust me' usually meant he was about to do something foolish. She had little choice but to follow him, the demons had closed the small opening they had had in the street behind them and were chewing up the distance between them. Even at a top speed, they had little chance of out pacing the creatures rushing along the torn streets. Their goat-like hooves seemed ideal for sprinting in this environment. She sent more fire after them, but each blast seemed less effective.

Charles bolted into the yawning archway at the base of the central tower of what used to be the college of Wizards. As she crossed the threshold behind him, she witnessed a strange event. The demons instantly stopped their pursuit. Something about the tower caused them to turn and flee back the way they had come. She didn't want to think what that something could be, anything that had that kind of effect on the nearly invincible demons was not something she wanted to cross.

Charles had disappeared into the darkness to her right, down the curving hall that circled the outside of the tower. She lost him momentarily until a sphere of red light sprang to life ahead of her. "We shouldn't be in here," she whispered harshly when she finally caught him. "Those demons wouldn't even cross the threshold."

"Good," he replied cheerfully. "We are safe then."

She shook her head. "I don't think you understand. They were afraid of this place." She kept her voice low, even if he didn't. "If there is something in here scarier than them, I don't want to find it."

"We won't be here long." He assured her, but she wasn't convinced.

Ardelle had been in the tower in its grandeur, nearly two hundred years ago, sent for a meeting with Ven's avatar. It had been one of her first tasks as Betala's mortal form, and would always stick with her. Ven's avatar was an arrogant man, chosen from the ranks of the powerful Wizards for his prowess with ritual magic. When Ven wasn't with him, he flaunted his power and the authority being an avatar granted him over his fellow Wizards. The meeting hadn't gone well, and it had soured her on all future dealings with the Wizards. The man had strongly come on to her and when she had rebuffed him, he dismissed her outright and refused any further dealings with the church of Betala. Her mistress had intervened directly, which of course soured things even further for Ardelle and Ven's avatar. She couldn't remember his name, but the experience would always be one she regretted.

"The circles are in one of these rooms, we just need to find one that is still active." Charles told her.

She assumed he was referring to the teleportation circles the Wizards had used to connect their colleges all over the world. It had been a marvel in its time, but after so many years of neglect, she had doubts they would find an active circle. The other colleges would have been quick to cut ties to this one, given its fall to the demons. "Please keep your voice down," she insisted.

Charles huffed, prying at one of the doors with his sword. Her master would have boxed his ears for such an offense, but she knew he was ignorant to the ways of the blade. The sword he carried was heavily enchanted, which meant there was little he could do to harm it. She let it slide for now, but she would educate him later, if they survived.

The door finally gave in to his ministrations, but not quietly. Groaning, the swollen timbers swung out into the hall where they were standing. A chorus of shrieks sounded from deeper in the tower, followed by the ominous thumping of wings. Her fears were confirmed when the first chestnut feathered Harpy rounded the corner behind them, hurling a ball of magical fire straight for them.

Charles dove for the cover into the room, but Ardelle merely raised her hand and redirected the flames into the wall next to her. The Harpies may have been masters of fire, but Betala still held dominion over it. Using her own pool, she sent a searing ray of concentrated fire directly into the face of the creature, disintegrating its head in a spectacular burst of blue flames. It wasn't alone though, and the trailing creatures learned quickly. Rather than repeat their sister's mistake, they chose instead to dive directly for Ardelle and use their talons.

With another pull on her pool, Ardelle sent two more of the creatures to the same fate as the first, then followed Charles into the room. The door was a lost cause at this point, the third creature to fall had crashed into it and tore it free from the wall. Little remained inside to act as a barricade so she had to settle for a wall of flames. It wouldn't hold against a sustained attack, and likely wouldn't slow the Harpies if they were able to get a good run at it, but the contours of the hall were in her favor.

"Whatever you are going to do Charles, do it now," she growled as the first Harpy attempted to breach the flames.

"I don't recognize any of these symbols," he admitted. "We need to get to another room."

"Charles, there is no chance we are leaving this room through that door and there are no other doors out of here. Make one of these work, or we're dead." It was harsh, but now was not the time for coddling.

The scarlet radiance she associated with the mages sprang to life around him, though it wavered greatly, in no way did it compare to what she had seen him wield on that cliff the day they lost Aurin. Charles crouched over one of the runic circles and began to examine it. He studied the lines intently before shaking his head and hopping to the next. The Harpies were beginning to gather on the other side of her flames now, concentrating their magic, working to undo her spell. It wouldn't be long before they succeeded. While she had them all beat one on one, the more of them that joined in, the less the odds leaned in her favor. Ardelle strengthened her magic as much as she could, then stepped back to fire more rays into the mass of winged bodies that gathered just outside the room. She would never be able to kill enough to prevent them from breaching, but she may just be able to slow them long enough for Charles to get them out of here.

The second circle also proved to be unusable to Charles, as did the third. Only one remained and with it their last hope of escape. Charles' aura dimmed again as he set about analyzing the final rune, but he managed to hold onto the little magic he had left. He drew on the magic of his sword, clutching the hilt with his left hand as his right worked over the spell.

Her pool was nearly depleted, and if it failed they would have a horde of Harpies upon them. She knew that if she was to call on Betala, her mistress could bolster her energy and likely incinerate the Harpies, but she just couldn't bring herself to do it. After one hundred and fifty years of isolation, it was hard for her to think of calling on an Arcana that essentially abandoned her. True, it was no fault of Betala's that Ardelle was imprisoned, but her mistress also appeared to do nothing to help her. If Aurin hadn't stumbled across her, she would still be sniffing about for game in her wolf's body.

"Hurry Charles!" she begged. "I'm almost spent."

"I..." He started, his hands working over the runes furiously. "I just don't have enough..." He looked up at her, tears streaming down his face. The aura vanished from around him and he pitched forward into the dust, sobbing.

It was over. Ardelle couldn't keep them back much longer, and Charles had once again exhausted his pool. She settled into the dust next to him and pulled his head into her lap. He was unconscious, but was still breathing. She fought back stinging tears and prepared to make her last stand.

"I'm sorry Aurin," she whispered to the empty room. "I tried to keep him safe." She drew on the fires within her to make Charles' end swift. At least he wouldn't suffer.

"Enough!" A voice boomed from the hall and stayed Ardelle's hand. "Minerva! Call off your dogs and leave me, these two are mine."

The Harpies outside the wall of flames turned to the voice, some hissing their disapproval. One revolved toward the voice and spat. "We had them first, Wizard."

"Should we take it up with the master?" the voice demanded. "Or your queen? I'm sure they would love to make a decision on who has rights in MY tower."

The Harpies shrieked. "This isn't over," the leader wheezed, rising into the air. With the rest in tow, she flew out of sight.

A large, black-robed man stepped in front of the flames as the last Harpy vanished. "You may drop the flames, priestess. I am not here to harm you."

She could barely keep the fires burning, but still hesitated. "Why should I trust a man in league with those monsters?" she asked.

The man chuckled. "What choice do you have? Your magic is nearly gone, and this wall wouldn't stop me anyway. Let us start out with a small measure of trust, lower the wall. Draw your blade if you must, but if I wanted you dead, I would have let the Harpies have you."

She was loathe to admit it, but he was right. Charles was still cradled in her lap, so drawing her sword was awkward, but once the steel was naked, she dropped the flames. "What do you want?" she demanded.

"Honestly, I want to be free, but I've given up that hope." He reached for his hood and pulled it back from his face. He was an older man, the grey had mostly replaced the black within his hair. His face was creased with the lines of someone that had seen much in their life and his blue eyes held no luster. From his build, she guessed that he spent a good deal of time working with his hands, an odd trait for a Wizard. "Do you know me?" He asked her simply.

"No." she admitted.

"That is for the best, those that do know me seem to only come to harm." He looked at the sleeping Charles in her lap. "You need to get him out of here. He has an important task to perform and isn't ready yet. I will activate the circle, but I can't go with you." He indicated the last rune circle that Charles had tried to use. "Once you are through, I will be sealing this side so that he is not tempted to return. A day will come when he is ready to return here, but that day is not today." The man spoke in an odd prophetic way that left little doubt that he knew it would happen. She didn't understand any of it, but she was without choice.

"Where does the circle lead?" she asked, unsure how to respond to him.

"Heimli Alfa, the home of the Oberons. Once you are there, take Charles to Darl, he will know what to do from here." The man stepped to the circle and gestured with his right hand. With no visible sign that he had called on his magic, the runes flared to life. "The Oberons will likely have trouble believing you mean them no harm, this gate has been closed for sixteen years. Be sure to tell them you are looking for Darl, and that you carry Chavox with you. Darl will understand." The man turned to leave, stopping at the doorway. "Take care of him, priestess. I have wronged him in so many ways I could never hope for forgiveness, but I still care for him." The plea seemed odd.

 Charles stirred at Ardelle shifted towards the circle. "M...Master...?" He muttered as his eyes opened, but he quickly dipped back into unconsciousness as she pulled him to the circle.

Arrivals

Her thin nightgown clung to her birdlike frame in the evening heat. Her wings were still tucked in close, even though she was within her homeland. She had grown so accustomed to the human lands that she kept them back, even now. They did little to push the heat from her as they were, made it worse in fact, but she didn't stretch them out. She couldn't say what had woken her, but it wasn't the temperature. Casting about with her magic, she brushed up against a shield in her sitting room. Someone had entered her chambers, someone that didn't belong.

There had been no alarm from her guards, so whoever this was either subdued them, or found some way to circumvent them. Her power wasn't enough for her to distinguish between men on patrol and men unconscious, she only knew that they lived. She cast the thin tendril of magic about her in the shield she had used most of her life and drew herself up before the door. Unless she stepped into the sitting room, she wouldn't learn who it was.

She relaxed her wings from her back and reached for the handle. Her wings hung loosely, not sending them to their usual flutter, but keeping the ready should she need to escape quickly. Like most Oberon rooms, hers had a large open balcony that she could leap from, should the need arise. Taking a deep breath, she threw open the door and nearly shrieked at the man she saw there.

"Hello mother," the thin human whispered. "How have you been?"

"I've asked you not to call me that," she responded. "I have no children."

"Not yet," he smiled at her, "but you will."

"So you've told me. Why are you here?" She had met this man twice before, but his presence still upset her. He had come to her nearly a year ago with stories of a prophecy and an altered history, but she had sent him away without heeding his warnings. Then some weeks ago he had returned and informed her that her inaction had sped up their needs. She had sent him away again, but he had refused to leave. It was then that he informed her of his status and their future relationship. She had slapped him when he told her that he was her son, a half-breed with some human that she was destined to meet. It didn't deter him.

He spoke of the fallen Arcana and the man that was to stop him. He told her that her grandfather was destined to die in the coming battle, despite the power he held. He revealed that even now a massive army was being raised in the south, an army of monsters and demons long thought gone from the world. Drawing on his magic, he showed her visions of what the future would be if she didn't act, visions so horrible that they had never truly left her mind. She didn't sleep for nearly a week afterwards.

The visions had shown her a battle-worn man struggling against a creature that he couldn't possibly defeat, a creature that no man could ever hope to overcome. The man died in his struggle as the Demon laughed over him. That was when she had seen the bodies. Thousands of bodies. Human, Gremen, Oberon, they were all there. She saw her own lifeless eyes staring at a blood red sky and she screamed. She could still see the bodies if she closed her eyes. This was why deep sleep eluded her, why the man's presence tonight had woken her at all.

It was even worse. Whenever the stranger left, her mind would drift away from him, as though it had been a dream, but each time he reappeared, the memories would be as fresh as if they had just been made. She could remember his directions after he left, but it was as though they were her own thoughts, not a suggestion from someone else. She tried to explain it to her uncle once, but had given up when he asked her if she needed to see a physician.

"I did as you asked, I went to my grandfather and warned him that there would be outsiders coming and that we had to do what we could for them."

"I know," the smile faded from his face.

"So why are you here then? I've done as you asked, leave me in peace!" Her voice rose as she snapped at him, loud enough that a knock followed her outburst.

"Are you alright princess?" The muffled voice of the guard asked through the door.

"I'm fine," she lied, "just a nightmare." She motioned for the stranger to follow her into her bed chamber, closing the door behind them. As they entered, something seemed to shift in the air, almost as if magic were at play, but her senses didn't detect any spells.

"I've just come to announce the travelers, they will arrive today." The grim expression didn't leave his face. "Also, please take this." He reached within his robes and drew out a leather bound tome. "The man I told you about will need it soon."

A small creature darted from within the man's hood to sit atop his shoulder. Though she had seen fljúga íkorna before, she had never seen one as a pet. The creature's small body was packed with fat, though it still had the ability to glide about her bedchamber. It was a well-kept pet, but a pet nonetheless.

"Don't go too far Scritch, we must be going." The man turned to leave, but paused just before he reached the door. "He will need you, mother, but for more than just his wife. The Oberon will scorn him and we don't have time for him to cow them into respect. Your grandfather was long dead when he arrived in my time, it made things easier. If he doesn't learn our ways he won't succeed. Teach him as you taught me, or will teach me that is. I know it is within you to do so."

The man left, closing the door quietly as his pet glided behind him.

She huffed at the departing shadow and made to follow him but stalked to the balcony instead. She had chased him during his first visit, only to find that he disappeared as easily as he appeared. Her senses confirmed that he wasn't in the sitting room, only the guards occupied the hall outside. Was her grandfather truly doomed to die in a war that her people still refused to accept? What would happen?

She knew the answer, she would have to take his place. That was why the stranger said it would have been easier if the traveler arrived after her grandfather died. There would be vast changes once she was on the throne. She had been plotting that since she was chosen as heir. Outsiders would no longer be scorned as they are now, especially those that served the Oberon. She had been to their villages, she had seen the squalor they lived in. Her people needed to come to terms with their place in the world. Their birth rate had plummeting in the last sixteen years, still births were on the rise. They needed the other races, more so now than ever before.

She stared out over the sleeping city, taking in the sight of all the flickering lights within the spiraling towers. It was a beautiful sight, even if she knew what lurked within those towers. The hatred her people had for those different than them, the other races of the world, was fascinating. Even now, a contingent from the major churches rested within a tower not far from her. Men and women that had come to rouse the Oberon into joining the fight against this army they had heard about. An army led by men who hadn't been seen in a hundred and fifty years.

Hudcoeden had fallen, as had many of the smaller city-states in the south. Krossfarin seemed to be the next logical target, but still her grandfather held his army back. She had met with him many times since the city of the Druids fell, but he was as implacable as a mountain. It didn't matter that so many had come to beg their aid, he wouldn't risk leaving the city without its army.

Shouts drew her attention to the low slung buildings surrounding the Wizard's tower. Something was happening within the old teleportation chambers and she had a good guess as to what it was. She turned from the window and slipped her nightgown from her shoulders. Her clothing from the previous day was still in an unceremonious pile at the foot of her bed, the servants hadn't been in to clean yet. She pulled the relatively clean clothes back on and went to the door. Her guards would report directly to the king if she turned up missing, but if she informed them of her intention to leave it was likely no one would think twice of it.

She pulled her chamber door open a crack, "I'm going for some air."

The guard closest to her raised an eyebrow. "Do you need an escort?"

She put on her best fake laughter. "Within my grandfather's city at this hour? I doubt it. I will return before my studies."

"Please do, your highness. I am still on my commander's bad side after your last excursion." The guard knew he couldn't stop her leaving and if he pressed to accompany her, she would just order him to stay. It was a tight corner to press the man into, but as long as she kept her word, he wouldn't face further reprimand. Plus, as her last excursion had been unannounced, he would be content with the warning.

She relaxed her wings once more and set them to a low buzz. "I will be back in time." Dashing back into her bedchamber, she leapt from the balcony, building speed as she fell freely through the air. She pulled out of the dive about three stories from the ground, turning that fall into a blazing, forward momentum. Her magic gave her a little boost to her speed, something that most Oberons could do, even those with limited access to magic. If she was to keep her word, she would need to make this a short trip.

Numerous other forms broke from between the buildings, all of them swooping toward the college in much the same manner as her. There were no guards at the college normally, so any alarm there would mean they would have to fly in from elsewhere in the city. She was quickly outpacing some of the slower guards, but a few managed to stay with her. One even signaled for her to stay back, but she ignored him.

She landed outside the building with the handful of guards that had kept pace and nearly sprinted for the open doorway. A large hand grabbed her shoulder and held her firmly in place. "Best you wait for the guards, niece."

She rounded on her uncle with murderous glint, but she knew he was right. There was no guarantee that it was her traveler in that room, or even if it was him, there was nothing indicating that he was alone. Truthfully he was her great-uncle, but being so much younger than her grandfather put him of an age with her father, so she had taken to referring to him as just uncle. She said nothing as the guards pounced on the chamber.

"It's safe!" one of them shouted after a brief moment inside. "Two humans in bad shape," he informed the crowd as he stepped from the building. "Fetch a doctor," he ordered one of his men, but her uncle had already stepped up.

"I'll handle it from here, son. You take your squad back to your patrol."

"Sir?" The guard looked puzzled.

"I'm a physician as well as a royal," her uncle responded. "Take your men and go, forget you were here."

The guard nodded once and signaled for his men to take flight. Her uncle waited until they had left the ground before springing into the building like a child being called to dinner. She followed him with the same excitement.

The inner chamber was dark, no lights had burned there in sixteen years, it took a moment for her eyes to adjust but her other senses were much keener. She could feel the magic within both of the humans, immense levels of magic that she had only ever felt within the greatest of the Oberons. The woman's power was clearly attuned to Betala while the man's was of Ven's stock. There was something familiar about the aura.

As her eyes adjusted, something else became clearer. She knew this man, or boy rather. She had been with him in Hudcoeden, on the day of the trials.

"Please," the woman begged. "We mean no harm."

"I know dear," her uncle reassured the woman. "Let's get you cleaned up."

She watched her uncle lift the unconscious boy from the floor and led the woman from the room. This was the traveler she had been told to watch for? The one that would save them all? He hadn't even managed to pass the rather simple test the Druids had given him, how could he ever hope to defeat something as powerful as Barrah?

Refugee

Water swirled around him as he fought for air. The fall had knocked all the wind from his lungs and he had failed to surface since hitting the water. The armor about his shoulders dragged him toward the bottom of the river, but there was no hope for removing it and he wouldn't dream of relinquishing the sword from his right hand.

As his vision blurred, he felt a strong arm wrap about his waist. He gasped as his head broke the surface, filling his lungs with clean, fresh air. His savior had a familiar face, he had met her in the streets of Hudcoeden, though she had worn more clothes then. As far as he could tell, she was completely nude. Even in his near drowned state, he felt heat rising in his cheeks.

"Again I save you, Human." The Gremen growled at him. "I think you would never live without me."

Even with her strength, they were floundering in the rapid current. He had little to offer to support her, and could not find words to tell her so. She seemed to understand without them though. With her arm about his chest, she swam for the shore, doing her best to avoid the rocks. Some of them were just too big to miss and the strong current battered their bodies against them. As her prodigious strength started to fail, the current began to slow. She had taken them through the worst of it.

With the last of his strength he helped her drag both of them from the water, but only just cleared it before he crashed into unconsciousness. His last vision was of another Gremen rushing to them.

White light filtered through the walls of the tent above him as he finally managed to open his eyes. He felt like he was laying on a cot but he didn't dare turn his pounding, throbbing head more than necessary to look. Slowly, tenderly, he moved his neck and took in his surroundings.

He lay alone in a tent emblazoned with the crest of the Druid Guard. He could see various other empty cots around him. The outline of the sun was almost directly over him, so he guessed it was nearing midday. If this was a military camp, he wouldn't expect any but the convalesced to still be abed at this time. His armor was gone, that was obvious, but the familiar sensation of his father's sword still hummed from his hip. Since he had used the blade in the Temple weeks ago, it had emitted a power that he had never felt before. It was odd at first, but he couldn't think of what it would be like without it now. His clothes were dry, but the feel of the fabric told him he still wore the tunic he had taken from Ardelle's house. Every part of his body ached, from his fight on the cliffs and the ride down the river. The armor had done its job well in preventing the beast's claws from gaining purchase on his flesh, but the impact from it and the fall still left their marks.

He relaxed back into the cot and closed his eyes once more, listening for the breath of a woman he knew wasn't there. Would he ever see her again? He longed to run his fingers through her flaming hair once more but she was likely far from here. She had crossed the bridge ahead of him. She was safe, at least he hoped. She would be with Charles now, heading to see Waliyt. Once they found the old man, Charles could carry out his destiny or whatever it was he had been babbling about in the cave. It hurt his head to consider his friend's story at present. He had other concerns anyway, like where was he?

Confident that he was at least safe for the moment, he pushed himself to a sitting position. A wave of dizziness nearly sent him back to the cot, but he fought through it. He could see the open tent flap and the camp that lay beyond it. Men and women were moving about on the grassy 'streets' between the tents, there were too many women in dresses to say that this was just a military camp. He could see baskets of wash, trays of food and pots of water being carried amongst the crowd. There were men in military regalia, both Druid Guard and Gremen, but they were the exception. This was a refugee camp, and he dreaded what that meant.

He let his head stop spinning before he stood to take stock of his injured body. His right leg was tender from the knee down and his trousers were torn away from the skin. If he had to guess, someone had healed a broken bone there. His ribs ached and it pained him to breathe deeply. He was confident they weren't broken, but the pain was still awful. His hands and arms survived surprisingly well, given that he had flailed about in the water trying to get to the surface. There were two lumps on his head, he must have struck more than one rock before they got free of the river. Those lumps were likely the source of his dizziness.

He stepped out into the sun and immediately regretted it, the bright light stabbing daggers into his eyes. He brought up his hand to shield them and took his bearings. He was near the outer edge of the encampment, on the outside of the military area. Directly in front of him were the haphazard rows of the civilian tents and their occupants. Behind him stretched hundreds of tents in orderly lines. If he guessed correctly, the command area would be somewhere near the center of those pristine rows. Steeling himself against the pain in his head, he set off for the center of camp.

After an eternity of walking, a shout stopped him. "What do you think you are doing, Captain?" A short Druid with a healer sash stepped in front of him and held up his arms. "You are in no shape to be walking about the camp, unescorted."

"I'm fine," he managed through clenched teeth. The pain was worse when he spoke.

"No you're not, you are lucky to be breathing. If it weren't for Castielle, you would never have survived." The Druid's voice rose with each word, ending in a near squeak. He cleared his throat, lowering his voice back to a more masculine level. "Now, back to bed with you. If you insist on moving around, I'll send someone to go with you so that you don't injure yourself further."

Aurin let the man have his way, it wasn't worth arguing. The Druid was right, he was barely able to walk a straight line. He followed the diminutive man back to his tent, sighing slightly at how little distance he had actually covered. It had felt like miles, but was closer to a few hundred strides. The Druid led him back to his cot and crossed his arms while his tiny foot tapped. He refused to leave until Aurin settled back into bed. The small man left him then, promising to send a supervisor so that he didn't die without someone to report it.

Aurin let the man ramble, thinking he would just rest for a moment before he snuck off again. His body had other ideas. When next he opened his eyes, the sun had moved down the far wall of his tent, almost lost behind the others in his row. Another person was with him now, Gremen by the armor. Their back was to him, but from the stance he guessed it was probably the woman that had pulled him out of the river. Two braids ran down her back, so he could say for certain it wasn't a man, not after his encounter on the streets of Hudcoeden.

"Are you my babysitter?" he grumbled.

"I told you human, without me you'd be dead." She turned and grinned. Her features had changed from what he remembered from Hudcoeden, she looked more feral now, with her long canine teeth and bright eyes. If he didn't know that she was there for him, he might even be threatened by that grin, it certainly showed a lot of teeth.

He leaned forward in an attempt to stand, but she put her hand to his chest and held him down. "I need to check in," he told her.

"With who?" she hissed. "Everyone who matters knows you are here already. Howlter will be here at sundown, with that big human guard, Dorne." She gave him a gentle shove back onto the cot and bent down close to his face. With her this close, he could see a beauty to her animalistic features, a wildness that was somehow alluring.

"What is this look you give me?" she demanded.

"May I help you with something?" he asked her, trying to sink deeper into the cot.

"Be still," she commanded, placing one of her warm hands to the lump on the side of his head. He yelped, but she paid it no mind. "The swelling is going down, you may yet survive." She told him flatly, staring directly into his eyes, her pupils dilating as she took in his face. He could see that the pupils weren't quite the round shape one would expect, they were closer to the eyes of a cat. "Again with the look. Am I hideous?" she demanded.

"No, you are just very close." Aurin admitted.

"You humans and your space." She scoffed, standing back. "Neesus tells me you tried to leave today."

"Neesus?" He asked, then remembered the little Druid that had sent him back to bed. "The little one?"

She laughed, a deep throaty chuckle that brought a smile to his face. "He is quite tiny." Her cat eyes sparkled in the setting sun. "I left him to tend you earlier while I sought out some weapons for myself. I had to leave mine in that cursed forest."

Aurin was lost for a moment before it clicked. "You've been here the whole time, haven't you?"

The laugh stopped. She looked down at him earnestly. "Where else would I be? If I wasn't around, you'd be dead." The conviction in her voice told him she wasn't joking.

"How long?" he asked.

"Two weeks you've been in that bed." Her smile returned. "Two weeks of nothing but your snores to tell me you lived."

He smiled back. "Did you say Commander Dorne is here?"

"Yes, yes." She waved her hand. "He arrived after we did with a force of guards that we thought had died in the city."

His features relaxed. "I guess you better fill me in on what happened in Hudcoeden."

She sighed. "I was not there, but I have heard the report straight from Howlter's mouth." Another deep breath. "Your city is gone, human. Barrah's army sacked it while you were in the forest. Howlter held them off long enough for most of the people to escape, but not all. We march now for Krossfarin, it is the closest city."

Hudcoeden fallen? A month ago he would never have dreamed of the day, but it made sense now. Barrah had infiltrated the guard and the Druids so that he could bring about the fall of the city from inside. An old tactic, but effective. With the Druids distracted by Charles' trial, no one would be looking for the intruders or suspect that an army was marching on them. With the Grand Druid's son's death, all facets of the Druid order would participate and with the gravity of the situation, the guard would have to be present as well. It was a perfect strategy and they had fallen for it.

Aurin suppressed his emotions, it wouldn't do to let them out now. "Please stop calling me 'human,' " he pleaded. "My name is Aurin, or if you insist, Captain."

"Very well." she conceded. "Aurin, my name is Crowlmer. At least that is what I am known by here." Something in her tone seemed vulnerable, not something he would associate with this woman.

"Would you prefer something else?" he asked her softly.

"Crowlmer was my father, I use his name to carry his legacy with me," she admitted. "My given name was Anissa." He swore a tear beaded in her eye, but she turned from him before he could be sure.

"May I call you Anissa then?"

"If you must," she sighed. "Just not in front of Howlter." She didn't turn to him, but there was a catch in her voice that confirmed his suspicions.

Revelation

Bright light filled the room filling Charles' eyes with a rough light. He was stretched out on a narrow bed, one that barely spanned his thin frame. A sheet of soft, white material was draped over him from his neck to ankles. His large, bare feet were exposed and nearly hung off at the end of the bed. He was tall, but he had never had a problem with beds being too short, this one, however, was close.

Tall windows lined the walls of his room, their glass frosted so that he couldn't see clearly what lay beyond them. A short stool sat in one corner of the room, but it was the only furniture present besides the bed. A single door to his right sat closed, though he couldn't see any locks. The walls of the room were a sparkling white, without any trace of dirt or specks.

A simple robe, also white had replaced his clothes. His skin had been scrubbed clean while he slept. The thoughts of someone man-handling him into the bath and then dressing him gave him an odd, violated feeling

"Hello?" He managed with a voice that felt like he had swallowed gravel.

It was enough, the door slid sideways into a pocket in the wall. An Oberon decked in the colors of the royal house strolled into the room and clicked at him. "You should relax, Charles. It will take some time for you to recover your voice, you've not used it in some time."

"How…" he groaned.

"Easy, boy." The Oberon moved to the bed and eased him back down. "You've been down for about a fortnight. You and your friend showed up in the old teleportation circles at our Wizard's college and right scared a room full of apprentices."

The man had an accent that didn't quite fit with the outward Oberon appearance, and his common tongue was absent any of the airs that were prevalent amongst the Oberon Charles had met. His confusion must have been apparent.

"Trying to figure me out, eh? Good luck!" The man chuckled, a deep rumbling laugh that brought a smile to Charles' face, despite the pain. The man's wings even fluttered slightly as he laughed. "I'm not from around here, well not in a long time anyway." The man didn't elaborate, he had busied himself with checking Charles over.

Satisfied that Charles wasn't dead, or dying, the man turned for the door. "Your friend will be back in a bit, she went for some lunch." He turned back to Charles, smiling. "I'll send for something for you too, don't worry."

Charles began to wonder if the man truly could read his thoughts. A short time after the Oberon left, a distraught Ardelle rushed into the room.

"You are awake!" She rushed over to the bed and gave him a once over, much like the Oberon had done. "And you are looking well." A glow sprang up around Ardelle, one that resembled the swirling flames of a campfire and Charles relaxed. He could still see radiances, which meant he still had magic. He hadn't tried to reach his pool since he had woke, but he reached for it now. A rush of magic washed over him and he allowed himself to breathe. His pool was intact, but something was different. Suspicious, he tested the pool again just to confirm. Not only was his magic still there, but he was stronger now.

He shook his head to clear it. During his training, it had always been explained that pushing yourself beyond your limits may burn the magic right out of you, never did anyone tell him that pushing himself that hard would expand his pool. He tested it again and found that he had increased his reserves so much that he easily rivaled Waliyt.

The thought of his master snapped him back to his current condition. He had a memory of Waliyt that he needed to understand. "Arrddd…." He was still struggling with his voice. She turned to look at him but lacked the Oberon's knack for reading him. He concentrated on his voice and pulled once again on his pool. The strain of actually using the magic sent a wave of nausea through him, but he fought through it. It has never been this strong before, it had strengthened after the ritual in Wylltraethel. He allowed the magic to pool there in his neck, about the muscles and tendons that controlled his voice. Once the magic was in place, he pulled, as Micah had taught him, until the pain in his throat disappeared.

"What happened in Falderal?" He spoke normally. The pain was gone, but the nausea from the magic wasn't.

"They told me your voice wouldn't be back for weeks. You took a hit to the neck some time during our run. What did you do?" she asked him, sounding almost like his foster mother, Desmira. "Did you use your magic?"

"Yes." He answered honestly. "Now please, I need to know."

"You shouldn't be using your magic, you are lucky you didn't burn it right out!" She shouted, as if he didn't already know. "You need to be more careful."

"Ardelle, please, I have to know, was Waliyt there?" he begged.

She looked away from him. "You called him master." She told him of the man in dark robes who had called off the Harpies and sent them here. She explained that the man had saved them, but as much as admitted that he was the one controlling the creatures there. He stopped listening.

Waliyt had been there, it wasn't a dream. He had saved them, but what was he doing with the monsters? Was he truly an agent of Barrah? His mind raced at the possibilities that would place his master in Barrah's service, maybe he was an inside agent for the good guys. Maybe he sought to undermine Barrah from the inside? Or maybe, it was exactly how it looked. His master served Barrah.

So many things clicked then. Micah's insistence that Barrah had interfered with Charles in Hudcoeden and sent him to the forest early. It had been Waliyt that told him to accept the banishment. Waliyt had insisted he take the Druid's test and had been instrumental in informing them as to his greatest weakness. Waliyt had been his teacher for many years but had never worked with him on that flaw, instead he had further cultivated it by keeping Charles uneducated.

Then there was his radiance. That obsidian taint that had swirled with the normal crimson of the Wizards. It had matched the creatures they had fought in the streets that day, but Waliyt had fought them, surely that meant something. Then the other shoe dropped. Waliyt had only stepped in when that fake Druid had sought to take his magic for good. Prior to that, the creature had killed several Druids and Waliyt had done nothing.

"Charles?" Ardelle looked concerned. How long had he been staring at the wall?

"I need some time," he told her. "I've got a lot to think about."

Concern etched her features. "I know, but we don't have time to spare. The physician passed along word that you were awake. We need to get you up and dressed so that we can take you before the king."

He fought hard to keep the tears back, but the battle was lost. "I… can't" He managed before he broke into a wracking sob that sent pain throughout his body. Clearly, his wounds hadn't completely healed. The strain of using that much magic would have sapped his body's ability to mend itself, so each and every bruise felt like a broken bone. His life had been turned completely inside out and now he had nothing. After they had lost Aurin, he had clung to the hope that Waliyt would know what to do, but now even that hope was gone. He was alone, truly alone to face a destiny he didn't want.

Ardelle wrapped her arms about him and brought his head to her shoulder. Her own eyes were wet with tears as she shared in his despair. She held him there and let him cry, patting his back gently and cooing softly the way a mother would to a child. They remained like that until Charles had composed himself. They set about the arduous task of getting him out of the Oberon bed. While he imagined the beds held a great deal of comfort for creatures with wings on their backs, they did little for him. He allowed himself a brief smile thinking about someone of Aurin's proportions trying to sleep on the slender table. The smile didn't last though, his friend was gone.

Charles decided to just keep his white robe on, rather than change into the freshly pressed scarlet robes that hung from a peg on the door. Between the lack of strength and the embarrassment of having Ardelle help him dress, he just couldn't think of changing now, even if he was to meet a king. He knew he should feel honored, but with all that had happened in the last month, he couldn't bring himself to feel anything but empty. Aurin was gone, his master was a traitor, and he had been banished from the only home he knew. How could he feel anything but alone?

As he settled himself back onto the bed to pull on his shoes, he noticed something nestled into the pile of clothing at the foot of his bed. It was a leather bound tome, though he had never worked out the language the book used, he knew the runes inscribed on its binding by heart. It was the book he had recovered from the chamber beneath Ven's home, the book he had fought that creature for. He had taken the book from the cave when they left but, like all of his other books, he had left it on that cliff when they fled. How was it here?

The mystery of its arrival would have to wait. He had a king to meet and if he didn't go soon, he feared he would have to be carried.

They left his room quietly, taking the stairs down an empty hall that looked suspiciously like a servant's corridor. The halls within the Oberon spire were well kept and wide, their wings wouldn't be tucked back here in their homeland. He knew that there was a strict hierarchy to the Oberon society, castes of people that operated the entire kingdom. The servant would use a hall such as this while they cared for the ruling and noble castes. They would handle everything from cooking to cleaning, and even assist in child rearing, but they had little say in the operation of the government. Outsiders were usually lumped with the servant's caste when determining their worth. Oberon society as a whole was haughty.

The artisan's caste would be next, with their skilled workers such as smiths and carpenters. They were treated very well by the upper castes, because without them there really wouldn't be a kingdom to rule. Tradesmen all fell within this caste, along with many of the merchants, though a good number of merchants were actually nobles. There were outsiders among the artisans, those that could craft at the level of the Oberon. They held no real power, and had no say in governance, but they were free to do what they wanted.

Nobles made up the smallest of the castes, but they held the most power, more so than even the ruling caste. Nobles could easily oust any ruler they felt was not performing as they saw fit, and with this power they were the true rulers of Oberon society. Economics all centered on the nobles, they set the prices and carried out most of the trade. A few merchants from the artisan's caste could rise high enough to be on par with the nobles, but they would always be just a step behind. Only those born to the noble caste, or raised to it by the rulers, could claim nobility and thus participate in the government. The nobility would select a representative from each noble house to sit in a court that would make the big decisions for the nation with the ruling caste having the last say in the decision making process. It was all very bureaucratic, and quite boring. Charles had studied the minutes from one such session as part of his history lessons, he had trouble keeping his eyes open from just the text. He couldn't imagine sitting at court during the proceedings.

The ruling caste was made up of a single clan of Oberons, currently the Fullvalda clan. Their patriarch, Driamati, had ruled for the last eighty years having taken the throne at the ripe age of thirteen. Charles had heard that Driamati had twenty-four children from four wives, all of whom he had outlived. His oldest children were now in their sixties and were seen as much too old to assume the throne. The children of his second wife were the current favorites for succeeding him, but the succession was not based on age but merit. Driamati would name a successor when he felt the time was right, a time that hadn't come once in the eighty years he had sat the throne. Many of his children had thought to usurp his authority or sway him to select them, but he had rebuffed them all. It was widely known that he had no respect for any of the adult children that currently served in some capacity within the government.

It was Driamati that Charles would meet today.

The long trip to the throne room left Charles feeling even weaker than he had when he first awoke. Ardelle bore the majority of his weight, which would have embarrassed him if he didn't hurt so much. His use of magic had left a feeling of nausea that just wouldn't cease. He wanted to vomit, but he hadn't gotten that lunch the physician promised and had nothing else to vomit. It didn't stop his stomach from occasionally heaving, which of course, hurt everything else on his body.

They were admitted to the throne room via a servant's door that led to a parlor just off the middle of the hall. He could see the lavish decorations, but didn't get his first look at Driamati until he was ushered into the hall by a stuffy Oberon in the livery of the Fullvalda's.

Charles' experience with Oberons had been limited in Hudcoeden, as they saw the college there as inferior to their own school, but he did see a master and a single apprentice every year when they attended the testing. This year it had been Darl and a young girl that Charles guessed was one of Driamati's many relatives. He couldn't remember her name though, he was horrible with names.

Driamati looked nothing like either of them. He was clearly tall, though he sat his throne, it was still plain to see that his limbs were long and had once been well toned. Hints of the muscle he had once held still appeared in places, but the years had taken their toll on him and left most of his skin loose and wrinkled. His tanned face bore the lines of a man that spent a good deal of time in the sun, and the wind, given the Oberon's ability to fly. His eyes were a different matter. They held the wisdom of a man of years, but still sparkled with a youthful intensity that belied his age.

"Kveðjur ungur maður." Driamati greeted him in the Oberon tongue. "Hvernig líður þér?"

Charles had studied the Oberon language, but was lousy at speaking it. His best phrase was: "Ég tala ekki álfur." Which meant 'I don't speak Oberon.'

The old man chuckled, blue eyes sparkling even more with the mirth. "Fair enough." He coughed slightly as he spoke the common language. "I trust you find your accommodations to your liking, young master Chavox?" His tone was grandfatherly, but there was something else to it as well, curiosity maybe?

"I am not accustomed to your beds sire, but I do appreciate that you have granted me the use of one." Charles forced his court speech, it wasn't something he used often in Hudcoeden. The Druids were rather informal, even given their strict hierarchy. "Thank you for your generosity and for the use of your physician." Charles attempted a bow but nearly toppled over, Ardelle struggled to hold him upright.

Another chuckle rang through the room. "Goria!" Driamati shouted to one of the servants stationed behind the throne. "Koma drengurinn stól." Charles missed the translation, but the context clued him in to the intent. A chair was carried in from the parlor he had just vacated and situated directly in front of the throne.

"Thank you, majesty." Charles breathed as he sat in the proffered chair.

"Your voice has returned in force I see, I was told it would be weeks before you could actually speak." The question was implied.

"A small healing spell I learned in my travels, majesty."

The king seemed unfazed by the statement but others in the room stared at him questioningly. Wizards weren't known for their ability to heal.

"Don't waste time with the honorifics here." The king motioned for the other man behind him to step forward. Charles recognized him as Darl, the wizard he had last seen in Hudcoeden. "You know each other, correct?"

Both of them nodded in agreement, though Darl hesitated to do so. "Yes, your majesty." Charles confirmed.

"Good, we'll skip introductions." Driamati adjusted his posture on the throne, rocking back and forth momentarily, then leaned forward. "We know who you are Charles, and we know what you are supposed to do."

The admission was a shock to Charles, he barely understood what Micah had told him those few weeks ago. How was it that the Oberon's were already aware of it? "Sire?" Charles queried.

"We're not so far removed from the affairs of the Arcana as the humans are. Vielk has already contacted us and bade us do whatever we could to help you. We are not in the habit of ignoring a direct statement from our Arcana." Driamati paused, adjusting his seat on the throne again. "We know what you are to do and who you really are. We are willing to help, but you must understand, we have been excluded from this war with Barrah to date and would like to keep it that way. Our race has suffered greatly in the last sixteen years and Barrah has the power to make it even worse. We cannot have this. Do you understand?"

Charles wanted nothing more than to respond in the positive, but he really didn't understand. "No, sire, I'm sorry, I don't understand."

Darl cringed at the response and could no longer hold his tongue. "Boy, if you are going to use the addresses, please use them correctly. He is not your sire, he is 'your majesty' or 'majesty.'" The unexpected outburst left Charles reeling for a moment. "Please show some respect." Darl snapped.

"That's enough Darl, he's young and not from here." Driamati excused. "What I'm telling you son is that we will help you, but once you have what you need you will have to leave. You can't stay here, once the agents of Barrah know you are here, then we will be back at the fore of his mind."

It clicked what Driamati was telling him. He would help, but only if no one knew they were helping. "I understand, si… your majesty."

"Good." Driamati sat back in his chair, though he still looked uncomfortable. "While you are here, you can't use your real name. You will be Mentor Maeryn Kairos, a traveling Wizard seeking training with our illustrious Wizard, Darl. 'Mentor' is a title used in the lands far to the east, it is the same as "Wizard" here. Do you understand Mentor Kairos?"

"Yes, your majesty." Charles was going to have difficulty with this. He had trouble remembering names as it was, now he would have to remember his own.

"We have much more to discuss, but for now you may return to your quarters." Driamati chuckled again. "I mean your real quarters, you won't be returning to that convalescent room." With a wave, he dismissed Charles and Ardelle.

"Well, Mentor." Ardelle whispered to him, smiling at his new title. "Let's find your room."

The March

Crowlmer fumed in her corner. The Druids and their endless complaints. They had made little progress toward Krossfarin since she and Aurin had joined the refugees, the blame lay entirely with the Druids. Howlter was far too soft with the old men for her liking, if this had been her command she would have left them three days ago.

"We can't break camp for another two days, Commander." The stogy old man, Drery, told Howlter. "Any sooner would put too much strain on the staff." The 'staff' were the servants the old men used to carry all their things. Most of those things were worthless artifacts they had taken from their temples before fleeing, a task that nearly cost the servants their lives. Howlter had barely kept the demons out of the city long enough to get the last groups into the tunnels and far enough away to collapse them. Not all the Druids bought into the old men's ideals though, she had to remember that. Some, like her new acquaintance Castielle, felt like the Gremen did. Leave the material things behind and save lives.

"If you would pack and carry your own things we could move faster." Howlter growled. "If we don't get across the Balen River before the rains get worse, we'll be stuck afield for the rest of the season. There just isn't any other way to look at it."

"It's time to make the hard decision," Aurin started from his reclined position next to her. He was still in bad shape from his fall, but he had insisted she bring him to this meeting. "I know you are trying to preserve cultural objects from Hudcoeden, but are they truly worth the lives of everyone here?" Aurin was technically in command of the Druid Guard, since his mentor, Dorne, had gone ahead with a scout force to secure their crossing in Balenford, a small village a dozen leagues from them.

"We simply cannot leave them behind." Drery insisted.

"If that is how you feel, then you must care for them yourselves." Aurin replied. "It is unfair to expect your servants to care for all of these things as well as their own families. The matter still stands though, there is a storm coming, your own Druids confirmed it. Once the river is swollen from that rainfall, we won't be able to cross in Balenford. If we can't cross in Balenford, we are effectively stuck. We have to leave first thing tomorrow."

Shouts of dismay rang through the tent. The other old men were on their feet now, shouting that Aurin had no authority to make such demands. Others insisted that Dorne be called back to settle the matter, which of course would give them the two days they wanted. Crowlmer was sick of it.

"Silence!" She boomed over all of the other voices. Every head turned to her. "There is no more debate. You carry your *cultural objects* or they are left here. Either way, we leave tomorrow." Her breath heaved within her chest and she had to fight the urge to bare her fangs to the assembled crowd. She hadn't fully returned to herself after leaving the forest.

No one spoke for several heartbeats before Howlter finally cut in. "You have your orders gentlemen, see that you are ready to depart at first light. I will station some of my men near your camp to relay any messages to me." The unspoken threat implied by his last comment didn't go unnoticed.

Howlter's men would ensure that the old men didn't try to force their servants to carry all of that useless garbage.

The old men left, not without a few glances her way though. They didn't appreciate her tone, and her physical changes put many of them on edge. She didn't care, she had long ago lost any desire to please those around her. After years of ridicule and ostracizing, she made the decision to live for herself.

She bent to help Aurin to his feet, but was waved off. The man was stubborn as a mule, but she had to respect his desire for independence. She never would have let anyone help her if she were in his state. That he bore her constant fussing with such grace was still surprising.

No Gremen would have stood for it, not from an unwed woman. In their culture, only a wedded woman would ever dare to care for a man, typically only the men they were married to. It wasn't unheard of for widows to care for others, especially if they had chosen to remain unmarried after their mate had passed. They called it 'Wearing Four,' referring to the symbolic four braids in their hair. She had never been married, and despite wearing two braids for months now, still had no suitors. Any man that would consider her likely had mental impairments, she wasn't like other Gremen women. Perhaps she had been among humans too long, or she was just unfit for married life. Others had given up on finding a mate, removing one of their braids and signaling their desire to remain unwed, maybe it was time for her to do the same.

She turned her attention back to the conversation. Aurin leaned heavily on the crutch she had given him before they left the tent, but remained on his feet while he and

Howlter discussed mobilizing their forces. "The Guard will be ready to march, but the villagers are going to need help." Aurin told her former commander.

"Send any that you can spare to assist them." Howlter told him. "It will be a long night, but we have no choice. I would rather a few of our soldiers were tired tomorrow than risk leaving anyone behind."

"He said send men to help them." She clarified for Aurin, knowing what he was thinking. "Not, 'Go yourself,' you still need rest."

Howlter smiled at Aurin. "I warned you to steer clear of her."

"You did." Aurin admitted, laughing lightly. He hid it well, but his ribs still caused him constant pain. When he thought no one could see he would grimace and grit his teeth. "I will send the men, I'm leaving the Druids to you." Aurin gestured to one of his men and sent the runner. Crowlmer was sure he wanted it to be done before his inevitable collapse. His somber tone returned. "I'm afraid they won't listen to the Guard, they never have."

"We'll make them listen," Howlter reassured him. "Or we'll leave them here. Either way, we march tomorrow with the rest of the refugees. Krossfarin is still a month away at our best possible speed, I don't want to be caught out in the open when the rains start in earnest and at this pace, the horde we left in Hudcoeden could be on us at any time." Howlter turned on his heel and left, heading out to issue orders to the Lieutenants still serving him directly. After her experience in the forest, and the subsequent return to the unit, Crowlmer found herself less and less interested in her former role. She couldn't say what drove her away, but she knew it had much to do with the looks her fellow Gremen gave her.

She had officially resigned her post shortly after Aurin first awoke, stating that she was going to see to her new mission before any others. She still didn't have the whole story of exactly what Aurin and his wizard friend sought to do, but she knew it was important. Anything Aurin put that much of himself into was important. She felt a heat in her cheeks as she watched the guard move about the command tent. She growled and forced herself to shake it off.

"Are you alright?" Aurin asked, turning to the sound of her growl.

"I'm fine," she snapped harshly. She sighed. "I'm just frustrated with the situation." Not a complete lie, which made it believable. She hoped anyway.

Thankfully, he let it drop. "I should lay down." He admitted, openly grimacing now. She knew that meant the pain was far greater than he let on.

"I told you to leave this one to me," she admonished.

"Yes, I saw how you handled them." He smiled at her in that charming way she hated.

"It worked," she spat back. "They stopped arguing."

He laughed heartily, immediately doubling over from the pain. "Yes, bed." He tried to walk on his own but nearly fell. She wrapped her arms about him and lifted him as one would a child. Sometimes her new strength surprised even her.

She carried him from the tent and across the path to his bed. They shared the tent now, more for convenience than anything else. She had been sleeping in an adjacent tent, but her constant trips back and forth bothered her tent mates there nearly as much as they bothered Aurin. Rather than have two groups upset with her, she decided to just bunk with him. Three times she had saved him, three times makes a law. He wouldn't survive without her.

She laid him on the cot that he had occupied for most of his time since they came to the camp. On the rare occasion that the procession moved, he occupied one of the numerous wagons that trundled along in the middle of the train. She stayed with him then as well, daring anyone to comment on her riding like an old woman. So far only Howlter had mentioned it, but it had been more of a fatherly observation than an actual denigration of her. The others said nothing, they feared her new self even more than the old and her old self had an infamous reputation. Ergon and Kary steered well clear of her outside of the command meetings, which was painful as she had once thought Ergon would take her offer of the two braids. He had been one of the only men not scared to death of her, but no longer.

Aurin passed out long before she settled herself into her chair to keep watch. He snored softly now, though she knew it would rise in volume the deeper he slept. He could wake the dead with his snores.

This was her life. Caring for a man that she barely knew, tending to his needs as a wife would. She had sought to know him better, but he had been resistant. He kept his deepest memories close to heart, and rarely shared more than an occasional joke or soldier's anecdote with her. On the off chance that he did share something, it was often centered on Charles or his woman, Ardelle. She could tell that he missed her, though why she couldn't understand. They had barely known each other for a fortnight. What connection could they have possibly made? She had spent every day with him for nearly a month and he had barely warmed to her. At least he didn't shy away from her appearance the way the others did.

She could admit to herself that she was jealous, but not in the way that a human would covet another's mate. In Gremen society, the females typically outnumbered the males two and three, to one so it was very common for males to have more than one bonded mate. Howlter himself had five wives. No, the jealously was more that he just didn't seem to notice her. This human woman, Ardelle, sounded interesting and they had clearly connected in that forest, but was it a true connection or just one of a caregiver and their charge? Wasn't that her relationship with him now?

She growled again and let it drop. Humans were strange, they only kept one mate. This was likely why he wouldn't look at her, she had been too late.

The following day was going to be difficult and she knew that he would refuse to travel by wagon for this move. Each march had been harder than the last on the civilians with them. These men and women weren't used to marching across the countryside, day in and day out. She could empathize with them, but they had to do this. Their city was gone, at least they had their lives. Howlter had prevented another Demensk.

The thought of all the Gremen lost when their capital fell left a sour taste in her mouth. Tens of thousands of her people were killed in the fall of their city. So many were lost that the nation never recovered and the Gremen had reverted to a nomadic, tribal society. Howlter's force was the largest assembled group of Gremen left in the world and without Howlter there to hold them together, they would all scatter back to their tribes.

The night passed without much sleep for her, but most nights did lately. She had grown accustomed sleeping like a cat during her time in forest; she slept for a few hours then rose to carry out mundane tasks in their tent, then slept a little longer. She went through this ritual most nights. Her senses were still those of her other self, heightened so that every movement in the camp around her drew her attention. In the forest they served her well, but out here they just left a very distracted woman.

Morning came far too early, but the sounds from the camp started even earlier. The civilians, some of them at least, had broken camp hours before the sun crested the distant hills. She gave up on any further sleep and moved outside to see if there was any help she could offer, knowing that most of these people would refuse her. She had to try though, it was her nature. Plus, there really was nothing else for her to do. The first family she approached grabbed their small girl and pulled her away. The next was much the same, shaking their heads furiously when she offered a hand.

A little boy ran when she turned her cat's eyes on him.

An elderly man threatened her.

Two guardsmen jumped when they saw her face, then hurried in another direction.

It was more than she could take. She turned between two tents, then sank to her knees. Tears rolled down her cheeks. She couldn't remember the last time she had actually cried. Why did she care? These people clearly didn't want her, but did Aurin want her any more than these people? She choked back a sob before it could get too bad, but the pressure of her changes wouldn't relent.

She cried to herself for several moments before a small hand crept onto her shoulder. "Are you ok?" a small female voice asked.

Crowlmer turned to see a young girl in a ragged dress standing over her. She rubbed at her eyes viciously to clear the offending tears growling, "I'm fine."

The clear blue eyes stared unflinching into her cat's eyes, "It's ok to be sad. We've all lost something," the little girl told her. Crowlmer looked her over. She looked a little older than twelve, with eyes that spoke of an old soul. Her clothing was dirty, as was her face and hair. She was thin, unhealthily thin. "Can I help?" the girl asked her.

"I..." Crowlmer hesitated. What could she possibly say to this little girl? "I was trying to help everyone get ready, but I guess they don't need me."

"Most folks have gotten pretty good about marching." The little girl assured her. "I find it best just to stay out of their way."

Crowlmer recoiled. The sentiment mirrored what others had said to her. *'Just stay out of our way.'* She had been told this on countless occasions, especially after she had resigned her position.

The little girl's eyes widened. "No, no, I didn't mean like that." She stepped up and took Crowlmer's hand. "I just mean these folks are very private. They won't let me help either."

The girl's hand was rough, the skin had seen its share of hard work. "Where is your family?" Crowlmer asked, letting go the small hand.

"I'm alone, always have been." The girl told her without a hint of sadness. "I have nothing to prepare, but I could come with you in case you find someone that could use help. At least we could keep each other company."

Crowlmer rolled the idea through her mind. This little girl wanted to help her, no one had ever done that before. She had always had to prove she deserved to be where she was. "How old are you?" Crowlmer asked, instantly regretting it.

"I'm sixteen." The little girl, or rather young woman, told her. "I know, I don't look it," she told Crowlmer, anticipating the next statement. "My name is Adla."

"Anissa." Crowlmer blurted, not sure why. She had only ever told Aurin her real name. Why had she told Adla? "But everyone calls me Crowlmer here."

Adla extended her hand. "It is good to meet you, Anissa Crowlmer. Shall we see if we can be of help?" Her blue eyes sparkled in the rising sun.

Crowlmer wasn't sure what had just happened, but she could honestly say that she felt better. With her new friend in tow, she set off for the poorer part of the camp to see if she could lend help there.

A New Master

Charles sighed into his textbook. Of all the things he had missed about studying to be a Wizard, copying texts wasn't on the list. Darl had tasked him with copying from a bloated work on the ritual casting of the Oberon Wizard Helk. He claimed that the rituals would be valuable in the upcoming battles and that Charles should know all of the nuances of casting each one. So far, Helk had ranted for nearly two of the six volumes about the futility of teaching magic to other races and how their work would never compare to the artistry of the Oberons. Charles had encountered this sentiment, many times before, when reading Oberon work. Theirs was the oldest race, but they had never really learned to accept others.

He sighed again and copied out some of the few pieces of the ritual Helk had used when setting the defenses of Heimili álfa. He was actually starting to miss his time in the forest, well, his time in Ven's cave anyway. Darl gave him little in the way of direction, instead he would just point Charles to a text or an anecdote of an Oberon that had solved some great problem of their society. Outside of the occasional review of Charles' work, Darl spent very little time with him and he never said anything positive. Darl critiqued his handwriting, his ability to memorize, and his ability to understand the meaning of the Oberon work as a whole. All of these things Darl found lacking.

The only saving grace had been Darl's other student. It had surprised Charles that Clornamti was still studying under Darl, despite having earned her Wizard title during the last test in Hudcoeden. Apparently, to the Oberons, a title granted by the human order of Druids didn't hold water. They were only deemed Wizard when their peers in the Oberon society thought they were ready. They would only attend the testing in Hudcoeden to prove that their training was as good as, if not better than, the human training that took place there.

Clornamti seemed uniquely able to withstand the cuts and jabs from Darl's critiques, and often would turn the negatives back around on their teacher. She would actually praise Charles' work from time to time, giving him the positive reinforcement that he needed to continue his studies.

His studies tended to suffer when she was present though. She was exceptionally beautiful, with deep brown eyes he would often lose himself in. Her amber locks fell to shoulder-length but were usually pulled back in a layered braid that accented her natural highlights. When she smiled at him, her perfect, white teeth would peek from behind her cherry lips in a way that caused him to sigh inwardly. Whenever they crossed paths he struggled inwardly waiting to see her smile, and when he would finally see it, his day would immediately perk up.

Her radiance held its own beauty as well, a swirl of colors swam evenly about her, instead of the usual crimson he saw about a Wizard. It wasn't a particularly strong radiance, but the fact that it was evenly spread about the whole spectrum lent beauty to even that.

When they were first reintroduced, he worried that she would recognize him from Hudcoeden and ruin his cover, but she either didn't remember him or she chose to participate in his cover story. She called him Maeryn or Mentor Kairos when they were together, but he longed to hear her say his real name. It was for the best that his cover was maintained.

In his limited exposure to others in the city, he had learned of Hudcoeden's fall and the subsequent evacuation of the populace. He had also heard the rumors that it was all brought on by the boy Chavox, whom they had long attributed to their foretelling of the fall of Barrah. It was odd that so many strangers knew his name, and more than a little frightening. Especially considering that he was being blamed for the fall of Hudcoeden. Driamati had been right to hide his presence here.

"Wake up, Mentor Kairos." Darl snapped his fingers. "I expect you to finish Master Helk's work by tomorrow at the latest and you are only on the fourth volume."

"Yes, Master." Charles responded.

"We will be delving into some of my own work tomorrow afternoon, I think you will find it to be superior to Helk's and ultimately more useful, but without Helk's work to act as a base, you wouldn't understand mine." Darl stated smugly.

The arrogance of this race was staggering. He doubted that he would have any more trouble with Darl's work if he was to tackle it today than if he had read Helk's first. True, Helk had offered a handful of unique ritual tricks that Charles could use, but it was hardly worth six volumes to cover the little pieces of information. "Yes, Master," he sighed back to his teacher.

He looked up to see Clornamti rolling her eyes behind their teacher and had to suppress a giggle. She was stunning today, as she was every day, wearing a dress of blue satin belted about her waist. The back was left open, as was the case with most Oberon clothing, to allow for their wings. Her diaphanous wings splayed out behind her, reflecting the sunlight in a shimmering wave that dazzled and captivated. The thin veins that ran through the wings were pale blue today, but he knew their color wasn't fixed. The color of the veins seemed to shift with the mood of the Oberon, but some had more control than others. He had meant to ask about them, but other than his teacher and Clornamti, he didn't feel comfortable asking any other Oberon. He couldn't ask Darl without risking a lengthy lecture on the subject that in some way would demean humans in general. He definitely couldn't ask Clornamti. For some reason any time he tried to talk with her about anything other than their studies, he would lose the ability to form sentences.

He sighed and turned back to his studies. For now, it would have to remain a mystery.

Some hours later he yawned, stretched and packed the single remaining volume of Helk into his satchel. He could finish the text in his apartment tonight and have some time available tomorrow to begin testing the rituals that he had copied down today. This had been his routine since he started his training under Darl, study all day and some more at night. Even though he was Mentor Kairos here, Darl and Driamati still didn't want him to spend much time among the regular populace of Heimili álfa. They feared he would be discovered and what that would mean for them politically. Since the rulers of the Oberon nation were appointed by the court, the political ramifications of every decision had to be weighed carefully. The court could decide, at any time, that Driamati was unfit to lead them and immediately oust him. Finding out that the aging leader was harboring the infamous Chavox right under their noses would be just enough catalyst to cause such a vote.

He had seen little of Ardelle since the night she had helped him to his new rooms, but he knew she was still around somewhere. She was allowed to come and go as she pleased since no one had heard of Ardelle, the priestess of Betala. Even the older Oberon still wouldn't recognize the name, though they should. It hadn't taken him long to find her in the records in Heimili álfa, and what he read left him with more questions than answers. Her story had been full of holes when Aurin first introduced them, but he had let them slide. There was little reason to press in the situation they were in. But now that he had no immediate fear of being imprisoned in a cursed forest for the rest of his life, he sought the answers.

She wasn't just a priestess of Betala, she was the Arcana's avatar to the mortal plane. The revelation had staggered him. He had thought to rush off to ask her about it immediately, but his conscience had won out. Who was he to pry into her secrets? The knowledge was killing him, but he had so far managed to avoid blurting it out on the few occasions he had seen her.

"Are you lost?" A female voice tinkled from behind him causing him to look up.

He was indeed in the wrong place, it was easy to do in the warrens of hallways the Oberon laid out in the lower portions of their towers, but it wasn't just that he made a wrong turn, this was clearly the women's baths. "I... I'm sorry" his cheeks were burning as he lowered his eyes back to the floor. He turned on his heels and attempted to beat a hasty retreat, but the woman stepped in front of him.

"Mentor Kairos?" Clornamti asked. "I didn't take you for the bath sort." She chuckled.

"I... thought... lost me then... I..." Wonderful! Now he was a peeper and an idiot.

Clornamti laughed harder. "It's alright, Mentor. These halls can be confusing. Here let me help you out of here." She took his hand, making his heart race in his chest. He tried desperately to keep the thudding muscle within his chest under control, but he feared it would burst forth any second.

"...Uh... thanks." He managed, as she guided him back toward the central hall.

She led him through the hall and out the back staircase without letting go of his hand. He didn't want to end the touch, but her closeness was causing his palms to sweat. He didn't need any more embarrassment with this beautiful girl. How did one let go of another's hand without looking even more an idiot? He had never puzzled questions like that before. Rather than spend his effort there, he allowed her to continue leading him up the winding staircase that twisted around the outside of the tower. While he knew he could reach his apartment from the outer stairs, it wasn't the most direct route. It did allow one to look out on the city of Heimili álfa as they climbed though.

The city was beautiful, alien, but beautiful. He had seen Oberon towers in Hudcoeden, but they hadn't been this tall, nor this numerous. Some of the structures lacked lower portions altogether and existed only by clinging to the massive suspension bridges that spanned from the neighboring towers. The entire complex looked much like a great hive, with Oberon flying to and fro on their insect-like wings. He didn't dare make this comparison to any of the Oberon here, he knew it was a great insult to link them to the bees they so closely resembled. Each of the spires held one of the great clans and all of their subordinate clans and family members. Thousands of individuals could live in any one of those towers.

The hierarchy of the Oberon nation was impossible for him to keep up with. Everyone knew exactly where they fell within the structure of the government. He had laughed when Ardelle told him that his first day out of bed, but the maid that serviced his room confirmed it. She could tell you exactly where she fell within her clan's political stature and the rank of every one of her siblings, cousins, and even more distant relations. It seemed so ridiculous, but it was how they measured their success. The Oberon had no formal currency, they traded only in political clout.

"I believe your apartments are just there," Clornamti broke into his thoughts. "If you ever need a guide again, I'll be here," she smiled at him, her white teeth flashing in the sunlight.

"Thank you, umm…" he stumbled for the words, "kind lady."

She laughed heartily and without restraint, "Kind lady? Am I an old matron now? Maeryn, you can call me Clornamti, or even Clora, I need no formal title."

"Ah..." he fumbled. Where had his tongue gone now? Why couldn't he just speak with her? "Thank you, Clornamti," he forced out finally, relieved that he managed that much. He bowed slightly to her then turned toward his apartments, cheeks aflame.

The following day was much of the same, but this time he asked her to accompany him as they left the small classroom, something he was immensely proud of. She agreed and led him up the many twisting halls to his chambers, humming sweetly as she did so. He didn't try to speak, instead he just took in the sight of the city and of her as she walked in her relaxed steps ahead of him. He continued this for two weeks before she finally said no, momentarily breaking his heart.

"Not today, Mentor Kairos, today I think you should see more of our city. You've been in that tiny cell for a month now, why not see what we Oberon have to offer?" The invitation was completely unexpected and he thought to refuse at first, but Darl had already left them and there was no one else to contradict him.

"I would love that." His tongue came easier now that he had spent so much time with her, even though he spoke little on their walks back to his quarters.

Her next move nearly took the breath from his lungs. Instead of simply walking ahead of him, she took his hand in hers and pulled him from the classroom. His heart was hammering so hard, he feared she might feel it in his sweating palm. She ignored his nerves and tugged him along through several corridors until they broke free of the tower at the base and crossed out into the cleared area that lay around it. From the ground, the Oberon towers were a daunting sight, with their spiraling heights passing well out of sight within the low hanging clouds above them. There were few actual paths along the ground as the Oberon had no need of them, but a few well-kept walks crossed between the towers, offering visitors a small reprieve in their hike among the buildings.

Clornamti took him down one such path, but not toward any of the looming towers. Instead she took him to a small complex of low buildings that housed visiting dignitaries. A wall encircled the complex, but it would offer little in the way of protection against the winged Oberon, it was more a formality grown from years of consulate buildings within the free cities. He knew the place from his brief reading of the history of Heimili alfa, but he had never actually seen it.

"I thought we would start here," she smiled at him as she released his hand. It felt as though he had lost a piece of himself as the breeze hit the surface of his sweating palm. "This is usually where our visitors from other lands stay, so that they are more familiar with their surroundings. When I heard that you had been given quarters within the tower, I knew you would be different but still, all land-bound eventually come here for a taste of home." She meant no offense by her 'land-bound' statement, but it still drove home that he was still an outsider to her. "Would you like to go inside?"

He considered for a moment, then noticed the looks he was attracting. Anyone could be within those low slung walls, including merchants he had met within Hudcoeden or worse, a sitting Druid visiting Heimili álfa. He had been nobody there, but it wouldn't take much for them to place him. He shook his head, "No, I should return to my quarters. The King and our Master asked that I remain in the tower for my stay. I'm violating that request already."

"Oh," she turned back to him. "I didn't know that, I'm sorry. I will take you back." Her face fell slightly, and he desperately wanted to change that but knew that he couldn't.

He let her guide him back to the tower, though she didn't take his hand this time. She left him at his quarters, as she had done so many times before, but this time she didn't say goodbye as she turned and left.

He stormed into his chamber and sank to his knees behind his closed door. Tears stung his eyes as he sat there, silently wishing he had never gone to his second trial. It was that event that had set him on this road. Now he was stuck in Heimili álfa, answering to a name that wasn't his and unable to enjoy the company of a girl that he truly liked. He longed for to sit under the tree at the center of the grove behind Desmira's house. He missed the peace that a night spent at the center of the magic in Hudcoeden would bring him.

Rules

It was hard to see him so downtrodden, but she still left him with a smile on her face. She had grown quite fond of Mentor Kairos, though the name sounded silly to her. His use of magic was unique, creative almost to a fault. He rarely wasted time on the prescribed methods and tended to just forge his own path, but it had worked for him thus far. There was wisdom in the teachings of the Oberon, but even she had to admit that it was sometimes hard to pull it from their writings.

She had hoped to see more smiles on his face today with the trip to the "lower" city, but he had been right in insisting that they return to the tower. Anyone could be present within the trading areas and if any of them recognized him from Hudcoeden, it could prove disastrous. She knew his secret of course, but she was confident that he didn't know she knew. It was a tangled web, but her grandfather had insisted that she play oblivious when around the young man. He was of a similar mind to Darl, he didn't care for humans and he didn't want any of them to think they had made an impression on a member of the royal family, no matter if it was true or not. She remembered his trial and his use of magic against the Druid's test. How could one forget the Grand Druid shouting and spitting as he and his fellows were being drenched by a water pipe? At the very least, it had been comical to see those pompous old men knocked down a peg, but his display of power in bringing that water up from the warded plumbing had been just as impressive.

She had shared the story with her grandfather when she met with him and Darl the night the travelers had arrived.

He had been unimpressed and with Darl's rebuttal to her statements, the story had negatively colored her grandfather's opinion of the boy. Darl had only words for the lack of respect the boy had shown his obvious betters and their distinguished guests. Of course, the stogy old man only cared for his mussed feelings, having to witness the embarrassment of the Druids first hand had soured him on ever making another trip to Hudcoeden, not that it mattered now that the city had fallen.

    She sighed to the empty hall around her. So much had happened in the last few months and if the prophecy held, there was far worse to come. The sages had long predicted Barrah's return and the subsequent battle for the mortal plane. Their prophecy spoke of a Chavox and his role in the final battle, but there were others as well, including a queen of the Oberon.

    Micah's warning also loomed over her. His dire words of her grandfather's death, the fall of the Oberon, and of her role in the Chavox's battle. She still had nightmares of the vision Micah had forced on her when she had refused his warnings the second time.

    She shook the thoughts of her body broken and lifeless on the battlefield from her mind. It wasn't right to dwell on things she had no control over. There were other things in her life to occupy her and wallowing in the fear of a future that was likely already written, would keep her from experiencing them. She was already struggling with new feelings lately, could she really be falling for the boy that had so recently entered her life?

    She smiled to herself as she entered her chamber, but the smile didn't hold. A brief wave of nausea struck her as she looked toward her chamber windows. The figure that caused her nausea reposed on the ledge.

"Hello mother," Micah greeted as she entered. His hair was messier than last she had seen him, and his eyes more haunted.

"Please don't call me that," she sighed as she moved out of her sitting room and into her bedroom, closing the door lightly behind her, blocking him. "What do you want this time?"

A short laugh bled through the closed door, "So blunt. You would have boxed my ears for speaking to someone like that." She could hear him moving nearer the door, but he didn't follow her. "I've not come for want of anything, only to see how things are progressing. Has Charles learned shielding yet?"

She moved to her closet to dress for the evening, "No, Grandfather assigned him to Darl. I'm not sure Darl has ever taught anyone the shield before and I don't think he has any intention of doing it now."

"That won't do, he needs to know the shields." She could hear him shifting around something in the other room. "Is there any way you can speed things along?"

There were ways she could teach Charles shielding, but it was a very intimate process, something typically reserved for children so that the risks of emotional imprinting were negligible. "I can make recommendations to Grandfather, but he may still say no." She finished dressing and moved back to the door, pausing momentarily to peer at herself in the full length mirror. She adjusted her hair lightly but left the rest of her appearance intact. She opened the door, "Why are the shields so important?" She tried to ignore the rearranged furniture.

"Shields are the gateway to Oberon magic, he will need that, and much more before he can complete his destiny. The timeline is starting to correct, but it is still too early. He was still with the Druids at this age in the history that I remember." He steepled his fingers in front of his lips and tapped them to his face lightly. "You are doing well, mother. We may yet recover from the changes."

"Please stop calling me that!" She whirled on the man, lifting her finger to point at his face, but lowered it slowly. "I will ask Grandfather to start the training for the shield."

"Thank you, mo… Princess." Micah swung his arms behind his back, clasping his hands one over the other. He moved to the window and stared out at the city. "Something is coming, I can feel it."

A knock drew her attention to the door, "Princess, you've been summoned to the king."

"Well, it looks like I'll get my chance to speak with…" She turned to see that Micah had vanished again. Even more disconcerting was that all of her furniture was back the way it had been before he arrived. She hadn't seen it move, there had been no noise and there were no traces of magic. Like before, her memories were clouded but she knew that she couldn't waste the opportunity to speak with the king. Maeryn needed to learn shields, or at least attempt to learn them. He was so cooped up in the tower, at least the training would let him go outside.

Her dress wasn't court attire, but she decided to just go. Her grandfather would just have to suffer her appearance. Her grandfather's disapproval didn't scare her. She left her chambers and fell in with her guards as they led her away from the center of the tower, toward the balconies that offered convenient take-off and landing platforms. She could have lifted off from her bedroom, but arriving to court without her escorts would cause even more of a problem than her current state of dress would.

She opened her wings and followed Dimitri, the leader of her guards into the air. Her second guard tonight was Alexi, but he didn't follow them into the air. He would maintain his position at the center of the tower so that their return landing would be protected. It was the standard tactic for her guards, one would always be with her while the other remained near her quarters. She had six guards in all, two of which were on duty at all times. Considering her rank, it was a small guard contingent, but it wasn't publically known where she stood. Her grandfather played that part expertly, no one even suspected that he had already chosen his heir.

They entered the royal chambers through one of the upper balconies that were for family use only. Though she didn't care what her grandfather thought of her current attire, she didn't need the scandal that would ensue should the general court see her in her evening wear. Dimitri landed first and saluted the guards on station before he waved her in. They could easily just take to the air again, but protocol dictated that they go through the motions. She smiled slightly at the thought of protocol as she smoothed the front of her nightgown and strolled into the royal chambers.

For the most part, this area was empty. Servants moved about on their tasks, but there were no other courtiers here, nor would she be likely to encounter any of her family, as they would all be attending court below. Her grandfather rarely sat on his throne among the others, preferring his private chamber to the din of the court, but her father, mother, and six or seven of her sisters would be there. The others were either married off to Oberon out in the world or serving some other capacity within the kingdom. While it was true that most Oberon families had only a single child, her parents had been especially prolific. She was the youngest of thirteen, all born over the past century. Her closest sibling was nearly twenty years her senior.

Oberon maturity was slower than other races, to fit their enduring lifespans. Though she was nearly twenty-five chronologically, to the Oberon she was just a child and she looked it. She had started her change to womanhood over the past few years, but it would be at least two or three more before she truly grew into it. To a human, she couldn't have been more than fourteen or fifteen, which was why they rarely allowed their children to interact with humans before adulthood. Some Oberon, especially males, didn't reach their mature bodies until well into their third, or even their fourth, decade.

"Good evening, favorite niece." A welcome voice purred from behind her, "you look... sleepy?" Her uncle smiled playfully as he wrapped his arm about her shoulder. It wasn't common for Oberon to show displays of affection, but her uncle had spent most of his life among humans and had adopted many of their customs. "Come to see my brother?"

"I was summoned," she told him, smiling once more now that she wasn't alone. "Any idea what I was summoned for?"

Her uncle roared his infectious laugh, "That would be cheating! You just have to find out the hard way."

She sighed slightly, but didn't let it dampen her mood. Whatever happened, at least he was here to support her. They moved further into the royal apartments until they came to a nondescript wooden door that would take them into the King's private audience chamber. Her uncle knocked, once, to alert the guards within that they had arrived. No guards stood outside to keep the chamber a secret, though she wondered how well it actually worked.

It was several moments before the door finally swung inward to admit them. "The King will see you now." The somber guard told them as he waved them into the chamber. No herald stood to announce them here, it was as informal as one could get when addressing the king.

"Couldn't even bother to get dressed?" her grandfather scolded. "My summons was not that urgent."

"I treat any message from you as urgent, dear grandfather," she demurred, then curtsied before moving toward his throne. The room was empty, save for the handful of guards stationed at every entrance. "What may I do for you tonight?"

She watched color flood into his face, "you can stop seeing that boy, immediately."

His comments were like a slap to her face, "you mean Mentor Kairos? I'm not seeing him…"

He cut her off, hard. "You most certainly are and it does no good for either of you! It stops, now!" He rose to stalk towards her.

"Brother, sit down before you faint again." Her uncle chimed in from his position near the door. "I'm sure Clornamti has kept their relationship purely platonic and is just showing our *guest* a good time." There was a strong emphasis on 'guest.'

"I don't remember inviting you, *brother*, and this doesn't concern you in the slightest." Her grandfather turned back to her and raised a finger to her face. "I've had many reports of you leading this boy around by the hand, to places we both know he wasn't to go!"

How could he possibly know that already? It had only been an hour or so since she had dropped off Maeryn. "I only wanted him to get out of that stuffy tower for a little while. He's been cooped up in there since he's been here, with nothing to do except read the dribble that Darl is forcing on him."

"You watch your tongue in my presence. I selected Darl to teach you and the boy personally. He is one of our most respected tutors." He moved back to his throne and sat once more, "It ends now Clornamti, or I'll have the boy removed."

"No!" she shouted a little too enthusiastically. She took a breath to compose herself, "perhaps a compromise. If he were to begin studying with our field mages, it would at least get him outside and give him a break to absorb what Darl has given him." It was only a small lie, she knew Maeryn needed no break to absorb what little Darl offered. "Basics would give him a practical application of our magic that he could build on later."

Her grandfather turned to stare at his brother before finally nodding. "Very well. I will arrange for him to begin basic field training, but you have to give me your word that you will no longer see him outside of the classroom."

She weighed her decision heavily before replying, "I promise." At least she would still see him in class.

"It's done then, you may go." He dismissed her with a wave of his hand.

She had accomplished what Micah had asked, but what had it cost her? She turned to leave and was quickly followed by her uncle.

"Training in the field, eh?" Her uncle whispered to her as they moved back down the hall toward the balcony, "that was what you were after all along wasn't it?"

She stopped dead in her tracks, "how did you know that?"

"My brother may be blind to your machinations, my favorite niece, but I am not my brother." He offered her his arm and patted her hand softly as they resumed their walk. "It will be alright, my brother can't keep you here forever, and he won't always rule here. In time, you'll be free to make your own decisions, even if they include a certain young man." He smiled at her once more before releasing her to Dimitri and their flight back to her chamber.

His words gave her comfort as she settled in to her bed, he was right after all. Her grandfather couldn't control her forever, despite his wish to do so. All she had to do was do her part while she was here, but once she had finished her schooling she would be free to pursue anything, or anyone, she wanted.

She was almost asleep when her hand drifted across a piece of paper that had been tucked under her pillow. She drew it out to read but didn't recognize the handwriting, not that she needed to bother. A single line was written on the page. *'Nicely done Mother.'* She was going to have words with that man, if she ever saw him again.

The Crossing

"Keep them moving!" Howlter roared to his drivers. The lead wagons slowed as they neared the deeper waters in the center of the Balen. They couldn't afford to delay, it had been raining since an hour before daybreak. "Drive them in!"

Behind the line of wagons stretched an endless stream of refugees ranging from rich to poor, old to barely out of the cradle. Most of the villagers from Hudcoeden hadn't had animals to pull a wagon, let alone a wagon to pull. The entirety of their possessions rode on their shoulders and the shoulders of their loved ones. It was worthy of pity, but not today. Today, Howlter had to bear the angry stares and pleas for help in the same token. He couldn't afford to stop his troop from getting the bulk of the infirm across the water. If the wagons didn't cross before the water was too high, they would never cross and the masses wouldn't survive the oncoming fall and winter if they didn't have the food that rode in the wagons. He had to put the needs of the many before the few that suffered.

He hadn't seen much of Crowlmer or her new charge today, but he knew they rode in one of these wagons. It had even looked like she had picked up another stray since he had seen her last. A young girl was with her the last time he had spotted his former lieutenant. He couldn't believe the fierce woman who had once vowed to lead every vanguard had given up her position for a human, and now seemed to be collecting them. He shook his mane and laughed. He was old enough to know that no man could ever truly understand a woman.

He knew she had faced some challenges since returning from the forest; a lot of the men shunned her due to her new appearance and he had to admit he had been taken aback as well. The feline eyes and nearly split lip, combined with her feral attitude, set him looking for a healer as soon as she had woken from her injuries. Instead they had all given her their blessing. She was perfectly healthy, just different now. Her physical changes weren't the only ones he had noticed though. Since she had awoken, his connection with Nezmas had told him there were other differences as well. It was different than his, but she had power now and he was confident she was unaware of it. He had never felt its like. He couldn't see radiances like many mages could, his gift only allowed him to feel that there was power there. Each gift felt different, but he travelled enough to know that there were still many things he hadn't encountered.

His thoughts faded as he turned his attention back to the snaking caravan that stretched out into the wide, rising waters of the Balen. The first wagons were being pulled up onto the far bank by a contingent of the Druid Guard, led by dour Samuel Dorne, who had met them at the river early in the morning and coordinated the movements. Howlter's force would remain on this side to guard their backs as the civilians crossed, while the bulk of the Druid Guard would dig in on the far side and assist with pulling the refugees out of the water. They had also started the camp and built up some large bonfires to aid in warming the bodies of those who had to swim across on their own. The rain wasn't the pleasantly warm spring rain, it was the bitter cold drizzle of autumn that just seemed to soak straight to your bones. From his platform near the water, he could see the faces of the first folks on foot that had to hop into that icy water. At a brisk pace, it was about a quarter hour walk across the river, and it was cold. If the rain soaked to your bones, the river went clean through you and the water was only getting deeper.

"Sir, from the rear!" shouted one of his sergeants from his right.

He turned and drew the spyglass from his hip so that he could see the ranks of his men arrayed nearly a league behind them. He could see the men undulating forward as plumes of dust and smoke obscured the foremost of their ranks. The demons had found them. Thousands of them spread out on the field across from his men, still several leagues away but close enough that they must know what he did here and how vulnerable they were.

"Get these people across the river." He told his men flatly, then bounded from the platform to find transportation to the rear. "Bring me a horse, a mule, anything with four legs that is faster than my waddle!" he commanded. A horse appeared within moments, a worn-looking, grey-colored thing that he would have volunteered to feed to his dogs, if it had any meat left. It was fitting for him to ride, it was likely the only creature in camp that understood old age.

The horse plodded along at a pace that barely met his requirements of 'faster than a walk' but soon the old horse picked up speed and rolled into a canter that threatened to neuter him. He had never been one for horses and riding on the back of this ancient bag of bones didn't change matters. It was perhaps the most painful league he had ever crossed, but he reached his lines before the demons did and proceeded to issue orders. Ergon fell into step with him quickly, but had to back off to keep from laughing. Howlter walked as though the horse was still between his knees.

"Get these men into a proper formation!" he shouted to the assembled officers. "We have to keep them away from our civilians and then give them a chance to cross. Do we know how many we face?"

"At least four thousand sir, though there are none of the harpies with them."

"Nezmas be praised for that." Howlter exclaimed, out in the open field like this the harpies would be able to harry the civilians without much fear of his soldiers. "Well, it's only four to one odds, we've had much worse." The men chuckled. "No heroics, just hold the lines and draw back to the water as the civilians cross. We don't need to kill them all." He smiled to the eager faces around him, then nodded to the officers to carry out the orders they had carried since leaving the tunnels. They had all known that the demons would catch them eventually, they had just hoped they would be on the other side of the river when it happened.

"Howlter!" A rather angry female voice shouted from behind him. "Where do you need me?" Crowlmer was decked in her armor for the first time since she had rejoined them, her twin curved swords once again on her belt.

"Right now, you need to get across the river." Howlter told her. It was painful to watch the shock cross her face, but she had given up her position and hadn't trained with his men or even marched with them for several months. She would be end up being a liability like the civilians

"You know I'm still the best blade here," she told him. "I can help."

Howlter shook his mane. "No, you can't. Go take Aurin and the little girl across, and see what help you can offer on the other side. There are only four thousand in front of us, the rest could be moving to flank or could even have crossed the river and are just waiting for all of these civilians to cross over without us." It was a thinly veiled excuse to give her some honor, but she didn't accept it.

"You're a fool," she growled. She didn't argue further, another sign that she had changed. The stubborn woman he had sent into that forest wouldn't have taken 'no' for an answer and would have led the troops onto the field. She stared hard at him with those feline eyes then turned and left the field, trotting for the civilian camp. Halfway there, she was joined by a small girl in ragged clothing with brown hair blowing in the wind and rain. It was the same girl he had seen before, but she looked even slighter in the full light of day.

"I never thought I would see the day that she backed down." Kary said from his right arm, Howlter hadn't even noticed the man approach. "That forest did something to her that she can't shake and I don't mean those strange eyes."

"Let it be Kary, get your men ready to fight." Howlter didn't want to get into the woman that Crowlmer had become, or what to do with her now. There were bigger problems to deal with. Kary's scouts would act in place of a traditional cavalry unit, riding out to flank when the enemy pushed too hard in any one place along the line. He hadn't brought cavalry with him, and the horses Kary's men rode had been commandeered from the Druid guard when they fled the city. Ergon would command the center with his force acting as anchor. The flanks were both commanded by his new lieutenants, Darceer and Greymane. They had been with him for many campaigns and had taken over for Crowlmer nicely.

He had sent several riders out the first night of the battle in Hudcoeden to get messages to the remaining cohorts that he had left the city, but he couldn't be sure if any had gotten through. His original plan had him in Hudcoeden until the following spring, however the early arrival of the army and the speed with which the city fell had changed his plans immensely. He still had a force of three thousand scattered all over the south, but he couldn't count on any reinforcements until Krossfarin at least. This meant he had to promote from the men he had to fill the hole that Crowlmer had left and he needed a fourth to pick up the partial cohort that had assembled before the city had fallen. Two of his units still reported directly to him and would remain in reserve for as long as possible, moving in to spell the men that would be doing the bulk of the fighting. None of them taking the field were full strength, any two combined would have a hard time claiming full strength. He had lost many in the streets during their final stand. A thousand Gremen remained of the better than two thousand he had taken into the city. He knew that number would shrink further today.

He led his cohorts to the rear of the line and waited. The demons were still nearly a league off, but their vanguard was on its way now. They came straight at his massed soldiers, no fear of the Gremen and their defensive position. When they reached a quarter league from his position they charged full tilt. He guessed there were around five-hundred in that force. With a crash, they collided with his front line, but barely slowed. The front ranks of demons blasted through his lines, leaping shields and spears alike, to land in the midst of the assembled soldiers to begin their killing.

If he faced any other force, he would lay odds on his men, even outnumbered four to one, but the demons were not like other armies. They tore into his center, collapsing the first few ranks in on themselves before the cohort there had a chance to push back. He ordered his reserve into the center immediately, he didn't wait for the rest of the demons. If the van was like this, he would have to commit everything he had just to holding them. Reinforced, the center pushed the demons back to the defensive line and held them there, but it cost them dearly to do so. He could see the bodies of those that had fallen everywhere, crumpled masses filled spaces two and three rows back from the front.

"Get the dead and wounded out of there, we're going to need room to move." He ordered his attendants and the message was relayed to the cohort commanders.

The majority of the enemy were closing the gap, arraying themselves in a half moon around the smaller Gremen force before marching forward at a measured pace. The van had charged wildly, but the main body would close the noose slowly, ensuring that his force had no chance to escape on this side of the river. He had made no plans to leave the bank of the river anyway, but it was unnerving to be pinned in. They would need to draw back to the banks quickly to avoid being completely encircled.

He took a moment to check on the progress of the civilians behind him and was rewarded with the sight of an orderly crossing. He had half expected the bulk to panic at the proximity of the demon horde, but they were momentarily calm. Smiling slightly as he watched their withdrawal, a large ebony-skinned woman seemed to be directing things from the bank, a tiny girl still at her side. Crowlmer was proving her worth despite him turning her away.

Turning his attention back to his men, he drew heavily on his magic and passed it out to the men on the front line. It was a simple magic, meant to steel them and strengthen their arms. Beast magic wasn't as showy as the spells the Druids and Wizards used, but it was effective. By using his magic, he could calm his men and strengthen their resolve, or even reassure them that they were in the right. He could even employ the magic on their horses or other beasts to calm the animals and keep them in the fight. It was extremely useful when facing a horde of demons spawned from the hellish lair that Barrah inhabited. His magic didn't affect the majority of the sentient races unfortunately, only the Gremen. A few more bestial tribes could be influenced, but for the most part he couldn't affect Humans, Oberon, Solterrans or Tu'rokians, though he had never tried to affect the latter, but his master told him it could be done.

Beast magic, like all magic, had a dark side, especially for the Gremen. The magic could influence the baser natures of Gremen, their desires, and their needs. There were many instances where the users of beast magic users were killed after influencing others into their beds, and many more stories of the bastards that came from such unions. Howlter himself came from one union.

A crash tore him away from the dark thoughts. The men were defending themselves as the demons attacked from all sides. The horde pushed forward, tightening their noose as they forced the Gremen back toward the river. Kary rode forth to push the demons away from their left flank, creating a retaining wall against their attempts to close the circle. The right flank spread out to match his efforts, but without the weight of horses beneath them, their push wasn't as effective.

Fire bloomed from the end of the demon lines on the right as Ryat joined the fight. He was alone, his apprentice lost his ability to use magic during the retreat from Hudcoeden. No other Wizards remained with the fleeing refugees. The fire scorched the flanking demons and drove them away better than the horses did, but Howlter knew the Wizard couldn't hold it. That much magic would sap his reserves quickly. The flames ate at the demons greedily before finally dying out as Ryat was forced to cut off the flow of magic, or risk joining his apprentice.

The demons quickly moved to reinforce their lines, but the Wizard had given Howlter's men enough time to close their ranks, withdrawing toward the water. The civilians were still moving much faster than he could ever have hoped, which meant his men could flee the field quicker. Once in the water, they could count on the Druid Guard, some four thousand strong, to cover their retreat across the rapidly rising river.

Howlter poured the last of his magic into his men to strengthen their resolve for one more charge of the demons. It was all he had, he hoped it would be enough.

The lines withdrew to the secondary position with precision, not a single rank had broken during the onslaught. The demons didn't charge wildly into them as he would have expected. Instead, they dropped back and reformed their semicircular lines, advancing slowly. Hundreds of bodies littered the field from the first clash, but the demons were unfazed. Their precise movements belied an undercurrent of control that rivaled Howlter's own.

He scanned their ranks and was surprised to see men amongst the demons. Humans in plain grey cloaks walked amidst the demons with unadorned armor of strange craftsmanship. They walked evenly, and seemed to be leading the lines of demons as they marched slowly across the intervening distance between the forces. Each man carried a blade with three tines along its length, sword catchers of some kind. He had seen a similar blade hanging from the hip of Caliban, one of Barrah's top generals. Were these his men?

Kary pulled the horse back to the rear and assembled them, readying for another charge. The civilians were more than halfway through their crossing, but the lines were starting to slow as the water continued to rise. Howlter ran his hand through his soaking hair and flung the sweat aside. The demons reached his front lines and the battle began anew. How long could they hold? Would it be enough? He drew in the last of his power and pushed it out to the men, praying to Nezmas that he could hold this bank.

Still Birth

"On the count of three, give us another push." Ardelle told the tiny human girl she was tending to. She had ended up in the small village about four leagues south of Heimili álfa. Ardelle had left early this morning knowing that this girl would deliver soon and that she would be alone. The girl didn't know who the father of the child was and her own parents had long left the picture.

The dirt poor humans that lived here typically served as maid servants to the Oberon. It was expected that the young ones would find an Oberon family of their own to serve by the time they were in their early teens, and would then move out to their own hovel. Some served such large Oberon clans that they were able to guarantee their children places amongst the servants; however most served lowly branches of society that couldn't afford to keep more than one or two servants and had to 'settle' for using humans. Oberon castes included a servant class, but even they had standards and held 'rank' amongst their brethren. The smaller clans had no such claim to rank and couldn't attract Oberon to serve them. The humans here and in similar villages would fill that hole, for an Oberon couldn't be without someone beneath them.

Ardelle had seen an immediate need for ministrations, these people had no one to tend to their medicinal needs. The temple of Betala wasn't known for their healing, traditionally that role fell to the Druids or the Clerics of Ori, the Arcana of Life, but she had grown up amongst the Druids and learned enough to help. Priests of Betala had the capacity for healing, but it typically dealt with things like infection and disease where a purging with fire could prove effective, as she had done when Aurin's wounds had festered after his fight the night they met.

Ardelle met this girl her first night in the village and knew that there were going to be issues. The young woman was severely malnourished, much too young to be caring for a child and it was obvious that she had a few parasites. Ardelle could have healed the parasites if the woman hadn't been pregnant, it was dangerous to use that kind of power around developing babies. It was going to be difficult for them for the first few months, but Ardelle didn't think she was leaving any time soon and could at least tend to this one baby and her mother.

"Okay," she told the girl. "One, two, three, and push!"

Screaming, the girl pushed with everything she had. Ardelle could see the crown of the baby's head, and with one more push she knew there would be another little life in the world.

"You are doing great!" she reassured the girl. "One more push and the baby will be here."

The girl took a deep breath and bore down as hard as she could, screaming again as the baby tore free. Ardelle smiled at the slimy bundle before she realized that something was wrong. She ran her finger through the baby's mouth to clear the airway, but it didn't breathe in. Laying her hand on the baby's chest she could detect no movement of a heartbeat. Frantically, she tried to start the baby's heart but it was no use. The baby was a stillborn, it had never drawn a breath.

Tears filled her eyes as she turned her attention back to the mother. "I'm sorry," she whispered to the little girl, trying to convey more in the words than simple empathy. The mother wailed into the dark, unforgiving night.

Ardelle busied herself sewing up the tears the baby had left in the mother, stemming a small trickle of blood. The mother would live, there was that small victory, but it was empty.

Once the mother was stable, she cleaned the baby and washed away the blood and birthing fluids. Ardelle handed the small, still bundle to the grieving young woman, who held the lifeless baby close to her body. The little girl who had already felt so much pain only to have this tragedy thrown at her as well. Standing, she took leave of the girl, holding the baby that would never grow to hold her hand, would never speak or laugh. It was too much.

Once outside in the cold night, she collapsed to her knees. Things hadn't changed, the world was still a cruel, evil place, full of sadness and loss. Turning her tear-filled eyes to the heavens, she bellowed, "Why?"

She let the emotion flow out of her for what felt an eternity before she felt that tingle at the back of her mind again. Betala was trying to reach her, but she couldn't face her mistress now. She hadn't opened herself to the Arcana since she had been freed from her curse, though Betala often tried to reach her. For now, Ardelle's hurts were too much to bear without letting in the Arcana that had left her in that forest.

She knew that Betala could do nothing to counter Barrah's punishments, but Ardelle had been so alone in that cursed wood. The curse had driven all hope from her and left her with nothing; and a soul without hope is a damned soul. A thought struck her as she wiped the tears from her face.

Souls.

There was a lone priest of Ori, the Arcana of Life, in Heimili álfa, he may know something of these births. This wasn't the first stillbirth she had heard of and if she was right, there were many more. Her instincts told her to remain with the mother, but she couldn't just sit idly when she may know what was happening. The exhausted mother was sleeping, her tear stained cheeks belying her grief. Even her grief couldn't compel her to remain awake after the birth. Ardelle removed the small, still bundle and placed it in the cradle at the back of the shack, it would be up to the mother to care for the remains and see to a burial by whatever beliefs she held. Before leaving, Ardelle checked the girl's vitals, then sought out the one midwife in the village and asked her to check in on the girl from time to time. The midwife was old, likely in her eighties, and didn't get around much, but she agreed to do this for in light of all the help that Ardelle did around the tiny village.

Taking small comfort that the girl at least would be cared for, she found her horse and set out for Heimili álfa. The trip was too long, considering that most of the residents of the tiny village were servants in the city. One in ten residents had some form of transportation other than their feet, but the Oberon laws prevented them from settling any closer to Heimili álfa. It bothered her a great deal that such segregation was allowed to flourish, but there was little she could do. She would have thought that things would have improved since she had first visited nearly two hundred years ago, but that didn't appear to be the case.

The ride gave her time to reflect on what she had seen and heard since she had arrived in Heimili álfa, the first major city she had spent any time in since leaving Wylltraethel. There had been hundreds of still births this year among the residents of the shanty town, many more than when she had last walked among the poor. She had heard mention of a small number among the Oberon, which was completely unheard of. The Oberon birth rate was incredibly low even during her time and to hear of a still birth within them was shocking. Oberon biology was the most evolved of the races and geared toward smaller family sizes, with each family doing everything in their power to see to the health of each and every newborn.

From her time in the temple, she knew that sickness or poor health of the mother could cause a stillborn, but that was an occasional thing more common among the poor. To have so many still-born in all layers of the social strata, she feared that the other possibility was the culprit.

The children had been born without a soul. A soul was vital to life, every living creature had a soul, though among the animals and plants of the world it wasn't as obvious as it was among the sentient races. When a mortal died, their soul was judged and those that had lived their lives as they should were reborn. If the soul was corrupt, or a mortal lived an evil life, they were condemned and sent to the realm of Lookai, an eternal torment that no soul ever left. In her time, it was Barrah's duty to decide what souls had lived a good life and those that deserved eternal damnation. It had been exceptionally rare that a soul was ever sent to that horrible place, but if she was right, Barrah had corrupted the process and rendered his judgment on all mortals. She hoped the priests of Ori would know the truth.

She left her horse within the lone stables that tended to the few animals present and pressed into the city. The visiting priests were quartered within the same tower as Charles, which gave her a good excuse to look in on him, though he was likely still with his new master at the moment. She made a note to stop at his quarters on her return.

The tower had no stairs to speak of, just a winding ramp that spiraled around the core of the structure stopping several floors from the top. Outsiders were not permitted at the uppermost levels. The visitors were somewhere near the top, they were kept as close to the Oberon as possible. She didn't know the full reason for their visit, but she did know that most of the major churches were represented. The chambers were empty, but she had expected that. The priests would be in the small common area at the center of the tower, where they would see to any local worshippers and conduct business between them.

The priest of Ori was a big Tu'roki man who stood nearly head and shoulders taller than Aurin. He was an older Tu'roki with a thin wisp of hair sprouting from his lip and extending past his mouth on either side, a common feature found in the older members of the race. His large shoulders bore the weight of the immense shell that adorned his back. Intricate runes of his church spiraled about his chest, carved directly into the solid flesh of his natural armor. He wore only a small skirt, or rok in the Tu'roki language, which hung from his waist down past his knees. He was currently speaking with a heavily robed priest of Mamrix, the Arcana of Knowledge.

Two guards watched the room from their perch on a balcony above the assemblage, but they knew to allow her entry. As an honored guest of Driamati, she had the run of the city. They nodded to her silently as she entered and one returned her quick salute with one of his own.

She took a moment to adjust her clothing, remembering that she was still covered in the blood and birthing fluids. To most of the assemblage she would be horrific looking, and likely had a smell to match. Too late to make a better first impression, she ignored the baleful looks and frightened faces as she marched straight for the big Tu'roki. She had met him once before, shortly after she arrived here but their conversation had been short and bereft of anything but pleasantries. "Master Ceh'ruk, may I have a word with you?" She bowed slightly as she spoke, ignoring the hand that shot up to the priest of Mamrix's nose. She had no care for his sensitivity.

The Tu'roki's moustache twitched as he took in her appearance, "Sister! Are you quite alright?"

"Please Master Ceh'ruk," she interrupted. "It is urgent."

"Of course, but let us adjourn to the balcony, I fear that your presence has upset some of our brothers and sisters." He inclined his head slightly to the priest next to him and moved toward the archway she had just entered.

"Master, I need to know about the still births," she began before he had stepped onto the balcony. "Is it Barrah?"

The big Tu'roki sighed, "Yes, sister, it is. When he returned sixteen years ago, he began to punish all mortals for the lives they lived. All were judged unworthy and damned to the domain of the dead. There are no old souls, no rebirth."

Ardelle had suspected the answer but was still shocked. "Is it everywhere?"

"In truth, I don't know but it is everywhere that the followers of Ori have been. Birth rates are down and the number of stillbirths are up. People fear for any woman that is with child." He turned to face out into the city, "At first our lord sought to stop Barrah, but he doesn't have the strength. The others tried to help, but they just don't have the power to overcome Barrah's influence over death and rebirth."

"There must be something," she started, but he stopped her with a hand.

"We have tried everything," he affirmed. "As long as Barrah holds dominion, the loss will continue. I'm sorry to be the one that bears this news, I wish there could be another way." He turned back to her, his eyes brimming with tears. "We are here to discuss our resistance to Barrah. Each city-state and every active church has sent a representative to negotiate our response. We must do something to stop the Demon of Punishment, and it will require all of us, you included. Perhaps, after you've a chance to clean up, you could join in our discussions with Driamati?"

She considered the implications of her presence at this council. True, she was the Avatar for Betala, the highest of all her priests, but she had no desire to return to the church life. She felt even less desire to surrender herself to her mistress, a fact that she couldn't share with the other members. To shun the will of the Arcana was the highest form of blasphemy amongst the church. Fallen Avatars weren't unheard of, Ezra was likely the most famous example, but they were also removed from any and all dealings with the devout. Their influence was seen as a poison to the church and quickly removed, in any way necessary. "I have no contact with my church, and my influence elsewhere is limited. I'm afraid I would be more of a detriment to this council than a boon."

"That may be, but you are an Avatar, sister, that carries a lot of weight." He turned his great head back toward the congregation within the tower. "To be honest, I would much rather hear what you have to say than another speech extolling the plight of the churches and their need for tithes."

She tried to keep the disgust from her face, but the sarcasm bled through. "Tithes? I wish I had the time to worry about gold."

Ceh'ruk's face perked up, "Some days, it is all they bicker about. Gold for troops, gold for the church for maintenance, and more gold for the workers needed for that maintenance, the list goes on. The city-states are almost as bad, though their needs seem more genuine given that they will have to house and feed the armies that we raise. We need someone to drive home the urgency of this fight, someone who understands what we will lose if we don't act, someone like you. The other Avatars hide in their great churches, surrounded by their guards, fearing that what has happened to Ven and Gelthar's Avatars will happen to them."

She had heard the speech before, from priests of her own church when she was first selected as Avatar, but his last statement gave her pause. "What happened to the other Avatars? This is the first I've heard of anything."

"I forget that you haven't walked freely for long, I apologize." He took a deep breath, "Ven's Avatar was slain during the sacking of Falderal and no one has risen to take his place. Some say that Barrah has sealed the legacy and that no mortal can ever hold the mantle again. During the battle in Hudcoeden, the Avatar of Gelthar also fell with similar results. The Druids have been unable to commune with their lord since then. Worship of Ven has completely vanished since his Avatar's fall, and some fear it will be the same for the rest."

She finally understood. "You don't need me, you need an Avatar to stand at the head of the army and shame the others into following. You seek to use me as your figurehead, the answer is no."

"Please consider the invitation, sister, you don't need to commit to anything today. We meet tonight at sunset in the grand hall." Ceh'ruk bowed his head as much as his great shell would allow, then left her to consider.

He had given her much to think about, even though their conversation was brief. She knew that Barrah was responsible for the stillbirths and she also knew that no alliance stood within the mortal races to counter the fallen Arcana. Barrah had been free of his prison for sixteen years, and in that time no army had been raised, no coalition formed to stop him. Had the world fallen so far?

The thought of being a figurehead appalled her. She had no desire to shame anyone into fighting, she truly had no desire to fight at all. After her flight from Falderal and her failure to stop the demons there, she had lost her will. She knew she could wield her sword and magic if pressed, but she didn't feel the drive to take the battle to the enemy. When Aurin had first told her the state of the world, she had been incensed, she wanted nothing more than to march forward and lay waste to Barrah's army single handedly. With her powers, and Betala's backing, she could stop the army on her own but she couldn't bring herself to open her mind to her mistress. She had lost Aurin since then and she had faced the enemy and failed. How could she lead an army? Any endeavor with her at the head seemed doomed to fail, she could never be the hero she had dreamed of. She tried to stop Barrah over a hundred years ago and had been banished for her trouble, what would make today any different?

She left the balcony for her apartments, she needed to clean up. At least the feel of the heated water would take her mind from the world, if only for a few moments.

Thief

Charles slammed the book closed a little harder than he had meant to, causing Darl to look up from his desk. "Please treat my books with more respect, Mentor Kairos. They are older than you are and I would say more valuable."

"Sorry, Master," Charles sighed.

Clornamti tried to hide a giggle behind her hand as Darl's head lowered back to the tome he had been penning for several days. She had been hesitant around him since their last outing, but was slowly warming back up. He had decided that he would ask her to walk with him again today, though he hadn't gathered the courage. The boring text he had just finished was slowly bringing his blood to a boil, six hundred pages of dribble about Oberon magic and its uses in place of Solterran spells. Why would anyone bother? It was far easier just to use a focus than it was to try to construct from stone using rituals designed to manipulate the air. Some Oberon felt it tainted their magic to change the focus, it somehow smudged their relationship with Vielk, though Charles was sure the Arcana could care less.

Darl really had taught him nothing. Oberon magic was no mystery, even with all of the pomp, it was identical to using Ven's magic. He had mastered their architectural rituals in less than a week and had moved onto their spells for travelling on his own, but Darl had reprimanded him for studying outside of his curriculum. He had even dragged Charles before Driamati in an effort to get the old king to scold him further. Driamati had dismissed them both for wasting his time, but not before publically shaming Charles, or rather Mentor Kairos, about his inability to follow simple directions. Charles was told to avoid digging too deeply into magic that he 'could never hope to understand'. So he was forced to study the magic secretly in his bedchamber every night.

The spells for travelling were what he truly desired from his instruction, but it was clear that Darl was never going to teach him. Charles often wondered if his master truly knew the spells anyway or if he refused to teach because he just didn't know himself. The tomes Charles had uncovered were old, even by Oberon standards. There were eight in total and they were written in a form of Oberon that Charles spent a full day deciphering. The works had also been absent any of the usual Oberon bloat, the author just spoke of the magic. He longed to try any of the spells, but they required a good deal of magic and his instructors had a tendency to leave him with nothing usable by the end of the day.

Darl had handed him over to the battle instructors two days ago. They claimed half of his day now, splitting their sessions between morning and afternoon. Today had been a morning session where they were supposed to teach him to utilize his magic without a ritual or focus, however they had failed to teach him anything. Their training was brutal, they constantly assaulted him with magic and offered little in the way of guidance. He had a fair idea of what went into the spells they were using, but he still couldn't repeat them. What made it worse was that he could only practice them on the field, with the instructor looming over him. They never offered anything in the way of positive reinforcement, only criticism of his spellcasting.

"Kairos!" Darl shouted from behind his desk, "is my time worth so little to you? You have the honor of working with one of the greatest Wizards in Heimili álfa and you just sit and stare out the window. The king will hear of your inability to learn, don't you doubt."

Charles hadn't realized he had been staring out the window but it really didn't matter. Darl wasn't teaching him anything, just assigning him more books to read, books he claimed to have written but Charles doubted the man could even prepare half of the rituals, let alone create them on his own.

"If, perhaps, you were to teach us something, I might be more inclined to pay attention. However, all you do is lord over us from behind that desk while we comb through these worthless books!" He shoved the books onto the floor to highlight his point but instantly regretted it.

"Teach you something?" Darl's pupils widened dangerously, "pay attention." His hands shot up and before Charles could react, a lance of raw magic flared out. Before it struck, the lance split to five separate tendrils, four grabbing one of Charles' limbs and the last wrapped around his neck. The force of the attack drove him from his desk into the back wall of the small chamber. The air left his lungs forcefully, causing him to gasp but the tendril around his neck didn't allow him to pull in much air. "This is Darl's hand, a spell of my own design. Effective wouldn't you say? Right now your lungs are desperately trying to pull in air but my spell is tightening about your neck. At the same time you might think to use your magic, but without your hands or feet you are limited to using what you can cast raw. Since I know you are such a horrible student, your ability to cast without a ritual is non-existent. So what do you do?"

"That's enough," Clornamti shouted adding, "Master," as an afterthought.

"No, I don't think it is." Darl told her, "He still hasn't learned that he is a toad trying to fly."

Charles pulled on his pool of magic and sought to channel his power to break the bonds. He discovered Darl had neglected to raise a shield about himself. His teacher was so arrogant that he believed Charles was completely helpless. While the spell was impressive, without a shield to protect yourself, or a pool large enough to completely stamp out your opponents spells, you were vulnerable. Darl's pool was rather pathetic. Charles drew on the bulk of his magic and began to form it into a lance of his own. He knew that Darl would be able to see what he was doing, but the lance was a ruse. With his remaining magic, he created an egg shape near his throat, at one of the healing points Micah had shown him. His airway immediately opened slightly. His instincts told him there were other uses for that little knot of magic, something he had never tried. He sucked in what air he could, his vision already starting to go black, then released the first spell. As expected, Darl scrambled to throw up a shield that just couldn't contain the bulk of Charles' magic. The grip of the tendrils started to wane, but rather than letting them go, Charles used the small egg of magic to grab at the rope that had been about his neck. He drew the power of Darl's spell into himself rather than allowing it to dissipate, then he fired the magic back at the stunned Oberon in a perfect copy of the original.

Darl sputtered and gasped against the bonds about his neck and choked out, "How?"

Swallowing, Charles rasped, "You finally taught me something useful, Master. You are right, this spell is quite effective." He released the spell and allowed Darl to breathe once more.

"Get out of my classroom!" Darl screamed in a high pitched voice.

"Yes, Master," Charles replied coldly. "I imagine you'll report this to the king, when you do, please let him know that I will be changing my schedule so that I am with my battle instructors all day. I've learned what I could from you." He left Darl sputtering on the floor as he made his way out into the hall.

Clornamti dashed from the room to stand in front of him, barring his path, "How did you do that?" she demanded, hands on hips.

"That spell was simple enough, and I had the magic to do it. Some of the real battle magic is still foreign to me." Charles admitted. He was starting to calm down and his ability to speak full sentences to Clornamti would soon fade away.

"No, not the spell, a child could do that spell," she blurted, then caught herself. "How did you take his magic and make it yours?"

Charles realized what he had done. He hadn't even thought of the spell to take Darl's magic, it had been pure instinct. The more he considered the magic, the more he thought of Aurin on that cliff. Aurin's sword had absorbed the magic of the Remnant and turned it into something Aurin, and through him Charles, could use. That transfer of magic had been what he was thinking of when he had set that small egg at his throat. "It's just something I saw once," he told her dismissively. "Nothing really, just a redirection of the magic."

"It wasn't nothing, Maeryn, you took Darl's magic and threw it back at him. I've never heard of such a thing and you can be sure no one else here has heard of it either." She looked around the hall as if there were Oberon watching them. "Magic like that could be very dangerous, in the wrong hands you could strip the power right out of anyone you chose!"

He didn't follow her logic, but he could see the implications of striping another of their pool. There were times when two or more people shared their magic, a practice called linking. During linking, they had to be very careful not to over use the other's pool or risk burning out their magic completely. If Charles was to use the magic he had just demonstrated in anger or without restraint, he could permanently strip a person of their gift. Just now he could have damaged Darl's magic if he had continued to pull from the man, instead of just absorbing the magic from the air. He had felt the briefest of connections with the Oberon when he had released the egg, but he had ignored it. "I…" he couldn't even finish the thought. Could he really use his magic to destroy someone's ability to use their own?

"I'm sorry, I didn't mean to worry you further." She reached for his hand and guided him toward his rooms. He was too shocked at his own magic to even blush over the physical contact with Clornamti. He just let her guide him from the scene of his latest crime. "Why don't we try to put this behind us? Would you mind if we take a brief detour? I want you to see something." Clornamti spoke sweetly, calmly. Was it out of fear or something else? "It will just take a moment."

"Umm…" he managed. His tongue couldn't form the words, so he simply nodded. His mind raced through the possibilities of her suggestion. Was she leading him to waiting guards so they could arrest him? Some secret path directly to the king so that she could share the news directly?

"You'll like it, I promise." She assured him, tugging him by the hand. "At the least it will help you forget what just happened."

They raced up two flights past his floor and turned to go back into the tower, her glittering wings just a span or two from his face. He was huffing with the exertion, but he refused to let that stop him. She was right that he needed to forget what had just passed between him and Darl, but he couldn't shake it from the forefront of his thoughts. She turned down two more hallways before entering into a large circular chamber at the heart of the tower.

The ceiling in this room soared more than ten strides up with great arches supporting its dome all the way around the outer part of the room. A single shaft of sunlight filtered through colored glass at the peak of the chamber, illuminating a tile mosaic that stretched the entirety of the floor. The light seemed to come from the peak of the tower, but he knew they were far from the highest floor. The building must have been designed with an open shaft from this point up.

"It's mirrored." Clornamti answered his thought. "The sun will shine into this chamber from dawn till dusk and the moon will even light the room when it is full." She released his hand.

He stifled a sigh as she moved away. Her brown eyes locked onto his briefly, sparkling in the light. Her hair had fallen loose in their flight up the stairs and the curled locks were framing her face, emphasizing the angular lines of her face. She smiled slightly as she turned away to look at the frescos that lined the walls around them, her ruby lips pulling back from her perfect teeth. His heart hammered within his chest and all thoughts of his magic and the fight with Darl vanished. "It's beautiful," he managed, but had desperately wanted to say *you're*.

"I knew you'd like it." She sighed heavily as if she hadn't known at all. "This is Vielk's chamber, this is where he chooses his avatars and where we crown a king. Sometimes they are one and the same, like Driamati," she turned to look at him directly. "This is the center of worship here in Heimili álfa. The Druids had a chamber like this in Hudcoeden, it was where the trials were held."

He hadn't known that. He knew that the Druids would use the large chamber for things other than just the mage trials, but had day dreamed during most of the historical sessions that covered what they actually did. "Interesting," he muttered.

"They keep the identity of Gelthar's avatar a secret though. No one outside the order knows who it is right now." She wandered about the chamber, awestruck. "It is just another tool here. Everyone tries to be Vielk's avatar, or at least get someone from their clan chosen. It carries a great deal of weight with the court."

Another political tool, he should have known. "Is everything political here?"

She turned back to him, quizzical. "Isn't it everywhere? Your Druids used their influence to run the city you lived in, even though there was actually an elected government. Falderal was much the same, the Wizards ran the place even though there was a lord. In all of the city-states where the Arcana hold sway, it is their avatars and the chosen followers that seem to hold all the power. There are, of course, exceptions. Nezmas, for instance, doesn't directly influence the Gremen, even though they are his chosen. Ori has little real influence in the world, his temples tend to be natural preserves more than places of power. All of the others though, they hold some kind of sway in the world."

"Maybe that is the problem." he whispered.

"I'm sorry?" Clornamti asked.

"It's nothing," he lied. "This chamber truly is beautiful. How often do you come here?"

"Personally?" she asked, then continued without waiting for his response. "I try to come here every day at sunset. The colors that reflect down the mirrors light the room in a way that I've never seen anywhere else. I was hoping we'd start to see them when we got here, but summer is still clinging and the sun won't set for a while yet."

"I've nowhere else to be," he told her, locking the uncomfortable subject away. He was honest and open, and the anger over the discussion had some to do with it, so did his earlier fight with Darl. He wanted to find something he could share with her that didn't root itself in negativity.

They sat together silently, enjoying the changing colors as the sun finally began its trek to the horizon. As the light dimmed, an array of colors danced among the columns around them. Yellows and golds, reds and oranges, all the bright colors of the sun swirled along the marble. The colors played about Clornamti's skin, changing the tanned flesh to the sun kissed colors that matched the swirls around them. It was far more captivating than any marble pillar, Charles thought. He caught himself staring into her deep brown eyes and losing himself there. He moved to turn away, but realized that she stared back. They were also getting closer, though he didn't know how.

As she drifted into him, their lips touched, but only for the briefest of seconds before a booming voice sounded from the chamber behind them. "What do you think you are doing here?" a stern female Oberon thundered.

They parted quickly and rearranged their features before turning around, "Matron Miatem! I was just showing Mentor Kairos the sunset from Vielk's chamber. He had never seen it." Clornamti offered, but the displeased look didn't leave the older Oberon's face.

"Well he's seen it now, you get back down to your family's quarters, immediately." There was no suggestion in the tone. "You." The woman turned on Charles. "I won't see you with her majesty unescorted again, will I?" The honorific threw him until he remembered that Clornamti was a member of Driamati's clan. Hearing that title meant she was a lot closer to the king than he was originally led to believe.

He didn't bother to answer, it was clearly rhetorical. Clornamti let herself be led away, a whispered tongue-lashing echoing from the matron as they disappeared around a corner at the far side of the chamber. Clornamti risked one last look over her shoulder before they vanished completely. He couldn't believe the day he had, first his field training had been a complete failure, then the fight with Darl and now he was likely to be called before Driamati for his actions here with Clornamti. Then there was the kiss.

It had been a brief contact, but it had been the most amazing contact he had ever experienced. He had never cared for a girl before and never been close enough to one for the thought of a relationship to exist. There were other apprentices that were female, but they had never even spoken to him. Most of his peers avoided him like the plague, his name was tainted throughout the college as one who would never move forward. The Druids had labeled him a troublemaker on his first day with them, calling him out for already using magic when most of his classmates had yet to even tap their pool. That had been little more than three years ago, now he had met this amazing girl and she reciprocated his feelings. He smiled as he left the chamber, at least the day had ended well.

His mind slowly drifted away from the happy ending and back to his larger problem. Darl had experienced Charles' new talent and the theft of magic. What were the ramifications going to be? Would he be allowed to continue his study or would it be immediate banishment? He couldn't dwell on the 'what ifs' though, he had to prepare himself for the larger conflict. The thought of going against a fallen Arcana drove any happy thoughts of Clornamti, and a relationship from his mind. It would be far better for her if she would just forget about him and go on with the life her grandfather and others had laid out for her. It hurt him deeply to think he would never have the happiness he had so briefly experienced today. What hope did he have of ever surviving against a being like Barrah? What chance at all?

Valor

"Crowlmer!" Aurin roared into the canvas over his head. "Get me out of his damned wagon!" He had heard the horns sound, he knew the enemy was at hand. He should be on the field with his sword in his hand, not strapped to a cot in the back of a wagon. The Gremen babysitter had tied him down in his sleep and abandoned him to the Druid Guard before he woke.

He jerked against his bindings again, trying to gain purchase on the leather, to no avail. He was stuck in this cursed wagon and there was nothing he could do about it. Damn that woman, she knew he wanted to be out in the field today and had decided on her own that he was better served here.

Somewhere, outside his canvas prison, men were fighting and dying but he laid here like an invalid, waiting for the inevitable. The horns had stopped, but that could mean anything. He knew from the rocking of his wagon and the lack of the sound of rushing water, that he had crossed the river. How many more needed to cross? Had the Guard deployed on this side of the river before the fighting had started? What did they face?

"Crowlmer!" He shouted again, though he knew it wouldn't do any good. She was probably where he should be, with the men fighting the enemy.

"Aurin?" A familiar voice rang from the direction of his feet. "Is that you boy?" Samuel Dorne's head came into view at the back of the wagon. "Well it is you!" He exclaimed, as he started to unbind Aurin's hands, chuckling to himself. "That big Gremen woman do this to you?"

Free of his bindings, Aurin shot upright and immediately regretted it. He had been on his back for more than twelve hours and the blood was rushing from his head, leaving him dizzy and disoriented. "Where is she?" He demanded of his commander, though he should have checked his tongue.

"Easy now," Dorne replied. "I didn't tie you up, don't you take it out on me." His master helped him from the wagon.

The grass around Aurin refused to stop spinning, but he ignored it. "What are we facing, is it Barrah?" He reached for his sword and was grateful that it still hung at his side.

"Aurin, son, take it easy. You know you aren't in fighting shape. Yes, Barrah's forces have engaged the Gremen on the far bank, they arrived shortly after we started our crossing. So far Howlter has held them off, but he's running out of ground to fight on. The river is still rising and the demons keep pressing."

"Did the archers make it to their positions?" Aurin asked again, trying to see through the drizzle.

"They did, but we had to abandon them. The waters surged about a quarter hour ago, the river is nearly half again as wide as it was when we started." Samuel stared off at the banks in the distance. Row upon row of Druid Guard assembled there, but there was little they could do when facing that river. The current had picked up, he knew that would make the crossing even more difficult. "I'm going to take some men across and see what we can see, but the last wave of civilians is just now clearing the water."

"I'm going with you," Aurin stated flatly.

"No you aren't." Samuel responded. "You are going to stay here and lead the men, just in case I don't make it back." The tone wasn't a suggestion.

Aurin couldn't argue with the logic, it made sense for him to remain as Dorne's second in command. It seemed like another prison sentence, but his duty was to remain here. "Yes, sir," he responded to his commander. "I'd rather be there, with a sword in my hand."

"I know son, but today is not the day for senseless heroics." Dorne continued to stare at the stream of civilians coming from the water. Some barely made the land before collapsing under the weight of their belongings. Others stood with their head in their hands, shoulders shaking with the tears of those that didn't make the crossing. He imagined that the old, the infirm, and the very young would have great difficulty crossing that raging water now that its level had risen so much. There would be parents grieving the loss of more children today. "Where are the Druids?" he asked Dorne, fearing he knew the answer.

"Gone, for the most part. The elders all left as soon as they crossed, heading north toward the village. Some stayed behind to help, but it was woefully few. Your healer, Castielle, she's around somewhere, as are a few from her sect. After the horns blew, I don't know how many are still here."

Rage boiled within Aurin, the Druids had the power to change the natural order of things, including this river. They couldn't stop it, but they could slow its rise or even divert part of the water. They had regulated the weather within Hudcoeden for centuries, keeping the temperature moderate through all four seasons, as well as bringing the rain and snow when it was necessary to do so. Why hadn't they diverted this storm, or at least redirected some of the water away from the river? These were their people as much as they were his, but they weren't here when it was needed most.

His head reeled as he clenched his fists at his side. He still wasn't well, the head injury he sustained when he fell from the cliff might never heal completely. Castielle had tried to alleviate the symptoms, but it only gave him a very brief respite.

Horns sounded again, but these were much closer and on the same bank. Shouts rang from the right side of the camp, devolving quickly to panicked screams and rushing people. He turned to Dorne and saw the same fear mirrored on his face. The enemy was on this side of the river, they were caught between two forces with a river dividing their own. They split without a word, Dorne going to the men on the bank and Aurin limping toward the right flank. Civilians dashed in every direction as he approached, some bumping and crashing into each other, and him in their haste. He had to stop twice and sit on the grass to recover before he finally reached the thin line of men that stood between all of these people and the horde marching against them.

Thousands of purple skinned demons marched in battle formation with a slow, determined pace across the plains toward their camp. Interspersed amongst them were humans in unadorned grey cloaks, carrying naked swords in their hands. The sword was familiar, he had seen it the night that Charles had attacked the temple. The man he had fought in the square had carried an identical blade. Were they a regular force in Barrah's army? Was the man he had fought here today?

Aurin tracked down the captain that commanded this flank and took over. Immediately he set the troops to forming a defensive rank, two men deep, along the perimeter of the camp. It stretched them thin, but gave the most coverage against the advancing demons. The line would never hold, the demons had better than three thousand arrayed against them. At best, there were four hundred guardsmen here. Dorne would redeploy from the river, but he couldn't abandon the bank altogether. If the Gremen were to try to cross it or worse, if they were to fail in their defense of the far bank, there would be more demons closing on them from the river. There just weren't enough men to stand against the coming demons and the terrain was too open to pull them into a bottleneck. The demons had waited until this opportunity to strike. They likely had reached here long before the refugees and began their preparations. It was the only way to explain their perfect deployment.

Another wave of dizziness struck him as he stared into the horde before them. He nearly lost his feet, but a strong, ebony hand wrapped about his arm and held him upright. "I told you to stay in bed," Crowlmer growled at him. "Did you think you could fight in your condition?"

"We're all going to need to fight, Anissa," he told her, jerking his arm free. "Have you bothered to see how many march against us?"

"And one crippled man is going to make the difference?" She was getting close again, her feral features very near his face.

"Ah...hmm..." a small voice sounded from behind Crowlmer. "I don't mean to interrupt, but perhaps we could argue later." A teenage girl stepped around the Gremen and stood on his other side, offering her own hand as aid. "I'm Adla," she told him plainly.

On instinct, he reached to shake her hand, but when their skin touched something passed between them that was far more than just greeting. He could feel power washing over him, much as it had when he'd fought the Remnant on the cliff. This power was different though, purer. He tried to release her hand, but he couldn't open his. Something was holding him in place, something far stronger than anything he had every felt. He looked up into the girl's eyes and found the answer. Something within those pure blue orbs held him fast, though he couldn't say what it was.

He could feel new energy within him, it was more than he had held before, far more. The power washed over his consciousness, invading his thoughts as it filled him up. When he felt he could stand no more, the connection suddenly broke. He dropped to his knees before Crowlmer could catch him. He was panting, but he felt better than he had in weeks.

The girl joined him on the grass, a confused look on her face as if she tried to understand what had happened. They shared the look for a moment before Crowlmer interrupted. "Get back to bed right now!" she screamed at him, hoisting Adla to her feet before grabbing at his arms.

Before she could lift him, he sprang to his feet under his own power. The dizziness was gone and he felt as healthy as he had on that last day in the forest. He also felt the power again, something he hadn't felt since he awoke within the camp. Crowlmer looked at him with her head tilted to the side. She was still holding him in her arms. Face flaming, he backed away from her and stretched his muscles.

"What did you do?" he asked Adla as he pulled his arms up behind his back in a deep stretch that would have sent him to bed only yesterday. "I haven't felt this good in a month." In truth he had never felt this much power before.

"I…" she started, "I don't know." She still looked lost, confused by the whole situation.

Horns blared, the enemy was approaching fast now. It was a controlled charge, but that didn't matter with such uneven odds. His men braced themselves, readying their spears and shields as the demons and the strange humans rapidly closed the distance. He rushed to rear of the line and placed his shoulders against two of the men. The demon line struck like a wave, crashing against their lines in successive blows. The men bearing shields at the front suffered heavy losses in that first strike, half their number tumbled to the grass under the weight of the demons. The spear men pushed back, but there were just too many creatures and they began to lose ground. He had never been in a melee so brutal. The demons didn't even draw their weapons. They simply pulled the men down and trampled them beneath their goat-feet.

He drew his father's sword from his hip and set into the creatures closest to him, cutting down several, only to have their compatriots fill the holes immediately. Two attempted to pull him from the line, but he removed their hands at the wrist and stepped clear. Thunder sounded from his left as Dorne arrived with what men he could spare from the beach, their numbers painfully small, but still a welcome sight.

"Collapse on me and form ranks!" he shouted into the din, but couldn't tell how many heard him. Crowlmer was at his side now, fighting like a demon herself. She alternated between one of her curved swords and her bare hand. Of Adla, he had no sign, but he hoped she had gotten clear of the fighting.

He ducked under a wild swing and brought his sword up to counter the follow up. Ducking under the man's outstretched arm, he used his elbow to smash the man's face before turning to the next opponent. This one didn't even get a chance to attack, Aurin simply struck its head from its body with a hard slash on the recovery from his last parry.

He was turning now, there was a gentle pressure to one of his shoulders from Crowlmer as she guided him in a leftward circle that carried him clear of the demon that had moved up to challenge him. It was suddenly facing Crowlmer and her wicked blade, the change threw it off balance and allowed her to kill the creature. Aurin found himself trading blows with one of the three-hooked blades, but the man wielding lacked the skill of the first man he had fought with the weapon. A simple parry and a hilt lock broke the man's grip and sent the ugly sword into the mud at their feet. Aurin finished him with an upward slash to the ribs. Then he turned again, encountering two more demons that pressed him hard, but ultimately were no more effective than the last.

Crowlmer had her second sword out and danced into two of the swordsmen, parrying and countering both of their blows with ease. She moved like a creature possessed, nothing came close to her. She dipped and slid, ducked and weaved between blows, hopping over the low attacks and countering with high slashes. There was a bubble of air around the two of them, but outside of that small clearing there were only enemies, he saw none of his men. His enemies pressed thicker upon them, driving Crowlmer back from the ranks of demons and keeping her back to back with him. They kept their feet despite the mounting pile of corpses below them, but the press was growing tighter.

His companion was growling and hissing now, sounding much like the great cat she had been in the forest. Indeed, her features were becoming increasingly feral by the moment. Her body became leaner, its muscles growing taut about her thin frame. Her left sword stuck in a corpse, but she left it there, slashing instead with thick claws that had sprouted from her fingertips. The second sword soon followed.

She moved with feline grace, despite her size. She kept close to him, but had reverted to moving about on all fours. This made it difficult to keep his back to her as she leapt about the demons, slashing and biting. A tail swept from between her legs as she moved, a long black thing that twisted and turned to maintain her balance as she bounced from demon to demon, slashing with her claws and tearing with her teeth.

He tried to keep the demons from getting between them, but there were just too many. A polearm swept inside his guard and sliced into his ribs, causing him to stumble and shout in pain. The power within him healed the wound, but the shock still drove him to one knee. The demons were on him now, pulling at his limbs as they sought to tear him apart. He swung at them as best he could, but they were too close for his sword to be much use. In desperation, he dove into his well of power and sought to use it as he did on that bridge out of the forest. A pool of white light was far beyond what it had been that day, he nearly lost himself, but managed to keep his wits. Pain shot through him from the outside world, but within the power he could ignore it.

He pushed a stream of energy out through his hands and was rewarded with the screams of the demons around him. His vision returned, though he almost wished it hadn't. The power from his hands ripped the creatures apart, sending rivers of their black blood into the grass beneath them. Their howls quickly turned into panicked screaming as those that survived the initial wave stumbled over the dying to escape. The humans among them tried to corral them back into fighting, but the horror of his magic outweighed their control. In the first moments of his attack, more than a hundred demons and their human handlers lay dead or dying on the field around him. Aurin pushed the magic out further and sought out more of the creatures, turning his attention to the humans with them first. The tactic was cruel, killing their officers first left them confused and without direction. He had passed beyond caring about cruelty, more than two hundred of the Druid Guard lay about the field unmoving. Two hundred men he had likely trained.

He poured the magic out into the demons, avoiding any guardsman that still moved. As the demons died, he followed the magic out into the surrounding countryside following the river to the Gremen engaged on the far side. He set about killing the enemy there as he had the others, killing their human officers first before turning the slaying energy on the demons.

You have to stop! A voice boomed within his mind.

The intrusion nearly caused him to stop, but there were still demons left. He had to kill them, kill them all. *No! You must stop! You are too far extended.*

Get out of my head! The magic was rushing through him, giving him a high he had never experienced in battle. He continued his assault, directing the magic into ranks with glee.

They are not all your enemy, look! An odd sensation over took him as the voice directed his gaze to one of the humans that he had already struck. At first he saw nothing, then clarity began to dawn. The blonde hair matted about the human's face, the brown eyes squinted in pain and the weak jaw opened into a slow scream. He had last seen this man, no he wasn't truly a man but a boy still, on the day he left Hudcoeden. He had seen him in the hall of the boarding house as he had led Charles from the building under guard. Brennan had been training to be a wizard then, why was he here serving the enemy?

The shock was enough to drive him back to his body. As his consciousness settled back into his own flesh, he felt the damage he had done to it in his usage of the power. He was as weak again, weaker than he had been before encountering Adla. The Demons had gotten to him during his assault, the shaft of a pike still protruded from his abdomen and his sword arm was badly broken.

He tried to steady himself and find Crowlmer, but his legs buckled beneath him and the ground rushed up to claim him.

Rest now my son, we'll meet soon. The voice told him before he faded away.

Coalition

There were hundreds of people assembled for the meeting by the time she arrived. Everyone from the priests to common military men were present, representatives from every city-state and active church. Ceh'ruk was easy enough to spot, given that he was one of only a handful of Tu'roki present. His moustache set him apart from the others of his race, hair was not a common trait for their people.

She moved to intercept him, but was cut off by a short man in the robes of Betala's church. He had a slight build, thin and wispy, but his eyes held a resolve that she could recognize. A path of scars covered the majority of his face, a common sight among Betala's priests, a reminder that the fire wasn't always in their control. For her, the scars reminded her of the gift that Betala had bestowed, her perfect mastery of the flames and immunity to their heat. The inner fire of the priests was impressive, but it didn't compare to the raging flames within her.

"I had almost called Ceh'ruk out as a liar," the little man blurted as he reached for her hand. His skin was burned along his arms, blackened in some places. "When he sent word that Ardelle had returned, no one at the high church believed him, but my curiosity is greater than most and I had to know." He spoke reverently, but barely contained a lisp that took something from his regal appearance. The burns on his face kept his lips from closing completely, the cause of his speech impediment.

She took in his robes again before addressing him, "Excuse me, Pyre, I must speak with Master Ceh'ruk." Each priest within the church carried a rank, a title to signify their standing within the congregation. Initiates were commonly called Sparks, but their official title was Ember. Sworn priests were Flames, which was typically where priests ended their ascension through the ranks. A chosen few rose to the status of Pyre, a rank that held much esteem as Pyres chose the legitimate head of the church, the Inferno. The Inferno was second only to Betala's Avatar, though sometimes they were one and the same. Within the ranks were individual standings, but she had little care for them today.

The little man moved between her and her quarry once again, "Surely you can spare a few moments for a fellow devotee of our Flaming Mistress."

She sighed. "What do you need, Pyre?"

"You may call me Basir, my lady." He licked the spittle from his lip before continuing, "You'll pardon my bluntness, but where have you been since your return? Our church is in ruins yet you failed to even send word that you lived, we found out through Ceh'ruk's letter."

She clenched her fists at her side, Ceh'ruk had moved off further into the crowd and closer to the dais at the back of the chamber. The assembly was about to start, if she was to meet with him she had to go now. "I really must speak with Ceh'ruk, could we continue this conversation after the gathering?" She was attempting to be polite, but her words were forced and tended to move through gritting teeth.

"I'm afraid I really must know, it may affect the outcome of this gathering." He turned his face down as he spoke so that he looked upon her from the shadow of his brow.

"I have my own duties, Basir, and they are no business of the church," she panted heavily as she lost control of her temper. "I was banished for over a hundred years, and not one of you thought to come for me, what could I possible owe the church? Now step out of the way!" Her voice echoed about the room drowning out all of the voices within the chamber. Every eye turned to them.

Basir lowered his voice, "We will speak after. Know that I do not appreciate being made a spectacle." He turned away, robes swirling behind him as he stamped off into the crowd.

The assembled masses continued to stare for several moments before the conversations resumed. Ceh'ruk waved for her to join him before he continued his march to the stairs of the dais. She huffed once to clear her head, then relaxed her hands and moved through the crowd. After her little outburst, everyone seemed to give her extra space, which made it easier for her to close the distance.

"Are you alright, sister?" The big Tu'roki asked quietly as she stepped up to him. "I'm sorry I didn't have a chance to warn you about Basir, he arrived after we spoke earlier. Have you thought about our conversation?"

Right to the point, *what can you do for us?* She couldn't remember ever being more frustrated with her lot in life. All she truly wanted to do was help those who couldn't help themselves, stand up for the good that she knew still existed. It was clear that she wouldn't get that opportunity as long as the world knew where she was. "I have, and my answer is still no. I only came tonight to reaffirm that, before you used my presence to further your agenda."

"Your words are sharp, sister. I would never put you forward without your permission, I can't say the same for Basir or others from your church."

"Yet it was you that told them of my return, curious." She couldn't help herself, the conversation with Basir rankled her.

Ceh'ruk dropped his large head, "I merely mentioned that I had seen you from afar in my regular communications with the heads of the churches, I had not meant to out you to the others." He ascended the dais and moved to the central podium. She moved to follow, but was stopped by one of his guards who indicated a set of chairs just behind the dais. As she sat, she tucked her skirt in, trying not to make a fool of herself for a second time. The dress was borrowed, from one of the only Oberon women likely to carry a similar figure to Ardelle, Driamati's bastard born, half-human daughter Anamti. Though she was older than Ardelle in practice, the woman was only in her thirties and had more access to gold than any city should. With that access came expensive tastes and many unused gowns. She had loaned Ardelle several outfits on her first few days in the city and then granted her use of her family's personal tailor.

"Friends," Ceh'ruk boomed from the central podium. "Brothers and sisters all, welcome tonight to the start of our coalition. I, as well as many of you here, hope that an accord can be reached and an end put to Barrah's tyranny. As many of you are aware, our attempts at reaching an amicable arrangement have failed for many years, but we can afford to delay no longer.

"Barrah's treachery has reached all of us where he can hurt us the most, our children. His tenant that no mortal has earned the right to be reborn has caused the rate of stillbirths to reach cataclysmic levels. If we can't stop him, our races will slowly die out and he will win without ever having to face us on the field of battle. His armies sew death and discord among all of the races, all of you have suffered from his evil. For every healthy child born in the world, fifty mortals die. We can't continue to ignore the threat, at this rate our races will all be gone within a century." Murmurs rolled through the crowd, shouts of dissent rang from every side of the assembly. Ceh'ruk raised his hand to call for silence, "Many of you will deny what I say, but I assure you these are the facts. My lord Ori has shown us the consequences if we do nothing. Through his Avatar, he has spoken to our congregation and beseeched us to act.

"More than a hundred years ago, we came together to drive Barrah from the mortal world. Every Arcana combined their wills through their Avatars and sealed Barrah within the realm of death, but it wasn't permanent. All Barrah needed was a mortal who was willing to sacrifice their own soul and he could once more touch the living world. He found that mortal sixteen years ago, in Falderal.

"Since the day Falderal fell, we've sought to create a coalition force to once more stop Barrah, but we've been unable to compromise. We can no longer afford to wait for a compromise, this is our last chance to stop the Demon of Punishment. Hudcoeden and the Druids have already fallen,

Krossfarin is next. Barrah's armies have been sighted marching in force toward the last free city in the south. If Krossfarin falls, Barrah could strike anywhere or simply push through to Utladalen and split our nations in twain. If he divides us, we lose all hope for stopping him.

"I have reports that Sozenra's Avatar marches for Krossfarin now to lead the defense, but he may not arrive before Barrah's army. Even if he does, his force is in no way strong enough to stop the horde on their own. Krossfarin needs us all, and they need us to march now." Cheers sprang from a group of soldiers wearing the colors of Krossfarin. Ceh'ruk roared from the dais, "Brothers and sisters, the time to stop the Demon is now!"

Further cheers erupted from pockets throughout the room, but more voices remained silent. After several moments of unrestrained cheering, the Oberon king stood and moved to replace Ceh'ruk at the dais. He raised his hand for quiet before speaking, "Passionate words, Master Ceh'ruk, but you provide little in the way of proof. We have spoken with Vielk as well, he doesn't agree with Ori's assessment of our troubles here and thinks there are other ways to stop Barrah, ways that don't involve the slaughter of our armies on a field of battle not our own!" Cheers erupted from the Oberon elite to Driamati's left. "Krossfarin may well fall to the demons, and our hearts bleed for them, but we can't afford to leave ourselves defenseless."

"That's typical of you Oberons!" One of the Krossfarin men shouted over the king, "we'll see how you feel when it's your city they mean to raze!"

Shouts of agreement rose up from across the room, the calm throughout the room was fading quickly. Part of her had hoped that Driamati would step forward to lead this coalition, since he was the only other known Avatar present. She could stop the arguing simply by opening herself to Betala, but she was done living her life for the sake of this rabble. A pushing match along the center of the room had broken out between the delegation of Gremen and the Krossfarins, it was time to leave. She stood to make her exit when a large hand wrapped about her arm.

"Is your answer still no?" Ceh'ruk asked her. "We need someone like you. You can unite everyone here."

"So could Driamati, but I don't see you pulling him aside," she snapped, "Please release me, I want no more of this."

His face fell and he released her arm, "I had hoped I wouldn't have to do this." He spoke quietly now, barely audible over the shouting. "When you arrived I thought I could convince you to lead, but I can see I was wrong. Go if you must, but please remain for what happens next. If you won't lead us, at least lend us your support. Even if it is only empty words." He turned from her and stepped back onto the podium, a vibrant green radiance sprang to life about him as he forced his way to the center of the stage. He shouted to the sky as a flash of green silenced the room, "I am yours, my lord!"

Ceh'ruk's radiance flared to immortal levels as Ori's presence settled within him. Ardelle had to drop her magically enhanced sight just to keep from going blind. "Mortal Children!" The great thunderous voice of the Arcana of Life filled the room and echoed far out into the night. "Be still your arguments and listen to my words!"

The men on the dais, save Driamati, scrambled away from the Avatar as Ceh'ruk raised his hand to point among the crowd. "Barrah must be stopped," he spoke simply. "We Arcana may take no direct involvement is this struggle against our brother, though we desperately wish to do so. He is within the tenants set down when the world was formed and therefore beyond our reach, but you have the ability to stop him. Within each of you is the power that can topple any of us, a power that every Arcana covets. You are free."

Odd looks passed among the crowd, there had never been an event like this in recorded history. No Arcana had ever spoken to the mortals of their desires, even in Barrah's decline there had never been a record of the Arcana coveting the mortal lives. "Each of us has our chosen, but it is not the same as the freedom each of you enjoy. We are bound by the tenants of creation to do only what we were made to do. Your freedom is why we are here tonight, if Barrah is not stopped all of you will die and never be reborn. Your eternal souls will be banished to the domain of the dead where you will be tormented for eons. When my Avatar spoke to you of the stillbirths, did you listen? There are a finite number of new souls created each generation, a number that dwindles with every passing century. I can do nothing more to perpetuate the flow of souls to this realm, without rebirth your races will all slowly die."

The words sank in this time. Ceh'ruk had given much the same speech only moments before, but with the power of an Arcana behind them they could not be denied. Driamati moved to interrupt the Avatar, but Ori glared at him through Ceh'ruk's eyes, "Do not seek to lecture us on the 'wisdom' of your Arcana. We all know what he thinks of the mortal realm. It is not his eternal soul that faces damnation, it is yours." He turned back toward the crowd. "Each of you must choose what is best for your people, but know that the fate of the entire world rests with those decisions." The Avatar's arms rose to the ceiling before a blinding flash of green erupted from his body. Ori had left him. Ceh'ruk dropped to one knee, panting heavily. His attendants rushed to his aid, but he waved them off and got back to his feet. "I had wanted to keep my lord from this affair, I hoped that I could persuade you to do what must be done without him but that did not happen. You are all faced with the same choice now, join with us in a coalition or stand alone against Barrah when he comes. Forces from Utladalen have already begun their march for Krossfarin, will any of you stand with us?" Some cheers rose from the crowd, but it wasn't everyone. The Oberon representatives kept silent as did a number of the churches, including Basir. The City-State delegations seemed more accepting and raised their voices in assent.

Ardelle was confident that it hadn't been the result Ceh'ruk desired, but at least Krossfarin wouldn't stand alone. She was also sure this wasn't the last she would see of Basir. She fled the room before any other outburst over her presence broke out.

She desperately wished Aurin was there, her hero to save her from the pain. Ardelle had never relied on anyone to save her before, but there was something about him that made her desperate for his presence. It was for naught, Aurin was gone. He gave his life to save them from the creature in the forest, gave his life for hers. She couldn't ask anything more of him, couldn't rely on him to save her again.

The air had cooled considerably since the sun set, autumn's touch was finally reaching the Oberon lands. Her borrowed gown carried a full back, unlike most Oberon clothing, but its fabric was still quite shear. She pulled her arms around her chest and hugged herself as she strolled to the railing of the balcony. Even the buildings built for the land dwellers bore grand balconies where Oberon could come and go as they needed. The architecture was strange to her, she had spent most of her time with either the officials in the High Church or with the Falcree in their cave homes deep in the northern mountains. The Falcree had once lived like the Oberon, soaring towers and lofty tree homes, but their war with the Harpies brought an end to that. Their tribe was the smallest of the bird-folk, but their skill with the magic of Betala was the greatest. Betala's Avatars often came from their numbers. She wondered if any of them still lived, there had been no mention of them since she had returned to society, nor had there been a delegation present tonight.

In her time, the Falcree had still been battling for survival with the Harpies. The remnants of Barrah's followers, the Just, had broken the siege of their last remaining city. It hadn't been enough to endear the Just to the coalition, nor had the Falcree sought to join. The coalition did nothing to stop the war within the mountains, even though the Tu'roki forces had been in a position to do so. Instead they marched south to battle on the Great Plains south of Falderal, a battle that was supposed to rid the world of Barrah and his forces forever.

She didn't know all the details of the battle, but it seemed that the Arcana had come together to banish their fallen brother sometime after that.

She sighed into the wind. It had been the Falcree that she had sought to hide from Barrah's punishments. They had begged her to do something against the Harpies, to use her power to crush their armies, but Barrah had protected the Harpies with his own influence. When he had stolen Ezra from Betala, he had usurped a good deal of her ability to influence the mortal world. When Ardelle had first come to power, Betala would have had trouble doing something as simple as what Ori had just done with Ceh'ruk. Her power had been broken, along with her heart. It had likely crumbled further when Ardelle had been banished. A pang of guilt rang through her at the thought of Betala's feelings over her loss. Was she not further punishing her mistress now? A small presence filled her as she dwelled on the thought, Betala's whisper that she was still there. Ardelle shook the feeling from her mind and turned to leave the Great Hall. The thought of letting Betala in, of surrendering herself again, was too much for her tonight.

She wiped at her eyes and fled before anyone could see her.

Repercussions

"He insulted me, in front of the Princess no less!" Darl practically shouted at the king in the private audience chamber. "I won't have him in my classes again!"

"You will if I decree it, Magister." Driamati's hand gripped the arm of his chair until his knuckles were white. "Tell me again what he did, granddaughter."

"He broke the laws of magic!" Darl spoke over her.

"I don't believe he asked you, *master*," she hissed at the old man, even her patience had worn out. "Perhaps it would be better if I were to speak with you in private grandfather."

"Yes, I think you are correct." He released his hold on the arm of his throne and gestured toward the door, "Darl leave us."

"My king," Darl sniveled. "I only wish to present to you the facts of what happened."

"And you think my granddaughter will tell me false? Be gone, now, or I may find a new place for you!" Driamati pointed toward the floor.

Darl bowed low, his head very nearly reaching the ground before he fled without a word.

"Now," her grandfather started, "tell me exactly what happened."

She recounted the fight as best she could, trying not to put Maeryn in a negative light, but keeping as close to the truth as she could. His feat of magic had been nothing short of spectacular, but it wouldn't do any good for her to brag about it to her grandfather. In her version of the story, Maeryn simply rebounded the spell back on Darl with a lucky shield.

"Darl would have me believe that this boy stole his magic and used it against him but you say it was a shield? One of these feats has never been seen before and Darl isn't exactly an objective observer." He stroked his chin, "but I wonder if you are."

She clenched her left hand at her hip to control her outburst, she had to keep her face placid. "It was only a shield. Darl underestimated Maeryn and lost control. Maeryn may only be a human, but his pool is still impressive. Raw power is useful in a direct confrontation."

"I suppose you are right, the boy is powerful. He's completely inept in actual spells, but what I wouldn't give to have that much raw power at my disposal." He rocked back into his chair, resting against the cushion as though the world had finally caught up with him. "When Vielk is with me, I feel that powerful. It's like I have the entire world at my beck and call, but when he leaves, I feel drained beyond belief." His eyes drifted to the ceiling, something wasn't right with her grandfather and it wasn't just his age.

"Are you well Grandfather? Should I call a physician?" She stepped closer to the throne but his eyes shot back to her face.

"I am fine," he snarled, snapping his gaze back to her eyes. "The boy will resume his classes with Darl, but only for half of the day, as before. He will continue with the field instructors, from what I hear, he needs it." He wiped at the corner of his eye, where she swore she had seen a tear. "You may go, send Darl back in when you leave."

She turned to leave but his next comment spun her around, "And don't think I don't know about your little trip to Vielk's chamber, Granddaughter. You made a promise to me and I expect you to keep it."

She forced her face to remain neutral. "I was only trying to calm the situation lest the human do something rash, nothing more. The matron was simply confused by my presence there." She could feel him probing out with his magic to search her thoughts, but she had learned long ago to guard her truth and lies from him. He would find nothing there, but the image of a beautiful field of flowers.

"See that you keep to that," his face carried all of the threat of that statement. He meant to see her kept from Maeryn. He waved in dismissal once more, sitting up and dropping his face to the neutral mask he wore in court. He was well practiced at keeping his emotions in check, which made his earlier loss of coherence even more worrying.

She made a mental note to check with her uncle when she next saw him to get a real gage on her grandfather's state of mind.

She ushered Darl back into the chamber, but didn't leave immediately. She pressed her ear to the door for a moment just to get an idea of what her grandfather was saying and smiled slightly when she heard the tongue lashing he was laying on Darl. The man deserved it, despite the humiliation that Maeryn gave him, he had started that fight. It was time that someone put him in his place.

She left the royal apartment by the most direct route, meeting up with her guard, Alexi today, before winging back to her chamber to change. After the day she had, she decided to shirk the rest of her studies and do some shopping. There was a need for a new outfit, and she knew where she could get one.

The march towards womanhood had started to change her figure, and it left her needing clothes frequently. Her girlish style would have to be retired soon as she would no longer be able to pull it off with any modesty. She had women's dresses, those selected by older members of her family, but she didn't have much day to day wear. Even though it pained her to admit it, she would need to start styling herself more like her older sisters and her mother. Especially if she was to retain the illusion of being the dutiful granddaughter.

She changed into her less formal attire, a loose fitting garment that she could slip in and out of easily when it came time to try on others, and left her chambers. Alexi made to follow her, but she waved him back, "I go to try on dresses Alexi, I don't believe your services will be necessary and I'd like to keep a modicum of my modesty." She had taken to using court speech to her guards to further the illusion of her conversion to the Oberon mentality. It felt harsh to do so, but it was how men of their political standing were treated here. Alexi would likely follow her anyway, given the current orders her guard had received, but at least she wouldn't have to let him into the changing booths with her this way.

Her favorite shop, a small place run by a Solterran dressmaker, was in the low city. Her family had insisted she use the Oberon Tailors, but their work was all the same. If she had to wear court dresses, at least she would have one that stood out among the crowd.

"Well hello Princess," the grey-skinned, hairless, old Solterran greeted her as she landed outside the squat building. "I wasn't expecting you," she winced as she dropped an arthritic curtsy.

"There's no need for that Granny," Clornamti told the woman. Everyone called her 'Granny,' though other than her age, no one really knew why. Clornamti didn't even know her real name. "And you don't need to call me Princess either, Clornamti, or just Clora is fine." She moved into the shade of the building and folded her wings behind her.

"What can I do for you today, Princess?" The old woman smiled at her as she moved behind the counter, her sapphire eyes twinkling at the small joke. "A new sundress perhaps? Or a new nightgown?" She gestured towards two of her displays.

"I need court dresses Granny. Can you help me?" She sighed at the woman's shocked expression. "My grandfather insists that I dress like a proper courtier, but I can't stand the Oberon style and their identical dresses. If I have to wear one, I want to feel like me while I'm in it." She gestured at her thin frame to emphasize her point.

The sapphire eyes took in her slight body and clucked her tongue, "You're too skinny for anything the Solterran would wear, but perhaps something in a nice silk?" Granny rifled through a pile of uncut fabric before producing a stunning silk that seemed to shift color in the different light.

"I've been saving this for years, bought it off a Gremen warrior woman that didn't know what she had."

Clornamti felt the exquisite fabric, marveling at its smooth texture. The color wasn't fixed. The light in the room, the heat of her hand and even just the angle she looked at it seemed to change its hue. She'd never seen its like. "It's beautiful Granny," she managed to murmur.

"I've only this one bolt, just enough for one dress. I've other silks if you need more dresses, but this one would be unique." The old woman lifted other bolts of cloth, beautiful in their own right, but nothing compared to the first. "I could make you five or six all alike from these others."

Clornamti didn't even raise her eyes, "I'll take one from this material. Two or three more in any of the other colors, but I want one from this." She touched the cloth lightly to her cheek, marveling at its luxurious feel.

The old woman cackled loudly behind her, "I thought you might. When do you need these dresses?"

"As soon as possible. Do you have any already cut that I could try to check the fit?" She carefully handed the bolt of fabric back to the old woman.

"No, I've not got a lot of business with you upper crust folks and the low folks don't buy dresses that would fit you." The old woman smiled down at her, "don't worry my dear, Granny hasn't let you down before and I won't start now."

After a quick measuring session, Clornamti left the old woman to her ministrations, and moved on to other shops among the lower city. There wasn't much in the way of court clothing, but she did find several pairs of comfortable boots and a belt. The leather goods here were superior to those produced by the Oberon, despite the common theory otherwise. The Oberon hadn't been hunters in centuries and to think that they knew much of anything about tanning hides was just conceited. Steel was another thing that other races did better, and it was a poorly kept secret that the Oberon imported the majority of their steel from the other lands.

She left the lower city and was heading for the artisans tower when Alexi suddenly appeared at her side, "Princess, we need to return to your chambers."

"What is it Alexi?" The concern etched years into her guard's face.

"Please follow me closely." His reluctance to pass along what was happening didn't go unnoticed.

She followed him at arm's length, keeping her small bundle close to her chest as they landed lightly on her private balcony. Dimitri and her other guards were waiting for them. They quickly ushered her inside. It wasn't until they had secured the doors leading out to the balcony that Dimitri finally turned to her, "a spy has been caught within the city Princess. We fear what they have learned and how far it has traveled. For now, I must insist that you remain here with one of your guards within the chamber. Once it is clear, you will be allowed back out unescorted but until then, please comply."

Dimitri was typically a jovial individual, to see him so distressed was more than a little unnerving. "Who was the spy?" It had to be someone she had come in contact with recently for her guards to be this on edge, but who? She had spent the majority of her time with Darl in her studies, or among the fools at court.

"I've been asked not to say, Princess, for your own good." Dimitri responded, then a hint of a smile crept onto his face, "asked, not ordered. Matron Miatem has been found in league with a band of Harpies."

Her hand involuntarily went to her mouth, Miatem was the one who had found her and Maeryn in Vielk's chamber. Was that why her guards were on alert? Had she been after Maeryn? "Miatem? What was she after?"

"I can't get into it Princess, I was ordered on that front. Just know that we'll keep you safe." Dimitri assigned Alexi to remain within the room and dispatched the others throughout the tower. Two of them were to remain in the air above her balcony while two occupied the hall leading to her chambers. Dimitri was to act as a rover and spell the others so they could rest in short shifts. It was a hassle for her, but it would be an incredibly long day for her guards.

She moved into her bedroom to drop her packages off in her closet before her arms fell off. Her arms tingled as the nerves came back, reminding her of her initial panic caused by Alexi's appearance. She moved back into the sitting room but somewhere had lost track of Alexi. He had been looking out the window across from her bedroom door, but the room was empty now, and the furniture was all in different locations. The light from the windows had turned grey, as though a storm had blown in.

"Micah," she whispered to the empty room. "Now isn't a good time." She looked around for her visitor or Alexi, but the room was empty.

"Your guards can't hear us this time, Clora." She noted he didn't call her 'mother.' "Something has changed, what did you do?"

"Only what you asked," she sighed as she scanned the adjoining chamber for her absent guard. She also couldn't yet see Micah. "Maeryn is studying with the field mages now, learning shields." She had nearly forgotten that it had been Micah that had pushed that decision on her. Whenever he left, her memory of him left too. She knew he existed, but when he wasn't with her, she had trouble remembering his name or what he looked like. She could remember something happening but it was ethereal, more dreamlike than any true memory. The instant he appeared it was as if the memories came rushing back, in vivid detail. The realization that she had lost the memories in and of itself seemed to be something she had experienced before.

"There is a ripple, something new that wasn't there before." He stepped from the window as though he'd been standing there the whole time. His hair shot in every direction like he had just woken from a fitful sleep. His eyes were heavy lidded and bloodshot. His robes were badly in need of a wash. Moving like a man possessed he strolled right up to her so that he towered over her small frame, smelling like he hadn't washed in days. "Tell me what has happened since we last spoke, everything!" His vehemence caused her to step back involuntarily.

"I went to Grandfather, as you asked, and spoke to him about Maeryn learning shields. He agreed and changed the schedule so that Maeryn was with Darl for half of the day and in the field the other half. Then there was the fight, but it was nothing really…" She trailed off at the look of rage in Micah's eyes.

"What fight?" he demanded, "Did you and he fight? Was there magic involved?"

She held up her hands, "No, he got into a fight with Darl. They exchanged some spells and Maeryn left. Then we went to Vielk's chamber and watched the sunset."

"Nevermind the sunset!" He screamed, his fists slamming into his sides as he stepped up to her again. "What spells?"

She weighed her options carefully. She had lied to Driamati about the magic that Maeryn had performed, but did she dare do so to Micah? He was more irate than she had ever seen him before and she feared what a mage of his caliber could do if he was truly angry. She decided to be honest, "Maeryn stole Darl's magic from him and turned it back on him."

"That's impossible!" Micah spun away from her, "that magic died off a thousand years ago. How could he possibly know it?"

The question was directed at the wall, she had no illusions that he believed she knew the answer. "He said he had seen it once," she offered.

"Seen it? Impossible!" Micah tapped his chin rather hard, "unless…" He turned back toward the window. "Don't let him leave. No matter what happens, he must be here when…" he trailed off clearly not intending to divulge what event he was to wait for. "Just keep him here!"

She blinked at the last shout and suddenly found herself in a well-lit sitting room with Alexi still at his post near the window. The furniture had returned to its previous state and she had a suspicion that she should remember something important, but her thoughts were only for Maeryn's training.

Forsaken

She crept quietly through the reeds along the river bank. The demons were only strides from her, a small group led by one of the human commanders she had seen during the battle. They had fled Aurin's display of power, as most would when faced with white fire that cut everything it touched to ribbons. Aurin slept now, under guard, back at the camp just north of that town, Balenford.

Her paws ached from the cold water. She still moved about on all four of her limbs, she had decided to remain a cat after the battle even though she now understood how to transform. Something within her changed after her escape from the forest, something that gave her a power she still struggled to understand. For now, she could ignore it while she hunted the few demonic stragglers left after the battle, but she knew she would have to confront it sooner or later.

Her fur still dripped silently onto the grass. The demons wouldn't hear her approach, and their human leader may as well have onions instead of ears for as well as he could hear. Humans lacked any true hunting spirit, they hadn't descended from the great hunters of the past. They were simply brought here by their Arcana, no lineage to anything that was natural existed, at least not as far as she was aware.

She eyed the camp menacingly, she knew they would soon be dead by her claws but she also knew she would have to wait for the right moment. The demons didn't sleep, but they seemed to have an insatiable appetite. They would feed six to ten times a day on any flesh they could find and if nothing presented itself, they often fed on one another. She had been following this group for three days and witnessed them consume no less than three of their compatriots.

It surprised her that she had been in this form and away from the camp for three days. It had been that long since the bulk of the forces she had fought so hard to protect had ostracized her. Howlter couldn't even look at her in cat form, and the others were worse. The Humans wanted her gone, insisted that she was as much monster as the things they fought. Howlter assured them that it was not unheard of for followers of Nezmas to revert to a beast form, though it was a lie. Devout Gremen were known to go wild when they were with Nezmas, but there had been no cases where they reverted to their distant ancestors. She was unique, and it was all due to that forest.

Wylltraethel had changed her forever, but she couldn't lie to herself and say that she would have it any other way. Her current form seemed more natural than her Gremen body ever had. She moved with grace as a cat, she could hunt and kill with impunity. Her fur was tougher than any leather she had owned and much harder to pierce. She had taken more than one arrow that day outside that worthless village, but none had pierced the meat beneath her fur. Her claws sharpened far easier than her swords ever had and they were just as strong. She could run for hours without tiring, needing only meat to survive.

It was the loneliest she had ever been.

Adla had vanished after the battle. The little girl was last seen running from the fighting as Crowlmer told her. No one remembers seeing her after that. Crowlmer couldn't say what passed between her and Aurin on that field, but whatever it was scared the girl. Adla was gone and with Aurin laid up, Crowlmer had no one. The Gremen didn't want her and the Humans feared her. It didn't matter anymore what she did, so here she was, hunting demons alone.

The demons never slept, but their commander did. She waited for the man to drift off before springing into action. The closest demon was dead before her back legs touched the ground. She tore its head from its shoulders with a swipe of her claws and a rip of her teeth. The second spilled its guts into the fire before it managed to get to its feet.

The third and fourth stood, but their attacks were clumsy and slow. She bounded off the collapsing corpse of the second and drove all of her weight into the demon closest to her, driving it to the ground. A quick gnash of her teeth severed the arteries in its neck. The last one standing rounded on her with a polearm, but she turned her neck at an odd angle and ripped the weapon from its grasp. She killed it before it could draw its sword. Two more lived but they remained seated through the slaughter of the original four. Something was different about the two. Their skin was a dusky color, rather than the violet color of the others. Their horns were more pronounced though they swept back from their faces like those of the hearty sheep from her mountain home. They remained motionless as she shook the gore from her face, their black eyes stared off into nothingness.

The human that had led them was awake now, scrabbling for his sword as he shouted, "Get it!" The large demons suddenly animated and stood, locking their black eyes on her as they marched forward. They held no weapons, but their hands ended in wicked claws that bore fresh gore from their most recent feeding. Their bodies were significantly larger than their violet cousins, well-muscled and completely hairless. No clothes, but they bore no genitalia that they needed to cover.

She stalked back away from their fire, gathering up her weight on her back legs. The creatures moved without fear, never slowing even as one of them walked directly through the fire. She saw no vulnerable point and had not faced creatures like this before. This was going to be a difficult fight.

She lunged at the creature on the right, thinking to take it down before its partner closed, but the thing raised a clawed hand and swatted her from the air. The impact thudded against her ribs with such force that she could feel one of them break. Snarling, she rounded on the creature again, dashing in toward its feet, but again it was too fast. A savage kick with its goat-foot tore the air from her lungs, sending her careening back toward their campsite. She rolled when she hit, hoping to regain her feet as she had on countless other occasions, but the pain in her left shoulder told her that her leg was broken. She stood on her three good legs, but her balance was gone. When she tried to flee, she tumbled back to the dirt.

The human had found his feet and stalked over to where she lay. "Thought you could take us unprepared, beast?" He sneered, the odd, three-hooked sword swinging absently in front of him. "My Rak'ternan are never unprepared." She assumed he was referring to the two demons that had turned and flanked him. "But they are always hungry." His cruel voice belied his intentions.

Her power was working on healing her broken bones, but she knew it would take hours before she would be at full strength. She had to get clear of the camp now, or she would be their next meal. She drew what magic she could from the well within her and transformed her body to allow her to run on two legs. The resultant form was new to her, but surprisingly comfortable. She stood up from the dirt, clutching her broken arm with her good hand. She could feel her tail, something new to her two-legged form. Her claws had remained, as well as her elongated back feet.

The human had stopped his march when her transformation had started and now stared at the creature before him with shock lining his face. He managed to bark out, "What are you?" before ordering his Rak'ternan to "Kill the freak!"

She didn't wait for their advance. With a leap that rivaled any cat, she bounded clear of the camp and its dead demons. She landed lightly on her spread paws, then sped off into the night. The demons pursued her for several hundred paces, but they were no match for her new speed. Her body was different, somewhere between the cat and a Gremen. It felt like she could run for hours as her legs rolled into the steps with ease. Her arm was mending as her magic worked, but still throbbed painfully as she held it against her chest.

Her torso was mostly Gremen, which meant the running would eventually prove uncomfortable as the weight of her breasts pulled on the muscles and flesh in her chest. She kept her arm tight against them, but the movement of her body sent pain through the wounded limb and her chest just wouldn't cooperate with her. The body felt good, but she would need clothes if she was to remain like this, at the very least something to bind her breasts so that her hands were free.

A soft, downy fur covered the majority of her skin, leaving off her stomach, down past her navel. The fur offered some protection from the chilly autumn night, but would do nothing if the wind were to pick up. Her hands had returned, but her feet still resembled the paws of a cat. They were elongated, much like any predator that ran on all fours. Only her padded toes struck as she ran on, her heels were well off the ground. The claws were gone from them though. It was odd that she had retained claws on her hands, but those on her feet had vanished. She still didn't fully understand this new power, and feared she never would.

She spent the remainder of the night curled in a tight nest of prairie grass. She had seen no sign of further pursuit and was grateful for that small piece of luck. After the sun peaked over the horizon, she set about finding a source of water to clean the stink of demon from her. The river was the obvious choice, but it was too exposed. Any pack of demons or their human coconspirators would see her from hundreds of strides away. The river also flowed from the mountains where winter had already set in, and that water was very cold.

She found a suitable pond a half league or so from last night's camp and set about removing the black blood from her soft fur. Her new skin prickled as she poured the water over it, cooling and soothing her body. The demon blood came away from her tough flesh easily enough, but she scrubbed at the congealed spots. The smell was harder to remove, an acrid, sour smell that just seemed to linger wherever it had touched. Upon inspection of the pond, she discovered a substance in a thin reed that not only held a stronger scent than blood, but softened her skin as she applied it. Her barely noticeable fur was thin, but it was enough to ward off the initial autumn chill. She still needed to find clothes if she was to remain like this, especially if she desired any companionship. It didn't bother her much, she had spent her life in an army camp where hundreds of other Gremen used the communal showers, there were few secrets among warriors. The other races though, they would take slight if she was to strut into their villages in her bare condition. The thought of it almost made her seek one out just to see the looks on their faces. After the ostracizing from the human camp, she had a need to exact some kind of revenge.

  Satisfied that she was as clean as she ever would be, she roamed back out into the countryside in search of any habitation that may offer her some protection against the human eye. Flexing her arm, she was delighted to discover she could still move it some, but it was still healing, so she kept it tight to her chest. Scanning the surrounding prairie for any signs of other demons or any signs of settlements, she kept her pace slow. She couldn't say how far she had roamed from the main camp of Howlter's army, but she knew it had been more than ten leagues at least. The demons had kept a run for nearly an hour, and she had matched pace. It wouldn't have surprised her to learn that she was closer to a hundred leagues from where she started three days ago.

  A single hill broke the monotony of the prairie, but she knew that it couldn't be much more than a league to its peak. No snow capped the rise, so the air up there wasn't much colder than it was here on the flat land. It was odd that there would just be the single hill. There were no signs as to how it was formed, but in a land where magic could do anything, she had a strong suspicion how it had risen. During the Great War, many such mounds were raised by the followers of Brokoom to provide defensible positions for the coalition of races. Barrah's forces outnumbered them greatly so any advantage in terrain was necessary to level the field. These plains saw a great deal of battles during the war due to their proximity to Falderal, which was the seat for the alliance.

With no other plans, she set off for the hill. She still hadn't seen any signs of habitation, but the hill at least gave her a better vantage of the surrounding plains. She increased her speed to a light trot, careful to keep her arm tucked so that the throbbing didn't get worse. She reached the hill shortly after midday and began to climb. A low stone wall circled the base, remnants of the defenses from the Great War, she guessed. The stones were quarried, with smooth edges and mortared fits, so it was not an ordinary farmer's wall. Time had worn down the structure, causing it to collapse in several places. The climb was a gentle one, with soft grass covering the entire face.

At the apex sat a single structure commanding a view of everything for leagues in any direction. It was a small, square building that appeared to be crafted of the same stones that made up the wall around the base of the hill. It was weathered, as anything that had stood for one hundred and fifty years in the open plain would be, but still sound. She circled the building and could see no obvious doors, but the northern face was decorated with a runic writing that was vaguely familiar. If she had to guess, she would say it was ancient Gremen. The Gremen had abandoned their written language shortly after the Great War, where the majority of their scholars had perished in one of the purges led by the Og'rai. It was a terrible loss mourned by the masses but little was done to preserve the culture. She could only read a little, what words she did know, she deciphered that this was a tomb.

    The runic carvings dictated where the entrance should be, but no crease or handle was visible along the face of the building. The words themselves offered little purchase, but she couldn't move any part of the rock. She slammed her fist against it in frustration and was rewarded with a minute shift in one of the letters. The door was sealed with some kind of pass phrase and these runes held the key. A sudden need to get inside the tomb came over her as she pawed over the rock to find each letter that would move. When she finally had the letters that moved, she was left with a new problem. There were eight characters, and just pushing all of them in, she found did not open the door. They would have to be pressed in order. The top most rune wasn't a letter in the common tongue, and she was sure it wasn't a single letter in ancient Gremen either, it was likely an entire word or a personal rune. Personal runes were common among the Gremen during the Great War, it gave them something to perpetuate their legacy. She touched the rune again and sighed.

    A flash erupted from the stone and a vision of the door appeared within her mind. The seven stones laid out in their proper order with the personal rune being last. A single word with the flash *Justice*.

She couldn't say were the image came from, but when it cleared she quickly pressed the stones. With a rumble, a crease appeared in the stone slab and it trundled back and then sideways into a concealed pocket. The inner portion of the structure was completely consumed by a staircase that led down into the darkness below the hill.

Training

"You have to keep the shield fluid or you won't be able to stop the attacks you don't see!" His trainer was a large Oberon bedecked in the armor they favored and carrying a spear in his right hand. Their armor was leather, a hardened chest plate with straps that ran around their wings. If offered no protection to their back, but they preferred to fight in the air where their backs were very difficult to hit. They didn't typically wear metal, since the added weight would hinder their ability to fly. They were drilling him on the use of his magic as a defense in battle. It wasn't going well.

His current problem stemmed from the type of shield they wanted him to construct out of raw magic. Almost every spell he had learned to perform had been attuned to one Arcana or another, never pure magic. The complex rituals he had used in the past all had attunements and foci that changed their properties to bring them in line with his goals. Using magic directly from his pool was severely frowned upon. The Oberon were coaching him to do just that.

His previous attempts at a shield had utilized foci from Brokoom, Gelthar and even Betala. Every time he had sought to stop a specific form of attack, he had always known it was coming. Today, they threw spells at him at random intervals, always while he was distracted. They derided his reflexes and clucked their tongues at his attempts to just leave a shield up all the time. It was extremely taxing to keep a complete shield about his person, especially when they attacked him with their spears or other weapons that would just pass through it.

"Mentor Kairos," his present torturer sighed. "You can't leave the shield solid indefinitely, even you have a limit to your pool. You have to keep it solid when you aren't expecting an attack, keep it flexible and fluid when you are alert. You can channel a small amount of power at a time to help you foresee the attacks, but you have to be ready to solidify the shield in the blink of an eye."

Their explanations were nearly as confusing as the use of the magic in general. "It doesn't feel right!" he whined at his tutor, "I've never done anything like it."

"That much is obvious," his teacher responded, "use your sight, watch me again." He drew on his pool, which in and of itself was shaming to Charles. It was just a tiny pool, and then cast out a thread of magic that swirled around him from head to toe. It was a miniscule thread, but Charles knew it was as strong as steel when it came to blocking incoming spells. He stared straight at the man's energy but couldn't see what he did to tie off the magic and keep it about him.

"How do you stop the magic from dissipating?" Charles asked, finally convinced the man was keeping something from him. Every attempt Charles made to keep the shield about him had dissipated his pool within minutes, whatever his instructor was doing was not the same as what he was telling Charles to do.

"Use your sight and watch! If you would only pay attention we could end this farce." His instructor, who hadn't even given Charles a name, instead insisting on just being called 'Instructor,' went through the spell once more then told Charles recreate the effect. Again, Charles was unable to see what the man did to keep the magic from fizzling out after he cast it. "Now raise your shield and defend yourself."

Quickly, his instructor launched into a series of attacks using a small lance of magic that Charles longed to copy. He threw up the shield for the first attack and stopped it, but the subsequent attacks came at random intervals over the course of several minutes and he only managed to stop one in five. It was a rather pathetic showing, even for him, but he was growing tired. His instructor kept up the attacks until Charles' pool was completely exhausted.

"You expect to battle Demons like this?" his instructor sighed. "We're done. Get some rest, tomorrow we'll spend the day working on holding a spell indefinitely, again." He turned on his heel and marched from the practice field.

Charles dropped to the ground, spent. "If you would only tell me what you are doing, I could be done with this," he whispered to himself.

"He won't tell you," A female voice said from behind him. "They are doing this just to embarrass you, they don't have any intention of teaching you the proper shield. It is a closely held secret of the Oberons, and has been for five hundred years." Clornamti stepped from behind a large tree and walked over to him, extending her hand to help him up.

"Do you know it?" Charles asked, breathless.

"Of course," she responded then stopped herself, "but it is difficult to teach. I would also have to ask permission to do so, it is a secret technique."

His shoulders slumped, "I wonder if my instructor has permission to actually show me."

"Oh, he does," she chirped. "I was there when it was given."

Charles tried to walk away, but his exhaustion got the better of him and he almost tumbled. "I'm tired of these games, I stayed here so that I could learn from your people. So far I've been assigned to a Master who doesn't seem to actually know any magic and then handed off to an instructor who hates me so much that he won't even give me his name." He huffed and clenched his fist, "It's time I moved on if they are done teaching me. There are other ways to learn."

She flinched at his vehemence. "No, wait," she started, then took a deep breath. "You can't leave yet, you aren't ready to battle. The Druids gave you nothing you can use when your life is in danger, just a few worthless tricks. I know, they tried to teach them to me as well." She turned back to him."I will teach you. Tonight after it's dark. Will you be able to recover any of your magic by then?" Her eyes sparked with unspent tears, what was truly bothering her? Was the thought of getting in trouble scaring her so much?

"I wouldn't want you to do anything that will land you in trouble." He wasn't sure how to react to her.

"Don't worry about me," she reassured him. "I couldn't live with myself if I let you leave without at least the basics."

Charles forced himself not to take offense at her statement, he knew it wasn't really what she had meant, "Tonight then, sunset, here?"

"Yes," she sighed, looking around to make sure no one overheard them. "Would you like me to walk you back to your room?"

Would I? She may as well have asked him if he'd like to breathe, but he couldn't say something like that. "That would be nice, thank you." He tried again to walk, but the dizziness returned with a vengeance and nearly sent him back to the grass. "Perhaps I should just rest here."

A dazzling smile sprang to her lips, "I'll go fetch some food and we can eat dinner together here, then train after. How does that sound?"

Like paradise, he thought to himself. "That would be wonderful, I'll just wait here," he let his weight carry him back to the grass. He sprawled out in an undignified way before he remembered he should compose himself.

Clornamti stifled a giggle before she skipped off toward the towers. "I will be right back." Her wings blurred as she crossed the yard, then shot up into the upper reaches of the towers.

He rolled to his back and stared up at the clouds, the blue sky seemed to glow brighter than ever. Was he truly this lucky? Not only was she going to teach him, but she had seemed excited just to have dinner with him. They hadn't spoken much since her watcher had caught them in the mirror chamber, though he still wasn't sure what had been about to happen. They had continued to have classes with Darl together, despite the fight with the man, but they rarely spoke. He had asked her to walk him to his rooms a couple of times, but she had politely declined, offering one of the servants instead. Not wanting to reveal his true motivations, he had accepted her offer though he felt the fool for doing so. He knew the tower blindfolded now, he hadn't needed a guide.

After the fight, Darl's lectures had grown more pointless, moving from rituals that may actually have been useful to spells that just didn't work. His treatise on creating architecture had been laced with so many faults that Charles couldn't bring himself to finish it. After his escape from the forest, he had at least a basic grasp on the materials and foci that were necessary to build with magic and Darl's book had been absent of all of them. Clearly the man had never actually put the rituals to the test, for if he had, he wouldn't be trying to teach them incorrectly. He wondered if the man was deliberately forcing him to read the worthless material in response to the humiliation that Charles had handed him. If Driamati hadn't insisted that he continue the lessons, he would have quit.

His other training came from various instructors throughout the city. One young Oberon taught him the tenants of travelling using magic, something that Charles could actually use, but forbade Charles from practicing them. Others taught him martial skills, like the sword or bow or spear, but he was hopeless when it came to physical combat. His lanky body refused to put on any muscle and he just seemed to get taller. He was head and shoulders taller than any Oberon he had met, he now had to duck his head as he moved through the tower doorways. He had perfected his Oberon language in his instructions, even picking up some of the undesirable phrases when he would get something wrong. The language was flowery and tended toward overuse of descriptions but you got used to it. Other training had taught him ways to attune his magic to Vielk, something the Druids could never teach.

Several visiting dignitaries also took time to mentor him in aspects of their magic. Two priests of Mamrix permanently resided in Heimili álfa, they taught him a spell to assist with his studies. It required attunement to the Arcana of Knowledge, but Charles had already found more uses for it than any ritual Darl had taught him. A lone priestess of Mormia had spent several hours with him trying to teach him the ritual for pulling magic from sunlight, but he was so distracted by her clothing that he didn't really learn much. How could anyone think that a shear gown of nearly invisible material was appropriate attire when around a teenage boy? Frankly, he learned more about anatomy than he had magic. Just the thought of her caused his cheeks to burn.

His worst lessons had all been with Oberons. Their inability to respect any race other than their own prevented them from instructing anyone else. It was true that Oberons started teaching their young folk magic much earlier, and that by the time they reached puberty they could outshine most mages in other parts of the world. What they didn't understand was they needed to start at the beginning of the training for others. No one learns from the middle, you have to start where everyone else started. He might be old enough to know all these tricks if he was an Oberon, but his instruction to this point had been reserved and far from anything they were trying to teach him. Fighting was strictly prohibited among the apprentices, he never learned to shield himself, nor had he learned a single offensive spell, the closest he had ever come was his flare. The flare he used to blind the wolf that first attacked them, but failed to even slow the guardian Micah had left to protect his book. On his first day at the practice field they had pitted him against a six year old

Oberon who had thoroughly beat him within a hair of unconsciousness before his instructor pulled the little boy off. Everyone on the pitch had enjoyed a hearty laugh at his expense.

    He sighed. The Oberon weren't all like that, he had met a few that were genuinely interested in helping him, but they had lacked the wherewithal to do so. He needed magical guidance from others attuned to Ven, not looks of pity from those attuned to Vielk. It bothered him that the spells didn't come easily as they had his entire life, but he knew a lot of that came from the Oberon's unwillingness for him to actually learn. If he didn't fear losing what miniscule respect he had amongst them, he would report their refusal to teach him to Driamati. The entire situation was undesirable and unsustainable, he had to learn quickly if he was ever going to help in the effort to stop Barrah. According to the prophecies, it was his destiny to do so but in what capacity? If there was ever anything to be learned, it was that things were never straightforward. It could be that his gruesome death sparked a fire under the mortals and causes them to rise up and stop Barrah, or something worse. Perhaps it would be his inability to do anything on his own that would propel others to greatness. In his present state of mind, the latter seemed the most likely.

    Clornamti returned bearing the traditional picnic. She hummed as she spread a simple blanket across the grass. He watched her with great interest as she began setting out various plates of food, far more than he would have expected from such a simple container. She giggled when she saw the expression on his face, he was nearly drooling. The food she had brought were some of his favorite examples of Oberon cuisine and his earlier training left him ravenous.

"Help yourself, Maeryn," she gestured towards the blanket.

He ate his fill, and then some before he had a chance to make a fool of himself in any other way. She watched him eat without partaking herself, staring intently at him. "I guess you were hungry," her eyes wide and staring as he packed away a large helping of their vegetables. "I can't say I've ever seen anyone eat with such…vigor."

He gulped down the lump of food in his mouth and gently lowered his plate. "I'm sorry."

"It's quite alright, I just may need to go get some more if I am to have any." She chuckled, a throaty giggle that he had never heard from an Oberon.

He joined in her laughter, enjoying what it meant. She had relaxed around him again, like she had those weeks ago before he had ruined it. "It was delicious, if that makes a difference."

She chuckled again, her brown eyes sparkling in the failing light, "I am glad you liked it. I wasn't sure what you ate, so I asked for a little of everything. I guess the answer to what you like *was* everything."

They laughed together for a few moments while the sun dropped below the horizon. When the mirth faded, Clornamti led him back to the training field by the hand and centered him within the pitch his instructor had used. She prepared him as his instructor did, but didn't give him any instructions.

"The reason we only teach this to children is that the training itself is very invasive." She stepped to the circle that his instructor had used. "In order for you to understand what it is to make the shield effective, I have to show you from within your mind."

Charles was momentarily stunned. "We have to link? Isn't that dangerous?"

Any hint of the earlier mirth was completely gone, "yes, very. If we don't do this correctly, we could end up stuck together or it could just destroy both of our minds. The real risk though is in your secrets." She stared directly into his eyes, "I will have to enter your mind. I will see everything you know and everything you seek to keep hidden, you will be an open book to me. Can you accept that?"

He had linked before, twice, with Aurin. The two had been under duress when they did it so there had been little sharing of thoughts, but Charles still learned more about his friend than anyone should be privy to. Could he trust Clornamti with his intimate secrets? She would know immediately that he wasn't simply a visiting mage from another land. She would also know about the prophecies and everything else he had learned since he left home.

Most frightening to him were his burgeoning feelings for her. She would learn that he wished for more than just a friendship between them. Could he live with that? Would he be able to bear the embarrassment? Did he really have a choice? He needed to know the secrets of the shield and how to further use his pool.

"I have to know," he decided aloud.

She sighed, almost relieved. "Our first step then is to link. Do you know how?"

His previous experience with linking had primarily been driven by Aurin, using that odd power that only he seemed to have. Charles was fairly confident he could repeat the process, but the risks of doing it wrong were too high to take any chances. "I think you should guide me, I have never initiated the link."

Her eyes widened slightly, fear crossing her face. It was then he realized that whoever initiates the link would host the other person until they pass control. She would have to let him see her mind. He could almost see the same inner battle raging within her that he had just fought with himself. Taking a deep breath, "I will start the link then pass it to you. First and foremost, relax, you have to open yourself to me or the link will never work. If you try to hide things, or keep things from me I won't be able to initiate the bond."

He sucked in air and tried to relax his mind, not an entirely easy prospect. "I think I'm ready," he told her, not entirely believing himself.

A glow sprang to life around her, one that he was confident even people lacking magic could see. "I'm going to erect a shield around us now. This will prevent anyone from taking advantage of our link to enter our minds without permission."

She began to release the spell but stopped, "Actually, this would work better if we were closer." She moved over to his circle, stepping so close to him that he could feel her breath. His entire body tensed at the closeness of her, so much that she noticed. "You have to relax, take a deep breath and think of anything but the spell."

He nearly laughed, he hadn't been thinking about any spell, except perhaps the one that she seemed to have over him already. He closed his eyes, took a deep breath and thought of open fields, of his tree back in Hudcoeden, and of his friend. When his mind was elsewhere, he nodded.

At first, he felt nothing but a small buzzing on the outskirts of his senses, like an insect you couldn't see but was close enough to hear. A pressure began to build at the base of his skull as the buzzing increased. He tried to keep his body relaxed, but the pressure soon turned to pain that lanced throughout his body like a thousand needles. He cried out once, but the tension just increased.

"You have to let me in, Maeryn. Let down your guard," he heard Clornamti whisper.

He dropped the natural barriers that he had erected between his conscious mind and the pain he had experienced throughout his life. Memories flooded in, memories of the loss he felt when he learned what it was to be an orphan. Thoughts of the parents that he had never known. The loneliness that never seemed to leave him, even when he was with others. He felt the weight of knowing that his parents had been killed by the minions of Barrah and that he was to be responsible for stopping the fallen Arcana.

He saw a burning temple, the bodies of Druids lying scattered everywhere. He heard his voice speaking to Frefel, as the man hung from the back wall of the chamber, bleeding from a dozen wounds. "What's the matter Frefel?" his voice sounded within his mind.

"Charles, no!" Desmira screamed as he detonated the house he had grown up in. More bodies littered the stairs behind him and the kitchen, the bodies of the guards sent to protect him. Above it all he heard laughter, a maniacal sound that filled his mind.

All of the emotional pain washed over him. He could feel Clornamti's presence now, a beacon of light within his dark thoughts. Much as Aurin had appeared that day in the temple, a glowing figure stepped within his mind and pulled him from the darkness. Suddenly he was awash with power, he could feel Clornamti within the magic but there was something else, something deeper. Suddenly he was standing alone in a field of wheat, the wind rippling through like waves on water. "Your sisters are gone," a voice told him from far off. The pain of loss hit him once more as memories, not his own, flooded into his mind. He could see the sisters, two little raven-haired girls playing in a flower-strewn meadow.

A wizened face flashed across the memory, a slightly younger looking Driamati sitting his throne with a sad look on his face. "Granddaughter, I am sending you to become a mage," the old Oberon told him, or rather told Clornamti. He felt younger, smaller in the man's presence, it must be a memory from earlier in her life.

He flashed to a day within the Grand Temple, though unlike his memory, this one was filled with joy. It was her Trial, where she had identified the magically manipulated animal from among the others. He could feel the pride flowing through her as she took her seat, two rows back from a handsome young man with curly black hair. He watched his own trial through her eyes, he could feel the laughter she had kept bottled up when the water had sprayed Frefel in the face.

He could feel something else from her, but he couldn't tell what it was. He was whisked away from Hudcoeden to a small chamber he had been in once before, it was Driamati's small audience chamber just off the throne room. "You can't let anyone know who this boy is, Granddaughter. He will be known as Mentor Maeryn Kairos for the duration of his stay. If anyone was to learn that he is the Chavox, we would all be in danger."

"I understand Grandfather," she had told him.

"You mustn't even mention to him that you know who he is."

The memories flashed again, he saw himself lying in that bed, breathing slowly. The feeling crept back into his mind, something akin to curiosity, but deeper. He saw her place the tome within his belongings, the book of magic that Micah had left him. The thought of the mage drove the memories to another place, a large sitting room high in a tower. A shadowy man stood before them, whispering something that Charles couldn't understand. Images flashed through the memory, a battlefield, a baby, a hopeless fight with the fallen Arcana, they all flashed by so quickly that he wasn't able to hold onto them. Even the vision of the shadowy man seemed to fade almost as quickly as it came.

So now you know, Clornamti's disembodied voice rang through his mind, much as Aurin's had during their link. Had she seen the memories as well? Who had the shadow been? *I know who you really are, Charles Chavox.* Emotions flashed within the link, guilt hit him as he realized that he could have said something to her, though Driamati had told her not to speak of it. There was still something else there, something other than the relief she was feeling now that the big secret between them had been brought to light. What was that other emotion trailing through her mind? *I'm going to pass the link now, I think we've learned enough about me.* He could almost feel her cheeks burning as she passed the link.

He braced himself as she entered his mind. He tried to stem the flow of memories, but the recent horrors still rang through. Despite his attempts to stop the memories, he flashed through the last year of his life in vivid detail. The memories of his first trial, Aurin's talk with him afterward, the Grand Temple on the day of his second trial, and the feelings of utter shame as the Druids failed him once again, all laid bare before her. The body in the street, the tribunal, and the night the other voice took control. He witnessed Frefal's death in brilliant flashes of horrific scenes. Hot tears fell from both their faces. He felt once more the battle with Aurin within the ring of fire and the subsequent binding of their power to flush out the voice.

Every detail of the forest suddenly burst into his head, the decaying trees, the smells and the sounds. He once again felt the terror of that first night when the beast attacked them and his resolve to learn how to defend himself. The cave of Ven, Micah and the books, and Scritch. The last memory brought tears to his eyes, the creature had left them suddenly and he had been unable to find it. Other feelings poured into his memories, recognition dawning at the sight of Micah and his small companion. Did Clornamti know Micah? Or was it simply recognition of Scritch's species? He could read from her thoughts that she knew what Scritch was and where he was from but there was more, much more, behind that recognition. Before he could dwell, the images roared into motion.

He flashed to the cliff face where magic warred in the sky above them, his power and the magic of the ritual battled the Barric spell that corrupted the banishment. He linked once more with Aurin, and felt the emotions his other friend poured into his relationship with the mysterious Ardelle.

He flashed to Falderal and the confrontation between Waliyt and Ardelle. Though he had barely been conscious, his mind held memories of the encounter. Then he was waking up within Heimili álfa with that strange Oberon tending to him. *Trianamati, My uncle,* Clornamti's voice rang out. Her intrusion caused the images to veer to the classroom where she sat in the sunlight, her eyes sparkling as she stuck her tongue out at Darl. The sound of her laughter rang within his mind. It was not the reserved giggle that he had heard from all Oberon, but the throaty chuckle he had heard earlier tonight. His embarrassment was rising as image after image of Clornamti flashed between them. The first day he had asked for her help, the anticipation of seeing her again the following days, the shame he felt when he couldn't share in her tour of the city for fear of saying too much, and other times where he had desperately wanted to talk to her.

I didn't know, she admitted to him as the disappointment of her refusal to walk with him finally collapsed the flow of memories. *I'm sorry that I hurt you, I just thought you didn't want me close.*

Of course I did, he admitted. *I should have explained why I couldn't speak of it. I should have known that you would remember me from my failure at trial. How could anyone forget that?*

He could feel her laughter, *it was a spectacular failure, and I've never seen a man so angry.*

He suppressed his own laughter, *Are we linked?* The question was rhetorical, he could feel everything she felt, and he could even see himself through her eyes. The experience was jarring, he could see through both their eyes. Since they looked at each other, it was an odd sensation, much like looking into a mirror image of a mirror.

He wanted to ask her about Micah, but she stopped him before he could pose it. *We should get to work, before someone finds us like this. I have shielded us, but it won't defend against an earnest attack.* He could feel her pull in a deep breath, with her senses and his own. At some point during the link she had pressed herself up against him. Fear washed over him from her mind, *Charles! Don't pull away, the link is not strong and it will be very difficult to restore if you break it now.*

He hadn't realized that he had been pulling away from the link or her. *Don't worry about our bodies, just focus on my thoughts. The first step to utilizing the shield is to forget what you know of foci.*

His confusion washed over both of them, *Forget?*

Yes, foci during rituals are well known, but you are about to use yourself as a foci. He started to interrupt, but she cut him off, *I know, it goes against everything you have learned but trust me. Draw from your pool, just a small amount it is all you need.*

He could feel her drawing from her own pool and matched her energy with his own. *You really are a powerful mage, I could cast for weeks with just your pool alone.*

Bewilderment rang through him, could she cast using his pool? *Yes, as long as we are linked, we are as one. If I was evil, I could make you do things from within your mind, like strip down or stand on your head.* She was laughing again, an infectious feeling that brought a smile to his face, until he remembered the night in the temple. The disconnected voice telling him he had no chance of breaking free, that his life belonged to the voice now. *That was likely a link as well, something done maliciously. We never learn how to do that here, but I have heard rumors that powerful spellcasters can enter your mind against your will if they have some connection to you, especially blood.*

He wanted to ask more, but they had work to do and it was already growing very late. *Can we talk about that later?*

Of course, she affirmed. *Now, with your power within you, collect it at your fingers but don't cast it.* She demonstrated using her own power. He watched her motions intently but the real insight came from within her mind. She used her body as the focus for the spell, linking the magic to her inner pool as though it were a staff. With the link in place, she created the shield and tied it to the pool within her. As spells or other energies collided with the magic, it would pull more from her pool to sustain itself. It needed little to maintain while she wasn't being attacked, and only drew enough from her pool to ward off the magic that it was stopping instead of dumping raw magic into the shield like he had been doing. He attempted the spell, but failed to link it to his pool. Clornamti interjected, *May I?*

Please, he replied, then let her take control of his magic.

The link is tricky the first few times you try it. When you release the spell, you don't fully let go, instead you pull it back into yourself. She cast his magic out around him, but he could feel her holding some small part of it back, a tie to the spell that she bound back to his pool. He had never seen it's like in any of the spells he had worked, nor had it been present in any of the texts he had read. *It's an Oberon secret,* she told him. *Only a handful of outsiders knew the trick and they were forbidden from passing it along. It is as old as our magic, something that our first Wizards used to protect themselves from the monsters that roamed this world before us. Some say it even predates Vielk, but the church deemed that heretical.*

He pulled his magic back to his fingertips and repeated her spell. This time, the magic kept its link to his pool and created the barrier that he had seen so many times about his instructor. *I did it!*

He felt her arms wrap about his body in a hug. *Congratulations! Now the real test is to break the link and try it again without me.* He feared releasing the link, of learning that this had all been a dream or worse. *This is no dream,* she reassured him then kissed him softly on the lips. His heart thudded within his chest but he forced himself to remain calm.

They practiced well into the night, finally deciding to retire when the first hints of dawn lit the horizon. He had never spent the night with a girl before and thought this was nothing like he had expected. He walked her to her chambers this time, then retired to his own for a short nap before his training would resume. His instructor would likely have many questions for him this morning, but Charles was resigned to tell him nothing. Let the man guess, it was what he deserved. He smiled to himself, then dreamed of Clornamti in a field of flowers, sunlight kissing her chestnut hair.

All thoughts of Micah had vanished from his mind.

Memories

Ardelle left her sleeping quarters well before the sun had topped the trees. She had meant to sleep late, but her body refused to cooperate. After several hours of doing nothing but staring at the ceiling, she had given up and dressed. Light fog mingled with the cool crisp air in the city. Determined as she was to spend the day on her own pursuits, ideas on what those could be were lost on her. She had long given up the idea of living for herself, a notion that the church told her was beyond selfish, given her status as an avatar. Knowing that they had abandoned her as much as anyone else had, she refused to let their doctrine continue to shape her life. There was no mandate from the Demon of Punishment that they couldn't find and rescue her, something that she hadn't really come to grips with until the night before, when the Pyre had sought to induct her back into the church.

Any churchgoer could have come to the forest and saved her, it wouldn't have taken much to break the curse. Just delving into that cursed place would have been enough to free her, but none had tried. No priest had risked themselves for her, not one had sought to spare their mistress the pain of being unable to contact her avatar, being unable to touch the mortal realm at all. They had all sat within their stone walls and kept their power to themselves. She learned that some had even suggested that they close their doors and simply take what they needed from the cities they resided. It had created a new fire within her, burning with resentment of all the time she had given to that institution, one that was supposed to bring heat and life to the world through their ministrations.

She descended the tower at a brisk pace, stopping only once to duck into an alcove when Charles and his young friend appeared arm in arm. Where had they been to at such an early hour, or was it a late one? It was none of her business, but she couldn't help the smile that crept to her mouth. It was good that he was finding happiness here, even if she wasn't. He deserved something to go well in his life, nothing else seemed to work for him. He had been banished from Hudcoeden, but only after the Druids had dashed his dreams. He had never known his parents and the only brother he had ever known had been lost when they left the forest.

She let the couple pass her without hailing them, and wandered out into the city. Despite the early hour, signs of life began cropping up around her, shops were dusting off their shelves and opening their doors, smiths stoked their fires and pumped the bellows, and the odd farm cart or two trundled by loaded with their autumn crops. She had already explored the areas along the ground level, but many of the towers were still a mystery to her. She doubted there was much for her within them, and most prohibited her entry anyway. The compound that housed the majority of the "land-bound" was much like any other city she had ever been in. There were exceptions of course, the Tu'roki, for instance, had a large presence here, unlike many of the human cities. Their skill in the smithy was a desirable trait for a civilization that needed lightweight arms and armor. Given their stature there was a common misconception that the Tu'roki were beasts of burden, but their bodies didn't bear weight any better than any other races. Their great shells protected them better than most armor but also limited their ability to move and lift, so any armor that made that worse was undesirable.

She followed her feet to their area, she couldn't say why but she felt like it was where she needed to go. The smithies were already glowing with their fires, fires that burned through most nights due to the necessity of even heat when working with steel. Two Tu'roki manned the forge nearest her, an older male and a young female. They worked in tandem on a single large piece, something long and curved, too big to be a weapon or a single piece of armor. Fascinated, she watched as they worked the glowing piece of metal into a more recognizable shape, the leading edge of a bow. She guessed this piece was a strengthening support for one of the big ballistae she had seen throughout the city. The Oberon didn't believe in outward shows of military power, but if you looked deeper you could see that they weren't without their defenses. Ballistae were mounted at regular intervals along their towers, camouflaged to appear as trees or other decorations. Close inspection would reveal their true purpose, but from a distance they were aesthetically pleasing.

The young Tu'roki girl acknowledged Ardelle watching her with a smile. It was still hours before they opened so Ardelle hadn't even expected that, but it was nice to be noticed. She watched the coals burn for several moments, fire at its core form. It was beautiful to watch, even if she hadn't been tied to Betala she was sure she would still take some joy in staring into the flames. The coals glowed brighter each time the girl worked the foot pedal that pumped their bellows, each puff of air would feed the flames and give them more energy. Fire was a remarkable element, you couldn't hold it or even really control it. At best you could direct its energy where you needed it, but fire was independent of all control. It lived only to consume, the fact that mortals could take life from an element that only had one purpose was wondrous. Fire had no soul, but it was vital to the binding of a soul to the body. Without fire's energy, life was cold and passionless. It was clear from the destruction fire reaped why others feared it, but for those that understood, fire was life.

She looked up from her study of the flames to see that the girl had addressed her and was awaiting a response. "I'm sorry," she started, "I was just admiring your forge." Not a complete lie, just not the direct truth.

"That is quite alright, miss." The girl spoke with the halting accent of a northerner, one not used to speaking in the common tongue. "Is there something I can help you with this fine morning?"

"I…" she started confusedly. Why had she come here? "I think I was just looking."

The girl's brow furled, "Well if you do need something, just ask." The girl turned back to her work.

Ardelle's cheeks burned as she turned to walk away, then she stopped cold. Directly across from the first booth was an older stall, one that had been on this ground for a long time. A single occupant worked the forge, a middle aged man with dark, soot colored hair. His eyes flashed as he looked up at her, black as the coal behind him. His ears tapered to points, like an Oberon, but no wings sprouted from his back, a half-blood. He swung the smithing hammer hard, sending a shower of sparks in every direction, his muscular arms flexing. He was big for a half-blood, broad-shouldered and thick-legged.

His most striking feature had little to do with his appearance. She knew this man, she had grown up with him, but why was he here? "Omar?"

The man looked up, "Omar was my grandfather. I am Omesh."

Of course the man she had known was long dead, everyone she knew was gone. She could see the differences now, Omar had carried a scar over his left eye from a knife and another on his neck from a burn, one she had given him when her power first manifested. It had been her hope speaking again, something she avoided. "I'm sorry, you bear a striking resemblance."

Omesh looked up at her from under his brow, "you knew my grandfather?"

She realized it would have been better to just walk away but it was too late now. "Yes, I knew him. We grew up together in Krossfarin, a long time ago."

He dropped the piece onto his bench and turned his attention to her fully. "You must be that Avatar everyone is speaking of, the long lost Ardelle. Grandfather spoke of you frequently, though I must admit I didn't believe his stories." He extended a soot-covered hand which she shook without hesitation. "I had heard a rumor that you looked young, but those stories just didn't do you justice."

Ardelle fought back another blush, "I may look young, but looks are not everything. Last I saw of your grandfather was in Krossfarin, close to two hundred years ago, how did you come to be a smith here in Heimili álfa?"

Omesh released her hand and stepped back into his stall, "Grandfather came here right after they took you. He told us of the fiery girl that he ran the streets with and how the church of Betala had come to claim her before he had a chance to ask for her hand. He told us a wild story of how the two of you sought to fight them to stay free but he had been captured and you sacrificed yourself to spring him. Is any of that true?"

It was close, though the part about asking for her hand was a stretch. She and Omar had been much more like brother and sister than a couple. The parts about the church were true, she had tried to keep herself from them, to stay free. When Omar had been taken she had no choice but to turn herself in, lest he suffer for her freedom. She hadn't thought about those years in a long time, her life started over when the church took her. "It's close, but I don't know about the marriage. Your grandfather and I were like brother and sister. The rest is true."

Omesh chuckled, "I never would have guessed. When I was a kid I believed all those stories and wanted to grow up so I could come find you." He laughed harder, "well, I guess I found you."

She couldn't help but join in. "You did. If only Omar was here so you could tell him."

"You know, he tried to find you once himself." Omesh explained. "When he heard that you had been banished he tried to get into the forest to free you, but the only way to enter is to be sent there." He paused, scratching his chin thoughtfully. "He told us he tried for a year to get into the forest, but no one would send him. Even some of the great

Wizards down to Falderal refused. My family thought he was crazy, but he swore he would have continued to try if not for the war. The war wasn't kind to him, he lost his right arm and most of his right leg. After that, he couldn't keep trying to get into the forest. He met my grandmother in the camp, she was a smith."

Ardelle nearly collapsed at the revelation. Someone had come for her, someone she never would have expected. Omar would have been in his middle years when he had made the attempt, his life extended by his half-Oberon blood, but he would still have been hale. "He truly tried to rescue me?"

Omesh thought for a moment, "If all the rest of his stories were true, then yes, he did." He looked her over. "Do you need to sit down?"

The dizziness had come on rapidly but she was able to take Omesh's arm and sit in the chair he offered. "Thank you," she said as he offered her some water. "I'm sorry to be a bother, I don't usually pry, but could you tell me more of Omar? I've lost so many people since I've been gone and I would appreciate knowing that at least someone found happiness."

Omesh sighed and gestured at the pile of half-finished work on his tables, "I would love to, but I have to finish an order today. Is there any way we could meet again tomorrow?"

Ardelle looked about the smithy. "If I was to help you here, would you tell me of your grandfather while we work?"

"Do you know the trade?" he quizzed.

"No, but I know fire," she smiled slyly.

Omesh chuckled again, "I bet you do. It's a deal!" He offered his hand again.

Shaking the dizziness from her head, she stood and moved to the forge. His heat was high, but she could do better. Using a small lance of power, she brought the coals from a cherry color to a white hot blaze. Omesh whooped as he saw the forge glow with its new heat. "I've never been able to get her so hot, can you hold it like that?"

She smiled again, "only all day."

Omesh grinned from ear to ear. "This is going to be fun."

They worked for most of the morning on his project, a large metal brace for one of the tower supports. It wasn't a glamorous project, but it was something useful. They finished around lunch with a story of Omar and the battle of the Just, his last battle in the war. He had lost his arm and leg to a Harpy's magic, but not before he had thrown his spear and killed the creature. Omesh told the story with a vigor that must have risen with the revelation that his grandfather hadn't been a crazy old man, but had actually lived a heroic life. He shared that Omar had lived to nearly one-hundred seventy-five, an extremely old age for a half-blood Oberon. He died quietly in his family home here in Heimili álfa, his eight children and thirty-five grandchildren all present. He died a happy man with only one regret, her. Omesh had been eight when his grandfather passed, it was hard on all of them and made harder when their parents told them that the grand tales they revered were probably just stories.

The smith was a welcome presence, he wanted little from her other than her help, and the reassurance that his grandfather really was a great man. It was refreshing to spend a day with someone who didn't have grand plans of how to use her best in the future, only how she could be helpful today. Omesh told her stories of his grandmother, another half-blood born during the height of Falderal and their peace, before Barrah's fall and the coming of the Demons.

"Well," he started, ringing his hands together, "that's it. That was the big project for the day."

She sighed, it had been a welcome change to work with her hands. "Have you no other projects we could work on? I am enjoying this."

"No commissions, but I'd love to see what we could do with a sword now that you've got the forge so hot. The steel we could make would be amazing." He grinned foolishly, like a child with his first sweet treat.

She laughed at his expression, then agreed to make the sword. Omesh immediately broke into another story of his grandfather's, one of his experience as a smith after the war. Not many customers trusted their work to a one-armed smith, but the few that did were never disappointed. He told her of a sword his grandfather had made, with the help of a real Wizard from Falderal. It had been of such steel that none could compare, except maybe the legendary swords of old. The Wizard had been a man who said little, but never spared in coin. The blade itself had been inscribed in magical runes, the hilt chased in gold with emeralds set in both the hilt and pommel. Omesh swore that the emeralds were magic, Omar had told him so. The sheath was also trimmed in gold, with a rampant golden dragon as its sigil. Ardelle had to contain her excitement. She knew the blade, Charles had it tucked under his bed at this very moment. She resolved to bring it to the shop tomorrow to give Omesh a glance at the work his grandfather had done, it was the least she could do after he spent the day with her reciting old stories.

They started their work with the iron, heating it as much as the forge would allow and then beyond. Omesh couldn't keep the smile from his face as they worked in the other metals that would transform the iron to steel. He added minerals and raw materials she had never seen before. He kept their origins to himself, 'trade-secrets' he told her. The stories faded as they worked, the process consuming all of their attention and leaving little room for idle conversation. They worked through lunch and into the evening. When she took a moment to glance outside the shop, she could see that the sun had dropped below the surrounding forests. Most of the other smiths had gone home for the night, their coals banked until morning.

Omesh worked the steel over the anvil several times between firings, folding the metal onto itself to add to its strength and to evenly distribute its alloy. It was full dark when he finally dropped the sword into the temper, rapidly cooling the metal and hardening it. She took the opportunity to infuse the length of the blade with aspects of her magic, an enchantment that increased the blades durability. The steel absorbed the magic hungrily, the metal was ideal for the casting. Omesh finished the tempering process over the next few hours, finally setting the blade to the grinding stone around midnight. The moon had passed its apex well before he sharpened the steel, their only light now was from the forge.

The sword was long and thin, bearing only a single edge along its curved blade. The tang was the full width of the blade, the length of her thumb from the first knuckle. The handle curved opposite the blade, though only slightly. Omesh sharpened the blade on the grinding wheel until he was satisfied with the edge. It would need further sharpening once they were finished, but for now he left it with the simple edge. With the fires work complete, Omesh banked the forge. He rested the sword on a stand on his workbench, eyeing it with reverence before turning back to Ardelle. "It's beautiful, isn't it?"

"What are you going to do with it?" It occurred to her that she should have asked that prior to making the sword.

"What would you do with it?" He scratched at his ear, shaking loose some of the ash. "I didn't actually get up this morning with the intention of making a sword and I'm no warrior."

"Perhaps we should make a stand for it and leave it here?" She smiled slightly at the thought of something so fine collecting dust on a shelf.

"Why don't we sleep on it?" It was clear he didn't like the idea of it just sitting. "It's nearly dawn now, I should get some rest anyway. It was just hard to stop."

Her smile widened, "I know the feeling. Thank you for the day, Omesh, I truly appreciate it. I needed this, a chance to get out of my own head."

"Any time you need to work the forge, I will be here." He smiled at her and held out his hand.

She shook it, "I appreciate that, Omesh. Thank you again." She left then, picking her way back through the darkened city to her chamber. She instructed her guard to keep everyone away until she woke and slipped into her room. She would see Omesh again, at least once when she brought Charles' sword for him to see. She took the time to wash the day's grime from herself, then climbed into bed without bothering to dress. She slept well that night, better than she had since her last night with Aurin in the forest. Thoughts of Aurin brought images of his sparkling blue eyes and his easy smile, but the tears didn't fall this time. Morning came and went while she enjoyed the rest she badly needed.

Mending

He awoke to the sound of drums. It seemed to be the only sound that would drive him from his unconsciousness. To call what he did sleep wouldn't do it justice. When his body ran out of energy during the day, he would just drop. There was no will that could keep him moving.

His nights were plagued with nightmares about the horrors of that day or, sometimes, with Ardelle's green, tear-filled eyes accusing him of murdering thousands. The latter always left him shedding his own tears when he woke. Could she really be with a man that could brutalize so many innocents?

He had spent nearly every day in his bed, something he had hoped to be free of but after his show of force on the field four days ago, he had nothing left to heal himself. At least his injuries from the fall had been healed, as had most of the cuts and bruises he had received. His malady wasn't something that could be healed with a bandage, he had used too much magic. Castielle had been to see him several times in his convalescence, but she had nothing but bad news for him. To her knowledge, there was no way to heal what he had done. In fact, most people that went as far as he did wouldn't have survived. The fact that he did and had maintained his ability to store and use magic fascinated her. It was nothing but a pain to him. Other Druids had come and gone as well, including some of the higher ranking healers, but none of them had good news. Most just came to see the show that he presented, like he was a traveling exhibit.

Most of the time, he was alone. Crowlmer had fled after the battle, driven away by the Gremens' reaction to her appearance. It felt odd to not have her around after spending so much time together. He actually missed her constant nagging and her sharp wit. Surely she knew that he didn't care about her transformation, after all wasn't he a freak as well? True he kept his appearance, but everyone still stared when he passed. No one alive had ever witnessed a display of power like his, nothing short of an Arcana had ever killed an entire army with a wave of their hand.

Castielle's presence often brought back memories of Ardelle, given their resemblance, but her visits also prompted more of the nightmares. Ardelle would hate him now, he was sure of it. He had killed hundreds, if not thousands, of innocents from Hudcoeden. She had given up her life as an Avatar and faced Barrah's punishment alone when she tried to protect mortals from his wraith, he couldn't even stop himself from slaughtering everything on that battlefield. How could such a noble woman ever love a monster like him?

He couldn't tell what time of day it was, or how long he had slept this time, but he knew that his body wasn't going to let him lie here any longer. He swung his legs from his cot, but a sudden lurch of the wagon underneath him sent him to the floor. So they were moving again, that was a good sign. They hadn't made much progress since leaving the river, but steadily crept their way closer to Krossfarin and the protection of its walls and legions.

Getting down from the wagon proved to be too much for him and he found himself eating dirt as the wagon continued down the rutted path. He propped up on his elbows and looked quickly to make sure no one was watching before he climbed to his feet. He felt better today, but still not himself. He attempted to walk, but the four steps that he took off the path to relieve himself quickly banished that thought.

Now he faced a larger problem. His wagon was out of sight by the time he finished and there was no chance he would be able to catch up to it. He had been at the back of the train, so there were no other wagons. Eventually the civilians would reach him, but his constant bouts of unconsciousness could allow them to miss him, or worse, leave him for dead. The Arcana knew there were civilians that would just leave him there on principle after his display of power and the destruction.

Some of those civilians had found their missing loved ones mixed in with the dead demons, blaming him for their deaths. He had no explanation that would settle their woes, no reasoning for why he had killed them, other than they were with the enemy. He also couldn't tell them why their loved ones had marched against them, which made everything worse. Those few that had survived his onslaught didn't speak, and soon after took their own lives in whatever way they could. Brennan had ripped apart his wrists with his teeth on the first night, he bled to death before anyone noticed. Many similar deaths had followed. Some of the captives had tried to escape by overpowering their guards, they were hopelessly outmatched, but they fought to the death nonetheless. He had wondered if it hadn't been an assisted suicide.

Thunderous hooves drew his attention in the direction his wagon had gone. Three horsemen approached him, each wore the uniform of the Druid Guard with the leader bearing the marks of the commander. Samuel Dorne had been his only friend since the battle, it was he that had brought the reports of the captives' deaths and the hatred that ran through the civilians. He looked haggard, somehow older as he pulled up to Aurin and jerked his chin to indicate his direction.

Aurin took his master's proffered hand and clambered up onto the horse behind him then muttered, "Thanks," between gasps for breath.

"Too proud to use the bed pan?" Dorne asked him, knowing full well the answer. "We've found the girl."

Aurin's heart lightened. The girl he spoke of was Adla, the strange little woman that accompanied Crowlmer on the morning of the battle. The girl that had healed him the last time. "Where was she?"

"With the civilians. She had found a family that had lost their daughter during the sack of the city and taken up with them. We found her changing diapers, are you sure this is the miracle girl you need?" Dorne thought Aurin's request odd when he first proposed that Dorne look for a waif mixed into the civilians, but she was the only hope he had of ever recovering from his overuse of his power.

"Take me to her," he demanded, overstepping himself.

"Easy boy," Dorne replied through gritted teeth. "It is the reason I was back here looking for you, we'll take you to her."

His relationship with his master had been strained since he returned from the forest. They had once been as close as any father and son, but something about the grizzled old warrior just didn't sit right with him anymore. There was something different, something deep down that he just couldn't put his finger on. It seemed to be the same man on the outside, but within there seemed to be an older soul, not the youthful, boisterous man he had been when Aurin was growing up. Perhaps it was the loss of the city that he had fought for most of his life, or maybe his age had just caught up with him. Whatever the case, Samuel Dorne was a changed man, even if it was only Aurin that saw it.

His head was swimming by the time they reached the forward command tent for the Guard, his body was nearing its limits. Two guardsmen had to help him from the horse when they stopped. He nearly collapsed at their feet when they set him down, so they each put an arm about his shoulders and carried him into the tent. They set him near the door and Dorne gave him a violent shake to keep him awake. It was almost not enough, his eyelids were incredibly heavy.

Adla sat at the back of the tent, legs crossed in front of her, her tiny hands resting on her knees. The worry that was etched on her face was quickly replaced by fear when she saw Aurin in his condition. Two guards flanked the little girl, hands on swords as if they expected her to do something that would harm them. She was so small Aurin doubted she could even swing hard enough for them to feel it through their armor, but he knew that somewhere inside her was a reservoir of power, much like he had used on the field. If he could destroy an army with a fraction of that power, what could she do?

"Hello Adla," he managed between grunts.

"Hello Aurin, you look terrible." She smiled slightly, "have you seen Crowlmer?"

"Not since the battle," his somber tone took the smile from her face. "We've been looking for you, have you been avoiding us?"

She flinched back into her chair, "No, well, not deliberately."

"I need your help," Aurin begged, "like you did the day of the battle."

Tears sprang from her eyes, "I can't!" She buried her face in her hands.

He was lost, what had he said? "Leave us," he directed the guards. Using the chair as a crutch, he lowered himself into the seat closer to the girl. "Did it hurt you when you gave me the magic?"

"No, that's not it," she whimpered into her hands, "All those people!"

It dawned on him. "You think you are responsible for what I did." He sighed and looked up into the filtered light of the tent. How do you tell a girl, one that knows she gave you the means, she wasn't responsible for the slaughter of nearly a thousand men, women and children from Hudcoeden? "Adla," he started, reaching for her hands to take them away from her face. She jerked at the touch, but relaxed enough for him to see her eyes. "What I did, I had to do. The people out there that day had been corrupted and sought to harm everyone else." He pushed the lump down in his throat, losing himself to tears wouldn't help the situation. "We can't let that day stop us from helping those that are still alive. If you can help me, I will make sure that we reach Krossfarin."

She looked up at him. "How can you be sure, Aurin? How do you know we'll get there and not lose everyone else before we do? Can you save the ones that were corrupted? Can you drive them from our city and give us back our homes?" With shaking hands, she raised a finger and jabbed it toward his chest. "You think the magic will fix everything and make you this unstoppable thing, it won't!" She huffed at him, "I saw what it did to you that day, and I saw your face as you killed them. You enjoyed it!"

Her ice blue eyes pierced his soul. He had enjoyed it, the rush of power as he leveled the enemy. "I... I wanted...," What did he want? He had wanted to kill them, and he did. Within that power he had lost all reason, he had only wanted to kill to stop the demons, from hurting any more of his soldiers, but he hadn't just killed demons. He had killed those that turned as well, people like Brennan who had been forced to be there through some means they didn't understand. Their humanity had been stripped away and they existed only to lead their demons and kill the refugees. The Demons' desires were the only words they spoke when Dorne's men had interrogated them.

"You wanted to kill!" she shouted into his face, "you wanted to slay and destroy so much that you drove yourself to use too much of your power and now you are back for more." She stood from the chair. "No, Aurin, I won't help you kill again, not like that, not ever!" She moved to leave the tent, turning back to him just long enough to see his face. Her features softened, but it didn't stop her. She forced her way through the flap in the tent and disappeared.

Aurin sank to the floor, the effort of simply sitting in a chair was too much. Tears streamed from his eyes as he considered her words. He had enjoyed it, and if it wasn't for that voice he would have continued doing it until it killed him. The power was intoxicating, was this why the Druids strictly controlled the Wizards? Was he truly any better than the demons he had destroyed?

He sobbed into the floor before he lost consciousness. When he came to, he was back in his wagon. He rocked back and forth as the wagon trundled along, the trees creating shadows along the canvas over his head that looked like the skeletons he had left on the field. He felt raw, empty of life. Adla had shown him his true self and left him a shell of a man. Who was he really? He had thought himself a hero, one of the good people to protect those that can't protect themselves, but he had slaughtered without compunction or thought. Could those that walked with the demons have been saved? Could he have used his power to do that? Charles had told him repeatedly that his sword was enchanted to break magic. Could he have used its magic to release them?

His body wasn't healing, and he didn't know if he wanted it to. If he died now, he couldn't hurt anyone else. If he healed, he would have power again and he knew now that he couldn't be trusted with it. He had sought out Adla simply to have the power again, not really to be healed. He missed that intoxicating sensation that you could do anything. It was overwhelming.

The wagon came to a stop some time later and a crew of Guardsmen boarded to take him to a tent. Dorne was waiting for him, looking even more worn than he had when last they met. "Your girl got past the guards, they swear they never saw her." His master wasn't one for greetings, or any sort of pleasantry, "I guess she wasn't the miracle you hoped for. What are you plans now?"

Aurin sighed. "Just let me die."

Dorne's head picked up, his eyes were bloodshot and there were bags under them. He hadn't shaved in days by the look of it. Aurin could almost see the man he had grown up with behind that pained look. The big man huffed. "Let you die? After all the work I put in training you?" It was an attempt at humor, but it fell on deaf ears. "What is wrong with you boy?"

"I left boyhood behind me a long time ago, Dorne. I'm a full-fledged monster now." Aurin tried to rise from his stretcher, but didn't have the strength.

"Monster?" His master snorted, "why, because you killed demons? Do you know how many things I've killed? Your display the other day was impressive, I will admit that I've never done anything like that, but I've taken more lives than you could ever dream of. We're warriors, it is our lot in life to kill."

"But we don't have to enjoy it," Aurin shouted, it was all he could do with the energy he had. "I enjoyed slaughtering those people. They were people from Hudcoeden, people I was supposed to protect and I killed them."

"Is that what this is about? Killing the turned?" His master turned away from him and raised his chin so that he was staring at the ceiling. "Would it help if I told you that you can't save them?"

"How would you know? We didn't even try!"

"But I have, many times I've tried to save them. They aren't really themselves anymore, their souls are gone." Dorne turned back to him. "Caliban uses a ritual that he fashioned a very long time ago to strip away their soul and leave an empty shell that he can fill with his evil. They only exist to carry his will, to lead the demons." He gazed seriously at the boy, but Aurin was still incensed.

"How could you possible know that? You've been in Hudcoeden your entire life, how would you know what this Caliban has done? For that matter, what do you know of magic?" He spat the words out, bringing on a coughing fit. It took him a moment to settle down and when he did, his master's face had gone dark.

"Sixteen years ago, I fought Caliban outside of Falderal. He led the armies of Demons out from the city into the countryside and I commanded the coalition defense. The Demons didn't move like they had before, they were organized into ranks and marched as units. When we engaged them, we found the men leading them. After the initial battle, we took several of these 'turned' as prisoners and tried to get information out of them. To a man, they killed themselves. Nothing remained that could be called human." His master sat at the foot of his bed, "The next skirmish was worse, we had to flee the field but not before capturing more of the men. This time one of my soldiers recognized his cousin among them. Soon others came forward to claim the men as relatives from Falderal and we started to piece together what was happening."

Aurin couldn't believe what he was hearing. His master had never spoken of fighting against the demons in the great diaspora that followed the fall of Falderal. He assumed that Dorne was already captain of the Guard in Hudcoeden by then and had stayed to defend the city. From the few books he had actually read, he knew that the Demons eventually came to Hudcoeden, but were repelled by a combined force of Wizards and Druid Guard.

Dorne continued, "Our Druids were called in to try and heal the men, but they couldn't see any magic in them. The Druids told us there was nothing to heal. We tried anyway, kept the men under guard for weeks trying to talk to them, make them see that they weren't monsters, but nothing worked. Eventually the men died, either by attacking their guards or simply not eating or drinking." Dorne stared off into the distance, recalling things Aurin knew he could never forget. "The worst was yet to come. Our final battle with the assembled army took place outside of Hudcoeden, our last line of defense before the Demons had clear access to all of the lands to the south. The siege lasted months, with thousands of men, women and children dying, catching the diseases that spread when people are kept so close together. The army we faced was far too knowledgeable about our defenses for us to muster any break to the siege. Somehow, they knew what our plan was before we did and always had a counter to our movements. In desperation, I assembled my best men and a stranger from Krossfarin and crept out under cover of darkness. We sought to kill their generals in their tent, cut the head from the snake as it were.

"We infiltrated the camp disguised as the humans we had captured, no one challenged us. In their camps, no one seemed to care if a few extra humans showed up. We found the command tent with equal ease, almost as if they were expecting us. We killed the guards at the tent, we hadn't needed to, they didn't even challenge as we approached. Our new friend thought it wise to put them down just in case we needed to flee quickly and I couldn't argue that point." Dorne inhaled deeply, "There were three men inside and one boy who couldn't have been more than two.

"I knew two of the men, I had served with them during my time in Falderal. Victor Chavox and Ashe Thormane, though they weren't themselves, not completely. Ashe recognized me, but Victor just stared. Ashe drew his sword as we entered, but didn't move to attack me. The stranger stepped forward before he could and revealed himself to be Ashe's third son, Eitan, who was supposed to have been lost in a skirmish with the Gremen. Eitan tried to reason with his father, but Ashe wasn't himself anymore. He wasn't a mindless follower like the others, no, Caliban left enough of his intellect for him to be useful. He wasn't human though.

"Victor was the same, his humanity was gone, but his knowledge was still there. Caliban had turned them and brought them along to lead the army. They were why our defenses failed, these two men that I would have gladly given my life for were serving my enemy," Dorne paused long enough to give Aurin too much time to think.

Aurin had learned from Charles that he was a Thormane, Ashe was his father and Victor Chavox was Charles' father, two men that had sacrificed themselves so that the refugees could flee Falderal. If they had been turned, anyone could be. What would cause them to turn against the very people they had laid down their lives to protect? What magic could possibly do that?

His master continued, "Caliban laughed as Eitan tried to reason with his father. He told us it was useless to try, but we were welcome to waste our time. He let us try to get through to the men for half the night before he finally grew tired of our attempts and ordered his slaves to kill us. Victor slayed Eitan before I could even draw my sword. He cut the young man down with that magic sword that was supposed to make him wise. Ashe ignored his son and rushed at me, it was all I could do to stop his sword. We fought for a long time, both knowing the other's style so well that there was little weakness to exploit. Victor took his time killing everyone else that had come with me. All of them eventually fell even after one of them sank his sword up to the hilt in the Victor's gut. Then it was the two of them against me and I knew I didn't have much chance, but Caliban called them off.

"He told me he could use me in his army, use me like he was using the other two." Tears fell from Dorne's dirty face, leaving streaks in the road dust that had accumulated there during their march. "I wasn't going to go down like that, I couldn't let myself be a slave. I ripped the sword out of Victor and took his head from his shoulders. It was one of the hardest things I've ever done, I had shared a tent and many an ale with the man during our training.

"Ashe was a harder fight, but I took up Victor's sword and used its magic to help. I disarmed him and pled with him to ask mercy, but he came on anyway. I killed him in that tent, drove this sword," he patted the weathered hilt at his side, "into his chest and through his heart." The tears fell more freely now, but Aurin couldn't understand why.

Ashe had tried to kill him, and was turned. Hadn't Dorne just told him it was what had to be done? What could possibly make his master sob so much for a man that was just a training partner? There had to be more to it. "Who was Ashe to you?"

Dorne wiped at his eyes, "Ashe was my nephew. I had taught him the sword, taught him war. I would have done the same for Eitan if I had known who he was, but the stringy boy I had known before he disappeared was not the man that I had walked into the camp with." He dabbed at his eyes again, clearing them before continuing, "Caliban was furious. He drew that ridiculous, three-hooked sword and charged me. After fighting the other two, it was all I could do to keep that thing from my body. I lost Victor's sword in the fight with Ashe and soon was unarmed on the floor of the tent. Caliban stood over me and giggled that hideous laugh before he started to chant. I looked around for anything I could use as a weapon and spotted the little boy. He was shaking Ashe and crying 'Daddy.' Then I saw Ashe's sword, under the chair next to me. I grabbed at it and stuck it as deep into Caliban's belly as I could, then ripped it back out. He fell to his knees and I should have taken his head, but I was so sure he was dead." Dorne shook his head again, "I grabbed my sword and the boy, and then I ran from the tent all the way back to Hudcoeden.

"The Demons broke that night, without Caliban exerting his control through his mindless servants they all scattered to look for easier targets. His human slaves all died on the field, all of them, as far as we could tell." Dorne coughed as he suppressed another sob.

Aurin already knew the answer, but he asked anyway, "I was the boy, wasn't I?"

His master looked him in the eye, "Yes, you were the boy, we're kin you and I." He bent down and lifted Aurin's sword from the floor of the wagon. "I knew your name already, from a letter I'd gotten from Ashe, but I couldn't have your surname known in the city so I called you 'Tor'." He rested the sword along Aurin's side in the bed, dropping the hilt into his open hand. "Do you understand now that there was nothing that could have been done for the turned? If men like Ashe and Victor could be turned and ignore their own sons, there is no hope for the others. Even the magic of your sword is useless, Ashe held it with his own hand when we fought."

Aurin was taken aback, Dorne had known about the magic of the sword and given it to him anyway. He gripped the sword, drawing on its familiarity to ground him back in reality. "There is something that can be done," he told his master firmly. "We can kill Caliban. At least that will set them free." His life had found meaning again, he had unfinished business with a man and his three-hooked sword.

Wolves

"Keep those fires high and your eyes sharp!" Howlter barked at his men as they sat lazily around their watch fires on the perimeter of the refugee camp. There had been a glut of wolf attacks since the battle, the animals seemed to be incited by all the wounded that had been left after the Demons had fled. There had been a dozen deaths just in the last three days.

His men grumbled, they often complained up the ranks about his leadership and wondered what they were being paid for this escort mission. Twice they had faced the Demon army for the citizens of Hudcoeden, and twice they had fled the field. His force had never fled from a battle prior to the sacking of Hudcoeden, they had never faced an enemy they couldn't defeat. His tactical experience and their unwavering loyalty had led to these victories, but that loyalty was waning now. Even with his gift from Nezmas, he had trouble keeping the men in line. If they suffered another defeat, there would be desertion or worse. The wolves were the immediate threat to his command, they struck quickly and left without witnesses, leaving only a mangled body in their wake. The Druids had been the first to identify the wounds, though they felt it necessary to inform everyone that the marks came for the largest wolves on record.

Howlter had taken to sleeping in his saddle as they plodded down the road and stayed up all night to act as guard. He had tried to use his power to sense the creatures, but they didn't seem to react to his magic. This was what worried him, all beasts were Nezmas' domain so if the wolves didn't react to his magic, they weren't beasts. Were they a new breed of Demon? Something worse? He didn't know, and he needed to know if he was ever to reassure his men. So he walked the watch fires, his eyes never leaving the surrounding country side. It was nearing midnight now, the time of most of the attacks. If the pattern held there would be screams soon, someone would either go missing or be found dead. There weren't enough men to patrol the entire perimeter, and those men he did have were tired, sore, and disenfranchised with the thought of giving up every night just to march the entire day after.

They had marched steadily north since the battle outside Balenford, moving as quickly as ten thousand refugees could move. His men had driven Crowlmer away, their prejudice of the 'impure' Gremen was common among members of his race. Since the time of the Just, Gremen have hated the thought of their 'more evolved' counterparts, those with tails or the ability to shape shift. Unknown to most outsiders, Gremen were born with tails frequently. Their parents would just remove the offending appendage before the child was seen by others. Having six children himself, he personally cut two tails off. When Barrah's last avatar had been chosen from the Gremen and her body adapted to the peak of its evolution, her tail had been nearly five feet in length. When the Arcana had changed her, she had set off the evolution of the Gremen race as a whole. Some, but not all, Gremen were born with tails from that day forward. Since Barrah's fall, any other child that bears the tail is either killed outright or banished forever even though every parent knows that the tail is a natural thing. If a child were to reach adolescence with the tail, cutting it off would prevent them from ever walking normally, let alone becoming a warrior. They became dependent on the balance of the tail.

The ability to shape shift is common, and usually borne by those with Nezmas' gift. Those with the gift, even in the slightest, feel a pull that they never understand, until the first time they transform. The desire to become a beast is even stronger in those with magic, though all Gremen have the desire. Had he not possessed the will of the Arcana himself, Howlter's strength in the magic would have long ago claimed his sanity and driven him to live as an animal. He often suppressed the urge when he was in battle, the pounding of his heart and the smell of blood brought the beast out of him. He slipped once, allowing the beast to take over, but was lucky that all of his companions had perished before he had done so. If any of them had seen his skin change, he would never have risen within the ranks of the army, nor led men to battle.

Even with this long history, his people could not accept one such as Crowlmer. It didn't matter that she had killed dozens of demons on the field that day, or that she had protected Aurin long enough for him to bring his magic to bear, all they saw was the tail and her feline features. He pitied her, she had always been an outcast, even when she was his lieutenant. Woman warriors among the Gremen were common, but not ones with Crowlmer's skill or her ferocity. Crowlmer had been the top swordsman in every competition he had ever held, including in ones he had participated. She outstripped every one of her peers in the blade and bested the majority of them in hand to hand as well. She lacked in the bow, never really applying herself to learning it, but it didn't matter. No other female had ever held the title of First Blade, and he doubted another would any time soon. Crowlmer was destined for great things as a warrior, but he doubted those deeds would be performed within any Gremen force. He missed her raw input, she never held anything back and was often right when criticizing his decisions. His other lieutenants would never be so bold as to question him, and they lacked the conviction to stop him from doing what he wanted anyway.

The screams started just as he reached the last fire on the eastern perimeter. They were close, but he knew he would never get there in time. Likely whatever had attacked would be gone before the screams started. He rushed anyway, his lean body carrying him through the tents faster than any human. He rounded a tent and saw the same scene he had encountered the last three days. A mutilated body lay in pieces across the path between the tents. He couldn't tell if it had been a man or a woman from the remains, but it had been freshly killed. He cast out with his senses but could only detect humans and Gremen in the area around him, as it had been every other time he had approached one of these scenes. He wished his power were more in tune with the emotions of mortals, but that particular realm didn't fall under any of the Arcana that he was aware of. To know the hearts of men had only ever been possible when Barrah stilled reigned as Arcana of Justice. Howlter wondered if it still held true given the Arcana's fall, but he didn't dare to consider using the Demon's magic.

Something was wrong about the entire situation in the camps. He should be able to feel the wolves, if they were truly wolves, but he could only feel humans and Gremen. There were no other animals within a hundred strides of him, save for one dog that barely moved. He needed another perspective, someone who had faced the world and won. He needed a Shaman.

He turned from the rapidly expanding crowd and disappeared into the darker areas of the camp. Shaman were the Wizards of his people, those born with Nezmas' gift and taught to use it to aid of their fellow Gremen. While it was true that all manner of magic was born within the Gremen, only that of Nezmas was given the place of honor among the people. Those born with other gifts, like Ven's raw magic or Ori's gift of life, were sent to other cities to train. The humans had always held the colleges for Wizards and Druids, the Tu'roki for Heliagurs, the priests of Ori. Betala's gift and many of the others just weren't common within the Gremen, but if one was born they were often sent to the churches of the Arcana. Only Nezmas' gift was kept within the Gremen tribes, only his secrets were kept holy and the Shaman were his priests. Howlter would have spent his life within the Shamanistic order had he not became Nezmas' Avatar. Though his lord rarely walked with him, Howlter bore the responsibility to speak for Nezmas when the need arose. This gave him freedom from the Shamans and a good deal of authority within the Gremen nation. If he had a formal nation and a city to call home, he would likely be their king, but a scattering of tribes living off the scraps of the rest of civilization needed no king.

He ducked beneath one of the only trees growing within their camp and disappeared into the darkness of the Shamans district. They burned no fires, kept no light against the darkness, relying instead upon their ability to see in the dark like the beasts around them. It was a small piece of magic within Nezmas' sphere of influence to grant yourself the ability to see without light, but to make it permanent came with its own costs. Half of those that performed the ritual, lost the ability to see in the bright light of day. They had limited vision, but it was like looking into a snow storm while the sun was shining in your face. Those afflicted with the sensitivity often wore scarves about their eyes during the day, or simply stayed within their tents.

He entered the largest of the tents, the home of the crone. The oldest of the Shaman kept council with few others, though her word held nearly as much sway as his own. While he was old for a warrior, she was ancient for any Gremen. There were rumors that she had walked the realm before Barrah fell, though he doubted their truth. She was indeed very old, she had known his grandfather when he was young, but to say she was better than two hundred years was a stretch. Most Gremen only lived to be thirty or forty given their warrior lifestyle, some into their sixties, but that was rare. It was never really discussed how long a Gremen lived, only what they accomplished while they did.

The overwhelming smell of incense enveloped him as he pushed through the hanging fur door. The breed of spice used in the incense was foreign to him, but having just come from a major city, it could have originated anywhere. Four Gremen occupied the tent, three robed men and an old woman in rags. Their robes were of the finest cloth and the woman's clothing was stitched together from whatever was lying around, but Howlter knew who held the real power here. The men were her attendants, they lived by her every word. The men never spoke their own words, only repeated her missives. They served as guards when necessary, but Howlter never witnessed them lifting a blade.

"I would speak with you, mistress." Howlter bowed low to the wizened figure in her rags.

"Of course, Silvermane," her voice rasped through her teeth like boots over gravel. "You've come to ask me about magic, Avatar."

Few knew he was Nezmas' Avatar, but the crone had always known. "Yes, I need to know about wolves."

"No, you need to know about skin changers." She smiled her toothless smile at him, her black gums sparkling with spittle. "If it were wolves troubling you, a torch and a bow would end your fears, but you need to know why you can't see them."

"Skin changers," he took a deep breath. If he was truly facing skin changers his magic would be useless. He couldn't see into the hearts of men like he could into animals, and some Gremen. "Tell me about skin changers, crone."

The toothless smile faded from her weathered face, "look upon them." She trailed a wrinkled hand through the steam over her cauldron. The image of a nude human appeared within the boiling contents. He ran through a clearing in the forest before slowly shifting to the shape of an enormous wolf. Howlter watched as the wolf downed a stag and tore into its flesh, even before it stopped thrashing. "When the enchantments of the forest came down, many of its tortured souls were released. This man was one of them, and his exposure to Barrah's poisonous magic has transformed him into something the world wasn't ready for." The image shifted to an attack against another human. The wolf creature tore into an unsuspecting human's neck, but didn't kill it. Howlter watched as magic roared into the victim, blackening its blood and transforming it into another wolf. "Its venom creates more like it, if the prey isn't killed during the attack."

Not only was he facing a shape shifter, but it was one that could pass on its abilities to others. There could be hundreds out there. "How often can it turn others?"

The crone's smile returned. "As often as it likes, Avatar, but avarice is its weakness. It doesn't like to share its prey."

"How do I stop them?" Howlter feared he knew the answer already.

"Seek you one of them, use a skin changer to find skin changers. The winds tell me there is one who walks among us now, use her." She waved over the cauldron and an image of Crowlmer appeared.

The Tomb

Crowlmer descended another flight of stairs. She lost count how many times she had descended, but knew with some certainty that she had long since passed from under the hill she had first entered. The complex was massive, each hall seemed to fork into four others with stairs at even intervals. Each floor was the same as the one above it, just steadily larger the deeper she went. She had passed more than one stone coffin within the complex, though they all bore human bones. Her heart told her that there was a Gremen somewhere within this complex, one of great importance that had been lost in history.

The language she had seen on the surface was easily more than one hundred years old, likely closer to one hundred-fifty, dating back to the Great War. Every corpse she passed was a warrior, and each had been bedecked in their battle regalia, but most of it had rusted or rotted away. The writing on each casket had been common, a change from the upper floors of the tomb where all of the script was ancient Gremen. This appeared to be even older than what had been on the door. She was no expert on history, but the stones nearest the top were more worn down than those further down. She guessed the tomb had been built from the top down, with new floors being added as the tomb grew beyond its capacity.

She knew that this was a tomb for the Avatars of Barrah, when he had served as the Arcana of Justice. That much had been clear when she first started encountering the common script. There were dozens of dead Avatars here, which meant that they did not serve long. She knew from the oral history of the Gremen that Avatars were granted longevity in return for their services, but the Avatars of Barrah never seemed to benefit from that gift. All of those buried here seemed to have died in their prime, long before old age would have naturally set in. When she began to recognize dates, she could see that most only served for twenty years or so before their deaths.

As she passed another level, the caskets began to change. While those above were simple affairs containing the bones of a warrior, this floor was opulent. The walls were studded with gems, the text gave more praise to the Arcana of Justice than any of the bodies buried here. The walls were also painted, rather than just plain stone. The years denoted on the caskets showed that these Avatars were from the last age that Barrah served as an Arcana. All of these men and women, with the majority being the latter, served Barrah during the years known as 'The Decline.' They all served after Barrah snubbed his long time consort, Betala, in favor of her Avatar, Ezra, Queen of the Harpies. He used his powers to make the Harpy an immortal creature, somewhere between the Arcana and mortals, but not belonging to either. Ezra could still walk among the mortals, but she could also cross into the plane of the Arcana, something that had never been done before or since. It was long thought that Barrah coveted Betala's powers and sought to usurp them through Ezra, but the plan never paid off for him. Crowlmer had always pretended to be Ezra when she played as a child, the thought of being a queen always delighted her. It wasn't until she was older and actually met Harpies that she learned their real nature. 'The Decline' hadn't been pleasant for them either.

If these were the Avatars from that time period, they were likely the last to be buried here. She still hadn't found a single Gremen, all of these were humans but very few were dressed as warriors. Most of the female corpses had very little in the way of clothing, as a matter of fact. From the remnants of cloth that she could see, these women wore mostly shear silk hanging from gold or silver adornments. Priests of Mormia often wore similar garments, if they wore anything at all, but Barrah's Avatars were the leaders of the Judgment. The current Avatar would be the Judge and the others would serve as Cavaliers, meting out Barrah's punishment and forgiveness throughout the world. Why would they wear clothes that served no practical purpose?

She also noticed that each of these Avatars served for only a single year. What really happened during 'The Decline'? Was Barrah really so fickle with his servants? The women in general served the shortest time, but the men fared little better. She pressed further into the tomb and finally came upon what she sought. Across from an empty alcove rested a grand onyx coffin with Gremen runes running the length of it. It was by far the most heavily adorned on this floor, and that meant something considering the opulence of the others. The casket was also the only one covered, a Gremen tradition. This had not been placed here by the priests of Barrah, this was a Gremen burial if ever there was one. Only the greatest of their race were buried, most were released back to the world in the pyres. The greatest were buried like this so that they may continue their glory forever.

She stepped up to the coffin and carefully removed the lid. The creature inside was not what she had expected.

Firstly, the Gremen was nearly perfectly preserved, her body was pristine. The wasting that was expected after so many years of decomposition were not present, the woman looked as if she had just passed yesterday.

Her preservation was one thing, but what really got Crowlmer's attention was the long black tail that snaked around the woman's right leg. Her preserved face also revealed the feline countenance that Crowlmer had seen in her own reflection. The woman's mane had a slight blue tint to its primarily silver hue and was gathered at the nape of her neck in twin braids. Her body was adorned with the armor of her station, a shining steel plate that bore none of the dints or rents that she would expect of battle armor. The breastplate was marked only with more of the Gremen script. Twin, curved swords hung from her hips in much the same fashion as Crowlmer typically carried. The resemblance was remarkable.

Crowlmer reached out gently to touch the face and was surprised by a flash of light. She quickly pulled her hand back, but could swear she had been on a battlefield.

She took a deep breath and reached out again.

*****

Her Cavaliers were arrayed along the base of the hill surrounding the last temple, their pennants flapped in the stiff breeze out of the north. Their armor gleamed in the midday sun as their horses pranced in place. It was the first and last time the entire order would be in one place, it wasn't likely that any of them would survive the day.

The Demons and Og'rai marched in tight formations from the east while a coalition of Humans, Gremen, and Oberon marched from the west. If she still had her power, still she would have judged them all, but Barrah's fall had left her with nothing. The two forces would battle here, and her Cavaliers would pay the price.

The leaders of both armies sought to destroy the last of them, the Demons for their new lord, Barrah, the coalition to wipe any last refuge of the Just from the mortal plane. Barrah had wronged the mortals, and her order was going to pay for it. They could hold this hill against either force separately, but she knew that a common enemy was enough to create peace between the two. At least until she and her fellows were dead, then they would return to tearing each other apart.

The Demons were being led by a huge Og'rai who wielded an equally large war hammer in his right hand. His left hand was a ruined mess, only two fingers remained and those were only stumps. She destroyed that hand, she used her own war hammer to mangle it when the creature had tried to stop her from leaving the central temple. It was healing though. When she had left the creature, the bulk of the hand had been removed. She had never seen anything regenerate so rapidly, it had only been a handful of weeks since she had fought it.

Her mount shifted restlessly beneath her. Unlike her fellows she sat astride a great mountain tiger, the only feline large enough and tame enough to serve as a mount in battle. She had learned of the creature from the Tu'roki several years ago, before she had been called to serve the Just. When she got her calling, she knew she had to find one of the creatures to carry her into battle. She had found Tremer as a kitten and immediately began his training. They quickly bonded and became loyal companions. Tremer was also her only real friend left in this world. She knew he could sense her apprehension and worry for her men, she also knew that he would ignore her feelings when it mattered. Sometimes she envied him.

The wind picked up as the Demons closed the last few strides between them. The tableau was impressive, the shining armor of the Just contrasting with the dark, violet skin of the Demons. Her men dismounted along the front line, horses were next to useless in holding a line. Their battle lines formed around a handful of low stone walls that used to encircle the entire hill. The walls themselves would offer little protection against the Demons, but her men had fortified them with fresh cut timbers, arrayed into a nest of spikes that would quickly dispatch any creature foolish enough to leap into them. It was a paltry defense for a long siege, but they had no hope of surviving a prolonged battle anyway. This fight was to prove that her order stood together to the end, and that they would not stand for the desecration of their most holy place.

Thunder rippled across the plains as the first lines collided. The immediate press of Demons forced her men back a step, but they quickly recovered and reformed their lines. The mounted reserve would wait for her signal before charging through the ranks to force the Demons back. It was an old tactic, but it was her only real option here. She had no superiority of the skies like the Oberon or the Harpies, no Oberon had ever served the Just and the Harpies had turned to Barrah. She would likely face both today, which kept her few archers out of the battle, staring at the sky above them.

The Demons pressed harder along the northeastern line, some even attempted to cross the trapped walls. She raised her arm to signal the horse, but waited. Something wasn't right about the Demons tactics. They clearly outnumbered the defenders but did not send their entire force against her. Were they waiting for the Coalition to engage her from the opposite side or was there something else going on?

She checked the progress of the Coalition, but their advance had halted. They waited for some shift as well. Their lines were thick, showing the superiority of their numbers as a haze of flying Oberon circled above them. As tightly packed as they were, one Wizard would level the bulk of their forces, but they knew she had no Wizard. Outside of a few former priests to Ori, she had no magic whatsoever. Her sword was enchanted, as were the majority of her officers' swords, but its power was nothing compared to the destruction one Wizard could bring to bear.

If wishes came true, you'd still be an Avatar and this whole matter would be moot, focus! Her inner self was far more realistic than she cared for. She couldn't wait for the surprise, her line was folding at the northeastern corner. She dropped her arm and the horse charged into the fray. The men on the front split their ranks to allow the horses to pass between them and quickly closed behind them. The lances of the men tore through the ranks of Demon and Og'rai, breaking their press and driving them away from the men on the hill. The foot soldiers quickly reset their defenses and prepared for the inevitable counter charge.

Her mounted men pressed until the Demon lines firmed around them, then withdrew to the north before crossing back behind the lines. The horses panted roughly as the men moved back into their formation in the center of what would be their second line of defense when the first line inevitably fell. It was depressing to know that there was no hope of victory today, no chance that any of them would leave this field alive. She was confident they could hold, and even defeat, either of the forces arrayed against them if they were alone, but combined there was just no chance. Even if the Coalition waited for the Demons to break themselves on her lines, they wouldn't allow her forces a chance to breathe before swarming in to finish the deed. If there were an Arcana left she could trust, she would have prayed for their guidance, but if even Lord Barrah could betray her as he did, what good could the others do?

Her heart dropped when she heard the first shrieks from above. The Harpies had arrived. Flames leapt from the hands of the bird women as they swooped in behind her lines to harass the men at the back. Her archers let fly, but there were just so few of them that only a handful of the Harpies were hit and only two fell from the sky. There were easily one hundred of the creatures flying over them and each of them let loose with a wave of flames that her forces could do nothing against. The dry prairie grass beneath their feet flared up, spreading the damage even further.

She signaled the first retreat and ordered her lieutenant to organize more archers to counter the bird-women, but it would account for little. Their first line of defense had crumbled moments after the Harpies joined the fray. She hadn't counted on the sheer number of Harpies arrayed against them, she knew they would be there, but not one hundred fire flinging monsters. It was a rare trait amongst the Harpies to even be able to control fire, but Barrah had rooted out a force that she just couldn't hope to counter.

She pulled her command to the top of the hill, near the mausoleum they sought to save, and issued another set of orders. Her men were to pull back to the top of the hill and implement her final defense. The stones and other debris they had gathered throughout the plain should keep the Demons at bay long enough to turn their few ballistae against the Harpies. She doubted it would turn the tide, but if she could just slow them long enough they might give up on such an unimportant target.

She checked the Coalition troops again before leaving Tremer with her squire. They hadn't moved from their original position, waiting for something that she just couldn't predict. Taking up her short bow, she joined the archers in their attempts to deter the Harpies. Her engineer set about deploying their trap as the Demons began their slow march up the hill. They had to know that the Just wouldn't let them walk up the hill unmolested, Harpies or no.

Blasts sounded high above them, well within the clouds that covered the sky. Flashes of orange and silver-blue erupted in every direction. Harpies fell from the air all around them as a new group of flyers joined the battle. At first glance, she thought they were more Harpies, but their coloring was wrong. The Harpies were typically a chestnut brown with splashes of red mixed among the feathers. These new creatures were a silver color, more like the great falcons the

Tu'roki trained in their mountain homes. Jets of silver-blue flame shot from their hands as they pursued the Harpies below the cover of the clouds. As they closed on the hill, she could see that they were all male. These were no Harpies, they were the Falcree.

She immediately ordered her archers to shift their fire to the Demons below them, the new arrivals had the Harpies well in hand. One of their new allies broke away from the rest and landed before her. His feathers were nearly metallic, blending seamlessly with the armor that fitted his lean frame tightly. His eyes were a shocking cobalt that sparkled with a deep intelligence in the dim light. His legs ended in the talons she had come to expect in the Harpy race, but his hands were free of the sharpened claws. A thin sword hung from each hip, hilts wrapped in silver.

He bowed low to her, "Milady, the Falcree are here to offer what help we can to the Just."

She returned his bow, dipping even lower than the custom, "Your help is greatly appreciated. We had feared we were alone in this."

"Your lord may have abandoned you," he started, staring deep into her eyes, "but we haven't forgot the aid your order gave us when our home was threatened. We will stand with you today to defend your most holy place. Our vile cousins have betrayed us as well as their Arcana, they sought to slay us but we have driven them from our mountains and sealed the entrances."

"I'm sorry to hear that, has Betala abandoned you?" The Arcana of Fire had suffered greatly when her Avatar was imprisoned. Her temples were some of the first to be attacked by the horde of Demons.

"No, we still have our power, but without her Avatar she is powerless here. We had heard that Barrah has taken your magic, is this true?" Concern creased the chiseled face.

"Yes, as a whole, the Just are powerless. We are truly no further threat to any in the world, yet they still seek to destroy us." An explosion drew their attention back to the battle. From the rear of the Demon army, a huge ball of fire roared to life. It spun slowly in place before flying from its location directly at their position on the hill.

The Falcree turned and raised his hands toward the flames. His own power leapt forth, but it seemed so small before that rolling ball of heat. His silver fire collided with the orange flames of the Harpies, and for a moment he slowed its advance, but he couldn't hold it alone. She longed to throw her power into the mix, but it was gone. More Falcree broke off from their fight with the other Harpies and threw their energy into the fireball, but even their combined energies couldn't stop it. With a thunderous burst, the ball erupted into flaming shrapnel that tore through the assembled troops at the top of the hill. She caught one shard across her ribs and couldn't help but cry out as it seared her flesh.

The shockwave of the explosion hit a heartbeat later sending the majority of her troops to the ground. Her tail saved her the indignity, she bounced and used its twist to keep her feet beneath her. The Demons roared in unison as her troops desperately tried to regain their feet. As one, the creatures charged madly up the hill swinging their ugly weapons before them.

The Falcree moved back to her side, his eyes trained to the back of the enemy camp. "Ezra is down there, she is the only one who would have that kind of power. We have to stop her, this may be our only chance. Can you fight with that wound?"

She gritted her teeth, "I've had worse. Can you carry me down there?"

"Yes, but only you," he replied stoically, "make yourself ready."

"Koen, you have command, don't let them take the hill," she told her captain and closest advisor. "I go to cut the head from the snake." The Falcree stepped up behind her and wrapped his arms about her chest. "I don't even know your name, friend."

"I am Gavyn, King of the Falcree," he whispered into her ear, "and you are Krelmer, the Judge. Let us go and slay Ezra so that everyone will remember our names." With a powerful downbeat of his wings, they were airborne. He soared high over the assembled forces, high enough that she could see the Coalition troops massed in their battle formations at the far side of the hill. If only she could see what it was that they were waiting for, did they seek to simply finish off the Just or were they only present to keep the Demons in check?

Gavyn flew them upwards at a steep angle before bending at his waist and shifting them into a dive. Their speed increased drastically, causing her legs to pull back and her eyes to tear up. The air felt cold at this speed, though she knew the temperature hadn't actually changed. On any other day she would have taken the time to enjoy the experience, she had never flown before, but today was not that day. If Gavyn was right, a former Avatar was down there right now, leading this force of Demons against her orders' most sacred place.

Four figures dotted the field at the rear of the army, two armored men, a stunningly dressed Harpy and a small boy. Gavyn sailed straight at them, shouting for her to prepare to land. Just before they bowled directly into the assembled strangers, he forced his wings down and halted their fall. He released her at the same time, dropping her lightly to the ground ten paces from the armored men. She drew the two curved blades from her hip as she stood from her kneeling position, her war hammer was still with Tremer at the top of the rise. Her tail whipped back and forth behind her, echoing the agitation she felt.

Gavyn dropped down next to her, drawing the swords from his hips in one fluid motion. "It ends today, traitor," he snarled at the Harpy.

She calmly replied, "Your pathetic tribe will never stand against me, *Falcree*. We nearly wiped you out before this bitch stepped in to aid you." She turned her vicious gaze on one of the two men, "Brenin, take Drech out of here, Tarian, you're with me."

The darker of the two moved to take the small boy by the hand and led him away from Ezra. The other flexed his hands and arms, then moved between the Harpy and Krelmer. He carried no weapon, but his forearms were adorned with a collection of blades. As he stepped closer, she could see that his armor was actually a series of scales that appeared to have been sharpened. If that man got his hands on her, she was done. The man smiled, then charged faster than she could react. His right arm shot out and grabbed her left by the bicep, twisting painfully as he did so. She brought her right sword around toward the man's face and broke his grip. With a hop, she dropped back into a defensive stance. She felt new cuts along her ribs on the left, he had scored straight through her armor.

Gavyn launched himself at Ezra, silver flames flying from his outstretched hands as her orange fire sprang up to meet them. They tumbled together before splitting and taking flight. She quickly lost sight of them as the armored man leapt for her again and her battle was back on. She brought both her swords in low, aiming for the softer armor about the man's knees, but he simply brushed away her blades with a flick of his steel backed fist. His other hand came in fast at her face, but she was able to drop low and avoid it. She split her attack, bringing one blade up between his legs while her second cut across his thigh. A twist of his knee stopped the first but he ignored the second as it rebounded off the scales of his armor.

He smiled viciously, "its pure iconel steel, nothing can pierce it." He stamped his foot toward her, narrowly missing hers as she hopped back again.

She knew the man was right, nothing short of magic would pierce the armor. Luckily for her, she had enchanted blades. With a thought, she activated their power, sending the stored magic out into the blades and giving them an edge that no blacksmith could replicate. The magic was finite, it would eventually give out, but she didn't think that would be today. The next time the man dove for her, she took his arm off at the elbow. The enchanted steel sliced clean through his armor and the flesh beneath, severing the bones and tendons as if they were tallow.

The man howled in pain as the bloody stump rained its fluids upon the field. He clutched at the remnant of his arm and collapsed to his knees. He fumbled until he recovered the severed hand and pulled it in close to his body. It would have been a comical sight, were it not for the screams and all that blood.

She didn't let him recover. Using her off-hand, she drove her curved blade straight through the man's chest and into his heart. The screams stopped. She sheathed her right sword and grabbed at her lacerated ribs. The wound was far worse than she had expected, her armor had only amplified the cuts with its ruined edges. She had already lost a lot of blood and soon wouldn't be able to stand. She dropped to her knees and let go her sword.

She would be no further help to Gavyn, though it looked like he desperately needed it. Ezra chased the silver Falcree through the skies above her, flinging fire indiscriminately in his direction. She watched the exchange until she couldn't hold herself upright, then dropped to her side. A shadow soon loomed over her, the dark man had returned from wherever he had taken the child.

"You slew my brother, only I may slay my brother." The man sneered, drawing the long sword from his hip. Its blade was an iridescent blue that actively swirled up and down the length. "He will rise again, our lord will see to that, but you will face his judgment and I'm sure he has a special place just for you." The blade whipped up and descended toward her neck.

Her last wish was for Gavyn to succeed.

******

Crowlmer screamed into the darkness of the tomb, suddenly back within her own body. The cold stone had sapped her body heat, so she curled into herself and drifted once more from consciousness.

Aftermath

"How could you possibly master the shield in a single night?" Charles' instructor demanded this morning. The man's first attack had met Charles' new shield and fizzled into nothingness before Charles had even shared his news.

"I opened my eyes, as you told me to." Charles had no intention of telling the man how he had actually learned, the man didn't deserve to know and he really had no desire to get Clornamti in trouble. "May we move on now? You had promised to show me the lance of power you were using if I mastered the shield, could we start there?" In truth, Clornamti had revealed that to him the night before as well, but he wasn't going to tell the man that either. Let him keep guessing.

"Very well," his instructor wound up to begin another lecture, but was interrupted by a messenger. The flustered Oberon handed his teacher a sealed letter then took to the air, his gossamer wings sparkling in the early sunlight. "The king summons you to his chamber, immediately. We will resume this lesson tomorrow, if you are still here." It was clear from the expression on the man's face what outcome he hoped for from this visit to the king. It was no secret that none of his instructors actually wanted him to learn. He had learned more in the single night with Clornamti than he had from any of the instructors, and likely more than he would ever learn while in Heimili álfa.

He took the proffered letter and made his way across the training grounds for the crown tower, the center most tower of the city and home to Driamati and his family. The guards at the gate were expecting him and quickly showed him to the reception hall inside the tower. Driamati's tower was unique in that it had a lift at its center, a great platform that rose and fell as the riders needed. It had been a work of one of Ven's avatars during the construction of the tower hundreds of years ago, and was the only one of its kind. The magic that powered the lift was a ritual that was never recorded, and though many had tried to duplicate it, there were no other lifts. Charles boarded the lift and waited for his escort to initiate their travel to the upper floors, but the guardsman just left him there.

He waited for several more moments before a familiar face entered the lift chamber from behind him. Clornamti was dressed in her plain Wizard's robes, but they had been freshly pressed. She smiled radiantly as she stepped to the front of the lift with him and commanded the magic to raise them up. "I couldn't wait for Grandfather to tell you, we've had news from the south! There was a great battle on the plains south of Krossfarin, near the Balen River."

Charles wasn't sure why she was so excited by a battle. "How does this involve me? I've been here this whole time, I promise." He smiled at his own joke, though she didn't seem to understand it.

"It doesn't, not directly, but we are pretty sure your friend was there! The one you told me about, Aaron or Adam, or whatever his name was!" Her excitement was palpable, though he hesitated to share it.

"How would you know if Aurin was there?"

She took a deep breath, "His magic!" She whispered dramatically, "I remember what it looked like from your memories, and from the description it was the same. One of our scouts saw the battle and reported in this morning, he never got the man's name, but he knows it was a young man from the Druid Guard that wielded the magic and how many could there be that can use that kind of magic?"

She was right, Aurin's magic was unique. Charles had never even heard of its like being wielded before. A broad smiled crossed his face at the thought of seeing his friend again, of telling him everything that had happened since they had been separated and of Clornamti. That last thought halted his excitement, Clornamti would be remaining in Heimili álfa. He tried to hide his disappointment, "when was this?"

"Nearly a week ago," she moved closer to him, taking his hand in hers and setting his heart pounding even harder. "Isn't it great?"

"It is," he told her, but it wasn't really. With news that Aurin lived, Charles had to go to him. Aurin was his only friend from Hudcoeden, and the only reason he was still alive today. There was also Ardelle to think of, she clearly missed his friend nearly as much as Charles and would insist that she be allowed to travel to him. Driamati would forbid it if Charles wasn't to leave as well, he wanted no one outside of Heimili álfa to know that Charles was here. It was too great a risk to his people should Barrah learn that the Chavox was here and that he was learning more secrets of magic.

"I thought you would be more excited, Aurin is alive!"

"I am excited!" He sighed, "I'm just going to miss you… I mean my time here."

She exhaled and looked up at him, her brown eyes dazzling in the false light of the lift, "So you are leaving then? I guessed as much."

"I have to go, Clora, he is my friend and I'm sure he'll need me, if not now then soon. Krossfarin will be under siege soon, if Barrah's plans hold, and Aurin will be fighting. I should be there."

She didn't get a chance to respond as the lift had reached the uppermost floor of the tower. She released his hand and stepped from the lift, all propriety and grace. "This way, Mentor Kairos," she curtsied briefly, before moving toward the two guards stationed outside of the king's chamber. He couldn't tell if the cold attitude was just a show or if he had really upset her.

One of the guards stopped Clornamti, "The king asked for you to remain here, Princess." Charles forgot that she was technically royalty, though so far removed from the succession that it didn't really matter, if he understood the line of succession correctly at least. Still, he should remember to address her properly when in public.

Clornamti fumed, "I think not, I will accompany Mentor Kairos to my grandfather as we agreed when I left this morning."

"I'm sorry Princess, his orders were clear, the Mentor is to proceed alone."

Charles stepped forward, "Did he give instructions that no one will accompany me, or just the princess?"

"No one may go with you, what he has to say is for you alone. Those were the orders. Please Princess, wait here."

Charles could think of no way to circumvent the order. He glanced at Clornamti over his shoulder and marched past the guards. The inner chamber was just as opulent as it was on his last visit, though there were more in attendance. Oberon lined the walls of the chamber, their fine garments sparkling near as much as their wings. It was odd that Driamati had insisted Clornamti remain outside when so many others were allowed in.

"Ah, finally," Driamati boomed over the din of the crowd. "Mentor Kairos, you grace us with your presence this fine day. How fares your training?"

Unsure how to answer, Charles bowed then replied, "I have mastered the shield sire, I hope to finish my combat magic soon and move on to your rituals of travel."

"Mastered the shield already? Impressive man!" Some throughout the crowd clapped, others merely frowned. "I'm afraid your training is at an end though."

Charles swallowed hard, "Sire?"

"You may have heard, there has been a battle to the south. The demons are massing again, this time they seek to destroy Krossfarin. We believe they seek to stop the city from being able to take in the refugees from Hudcoeden. There is a race across the plains going on right now and we seek to influence the outcome." More applause rang through the crowd, though it was reserved, controlled and cut off quickly. "Our generals are readying a force to send to the aid of our human brethren to the south, it will join with additional forces from the Tu'roki and Solterran regular armies at Krossfarin. We seek to stop the Demons there, and I mean for you to assist."

Charles finally understood why Clornamti had to wait outside, she had known nothing of this. "You are sending me away?"

"I can think of no greater need than that of our human allies, should another of their cities fall the Demons could run the entire southern part of the continent unchecked. This is why I am sending you, to act as a liaison between our forces and theirs. You have trained with our soldiers and mages and know the intricacies of our combat magic, you even just informed us that you have mastered the shield!" Driamati's sly smile spread wider as he continued, "Once the Demons are destroyed, we will have the freedom to once again begin your training, even teach you some of the travel rituals you desire."

Charles couldn't argue against the point, he already decided to leave, but he couldn't help but wonder what Driamati's true goals were. The man was too clever by half and no simple mission to aid Krossfarin would be enough for him to break his deal with Charles. There was something else going on here, something he would likely only know when it was too late to stop it. "When do we leave?"

"Two days, please say your good byes and prepare yourself. You may outfit yourself from my personal armory, please take anything you need." He waved a hand, clearly finished with Charles.

"Sire," Charles piped in, not wanting to let it go so easily. "Who will be leading this force? How will I be travelling as I lack the wings your people share?"

Driamati stared levelly at Charles, his face losing all semblance of joy, "General Kalemet will lead the force and will arrange for a carrier for you, now please excuse us Mentor Kairos, I have important matters of state I must see to." He waved his hand once more.

Charles moved to speak again, but a familiar Oberon broke from the crowd and took his arm. "This way my good sir," Trianamati led him from the center of the chamber toward the rear. "You walk a fine line, *Mentor*." The Oberon whispered, "My brother doesn't care for those that don't know their place."

"What do you mean?"

"He dismissed you, yet you continued to speak." Trianamati turned Charles so that they were eye to eye, "He also learned of your training and does not approve. He dotes on Clora though she is not the heir. He knows that it was her that trained you and he knows the only way to train is the link. Why do you think he is dispatching you after making such a show of bringing you here in the first place?"

"How could he know about that? We were alone," Charles insisted.

"There are eyes everyone, young one. Even when you think yourselves alone, some can still see you." Trianamati's eyes narrowed, "He is also furious at the Tu'roki for bringing their Avatar here without warning, and for their use of Ori as influence over his decision to send troops. That is why he is sending troops at all, but the coalition is going to be saddened when they realize just how few he has committed."

"You mean he isn't sending the army?" Political intrigue was not something Charles had any feel for, nor did he ever want to. "How many is he actually sending?"

"Less than one hundred," Trianamati replied. "Ninety-three to be exact, the number of Oberon lost when Hudcoeden fell." They exited the chamber and were greeted by a very flustered looking Clornamti.

"What happened?" she demanded.

"I will leave you in my niece's capable hands, Mentor Kairos. Come see me before you leave, I am quartered in the same tower as you, I may have something you could use in your travels." Trianamati bowed slightly, then retreated back into the throne room.

Clornamti tapped her foot, "Well?"

Charles told her of the brief encounter and the command to travel with the troops when they left in two days. He explained that he tried to get more information but Driamati had been dismissive. "I had to go anyway, I just wanted to know why he was forcing me. Trianamati told me it was because of us."

Clornamti forcefully led him to the lift. She sent them descending through the tower before replying, "He knows?"

"According to your uncle, he has eyes everywhere and knows it was you that trained me in the shield." Charles took a deep breath and took her hand, "I'm sorry Clora, I didn't mean for you to get in trouble. Perhaps it is best that I go so that I don't make it worse."

Before he could continue she raised herself up onto the tips of her toes and kissed him soundly on the mouth. She lingered for a moment allowing him to relish in the feeling of her soft lips before she broke away. "It was worth it," she told him breathlessly.

Too stunned to speak, he tripped over his tongue until the lift came to a stop on the ground floor. He had longed for another kiss, but for her to do so in such a public setting had left him speechless.

As the lift stopped on the ground floor, she deliberately took his hand in hers and sauntered out into the open. One of the Oberon guards nearest the door split from the group and dropped in behind them, a single eyebrow raised as he passed. Others were murmuring behind their hands as they passed through the crowd. It wouldn't be long before this got back to Driamati, he was sure he caught a glimpse of a courtier smiling as he entered the lift just before they rounded a corner and lost sight of the door.

"If he already knows about it, no reason to keep it a secret any more then!" Clornamti shouted to no one in particular, laughing gaily as their guard snorted behind them. "Something to say Dimitri?"

"It's not my place, Princess." The man smiled from ear to ear. "But the curfew still stands, we should get you back to the tower. Last night's…excursion… has earned your guards the ire of your grandfather."

"Is the ball still on for tonight?" Clornamti asked, not releasing Charles' hand.

"The dignitaries insisted, the Avatar of Ori is supposed to make an appearance." Dimitri's face fell as some realization dawned on him, though Charles couldn't say what that was. "Your highness, the king will be most upset if you were to attend this prestigious function on the arm of a human."

"He'll go apoplectic!" She cheered, "serves him right too."

Charles was lost, "What ball? Are you talking about me?"

"I believe she is, son," Dimitri told him. "Now, Princess, your dastardly plan will have to wait until later, we have to return you to your chambers."

"I'll send for you in a couple hours," she reassured Charles, though he still had no idea what was happening. "You should go see your friend, I bet she'll want to know about the battle."

He had nearly forgotten about Ardelle and it shamed him to think that he hadn't immediately run off to tell her that Aurin was alive. "You're right, I should have gone there first." He moved to leave her, but Clornamti didn't release his hand.

"Watch for me in a couple hours," she told him again. "I'll have it figured out by then." She kissed him lightly on the cheek and finally let go his hand.

He sighed as he watched her disappear into the distance before breaking into a trot towards Ardelle's tower. He thought they were within the same tower, but one of their few visits he learned she was being housed with the delegates from the various churches. It was a close tower, but one would have to cross three of the "sky bridges" to reach it from his apartment. Those bridges spanned the open air between the towers and gave the land bound a way to traverse between them without having to go all the way to the ground floor, but they made him ill. The thought of being that high up with only a few planks between him and the open air terrified him.

The climb to Ardelle's apartment took him longer than he had hoped, when he eventually reached her floor, he was rebuffed by a guard. "The lady got in late last night and asked that no one bother her until after midday."

"It's very important that I speak to her, is there no way you can let me through?" The guard shook his head and stood his ground. His guilt was assuaged slightly by his blocked entry, even if he had come straight here, the guard would have sent him away. It was close to midday, but he would need to find something to occupy himself until then. If he didn't find some way to apply his restless energy, he was likely to hastily dart for Clornamti's chambers. He knew she was in this tower, near the top, though he couldn't say on which side of the tower or the exact floor. He had several spells that could locate her, but he let it drop. She was busy and from the sounds of it, in some kind of trouble that kept her on a curfew.

He mulled the last few hours through his mind carefully. Just this morning he had been ecstatic about his progress in learning the shield, but that had been overshadowed by the news that his friend still lived and was moving with a large force from fallen Hudcoeden. The city hadn't been completely lost after all. Aurin would make sure they reached Krossfarin, Charles was certain of that. His friend was the strongest person he knew. What would it be like to be reunited with Aurin? Would they pick up where they left off or had too much happened for their childhood friendship to endure? He liked to think that they were lifelong friends, but could such a bond survive the ordeals that they were going to face?

What of the other consequence of this morning? He had to leave Heimili álfa, which in and of itself wasn't bad, but he had to leave Clornamti. If the battle for Krossfarin went well, he could always return. Assuming, of course, that Driamati didn't banish him forever after Clornamti's plans for tonight were carried out. Could he handle the loss of Clornamti so soon after discovering her feelings for him? Did he have to leave her behind?

He let that thought lie. It would do no good to dwell on any of the information from this morning until everything was at hand. He had two days left within the city and he should make the best use of them. Tonight, there was a ball, tomorrow, who knows? Perhaps the sky would fall and he would have nothing further to worry about.

If perhaps, the sky didn't fall…His thoughts drifted to a vague memory of a battlefield and the body of an Oberon staring blankly at the blood red sky. He couldn't take her with him, not if it meant that vision would come to pass, but if he had a way to keep her safe…

He smiled to himself as he paced back toward the guard and received an approving nod to approach Ardelle's door.

Preparations

Ardelle stirred sometime after the sun crested the trees in the east, she had been sleeping so soundly that she hadn't even realized the day was leaving her behind. Her night in the smithy had been therapeutic, exactly what she had needed to brace herself for another day of intrigue and posturing. Ceh'ruk had summoned her to a grand ball this evening and that worm, Basir was insisting on an audience. She showered and began preparing herself for the day but was interrupted by a loud knocking. After her late night in the forge, she had no desire to greet anyone, but the knocking didn't cease.

A shout rang through the door, "Ardelle! Please open the door, its Charles, I must speak with you!"

She paused briefly. She hadn't seen much of her companion since they arrived in the city, and she was fairly certain he had never visited her rooms. Had he only sought her out because he needed something? Where was he when the coalition demanded her attendance? She nearly turned away from the door, but a begged "Please!" tugged at her heart. He was clearly upset and needed her, who was she to say no? Hadn't she come here specifically to see that he was cared for? She turned back to the door and opened it a crack, concealing her half-clothed body behind it. "Oh, thank goodness!" he shouted and attempted to push open the door.

"Charles, I'm indisposed, what is it?"

His head jerked up, "Its Aurin! He's alive!"

She let go the door and pulled the boy into a hug, propriety be damned, "Where, how?"

"He's with the refugees from Hudcoeden, I'm not sure how. There was a big battle on the Balen, south of Krossfarin, a man matching his description used the same magic he used that day on the bridge. He is the only person I've ever heard of with that kind of magic." His face grew more crimson as he realized that she was naked from the waist up.

She stifled her own blush and turned to her sitting room. She pulled a loose tunic over her head and spun back to Charles to see that he wasn't alone. A young Oberon girl stood behind him, furiously stifling her own blush. This was the same girl she had seen Charles returning with yesterday morning. Her brown eyes were boring into the back of Charles' skull, but he hadn't noticed. Had he really found a girl? "I'm sorry, my name is Ardelle, and you are?"

Charles looked nearly as startled as she did at the presence of the girl, "Umm... ah..." he stammered.

The girl shook her head to clear the look of jealousy before speaking over the stunned boy, "Clornamti. Charles and I trained under Master Darl together."

The 'amti' moniker didn't slip past Ardelle, this girl was a member of the ruling family. What had Charles got himself into? "When do we leave?"

"I, uh," Charles looked between the women, a deer caught staring down two great cats. "I've been ordered south with a contingent of Oberon in two days."

"Just you?" Ardelle couldn't keep the anger from her voice, how could he think to leave her here.

"Driamati insisted that I act as his liaison to the coalition force. I think he is just trying to get rid of me." Color flooded into both of their faces as they shared a knowing look.

"I see," she turned back to the window. Aurin was alive, did it matter that she would have to ride south to see him again? "I will follow on horseback then, it will take me weeks to catch up, but I will survive."

"Across the countryside?" Clornamti blurted. "Alone?"

"Yes, Princess, I am quite capable of handling myself." She hadn't intended to sound so harsh, but she was on edge. These two were planning something, what, she couldn't say but they were up to something. Her gift had always allowed her to see into others when their emotions ran high, the heat of their bodies revealed when they were lying. She could pry but it really wasn't her place to do so, if they wanted to involve her in their scheme they would, but for now she let it drop. She had other things to worry about and plenty to do.

"Do you need anything?" Charles asked, pulling her back into the present. "I have some gold they gave me for my stay, I haven't used any."

She had a stipend that was allotted to her as well, though she had spent some. Clothing hadn't been something she had managed to save after their flight from the forest. Her pack was still on that cliff. "No, I've got enough gold for this. Did you two need anything else from me? I've a lot to do and I'd best get to it."

"Well there is one thing I could use help with," Clornamti started, with a suspicious look in her eyes. "Maeryn and I will be attending the ball tonight and I fear he has no formal attire."

"The ball," she puzzled, "together?"

Charles looked panicked, "Together?"

Clornamti smiled a devilish, toothy grin that left no doubt of her intentions. "The secrets already out, why try to hide it further?"

"I don't think this is a good idea," Ardelle argued, though she knew she would regret it. "Driamati isn't exactly progressive in his attitudes toward the other races and his granddaughter prancing about on the arm of a human is going to set his teeth grinding."

"Let him squirm!" Clornamti blurted but quickly covered her mouth. "I'm tired of having my life dictated and I'd like for Ch… er…Maeryn, to have a nice time."

Ardelle sighed, "I understand wanting to act out, Arcana know I did my fair share of it, but don't push things too hard. Show up to this ball separate, spend the night together if you must, but arrive separately. Driamati wouldn't risk a scene during the ball so you'll be free to dance and laugh at his face as he watches you together, but if you try to enter the ball together, the guards will stop you. The king may be old, but he is still crafty and he will expect something. Especially if, as you say, he already knows about the two of you."

The two of them turned to each other silently for a moment, then turned back to her. "You're right, but Maeryn will still need formal attire." Clornamti repeated.

Her role as coconspirator set, Ardelle nodded her agreement and plopped into one of her sitting room chairs. She pretended not to notice as the two embraced and shared a brief kiss. Once they were confident she hadn't been watching, Clornamti excused herself and left to prepare for the ball. Charles remained, fidgeting near the door.

"Have a seat," Ardelle finally invited. "Are you sure you know what you are getting into? She is a princess here and to the Oberon that means something, even if the succession isn't by blood."

"I guess," he muttered without looking her in the eye.

She sighed and stared up at the ceiling, "Charles, you need to take a stand for yourself. You've been letting the world push you around for too long, your entire life if I had to guess. Always doing what you are told or what is expected of you." She wasn't sure why she felt the need to give the advice, but she felt better having said it. "I know I haven't known you for long, but I've seen the way you act around those you think have authority over you. It needs to stop. If you really are this destined hero, you need to step up and make everyone see it." She turned her gaze on him and forced down her laughter. His face looked as though she had just snuck a lemon into his mouth.

"I… uh… I..," he stammered.

She let out a small chuckle so she didn't burst, "It will take time for you to build up the confidence to step out of the shadows, but you need to start thinking about it. Use Aurin as your role model if need be, Arcana know he's got more confidence than any two men should." The memory of her hero with the easy smile and strength he displayed in the forest came rushing back. She missed him even more now that she knew he had survived the fall.

"I miss him too," Charles admitted, correctly reading her face.

She smiled, "Now about tonight..."

Charles left more than an hour later, still bearing his lost puppy look, but she had given him a written list to follow for his preparations so he could figure things out from there. She had carefully steered the conversation away from the obvious joy of hearing that Aurin lived, and kept it focused on the current problem. It had been difficult to do so, but she couldn't juggle that many things at once and she had her own problems concerning the ball.

She left the apartments and sought out those of Driamati's bastard born daughter. She would need another gown for tonight, and she didn't feel up to shopping for herself. Anamti wasn't in, but her maid was more than happy to help find her a dress that wouldn't be missed, a beautiful, emerald green, sleeveless number with tasteful white embroidery that framed her breasts and hips, but bared little to no cleavage. It was something she was sure the owner would never wear. Anamti was one for show, she liked to flaunt the curves her human heritage gave her. Anything to make her father, the prudish dictator that lorded over his family about their interracial relationships, see her. Driamati was the epitome of hypocrisy when it came to race relations. He had two bastard born children with two different human women, a boy who had left to live in Krossfarin a number of years ago, and Anamti who was kept close, but still at arm's length. Even with these bastards in his own house, he still felt the need to bid his family to steer clear of the "lesser" races. Anamti was constantly shamed in his presence, a pastime that Ardelle had come to think the woman desired. She would dress provocatively just to get a rise out of the old man. The dress she was borrowing was likely a gift from her father, or some other relative, given as a not so subtle hint to cover up.

Having secured her evening wear, she slipped back to her apartments to drop off the dress, nearly trampling Basir as he came running from a side corridor. The ugly little man scowled at her before smoothing his robes, "I must speak with you, my lady. It concerns this coalition army that Ceh'ruk means to assemble."

"I will not be a part of the coalition, I have responsibilities elsewhere. Perhaps you should take your query to Ceh'ruk himself." She attempted to side step him, but he placed himself in her way.

"You have no responsibilities greater than the church, none of us do. It is time that you return to us, past time." His eyes burned with desire as he stared at her, something lurked within this man that she wanted no part of.

"As I told you at the gathering and in the letters I have sent since then, I have no desire to return to the church and you have no say in what I do with my life. Especially not after I spent one hundred and fifty years in exile, alone." She had been fending this man off since the Coalition was first established, but it just didn't sink in that she was not as fanatical as they hoped.

He clasped his hands in front of him, "We will not be sending a delegation to this coalition army, and we refuse to allow you to join with any army that they support. Our church will remain neutral in this war, we won't allow you to drag us into things like you did so long ago." He reached within his right sleeve and produced a rolled parchment that she assumed carried the edict directly from the Inferno. "By this writ, I do thee command, Ardelle Atretis to return to the church at once where she will face tribunal for her crimes against the Flaming Mistress."

"My crimes?" Ardelle shouted into the man's face. "Get out of my way Pyre, or I swear to Betala that I will finish what the flames have already started with your face." She summoned her magic to the palm of her hand, creating a ball of fire that pulsed with heat.

The man drew heavily from his pool of magic as he backed a step. "I will not stand for threats or blasphemy! You will report as ordered or you will be branded a heretic and forever denied succor from the Flaming Mistress." There was something about the man's magic, a taint that swirled within the flames and gave them an almost obsidian hue. It wasn't the pure fire that she would have expected from a Pyre within the church, theirs were typically the purest of magics.

"Brand me as you see fit, I will not submit to the church again!" She didn't dare attack the man directly, not within Heimili álfa. "Be gone, or I will see to it that Betala strips her gift from you personally." It was an empty threat, but it had the desired result.

"We do not mention that name!" The man was incensed. "Shut your filthy mouth you gutter whore!" He hurled his magic at her, a blast of fire and heat that she essentially ignored as her own power snuffed it from existence. His eyes widened with shock as his magic fizzled, "I will report this to the church! Your days of living like a queen are over, false Avatar. Not even a traitor like Driamati will shelter you!" She lifted her hand threateningly and the man nearly fell over himself in his attempt to flee.

What had he meant, 'they do not mention that name'? Was he referring to Betala? The entire experience was unnerving. She had never been attacked by a member of the church like that, not even when she had ordered them to go to war against Barrah. What had driven him to do so today? And what of the taint on his magic, surely others within the church had noticed?

She bent to pick up the parchment the man had discarded. It was singed from his attack, but the text was still legible:

> *Ardelle Atretis, you are hereby stripped of your rank within the eyes of the Flaming Mistress and ordered to present yourself for tribunal to face crimes against the church.*
>
> *Your crimes are too numerous to list but first and foremost you will face judgment for your false claims as Avatar. There is only one Avatar of the flames, the queen of all and consort of him who shall rule.*

The scroll dropped from her fingers. The taint on the man's magic had been Barrah's. It was clear now that the church had fallen. A pressure exerted itself on her mind once again, forcing her on her knees. Betala was seeking her out, but she denied the Arcana. She wouldn't allow guilt to drag her back to the mistress she had known. She forced the presence from her mind, though it took every fiber of her control to do so. Not again, not like this and not when her life was finally her own. She wouldn't allow it to pull her in.

At least she understood the man's reactions and his zealotry. There had been dissenters in her time, followers of Ezra and her corrupted Harpies, but they had been few in number. Clearly, their support had grown since then.

The Harpies had been Betala's creatures once, serving as her messengers during the founding of the great kingdoms and carrying the gift of fire with them. Harpies were one of the original races, brought here shortly after the Oberon when Betala first gave her gift to the world. Originally, there were dozens of tribes, but through intermarriage and joint rule, they combined to four greater tribes; the Sparha, the Ospa, the Egla, and the Falcree. Each tribe had their own rulers, but it wasn't uncommon for them to wed one another to ensure their alliance. They lived apart from the other races, though not to the extent of the Oberon. Theirs was a simple life spent in worship and love.

During that time, Barrah and Betala were consorts, but it didn't last. As the demon started his descent to madness, he took the matron of the Sparha, Ezra, as his new consort and drew the bulk of the tribe away from Betala. Their union produced a single child, Drech, who quickly grew to share in his father's view of the mortal world. His first act as he came into his majority was to lead the Sparha against the rogue members of their tribe, killing any that did not join them.

Others followed quickly, through conquest or capitulation. The Ospa were the first to fall, and the Egla fared no better. Only the Falcree survived the onslaught, due in large part to the intervention of Barrah's former church and their knights, the Just. Theirs was a life under siege and by the time of Ardelle's banishment, the Falcree were nearly extinct.

Ezra's power had grown under Barrah, until Betala stripped her gift from the Harpy queen. Ezra was one of the few Avatar's in history to have her powers taken from her while she lived. Barrah had been quick to replace it with a boon of his own, but the vile magic of the demon came at a price.

The race of Harpies became cursed, driven by an insatiable blood thirst. The cursed creatures must kill, or face madness and a loss of control. Most thought the curse had been placed on them by a vengeful Betala, but Ardelle knew the truth. Their thirst for death and destruction grew from Barrah's hatred of the mortal plane, and only grew stronger the more it was satiated. The rumor that it sprang from Betala had been perpetuated by Barrah and his followers to further sway the Harpies to their cause, and it worked. The Harpies believed that their demon lord could save them, spare them the madness of those they saw around them, but it was all lies.

A few among Ezra's followers did turn away from her eventually. They lost their wings but Betala freed them from their madness. A few had even lived long enough to see Ardelle rise to Avatar, the Inferno of her time had been one of them.

With the loss of the Harpies, Betala's church suffered greatly. The masses blamed them for the Harpies new war, and for the death they rained down from above. Most worshipped in secret, or they had in her time. Only two of their churches had survived the fallout, the cathedral in Krossfarin, and the grand temple in Marimensk. If the church had succumbed fully to Barrah, she doubted the ruling faction in Krossfarin would have suffered them. It was likely that Marimensk was the last temple of the church, though she couldn't imagine worship of the true Arcana of fire had simply vanished. Surely there were others out there that still shared their love with Betala. Or were there?

    She longed to know, but her only source of knowledge would be the Arcana herself, and Ardelle just wasn't ready for that. Her hero lived, somewhere far to the south, travelling with the remnants of Hudcoeden. She had to see him at least one more time before she let her old life back in. Those problems could be dealt with later. For now, she had to focus on tonight. Ceh'ruk was going to need an ally and there appeared to be no one else.

Darkness

The scent was so familiar it couldn't be anything else. The cat was in these caves, or at least she had been recently. He growled to his pack mates before he moved into the dark caves. When he had left the forest he had been alone, but his new power gave him more than just the ability to become a man at will, it also gave him the power to create others like himself. It took a great deal of his power to create another like him, but he found the additional companionship to be useful. He needn't risk himself first, his pack were completely obedient, they would do anything he asked, and now there were twenty just like him.

The catacombs stretched forever beneath this rise, they served as a burial complex for some group of humans or another. He was sure there was a connection between all of these corpses, but he really didn't care what it was. Somewhere down here was a creature that he owed a death. Twice the cat had stopped him from killing those fools and their woman, if he could kill her twice, he would.

Three of his pack followed him into the cave, each turning down a separate hall on the first floor but eventually meeting as the halls converged. The others all remained outside the mausoleum per his direction, he didn't want any of them to steal his kill. He wasn't particularly attached to any of his pack, but they were difficult to make so he would regret having to kill one of them.

They descended rapidly into the cave, each floor was larger than the last, but it became clear that the cat hadn't stopped on any of them. She must have been searching for something on the lower floors, or she knew that was where the treasure was. The halls on these lower levels would fund an army or feed a small nation. Precious stones bedecked every open space and every casket was trimmed in gold. His pack mates drooled at the thought of looting the place and living off the wealth. They had no ambition, not like him.

The scent grew stronger as they reached the last floor, as he thought it might. She was still here. The pack split among the corridors while he moved directly down the main hall. His instincts told him that he would find her at the last casket, the last soul to be put to rest here.

The casket was on a dais, raised above the floor, unlike the others he had passed. It was also constructed of obsidian, rather than the plain granite that adorned the others. Its lid had been removed, but the woman interred there appeared undisturbed. She was odd in appearance, somewhere between a Gremen and the cats they revered, but perfectly preserved. If he had to guess, he would say she had been dead less than a week, but his other senses told him otherwise. This body had been here for a very long time, almost as long as he had walked the earth as a wolf.

The nude body was covered with a fine fur, not unlike a cat's. The fur ringed her stomach and left a small patch of dark skin naked around her navel. She would have been attractive, in a feral way.

A howl tore him away from the corpse. He rushed around the nearest corner and witnessed one of his pack mates being cleaved in twain by an armor clad woman with a long black tail. The second wolf lunged for her back, but was brought up short by a backward stab of her second sword. She casually dropped the corpse behind her without ever turning to look at it.

He growled deeply, but backed away from the warrior. The smell confirmed that this had once been the cat he fought in the forest, but in her present state he was far outmatched. As sharp as his fangs were, they wouldn't pierce that steel. He howled for his third pack mate, but did not hear a response.

"If you are calling for more help, don't bother." The woman told him through clenched teeth. "I killed the other first. He didn't make a sound." She stood straight as she turned toward him, blood dripping from both of her curved blades.

He knew the woman wasn't bluffing, even the dimmest member of his pack would have responded by now. He darted back toward the obsidian casket before she could close with him and barreled toward the stairs. It was an obvious play, one that she anticipated as she appeared from the other end of the tunnel, but what she didn't expect was a naked man rushing toward her.

Capitalizing on her shock, he bowled into her, carrying them both to the floor in a tangle of limbs. Her swords were pinned between them, too close for her to swing, but deadly just the same. He rolled with the impact and leapt clear of her, drawing on his power to revert back to a wolf. She screamed in rage as he bolted up the stairs, her upright body wouldn't be able to catch him now.

He sent part of the pack back into the tomb once he reached the top, but he knew they had no more chance than the others did of stopping her. Revenge on the cat would have to wait. It had been a nice distraction while he waited for the refugees to move, but she was more than his wolves could take at present. His new ally had set a trap for the pitiful masses and it was up to his wolves to spring it.

Return

She killed more of the creatures than she cared to remember, but none were the one she knew from the forest. These were all weak copies of the original. The creatures taint was spreading now that it had been freed from the prison of Wylltraethel. There could be any number of these freaks out there, and each of them could be as deadly as the original.

Krelmer's armor fit her perfectly, better than any armor she had ever worn. Most armors were not made for a woman's build, and thus tended to pinch and bind. Despite hundreds of years of women fighting alongside the men in the Gremen nation, armorers still just made one type of armor. Even the more supple leather armors left much to be desired for a woman's physique, but Krelmer's plate was cut and fitted her body, moving with her like a second set of skin.

The twin curved blades were perfectly balanced and from what she could tell they were the same that Krelmer used over a hundred years go. She had even activated their enchantments using the method she had gleaned from Krelmer's memory. The beast she cut in two had seen their wicked edge first hand. She knew they had a finite amount of power, and disabled the enchantment since then, but she had to know if what she saw was real. The magic proved it.

The bodies of wolves were piled before her, the result of their last attempt to bring her down, but even with six of them, they had failed. Krelmer's armor kept their claws at bay and her ever sharp swords cut through their flesh like a scythe through wheat. She hadn't heard any other signs of life within the tomb, but there could still be more of the abominations.

Her arms ached from her grim work, but the creatures still couldn't stop her.

The original wolf, the one she had fought in the forest, had escaped the tomb. It never would have fallen so easily, even with her enchanted swords. Was that wolf the reason these others existed?

She hadn't eaten for more than a day and the little water she had consumed before coming here wasn't enough to stave off the parched feeling of her lips. The desire to find meat and water to sustain her body was strong. Her basest instincts almost drove her to consume the multitudes of meat before her, but she knew what these wolves really were. The thought of consuming their meat was worse than the idea of starving. If she could get clear of the tomb, she might get lucky and find game on the plain. It was a slim hope given the vast empty fields about her, but even a rabbit would hold her for at least a few days. She slowed her breathing and listened to the silence of the tomb for any hint of more creatures, but nothing stirred.

She crossed the threshold into the uppermost layer of the dungeon and marched for the entrance. This layer was the smallest of all of them and held only a single casket of plain stone. Runes covered every wall, glowing faintly, giving the room an odd light. She hadn't realized the rest of the tomb had been dark until her eyes started to adjust to the light. Her new form gave her many gifts, though it had cost her much more. Even now she longed to be among the Gremen again, though she knew they wouldn't accept her. Even Howlter had turned her away when she had tried to return. Why did everything come back to her appearance? Was she truly that hideous?

The dust on the floor had almost been completely swept away in the passing of the creatures, giving credibility to her estimate of well over twenty of them and more still loose in the world.   How many of the creatures were there? Why had they come into the tomb? She couldn't help but think they had come for her, there was really nothing else here for a pack of shapeshifting wolves. They may have come for Krelmer's magic, but she doubted anyone still lived that knew the last leader of the Just had been buried here with her enchanted swords.

A sense of dread crept over her as she approached the yawning door that had first brought her within the tomb. How many wolves were just waiting for her to leave? An ambush as she exited the tomb would give them a definite edge, they would be able to come at her from every side. Inside, she could use the features of the tomb to shield her from attacks, but out on the top of that hill there was nothing to hide behind. She couldn't stay here, there was no fresh water within the tomb and the only food was the flesh of the wolves she had killed. Having no other choice, she ducked through the arch and prepared herself for the attack.

But no wolves leapt at her from the shadows, no growls filled the air. The hilltop was empty.

She scanned the earth and found the tracks of many wolves. Some had entered the cave and never returned, but six sets of tracks led back down the hill and out onto the plain. From the direction of the tracks she guessed that the wolves' lair was somewhere northeast of her, not far from where the refugee camp would be by now. How many more wolves would be in the lair? She couldn't just let them roam free. She had seen what the creatures could do and the thought of a pack of them that close to the relatively defenseless refugees was frightening. Even if they had ostracized her, they were still innocents. At least she could warn them of the danger.

She set off quickly, covering the length of the hill in moments and stretching out into the plains so that she was nearly sprinting. Her new form kept the stride easily, even in the Krelmer's armor. It felt as though she could keep the pace all day, however without food, it wouldn't last long. Nothing stirred in her immediate vicinity, but she knew there were some small animals near her. Their smell was in the air and their comings and goings had left signs in the grass. She could stop and feed on one of the creatures, but it would probably take her hours to coax one from its hole and she just didn't have the time. The wolves that had fled the tomb had a significant lead on her and she wasn't likely to close it. If they had reached the camp... she let the thought drop. She didn't know how long the creatures had been hunting in this area. They probably found the camp and had only sought her out because she had gone off by herself. The true predators always sought out the prey that was separate from the packs. She was counted in that list now.

As the sun set, she left the relative flat land around the hill and descended into the valley of the Kross River. It was a deep ravine, the river wasn't very wide at this point, only ten strides or so. As it wound its way to Krossfarin, the river widened greatly. Nearest the walls of the city, it was close to half a league across. She had seen it once, it seemed like a lifetime ago but was actually less than a year. Howlter had marched them through Krossfarin during their search for Barrah's hunters, the men he had sent to root out where the boy Chavox was. They didn't know at the time that the hunters were looking for a boy, they only knew they had been dispatched and where they were sent usually meant something important was near.

    A herd of the small plains deer were grazing on the hill across the river from her, still unaware that she had entered the valley. If she was lucky, she could get close before they spooked and take one to satisfy the near constant grumbling from her stomach. She rushed down the hill, her legs pumping wildly as she reached the banks of the Kross. With a perfect leap, she cleared the river and rushed up the hill on the far side. When she got to within twenty strides of the deer they spooked, scattering in every direction as their spring-like legs sent them bounding. One unlucky yearling bounded toward her instead of away in its haste to flee the predator they smelled. Her instincts told her to use her teeth to take the beast, but her higher mind knew that she couldn't afford to wait for the creature to slowly die from its wounds. Without missing a stride, she drew one curved blade from her hip and struck the head from the deer. With her trailing hand she caught the carcass and pulled it to her. Blood soaked into the armor but the smell was intoxicating to her predator's senses. She ripped into the deer with her teeth and claws, finally allowing her legs to stop moving long enough to revel in her catch.

    The meat was hot, steaming in the cooling night air around her. The flesh was exquisite, nothing could top the taste of a kill you made yourself. She savored the meat as she ripped it from the bone, swallowing most of it without chewing. The blood and viscera of the deer splattered her new armor and her skin as her instincts drove all rational thought from her head. She could only think of the meat in front of her, the fresh blood leaking from the animal and the feel of the nourishing flesh sliding down her throat. Her heart hammered in her chest and she longed to chase the other deer before they had a chance to leave the valley.

A cold voice echoed within her mind *Stop, daughter of the crow. You are not a beast.*

Reality struck her like a hammer. She dropped what was left of the carcass and looked for the source of the voice, but there was no one on the hill with her. The deer had long ago fled from the carnage she had wrought and any other creature with any sense of smell could likely pick up on the death from leagues away. She hadn't been gentle in her feasting, bits of gore clung to every conceivable piece of her.

We need you, daughter of the crow. The Silvermane has been seeking you for days, the wolves have come. The voice sounded old, even within her mind. The words weren't just words either, images appeared in her mind with certain key phrases. She knew that "The Silvermane" was Howlter, even though she had never heard him referred to as such. She knew his clan was Silvermane, but he had never used the honorific. She also knew that the wolves were the shapeshifters she chased.

A sane person may have run from the implication of a creature with magic that allowed it to speak directly to the mind, but Crowlmer had left her sanity behind when she had first stepped into Wylltraethel. *Why would I care what the*

Silvermane wants? He and his as much as banished me for my appearance and this new power. She wasn't sure how she knew to respond, but it felt right.

Fools will do as fools will, but your people need you. Images of children rolled through her mind, both Human and Gremen, the weak and infirm. *Others try to stop the wolves, even as we speak, but their gifts are nothing compared to yours. Please, daughter of the crow, return to us and end this blight, before the Lord of Demons catches us.*

A pressure lifted from Crowlmer's mind, one that she hadn't realized was there. The voice was gone.

The smell of the gore and viscera covering her was suddenly too much. She ran for the river and plunged into the icy waters head first. The blood began to dissipate immediately, but the other pieces of the creature clung to her and forced her to scrub herself to shake them loose. The river ran red around her, the lifeblood of the creature she had consumed overwhelming the slight coloration of the silt. She burst from beneath the babbling water to suck in a breath of chill air, her lungs burning. Most of the gore was gone but she could still feel it clinging to her skin as she scrubbed her arms and legs. She scoured the skin of her hands until her own blood joined the creatures in washing down the river. Ducking beneath the water once more, she vigorously cleansed the blood from her mane and face, though she could never be certain she had gotten it all. Crawling from the river, she collapsed onto the banks, shivering in the night and wiping at her face in an attempt to dry the never ending wetness there.

Tears that she had kept bound up for years beyond reason were finally released. Her body ached in the cold and she knew that she had to get up, but the weight of her life kept her pinned to the grass. Her old life was completely over, there would be no going back to the carefree life of a mercenary sergeant. Was that what she wanted? She could hear Krelmer's voice in her head, the defiant cry at the injustice being wrought against her men and her powerlessness to stop it. Crowlmer had power though, she could feel it even now as she shivered.

Before the voice, before her kill, she had resigned herself to returning to the camp. Why was it harder now to do so? Knowing that she would be welcomed, at least by Howlter, was actually more difficult than if she was still being shunned. Who was behind the voice? It wasn't Howlter, he was confident but not vain enough to refer to himself in the third person. Who else would refer to him as "the Silvermane?" Formal clan names weren't bandied about typically, especially not in Howlter's mercenaries. Gremen didn't want to risk any bad blood their clans may have once held. The honorific meant that whoever was using it knew that he was the head of his clan, something else that wasn't common knowledge. The possibilities narrowed with every clue, but there were still too many to account for and she hadn't the time to dwell anyway. She needed to return, people like her new friend, Adla, had no one else to protect them. Knowing that still didn't make it easier to lift her face from the damp grass.

Willing herself to stop the flow of tears, she lurched from the bank of the river. She took stock of her surroundings, she needed to move to get the blood flowing again, and there was still had a lot of ground to cover to reach the camp. Her body wasn't injured, but she hadn't bothered to return the sword she had used to kill the deer to its sheath. Scanning the dark hillside with her new eyes, she saw the silhouette of the blade standing erect from the earth near the remains of her meal. She didn't remember driving it into the dirt, but there it stood.

    She loped up the hill and retrieved the blade, not sparing a look at the kill she had left there. Her other senses weren't fooled by the simple turn of the head. Her mouth watered involuntarily as she smelled the still cooling blood, her ears perked up at the sound of the fallen animals herd, calling from the distance. Part of her longed to return to her feast, to lose herself in the indulgence and to forget everything else. When she surrendered to her instincts, nothing else seemed to matter. When you lived to eat and just survive, the cares of others didn't matter. To her feral mind, banishment was nothing to worry about. She didn't need those that couldn't survive on their own, but a cool rationality overlaid that instinctual part of her now. It was, in and of itself, another distraction, a way to see the world so that others couldn't interfere with her but she could maintain control. The feeling was similar to the detachment Krelmer had allowed herself when she looked down that hill, on not one, but two, enemy armies surrounding her. Kelmer knew her fate was sealed and that all of her order would perish, but none of it mattered. She would bloody anyone that came up that hill, they would fight to protect their last vestige to the final man.

Crowlmer allowed the sensation of Krelmer wash over her. The woman had been a giant among her people, all people really. Was there a better example of how she could handle her situation? Before she knew it, her feet had carried her from the valley and set her on a path to the camp, straight as an arrow. Her legs pumped furiously, a pace only possible because of the meal she had admonished herself for. She flew over the plains, headed directly for the camp.

Fires lit the night ahead of her, many fires far taller than necessary for cooking. The refugee camp was more crowded than their previous campsites, likely for better protection against what roamed the darkness. She could feel the tension of the people through her new gift, something that hadn't occurred before. Indeed, now that she approached the large gathering of people she could feel other things as well, sense their pasts. She could see into their hearts.

She blew past the guards standing watch before they could even raise an alarm. The two moved to follow her, but they would never be able to match her speed. Shouts rang out all around her, but they were meaningless mumbles too distant for her to understand. She had a mission tonight, she was going to let no one stop her. The command tent stood sentinel in the center of the packed rows of tents, its banners hanging limp in the dead air. She could feel the men inside before she even drew close to the pavilion, but she didn't understand the complex weave of emotions that poured out of them. One of the guards at the door managed to get between her and the tent and leveled his halberd at her chest. She growled deep in her throat, baring her fangs at the man before she could stop herself.

The second guard seemed to catch up with the action, shouting "Halt!"

"I am 'halted.' Fetch Howlter," she turned to each of them in turn, letting her feline gaze linger on their eyes, "now."

They turned to look at each other, pausing briefly before the first guard nodded. The slower of the two ducked into the tent and returned a moment later. "You may proceed," he told her somberly, never taking his eyes from hers. She ducked her head and stepped into the tent. The interior was lit by several lamps, though the shadows were still deep. Her eyes adjusted quickly to the flickering light.

Howlter leaned over his table, studying the maps. A jumble of *skâk* pieces marked where the camp was in relation to a child's wooden block fortress that she guessed was Krossfarin. The checkered *skâk* board lay discarded in a corner of the mess, some of the unused pieces half-buried in the dirt floor. Howlter had tried to teach her the game once, when she first came into her rank, but she was terrible. Each piece had its own rules and tactics, and she could never remember if the knights moved two and then one or if that was the clerics. He eventually gave up on his teaching, which was a boon for both of them.

"Tidy as usual?" She chided, a harmless attempt to ignore the 'Org'rai in the corner,' or so the expression went.

"Where have you been?" Howlter asked, not taking the proffered light-hearted start of the conversation. "I've had men searching for you for three days!"

She hadn't realized that her hunt had gone on that long. If Howlter had been looking for her that long, it meant that she had spent at least two of those days within the tomb. "Maybe if you hadn't driven me out, I would have been closer at hand," she spit back at him acidly. "You made it abundantly clear that *my kind* weren't welcome here. Seems you may have found a use for me. Tell me, *Silvermane*, who is your witch?"

Howlter's eyes widened slightly at the honorific, "The Crone was the one that explained your… gifts." He couldn't keep the derision from his voice on the last word. Clearly it hadn't been his idea to summon her back. The Crone was a mysterious figure in their society, but she knew her magic. If she had told Howlter to fetch her, he had been right to listen. "We don't have time for pointless fighting. My sentries have seen wolves prowling everywhere along our western flank, what can you do for us?"

Crowlmer pulled the steel from her hips, "I've found that these work well on the abominations."

Howlter seemed to take in her appearance for the first time. "Where did you get your arms?"

"A gift," she replied, "from a distant cousin." It was technically true, Krelmer would have been a great-great-great-great Aunt, on her father's, mother's side. The 'mer' denoted their blood line, on their mother's side. Their clan came from their fathers.

"That is all you can bring?" Howlter's frustration dripped from his voice. "The Crone would have me believe that you are some preordained hero that will destroy all of the wolves and save the Gremen from extinction, but all you have are a couple of swords." He threw up his arms and stomped back to his table. "I already have a thousand swords at my call, what I need is magic. After Ryat and his wounded apprentice left I've only had Druids to counter magic and their talents just aren't enough. The shape shifters are always among us. Your kind has been able to sniff them out one by one, but whenever we kill one, two more take more of the refugees."

She hadn't realized the problem was so bad. Every encounter with the creatures, even the one that had transformed into a human, supported the notion that she could inherently sense them. She knew they were shapeshifters, something deep down had always told her so. "How many have they taken?"

"More than three hundred have been reported. Some had no kin and we only find what is left, we can't tell if there is more than one body most times and sometimes we find nothing. The first few nights it was only a few, but the numbers grew. They have been taking since you have been back from the forest, but they only recently started taking large numbers. For months they have been raiding us, but the refugees only made my men aware of it last week and with the Demons so close, we couldn't devote men to it. After the battle, we discovered just how bad the problem was." Howlter's head hung low as he finished.

She considered the weight that must be pressing on him, the sheer force of his responsibility. Still something didn't seem right, "Did any ever come back?"

"In the beginning there were a few false alarms, but none have returned in the last week." Howlter looked puzzled, "why do you ask?"

"The ones that came back are the wolves in your midst," she stated bluntly. "The leader of their pack is passing along his curse."

Howlter's eyes widened. "How would you know that?"

Crowlmer sighed. "The creature was in the forest with us. I fought it there and I fought it again this morning."

"That explains why it didn't start attacking until we were clear of Wylltraethel. How do we stop it?" The question was open-ended, but he didn't wait for her to respond. Instead he turned to his map and began studying the terrain around the camp.

"I was coming to warn you of the wolves, when I fought them this morning they fled to the swamps not far from here." She pointed to the greenish etching on his newly drawn map, "I tracked them heading in the direction of this area."

Howlter bared his fangs in a smile that would frighten most folk, "We have them then! All we need do is send a battalion into their den and kill them where they sleep!"

"No," Crowlmer shook her head. "They will just scatter when they hear you coming and they move much faster than you give them credit for. That's why I came here instead of just going into their den alone."

"Then what do you suggest?" Howlter sneered, his frustration bleeding into his words. "We just let them continue to kill us?"

Crowlmer studied the map once more, really seeing the camp for the first time. Howlter had nestled the refugees into a natural bowl in the landscape, presumably to keep their back away from the forest around them, but it did more than that. "Where are the Demons?"

"My scouts haven't seen them in days, seems their army turned north sometime after crossing the river, probably trying to reach Krossfarin before us." He looked down at the map and picked up on what she saw. There was only one way out of the bowl for the refugees. "Guards!" Howlter shouted for the men outside, but it was too late.

Somewhere to the north of them a horn sounded, followed closely by many more. Crowlmer felt her heart thud in response to the horns, but they were only part of the threat. From the rim of the hills surrounding them, the howl from dozens of wolves drove the fear deep within her. They were trapped here, Howlter had sought to gain refuge from the immediate threat and had invited a disaster that they likely wouldn't survive.

The Ball

"Best behavior tonight?" Her mother asked her in her childlike voice while she fussed over her hair, "Grandfather is going to need our support."

"Grandfather should have thought of that before," she snipped. "This is the last time that I will be able to see Maeryn and I mean to make the best of it." Her mother's face fell at the mention of the human boy. It was clear that everyone in her family knew about her feelings.

"Clora, we must be united behind our king. There will be delegates there from every free-city and all of the nations to the north." Her mother continued to fuss over her hair. "With all of the troubles lately, we need to show support."

"What troubles? Did grandfather upset another ruler? Kill another trade route?" She pulled away from her mother before she could further muss her hair.

"Clora! We don't speak of your grandfather in such tones!" Her mother sighed and smoothed the front of her dress. "We have patrols missing from the areas around Heimili alfa and there are reports of Harpies in the area. We've kept the rumors quiet till now, but grandfather will have to address the situation soon or risk a public outing by one of his rivals. The balance of power here is tipping away from Driamati."

"Grandfather has ruled for a long time, I'm sure he has a plan to get through this." She checked the lay of her gown in the full length mirror hanging near the window. Granny had outdone herself this time, the fit was perfect and complimented her figure wonderfully. She lacked the curves of a human, but carried herself well for an Oberon. She took a turn to check the back of the gown and smiled at her reflection.

"Clora are you even listening to me?" her mother muttered quietly.

"Of course mother, I'll be on my best behavior," she assured the woman.

"If anyone asks about the disappearances…" her mother continued her diatribe, but Clornamti tuned her out. She wouldn't actually be on her best behavior, but if it got her mother to leave she would promise anything. Maeryn was her focus tonight, not some missing patrols or the mythical Harpies.

They were escorted to the ball by Alexi and Dimitri, both of whom wore somber expressions despite the festivities around them. Something was bothering them. Their typical approach to their assignment was to simply guard her from site to site, they didn't pay too much attention, but tonight was different. Their eyes darted left to right, scanning the entire horizon and Alexi flew with one hand on his sword, something she had never seen him do. They were all on edge. Was it these reports that her mother had droned on about? Could they really fear an attack here at the heart of the Oberon nation?

She pushed the thought from her mind and flew on. Nothing was going to ruin her night. Ezra herself could crash the ball and Clornamti would just ignore her and continue dancing with Charles.

"You really are useless Charles," Ardelle was straightening his robes for the hundredth time. He had attempted to dress himself without her and he just couldn't figure out the tie so he had sought her out, but he was regretting it now.

"I think it looks fine," he tried to push her hands away from his collar, but it was like she had four hands. He couldn't keep them all away.

"You've wrinkled this terribly," she sighed, "didn't you just buy this?"

"It must have been wrinkled on the hook," he tried, but he knew she wouldn't believe him.

"Nothing for it now I suppose." She let her hands fall, smoothing her own gown as she did so. She was beautiful in a stunning emerald green flowing gown of modest Oberon style. He had seen similar cuts on other Oberon within the city, but they hadn't sported the full back that Ardelle's did. Her red hair was coifed about her temples in a tight braid that eventually turned to loose locks that fell down her neck. The dress set off the green in her eyes so much that they seemed to sparkle.

She was a beautiful woman, something he had missed when he had first been introduced to her in that cave. She had been covered in grime, wearing the majority of a swamp in her hair and clothing. Aurin had known of course, but Charles had been preoccupied with his magic at the time.

She smiled at him and ruffled his untamable hair. "Let's go, the party starts in an hour and it is quite the challenge climbing to the top of the tower in a gown." It was an honest statement, even his robes gave him troubles when climbing some of the steeper places in the ramps.

He awkwardly offered his arm to her and they left her chambers. The ball would be in Vielk's chamber, high above Charles' apartment in the tower next to this one and given that they were fully half way up the tower already, the walk meant crossing one of the sky bridges. The bridges were not something he was comfortable with, given that they were almost entirely glass and one could see the towers swaying in the wind as they crossed.

"I've been meaning to ask a favor," Ardelle started as they climbed the ramp that wound around the outside of the tower. "It's about your sword."

Confused he asked, "What about it?"

"May I borrow it tomorrow? I think I've found a descendant of the smith that originally crafted it and it would mean the world to him to see it."

They crossed onto the sky bridge and it took an act of will just to keep his mind on the conversation as they stepped out into empty air. "Ah… yeah… go ahead…" he stuttered as he desperately tried to stare at his feet.

"I hate these things too!" Ardelle accurately read his face and smiled as she quickened their pace across the bridge. She giggled as they nearly ran into the other tower, tripping over the hem of her gown and catching herself on his arm. He stumbled with the extra weight and barely managed to prevent them both from tumbling to the floor. They were both laughing now, drawing a long look from a passing Oberon nobleman which only set them to laughing harder.

He wiped at the tears in his eyes, "I'm glad I'm not the only one that can't stand those things."

"I usually hold my breath all the way across," she admitted, holding her hand in front of her mouth. "So about the sword, do you know anything about it?"

"I know more about its magic than anything else," he conceded. "Aurin and I found that in the forest after our exile. I've always meant to research it further, but there has been one thing or another stopping me since then."

"I couldn't imagine what," she smiled again, her ruby lips pulling back from her sparkling teeth. It was good to see a smile on her face again, she had been withdrawn since the forest. With the revelation that Aurin lived, he guessed that her smile would make an appearance more often.

The climb took the better part of the hour, and they discussed what had transpired since arriving in Heimili álfa. He was stunned to learn of the churches' decision to excommunicate her and further floored when she told him of the stillbirths and Barrah's curse. The smiles faded from their faces as she related her relative loneliness in this new world. He kicked himself for not seeking her out more often, it was clear she could have used a friend.

He passed along what he had learned from his Oberon tutors, glossing over his fight with Darl and the resulting change to his schedule. It wouldn't do for others to know about his strange magic, even his friends. After seeing Clornamti's reaction, he feared what the world would think of his ability to steal the magic of others. There would come a time when everyone would know, but this wasn't the night.

The herald announced them as High Priestess Ardelle and Mentor Maeryn Kairos, neither of them would be themselves tonight it seemed. The chamber held little resemblance to the empty temple he had visited just the other day, though he knew it was the same. Magical decorations had been hung throughout the room, glowing with a different light to represent the multitude of peoples assembled and their Arcana. Bright white light for Sozenra, deep green for Gelthar, grey for Vielk, blue-green for Chelan and even a fiery red-orange for Betala. There was no sign of the priest that Ardelle had warned him of, but it was a large crowd and one could hide easily.

Ardelle left him with the food as she moved off to speak with a large Tu'roki near the throne. She had mentioned something of a meeting between the churches and the free-cities concerning a coalition force that was to march south to Krossfarin. She had been asked to accompany them, but had declined. The big Tu'roki must be the priest she had spoken of.

Driamati stared at Charles from his perch, but did not call him over. It was a cold vicious gaze that Charles wouldn't wish on anyone. Clearly the king had expected something tonight, Ardelle had been right in her suggestion that he and Clornamti arrive separately.

Charles scanned the crowd, but could see no sign of Clornamti. He had no idea what she would be wearing, and there were just so many Oberon here that she could be anywhere. He took a deep breath and sent his power out, every person's aura would be different and hers would be easy for him to spot. He was careful not to push too much power forth. However, he may have used a bit too much. Some of the guests around him were looking about and their auras flared as he had passed over them. Clornamti wasn't present in the crowd. Others from her family were there, but she hadn't arrived yet. Anticipation built within him, would she still be here? Had something happened to keep her away? Had her grandfather simply told her that she couldn't attend so that there wasn't a scene? Perhaps she finally came to her senses and realized that he was just a human and could never live up to Oberon men.

His thoughts spiraled downward while he switched between wringing his hands and wiping the sweat from them onto the legs of his robe. His heart raced within his chest and he struggled for breath until the herald boomed, "Princess Clornamti and her mother, Princess Saranamti." He whirled toward the door and nearly swooned.

Princess Saranamti entered first in a teal gown of modest cut, much like Ardelle's but his eyes slid over the older woman to stare in awe at Clornamti. She wore a gown of silk that seemed to shift in color as she moved about the room, much like her aura. Her hair had been pulled up perfectly, not a strand out of place. Where most Oberon had taken to wearing paint on their faces to give them color, she had allowed the paleness of her skin to shine through. Her brown eyes sparkled in the false light of the chamber as though thousands of stars had taken up residence within them.

He stared openly, not caring what those around him thought until he felt a sharp jab to his ribs and a playful finger pushed his jaw closed. "Best not to stare, Mentor Kairos." Ardelle chided, barely containing her giggle. "She is quite beautiful tonight, I've not seen Gremen Silk since before I was banished. I wonder where she got it from."

Charles heard very little of what she said, but the distraction was enough to bring his feet back to the ground. Their plan had been simple, they would wait for the dancing to begin before 'accidentally' meeting on the floor. He couldn't approach her before then, even if the ache in his chest pulled him toward her. Ardelle took him by the arm and led him back to the food. "Eat something now, once you are on the dance floor you aren't going to want to leave."

He ate for what felt like hours, but was likely only a few moments before Driamati stood from his throne and boomed out to the crowd, "Friends! We have gathered here tonight to celebrate the new coalition and the coming end of the Demons!" He paused to let the applause die, "soon we will be able to trade with the south again and those here with us will be heroes! For now, let's dance!" Charles nearly leapt from his place near the food, but the look on Ardelle's face cemented his feet.

Something close to rage was boiling under the surface. "What's wrong?" he asked tentatively.

She shook her head and forced a smile, it held none of the warmth from before, "Nothing." Even he could read the lie on her face, "Go and be with your love."

The guilt of his neglect held him in place, "Ardelle, you can tell me. What is it?"

"The men that go south are more likely to not return than they are to be heroes. The world has a way of forgetting the sacrifices of those that go to war." She wiped her eyes, "I know, they forgot all about me." She smiled sadly, "don't let me ruin your night, Ch… Maeryn. Go, have fun, I'll be alright."

"Are you sure?"

"Go, Mentor Kairos, quickly before you lose your chance." She bumped him lightly with her hip before she moved back to the Tu'roki.

Charles watched her go, debating whether or not to follow her, but Clornamti caught his eye and winked at him. Decided, he moved off to ask the most beautiful woman in the world for a dance, but made a mental note to catch up with Ardelle after. Bowing low to her mother, Charles extended his hand to Clornamti, "May I have this dance?" Clornamti smiled, but it wasn't her that grabbed his hand.

"Of course, Mentor Kairos, it would be an honor." Princess Saranamti pulled him out onto the dance floor. He risked a glance back at Clornamti, and saw his fear reflected there. "I trust you know the Oberek," she asked, but didn't wait for a response before she launched into a fast paced dance set to the tempo of the song. He was familiar with the dance, but his partner was far more skilled than he was and he soon found himself following her lead rather than leading himself. The Oberek was a lively dance full of spins and jumps, and some of it even included lifts. Saranamti spared him this, lifting herself with her wings instead of expecting him to launch her airborne.

"I know what you expected tonight, Mentor." Saranamti told him between spins, "my daughter is as transparent as they come."

Charles panicked for a moment but remember Ardelle's advice, it was time for him to show his spine. "You're right, Princess. We had conspired to dance the night away, a truly heinous plan that could erode your very society."

The older Oberon shot icy daggers from her cold blue eyes, "it may seem harmless, but you could be jeopardizing her place in the succession."

"The grand hypocrite has a problem with humans and Oberon? Surely his son and daughter should be notified immediately." He dipped the woman then spun her loose, keeping perfect time for once. He caught her on her return and continued the spin with her, as the dance demanded. "We simply wish to see what becomes of our feelings, your highness. I give you my word that there will be no contact that would scandalize your family. Not without first seeking official courtship, as is your custom." He couldn't say where this confidence was coming from, perhaps he was channeling Aurin, though he couldn't imagine his friend attempting this dance. Aurin couldn't keep time to save his life, not on the dance floor anyway. Put a sword in his hand and he was a perfect dancer, but throw on a tune and he was all left feet.

"I will hold you to that, Mentor, though I've heard that you have trouble keeping your word." She was likely referring to his promise to Driamati concerning Clornamti a few weeks ago.

"I was a fool to promise what wasn't mine to give," he admitted as they spun together again. "I will be leaving the morning after next and there is a strong possibility that I won't return, surely you can let us have this night."

The cool gaze dropped from her face, replaced by sadness. The dance ended as she came back into his arms, "I can understand that, better than anyone here. I will allow you tonight, but we still need to speak of the future." She curtsied slightly, then left without waiting for his follow-up bow. Freed from his dance partner, he let his breath out slowly. He felt good, she had ambushed him, but he had held his ground. Even Ardelle would have to admit that he had improved.

"I can't believe she did that!" Clornamti huffed as she took his hand and pulled him back onto the dance floor. Her eyes were locked on her mother, but her feet found the rhythm of the song perfectly. After staring daggers at the woman, she turned her big brown eyes on him. The anger faded instantly, replaced by a stunning smile that nearly sent him toppling into a couple dancing behind them. Clornamti giggled lightly at his antics before helping him recover and starting their dance anew. "You dance well, Mentor Kairos and you look very handsome tonight." Her cheeks colored slightly, "not that you don't look handsome all the time…" The pink color darkened to a deep crimson. "I mean… uh…"

He smiled and tried to keep his own blush to a minimum before leaning in. "You look wonderful." He avoided gushing about the starlight in her eyes, or the perfect unison of her magical radiance and the silk of her dress, shoving away the inane comments about the Arcana and their lack of beauty compared to her. His life was on the line. He kept his statement simple and clear.

The Oberek ended as all the dancers bowed to their partners. The next song was a slower tempo with fewer spins and lifts, but far more complicated foot work. It was a

Solterran song, methodical in its composition but with stunning refrains that lent to the mental imagery of finding the gems among the stone. The dancers around them changed, most Oberon abstained from dancing to anything but their own works, but the others in the room had no problem with the new music. Human and Solterran, Gremen and Tu'roki, all took to the floor to stomp out the forms and smile to those around them. As the song progressed through its movements, the tempo increased until the dancers became a frenzy of stamping feet and laughter.

Charles and Clornamti were caught up in the wave of excitement as the music played on through the night. They spared a glance for no one but each other as the night slowly slipped away, so they missed the fire cast in their direction from one old man on his lonely throne.

Departure

She watched them spin about the floor and couldn't help the slight pang of nagging jealousy. Charles was far more graceful on the dance floor than she would have expected, given his inept performance in the sword ring, and his partner was loving it. Clornamti smiled brightly as they circled the floor, completely lost in their little world. If they had any awareness of their surroundings they would have noticed the icicles forming in Driamati's eyes, or the looks of disgust on some of the Oberon nobility's faces. There was nothing anyone could do about it here, not with so many foreigners present. Driamati would lose face with far too many dignitaries if he made a scene over his granddaughter with a human. In fact, if he would just let them dance and not give them the death stare, he might actually help his standing with the other races.

She chuckled to herself. Driamati accepting his granddaughter's affection for a human was as likely as a lion becoming friends with a cow.

Ceh'ruk smiled at her. "What's funny?"

She let her smile fade and returned her attention to the Tu'roki. "It's an inside joke."

"Someday you may allow me to become your friend, and then I too can smile at the jokes." He returned to a conversation with a delegate from the church of Sozenra concerning reports of a northern army massing under Barrah's twin generals, Brenin and Tarian. They were known for their ferocity in battle, but not for their strategic talents. Typically they served as bodyguards for Drech and Ezra, but Barrah lacked strong leadership in his armies. If he had the leaders he needed, the world would be in ruin. It was hard to attract talented leaders when your goal was the complete destruction of all living creatures on the mortal plane.

Ezra hadn't been seen since Falderal had been sacked some sixteen years ago, but Drech had taken the field alongside Caliban on several occasions in the south. He was at Hudcoeden, serving as the leader of the assault force that penetrated the city. There had been rumors that Ezra had been with him, but they were unconfirmed. The church of Sozenra feared the Harpy queen had her own plots. In Heimili alfa it was rumored that Harpies were active in the area and missing patrols to back them. She pushed the thoughts of the Harpies from her mind. Any time she thought of the fallen Avatar, Betala made her presence known. Ardelle didn't need the constant pressure of the Arcana ruining her evening. Her longing for a man she barely knew was already doing that.

"The reports don't lie Ceh'ruk, the hero of the Balen is still abed with his injuries. The Druids fear he may never recover, we can't count on him for the coming battle." The statement yanked her attention back to her companions. The hero of the Balen was Aurin, at least that was what Charles suspected.

"We only learned of the battle this morning, how is it that you know his condition?" Ardelle blurted, drawing many open-mouthed looks. It was the first time she had addressed the assembled dignitaries.

"Where there is battle, Sozenra has agents," the old man assured her. "We have known of the battle for a week, but it didn't seem pertinent to the discussions with the Oberons."

She wanted to throttle him. They had known that Aurin lived for a week and it wasn't pertinent? She opened her mouth, but snapped it closed as her better judgement won out. These men had no idea that Aurin was someone special to her, she had told no one of the man who had saved her from the forest. She didn't want to let any of them into her life.

They continued their discussion when it became clear that she had made her peace. It drifted away from Aurin and on to more mundane topics, like the provisioning of their coalition force as it moved south. She wandered away from them, taking a place along the railing of the balcony to contemplate her next steps.

She would ride out for Aurin, that much was assured, but what would she do once she was there? Did they have a future together? They had only spent two weeks together and while it had been wonderful, did it mean they were compatible for life? Did he even want to marry?

She struggled with the decision that she knew she had to make. If she stayed with him, she would inevitably lose him. He was a warrior, and now a figurehead, in an army that was fighting against the greatest threat to ever face the mortal plane. The chances of him living a long life were slim. She had already lost him once, could she go through it again?

She dabbed at her eyes with her scarf when she heard footsteps approaching from behind. "Are you alright?" Charles whispered, as he moved to stand next to her at the railing.

"I'm fine, just a little overwhelmed." She forced a smile although she knew it wouldn't touch her eyes.

"Thinking about Aurin?" He asked tentatively, staring out over the expanse of the Oberon city.

"A little," she dabbed at the remaining tears at the corners of her eyes. "I saw you dancing with Saranamti, you still have your head so you must have done something right."

He smiled brightly, "I just took the advice of a friend."

"Shouldn't you be with Clornamti now?" She looked for the tiny princess among the guests, but couldn't spot her from this vantage. "There won't be another chance to dance with her before you have to leave."

"I guess you didn't see the ending just now." He sighed and turned back to the ball. "Driamati announced that he has changed his mind and is sending a larger force south to aid the coalition. We are to leave tomorrow afternoon, instead of the following morning." He gripped the railing behind him until his knuckles were white, "I guess I got to him."

The man was truly something, he would send his country to war, just to prevent his granddaughter from falling for a human. "I'm sorry Charles, I didn't think he would make any move tonight."

"It was masterful, and I walked right into it." He huffed, "he interrupted the dancing and came over to stand between us as he announced my appointment as his ambassador. Saranamti collected Clornamti after that and led her out the back. I don't think I will see her again." His eyes were wet, but he forced the tears back. He was determined to be strong.

With the truncated time table, she had some things she would need to attend to immediately, including a promise to a new friend.

"Do I have time to borrow your sword with the new departure?"

"I'll need it back before I leave, but yeah," he sighed again despite her smile.

"Where is it now?" Her excitement was building, at least she could do something for someone that didn't involve going to battle.

"My quarters, would you like to go get it now?" He looked at the dance floor longingly, "I've nothing else to do."

She took his arm once again and let him lead her back down the tower. The trip away from the party was far more somber than their run up the tower had been, but it was still nice to spend it with a friend. Within his quarters, she saw the beginnings of a travel bag sitting on his bed, stuffed to the seams with clothing and other articles from around the room. The sword stood in a corner that was difficult to reach, due to an inordinate stack of books that had toppled over at some point.

He handed the blade to her as he balanced atop the shifting pile, "Please get that back to me. I've grown quite used to it and I don't know what I would do without it."

"Where are you assembling tomorrow?"

"Parade grounds, should we meet there?" He climbed down from his perch and began to strip his dress robes off. Once removed, he stuffed them into the bursting bag, but it no longer closed. She guessed he hadn't packed for himself much, in fact leaving that cave was likely the first time he ever had to pack his own bag.

"Charles, why you are bringing dress robes to a battlefront?" She couldn't help but interrupt his furious shoving.

His cheeks colored slightly, "Well I won't be returning here, I need to take everything with me, but they told me I can only have the one bag."

"And you fear that you will suddenly need dress robes? Leave them, and most of your other clothing. Take two outfits, your sturdiest, pack one, and wear the other. Then switch on wash day." She turned to his other belongings scattered around the room, "Leave the books, you won't have a chance to study them on the battle field and they will just slow you down. Pack the most important one, just in case you have need of it." She looked at the volumes arrayed on the bed and in the pile by the corner, most of them bore Oberon writing. "Leave anything written by Oberon, just take from the volumes you managed to save from the cave." They had left most of the books on that cliff, Charles had been in no shape to carry anything once his spell had finished, but a handful of them had found their way into his bag prior to the casting and were saved when they escaped. "Just remember that you have to carry that bag once you get where you are going."

Charles sighed heavily, then began pulling things back out of the bag. He had never been forced to give things up, so it was hard for him to just leave his things behind.

She left him to his packing and returned to her quarters. He would likely be at it all night at the rate he was going and she couldn't bring herself to watch. She removed her gown and pulled a night dress over her head. She hung the beautiful garment near the door for the maid to collect tomorrow, then saw to her own packing.

She decided that tomorrow was as good of day as any to leave the city and the coalition with it. If she stayed, she knew she would be tempted to join them on their march south, but the girl within her couldn't wait that long to see Aurin again. With a simple travel bag prepared, she laid out her clothes from her trip out of the forest. They were the sturdiest clothes she had. With their magical nature, they offered her the most protection from the elements. They had been repaired since arriving in the city, the Solterran woman who had done the work did so with such skill that you couldn't even see the patches. The mud had all been removed, but she could almost feel it clinging to her. The swamp had been terrifying, but at least the cleanup had been nice, with Aurin there to scrub her back.

She climbed into bed but slept little, nightmares of Aurin's fall plagued her along with visions of the Demon horde she would face once she found him again. She gave up on sleep shortly before dawn and made use of her shower for the last time. At least she would be clean when she left.

She lingered under the hot water longer than she had expected. Drying off, she saw the sun had crested the trees surrounding the town. Charles' sword in tow, she ran from the tower toward the low areas of the town. Omesh should have the forge up and running in full heat by now, which meant it would only be a quick stop. Midday would arrive too soon and she meant to grant Omesh his one wish. One and a half hours, if she was conservative, and she could be back on the road, away from the Oberon with their stuffy politics and their class system.

Aurin was alive, or at least he was on last report. He had been injured during the battle, but still lived. She needed to find him, to see him for herself. Would they be together again? Did he miss her at all? He hadn't sent a message or contact, not that he would know where they were.

She decided just to leave it, it wouldn't do to worry about it. If they weren't together she could still be useful on the front. Even without Betala's presence, her powers were enough to make a difference. On a battlefield, fire was often the key to victory and she could use that fire to ensure the victory was theirs. It wasn't a common gift, even among the Avatars of Betala, but she could pull the fire from anywhere and use it to fuel her magic. She had only had cause to use it once, but the power was still there.

She crossed the grassy area between the towers and the low swept buildings of the forges at a run, not even bothering to use the paths, despite the looks she received from the passing Oberon and their land bound guests. She passed the smoking stall of the Tu'roki father and daughter and dashed into Omesh's stall, but the forge was still banked. It had been stoked this morning, but there were no fresh pieces in the coals and Omesh wasn't present. The sword they had forged was gone as well. Had he found a buyer already?

She pulled the baldric of Charles' sword over her shoulder and resigned to just fetch a horse for herself. There was a standing arrangement with the stable owner for the brown mare she used to ride into the countryside, but getting him to sell may lighten her purse. She passed the many shops that catered to the land bound, from tanners to goldsmiths and even a single wood carver, though how a wood carver could compete in an Oberon city she didn't know. A single temple dotted the lane, a low building of Solterran construction with decorations of all the Arcana adorning its stone walls. Vielk even had his place, though she doubted there were many who would choose this church over the grand temple of the Oberon. Outsiders were permitted to attend the regular ceremonies of the church, even though it required them to scale the tower to its peak.

  She was studying the worn symbols of Betala when the first rays of fire rained from the sky.

Awakening

Everywhere he turned there were the bodies of his loved ones, torn to pieces by the magic he set loose, their accusing faces staring blankly. He had lost control again and his friends paid the price. There was Charles, pale from the lack of blood and nearly severed in two from the blast. Ardelle was merely a shadow of ash against the bark of a tree, her green eyes gone forever. Crowlmer still writhed on the ground, but her fight would soon be over, a pool of blood much too large to survive, spread into the forest floor around her. Others flashed through his mind, Samuel Dorne with his smiling face blasted off, Howlter with his guts in his hands. His guardsmen in a ring around him where they had sought to contain his power with their shields. Helpless refugees spread out as their eyes all stared at him.

He ran, but there was no escaping the carnage. Bodies lay everywhere, women, children, the elderly and the spry, all of them dead by his power. Demons moved among the bodies and as they saw him pass they cheered, he was their hero now. He did what they couldn't, he killed the last of the mortals. A large violet-skinned demon with a Harpy on his arm smiled and clapped as he passed, Barrah had won.

He pushed deeper into the forest, but still more bodies appeared. Castielle, her dark red hair plastered to her face in blood, lay crumpled against the trunk of a pine, her arm raised to point at him as she struggled to draw her last breath. The Druids lay around her, all of his healers dead. Hundreds of their white robes sprinkled the forest floor like snow in early spring. Crimson lines ran throughout the white cloth, spreading slowly as their hearts ceased to pound.

The trees closed in around him as he tried to escape, but there was nowhere to go. He had killed them all. He broke into a clearing that was dominated by a single figure wreathed in an ice-blue light.

"You killed them!" Adla shouted in a multi-toned voice, "You couldn't resist the magic and look what you did! I judge you traitor Aurin Tor, die a traitor's death!" The small girl raised her head to the sky and howled, but it wasn't her, it was the wolf from the forest.

"You did what I couldn't." The wolf told him. "You killed them all, rid the world of the human scum." It bared its fangs to him in a grotesque imitation of a smile, "now to finish the work." The creature lunged for his neck and tore at his flesh, pulling the scream from his throat before he ever gave it sound.

"Aurin!" Someone was shaking him violently.

He roared and leapt from the bed, only to collapse on the rugs, his body still weak. "Ugh..." he managed, as he rolled to his back and took in his surroundings. He was still in his tent, not the forest of his dream. Castielle was the one shaking him, which gave further credence to it being only a dream.

"What are you doing?" Her voice wavered, she was worried, and not just because of his nightmare.

"What's wrong?" He saw that the lanterns in the tent were lit, it was the middle of the night.

Screams pierced his tent, followed by rushing feet. "The Demons are here," she started but a howl from far off cut her short, "And they've brought friends. We need to get you ready to move."

"Help me into my armor." He struggled to get to his feet and took one shaky step toward his foot locker.

"Are you mad? I'm getting you onto a horse and away with the rest of the refugees." She took his arms like a mother would a small child and guided him back to the bed. He offered no resistance, his arms were useless and his legs only marginally functional.

"No! I belong in the battle, it's all I have!"

She turned her green eyes on him, "You can't." He could see tears threatening at the edge of her eyes before she blinked them away and stamped her foot. "I've not spent this much time on you for you to run off and die uselessly. You may still recover someday, don't give up so easily."

"I'm not giving up! I should be in the fight, it is all I know and…" he couldn't even finish his own thought. And what? He could slow the Demons down with his corpse? He couldn't even lift his sword up to eye level. Using magic ravaged his body to the point where he could do little for himself. Mobility was limited, he got winded too easily. He couldn't fight and he would just be in the way if he was to try and join the formation. She was right, he was no better than the children he would be fleeing with. The bed groaned briefly as he collapsed into it, feel useless in the face of need. There was nothing he could do to stop what was coming.

Not for the first time since his injuries, tears ran down his cheeks. Castielle patted him softly and urged him back to his feet. The now useless sword belt was carefully placed around his waist, more for peace of mind than functionality. She closed the foot locker with his armor still inside, a poignant reminder of its uselessness, and handed him his crutches. He could walk without the crutches, but not for long periods, it gave him something to lean on in between his small bursts of energy.

Heads turned when he emerged from the tent. Having freshly wiped his face of the tears, but he was sure it was still evident that he had shed them. Many people whispered to each other as he passed slowly by the mass of tents and pavilions. From the snippets he could catch, half of the people wanted him to just die, others were hoping for another grand show like the Balen. Some voiced concern, though purely for selfish reasons. This was what happened when a man tried to reach too far with magic. At least they were saving their food this time. After the bodies of the humans had been recovered at the Balen, riots had erupted from his presence. It didn't matter to some that he had saved their lives, or that the Demons would have slain them all that day was evident to anyone with a military mind. It didn't matter to the common populace, they only saw him slaughtering their kin.

No harsh words could ever drive him lower than he was doing to himself. Regret for his actions at the Battle of Balen enveloped him. The power he wielded and the feeling it gave him would always be at the back of his mind. He had been drunk on many occasions in the guard, but it was nothing compared to the euphoria he experienced as that pure white light poured from him. Demons had been slain by the thousands as he released the power, their human escorts along with them.

A shout tore him from the memory, but only just, "Tor!" A bear of a man stepped from his tent and slapped him on the back, nearly sending him to the earth. "What's the matter man?" He scratched at his thick, unkempt beard, "Dorne grumbled somethin' 'bout you gettin' hurt but I guess I didna believe him." His beady black eyes trailed over Aurin's hunched form, pausing at the crutches he was using to hold himself up. "What did you do?"

"It's a long story Bjorn, and I've no time to tell it now." Bjorn the Black was a friend of Samuel Dorne from Krossfarin, the leader of their equivalent to the Druid Guard to be exact. Aurin had met him on several occasions, both in the field and while staying in Krossfarin. He had even trained under Bjorn for a brief stint when Dorne wanted him to try his hand at the battle axe. It had been a terrible experience and Aurin sill couldn't see the wood and iron training axes without flinching. Bjorn was a mountain of a man with more muscle in a single arm than Charles did in his entire body. When he fought, his great strength passed into the battle axe flawlessly. A sword would be wasted on man like Bjorn, he had no finesse.

"Yer right there, the Demons be close. My men still half day's march from you, but if you can hold out that long we can spring ya."

"How many are there?" Aurin had been kept from any details, he suspected it was deliberately.

Bjorn scratched at his beard again, "Better 'an ten thousand, if scouts can be believed. But you took that many at t' Balen not long ago, you can handle a half day, righ'?" His great belly jiggled as he laughed at his own joke. He slapped Aurin on the back once more, this time taking him to his knee.

"We don't have the same power we had at the Balen, Bjorn, we've lost… our magic." It took every fiber of his will to not say 'my magic.'

The guffaw continued, louder, "Magic ne'er won nothin' boy, you still got the men here to stand for you."

Aurin stood and gripped the crutches harder, turning his hands white. "You just don't understand, Bjorn. If it wasn't for the magic we'd all be dead on the banks of that river. They had us out numbered ten to one."

"Captain Tor," Castielle came to his rescue. "I really must see you to the medical wagons, I've others that will need my help."

He let her lead him from the confrontation, his anger bubbling under the surface. More horns sounded from the north and east, closer this time than they had been moments ago. The demons were advancing quickly. The howls from the mountains to the south and west had quieted, but that didn't give him hope. Wolves don't howl while they hunted and stalked their prey. It was enough to know that they were out there. He itched to pull his father's sword from his hip and charge off to the battle, but fate had other plans for him. This wasn't his fight, not today. He would have to learn to rely on others to do his fighting for him.

Not for long, my son. The voice boomed within his mind. *Soon you will be whole, but will you be ready?*

Who are you? He demanded, or at least did his best to demand of the voice within his mind.

Soon, we will meet soon. He could feel an absence as the voice left.

"Captain?" Castielle was staring at him from a short distance. His internal conversation had stopped him in the middle of the path. He resumed his hobble behind Castielle, his chin to his chest as he fought the urge to weep. His crutches clicked and popped as he shifted his weight during his crippled walk, he'd never sneak up on anyone with them, but at least he could move under his own power.

Men rushed by in every direction, farmers with their children heading to the center of the camp, half-dressed soldiers to the front lines on either end of the camp. They all sported the same fearful look. Screams rang up the street behind him, another victim of the wolves had been found, or so he thought. A knot of Gremen with spears rushed into the path toward the sound, their ill-fitting armor clanking loudly. These were conscripts from the Gremen camp followers, not regular soldiers. Seconds later, another Gremen rushed toward the south, though this woman bore armor specifically fitted to her. Two identical blades hung from her hips, but the tail that swung back and forth as she ran drew far more attention.

Crowlmer's step stuttered as she spotted him and his crutches stopped her dead. "What has happened to you?" True concern lined her face.

"Nothing I didn't bring on myself," he admitted. "I hadn't heard that you had returned."

"I came to warn of the wolves, but I was too late." She eyed the far end of the camp where the others had rushed off, "I must go. Take care of him Castielle, he seems unable to do it himself." A small smile crossed her face, but it didn't last. She had allowed herself that brief joke but something nagged at her, much as it did him. Briefly, she put a hand on his shoulder and vanished into the crowd at a trot.

Aurin longed to follow her, to have her at his side again would ease the pain he was feeling, the loneliness he had surrounded himself with since the Balen. He knew it was just wishful thinking to long after something that would likely never be his again. He wouldn't be the one charging into battle at the head of the troops or leading the scouting missions into enemy territory.

Castielle took him by the arm and led him toward the center of camp where the other non-combatants were housed. They couldn't flee, there was nowhere to run, but they also couldn't be underfoot when the fighting started. Aurin was one of them now, though he wouldn't go down without at least trying to stand.

More screams from the direction Crowlmer had disappeared to, turned him around. The crowd rushed away from something moving up the street, but not all of them were clearing the press. The bodies at the back started to drop as something systematically dragged them down. Aurin was bowled aside as the citizens of Hudcoeden lost all composure, fleeing whatever hunted them. Castielle helped him back to his feet, but it was too late. The wolves were only strides away from them now, malice lighting their human-like eyes. Dozens of the huge creatures filled the street, some feasting on the bodies they pulled from the crowd, others turning their attention to those still standing. Aurin dropped his right crutch and gripped the sword at his waist, but he could barely maintain his balance without the support. Castielle pulled at his other arm in an attempt to lead him from the creatures, but he shook her loose. He couldn't just leave these things, by his reckoning it was his fault they were even here. Before he and Charles broke free from the forest, the wolves had been contained within its boundaries. To see them here and now, free from the banishment, but still cursed with their lust for the hunt, he knew it must have something to do with him.

Calling on what reserves he had, he pulled the sword from his hip, and swiped it into a block directly in front of his body. With his one crutch, he turned the rest of his useless limbs away from the approaching creatures. He kept the point of the sword up, more for the balance it gave to his quivering arm than for any preparation of defense. Ideally, he would keep the point low to strike at the creatures' relatively unprotected bellies, but just the thought of bending his body that low sent a wave of pain through him. Shouts from behind the wolves announced Crowlmer's return with what was left of the wolf patrol, a sparse three man pike assembly. Crowlmer tossed her blade to her left hand and ripped the second free of its scabbard. She whispered and the blades lit with an icy blue glow. "Press your backs together and keep your spears low!" she shouted to the men, then charged the nearest wolf.

The first creature had no chance, her glowing blades struck the head from its shoulders before it could even open its mouth to snap at her. Others followed it, but more were slowly closing in on her. The three spearmen followed her instructions, but there were just too many wolves. Two spearmen went down with the second wave of creatures and the third soon followed. Crowlmer was being pressed hard now, three of the creatures kept up their strikes directly at her whirling blades, leaping clear before she could catch any of them. Others circled her to close their trap, a common pack tactic.

Take the Druid's hand, son. I will help you. The voice nearly sent him to his rear.

He couldn't say why he trusted the disembodied voice, but with little other choice he called to his Druid escort, "Castielle! Take my hand!" Apprehensively, she reached out and took the hand from the crutch.

Now, you must be careful, she has very little power that she can give you, but it is enough for this. Aurin anxiously watched the wolves closing on Crowlmer and willed the voice to hurry its instruction. *Do you see them now? Their true forms?*

Aurin concentrated on the wolves and could almost see a hazy male spirit hovering behind each one. He knew they were men already, but why could he see them now?

I've given you the ability, but I can't maintain the connection, I'm still linked to another. If you weren't so strongly rooted in my magic, I couldn't even do this much. Carefully draw some of the magic from the Druid into yourself and use it to throw your sword at the nearest creature. Then let go, lest you drain her completely.

Aurin, deeply confused, didn't stop to consider any of what the voice had told him, but he could feel the power within Castielle. He drew a small thread of the magic from her and sent it straight to his arm, he couldn't explain how he did it, but it felt right. Strengthened by the sudden rush of magic, the weight of the sword vanished. He threw the blade as hard as his borrowed strength would allow and let go of Castielle.

Her eyes rolled into her head and she collapsed to the earth behind him, taking his crutch with her. The strength left his legs and he dropped to his knees.

The sword spun away from him impossibly slow, spinning end over end before finally striking its target. His aim had been true, but the flat of the blade struck instead. The creature stumbled from the impact. Unhurt, it turned to him and growled as it lunged for his pathetic form. Mid-leap, a lash of magic leapt from the fallen sword and slammed the creature to the earth. As the creature struggled to stand, a flash erupted from the sword and revealed the wolf's true form. A naked man thrashed about the trampled grass of the roadway, clutching at his limbs and howling in pain.

Now reach for your sword. The voice sounded almost smug.

Aurin held out his hand toward the shining blade and willed it to come to him. At first, nothing happened, then something within him tore loose and the blade leapt into his outstretched fingers. A wave of power flooded into him from the sword. Whatever magic that had cursed the creature, was now purified, much like it had been that first time on the cliff top. The magic rushed through his limbs and infused them with a strength he hadn't felt since the battle of the Balen. It wasn't the same as it had been when Adla had touched him, but it was enough. He shook his left hand loose from the crutch's strap and pushed himself to his feet. The writhing man had stopped moving altogether, simply staring at Aurin as though he'd seen a ghost.

Free the creatures from their curse and they will panic, but not all of them are as they once were. Some of their minds will have broken due to the magic, those, I'm afraid, are lost. I must leave you now, my son, but soon we will be together.

Aurin felt the familiar lifting from his mind as the voice retreated from whence it came. His body was his once more, he felt whole. Not euphoric like he had been after Adla's touch, but more like he had been before the forest. He tossed his sword to his left hand and charged to Crowlmer's side, swatting aside two more wolves with the flat of his blade. The raw power welled inside him again, but instead of the blast he had used on the Balen, he concentrated on his sword instead. He could feel the enchantments within the blade now, the power that had been stored there when it was forged. Thrusting the sword above his head, a soundless thunder erupted from the clearing, sending everyone to the earth once more. Dozens of naked men rolled about in the grass around them, some with fear in their eyes, others with nothing but hate.

A few, those that the voice had warned him of, rushed at them once more. Their minds were gone, replaced with the simple need to kill and feed. He couldn't see any humanity in their eyes, only the lust. Crowlmer took the first two, easily striking their unarmored forms down. He took the last, though only in mercy. The others took the opportunity provided by their brethren to flee from their armed foes, without the strength and speed of the wolf, they knew they were no match.

Crowlmer spun on him as the last of the men disappeared, "Where did that come from? Was the crippled look just a ruse?" She huffed through her nose as she stared balefully at him.

"No, it wasn't a ruse. It has to do with my magic, or lack thereof, it's a long story that I'd love to regale you with but we can't get into it right now." The magic was humming through him, but it wasn't like before. He felt no need to let it loose, to destroy his enemies with it. "Castielle!" He dashed for the crumpled Druid and slid to his knees next to her. Her breathing was slow but even, almost as though she slept. He had no idea what to expect from her, he'd never taken magic from another like that. Was she going to be alright? Had he permanently damaged her? Panic rushed through him as he checked her pulse and shook her to rouse her.

Castielle's eyes fluttered open and she groaned, "What did you do to me?" Her words were mild, but he thought he could hear anger behind them.

"I borrowed some of your magic so that I could fight, I should have asked you but there wasn't time. I only took enough for that one strike."

She scanned his face, "it feels like I've just spent a night in healing. I'm exhausted. One strike?"

He nodded slowly, "I just needed enough to hit the wolf with my sword. That's all I took, I promise."

"I can't remember the last time I've felt this drained, how do you function?" She took a deep breath, "What I mean is, if you needed that much magic just to throw your sword, how did you get through the day without it?"

"Not well," he sighed at the thought of being a cripple again. "I don't know much about my power, I don't know where it comes from or why I seem to be the only one with it. I wish I could tell you more, but I just don't know." Horns blared from the northern end of the camp, reminding him that he couldn't delve into the mysteries of his power right now. "Come on, I'll take you to the medical area."

She laughed, a hearty bark that stopped him short of picking her up. "And to think, not but a moment ago I was taking you to the medical area."

He smiled down to her and lifted her from the ground. She was a feather in his arms, he worried that a stiff breeze would carry her away before he remembered the vast well of magic swirling within him. Everything was lighter than he remembered as power infused his muscles. Crowlmer stepped in beside him, resting one of her hands on his shoulder before moving with them into the center of the camp. He felt whole, something he had feared would never return to him. The horns sounded again, and he couldn't help but wonder how long the feeling would last this time.

Shattered

Screams pierced the air as the fire rained down all around the practice field where Charles' troop had gathered. Harpies soared everywhere, hurling great flaming spheres into every building they passed. His escort kept him penned in around the carriage that he was to ride in on their flight to Krossfarin. Their leader ordered him to stay put as they made their final preparations for flight, intending to continue with his mission, despite the attack. Most of the soldiers that had been assigned to the escort were currently in the air, protecting the carriage and the practice grounds with their crossbows and spears. Guards buzzed around most of the towers where spectacular aerial battles were being waged between the nimble Oberon and the Harpies with their great bird-like wings. Most of the buildings were aflame, including the majority of the towers. Only the crown tower was untouched as the primary force of the guard fought off the Harpies close enough to set it alight again.

A roar of wind signaled the close passage of one of the harpies to his carriage, it was quickly followed by the buzzing of an Oberon's insect-like wings. There were thousands of Harpies overhead, many more than anyone would have speculated still lived, and every one of them was flinging fire, marking them as a mage. The entire college of Wizards in Hudcoeden couldn't have fielded more than a thousand magic wielders and they were drawn from many races. The fact that the Harpies had so many was just unbelievable.

There were no supporting forces on the ground, the Harpies attacked solely from the air. History had always shown them as the air cover for the greater forces under

Barrah's command, there were no documented cases of them raiding without ground support. What were they after? Their numbers were impressive, but it wasn't a large enough force to sack the city. Though they could inflict a good deal of damage to the buildings, there were few Oberon casualties. So far, only the visiting dignitaries and common folk from the land bound races were suffering as the towers burned, unable to flee the flames from such heights. The Oberon simply took wing. One such Oberon was flying from the upper reaches of the tower he had called home these past months now, her dark blue dress fluttering about her legs as she leapt into the air; Clornamti.

  He watched her bank away from the tower then screamed, "No!" Two Harpies trailed her as she dived to gain speed, their chestnut colored wings flapping frantically in an attempt to close the gap. Twin balls of fire shot from the Harpies as Clornamti pulled out of her dive just before the ground, the flames bursting up and singeing her clothing, before she blasted clear of them with a new surge of speed. He suspected she just used her magic to increase her speed, but at this distance he couldn't be sure. She was making for the crown tower, but the Harpies were quickly closing in on her. Even with her heightened speed, they would catch her long before she made the tower and its defenses. She must have realized this because she banked hard around the closest tower, turning too sharply for the Harpies to keep pace with their great wings. Like a shot, she flashed back the way she had come, toward the tower Charles had left her in earlier. Her pursuers quickly resumed their chase, flinging more fire at her. The fire barely missed her as she hastened to the relative safety of the tower. Charles could almost see the small threads of magic maintaining the shield about her.

The Harpies closed to within bow shot and let loose a barrage of fire that her shield couldn't completely deflect. Clornamti's screams reached Charles as she lost her controlled flight and tumbled through the air. Her forward momentum kept her aloft, but it wasn't enough. She was soon spinning wildly toward the earth. Charles drew everything he could from his pool and instinctually cast it toward her. He had no idea what spell he had just released but the magic sped away from him, colliding with Clornamti three stories from the ground and sweeping her up. The ray of magic propelled the small girl toward the tower, bearing her within the structure and smashing everything in the way. He lost sight of her within the debris, but the Harpies didn't stop their pursuit. They swooped into the tower, two levels above where he had sent her and rushed down the ramp that circled the central structure. They would be on her in moments and he still couldn't see her.

He burst from the carriage, careening into his guard and rushed toward the tower. There was little hope that he could reach her before the Harpies, but he was going to try. Shouts rang out from his escort as he sped across the intervening grass, but the message was lost on him. He drew from his pool again and set the magic to work within his own body, forcing it into the healing points along his frame and pushed the power into his muscles. A surge of energy washed over him as the magic took root, giving him a speed that would frighten the great cats of the plains. Despite them hanging limply from their battered and burnt hinges, he blew through the doors of the tower. Screaming furiously, he ran up the ramp, covering two floors in a heartbeat. He could hear a struggle above him, but he didn't stop long enough to process what was happening.

He twisted around the last turn and dumped the magic from his limbs. As he turned the last corner of the tower, he threw up a shield as a ball of fire crashed into him. One of the Harpies was waiting with more fire as the smoke cleared from its first attack. A torrent of flames leapt from the Harpy's hands, washing over his shield, completely obscuring his vision. He had never practiced his attack spells without sight, but he knew generally where the Harpy was and used that as a reference. He also knew how Clornamti's height and worked that into his estimation for where to send his magic. He didn't dare let loose a wide attack from here, it would likely collide with the girl he was trying to save.

Keeping the thread of magic feeding his shield, he pulled in enough to let loose with an arc of thin magic, roughly the span of his arms. He fired the spell at eye level, hoping that Clornamti hadn't taken to wing again within the confines of the ramp. The fire stopped. As the smoke cleared, he watched a headless Harpy corpse tumble from the ramp out into the open air. The second Harpy turned and shrieked at him, bringing her arms up before her to let loose with more fire. She didn't have the chance. Clornamti, recovering from her fall, leapt onto the Harpy and drove her fist into the bird woman's head repeatedly until the creature finally stopped thrashing.

Relief flooded Charles. He rushed to Clornamti and pulled her clear of the unconscious Harpy, wrapping her in his arms as he did so. He looked down into her sparkling brown eyes, and bent to kiss her as she raised up on her toes in response. The world stopped as they remained there for what could have been an eternity. The sounds of battle finally broke their embrace.

"Why did you come back?" Clornamti asked him tearfully.

"I saw you fall," Charles started. "I couldn't leave you to the Harpies. My magic got you to the tower, but anything I cast from so far away would be like throwing hammers in a glass shop to kill a bug. I had to make sure you were alright."

An explosion erupted at the base of the tower, causing the whole structure to shake. "We need to get you out of here," Clornamti grabbed his hand and pulled him toward the ground floor. More explosions ripped through the tower as they tried to exit, and fire leapt up directly in front of them. Charles felt a rushing wind before the Harpy crashed into them from the other side of the fire. Clornamti was ripped away from him, and sent farther up the ramp than where they started. The Harpy slammed him to the ground, bashed his skull against the floor twice, and then struck him hard across the face before leaping clear and chasing after the Oberon. Charles' head spun as he tried to right his body, his right arm was pinned beneath him. It was painful, but unbroken. He couldn't seem to stop the ramp from spinning long enough to gain his feet.

A blurry image of the Harpy standing over Clornamti flashed before his eyes and then his vision was gone. His skull was pounding, sending lances of pain with every beat of his heart. "Bring the boy too, Ezra may have use for him," A high pitched voice sounded from above him.

A pair of rough hands lifted him from the floor and flung him over what he guessed was a shoulder. "He had best be worth something," a second voice replied.

He tried to draw from his pool, but the pain in his head was making it difficult to heal himself. The Harpy carrying him began to trudge up the ramp, bouncing Charles with each step and sending more shocks of pain through his head. They travelled for an eon before the Harpy finally dumped him back onto the floor. His vision was starting to return, but everything was still a blur. He could make out the shapes of at least a dozen Harpies moving around, their chestnut wings pulled back to resemble a cape. They were in the chamber of Vielk, the decorations from the ball still hung from the ceiling. He could see Clornamti now, bound hand and foot but still conscious. Something had been stuffed into her mouth, muffling her screams.

"Stop your screaming wench," one of the Harpies kicked Clornamti in the stomach with far more force than necessary. She doubled up about her middle and sucked hard against the gag, trying to refill her lungs. "Where is Ezra?" the Harpy asked one of her compatriots.

"Still having fun with the Oberon around the crown tower, they refuse to give ground so we kill them one at a time." A Harpy across the room chimed in, laughing maniacally.

A larger bird woman stepped to the center of the room, "We have the princess, Driamati will come to us. Someone signal the queen and let us end this farce."

Charles shook his head in an attempt to clear it with little success. The magic was there, but it was too faint to respond to him. His hands had been left unbound, likely due to his semiconscious state but he could do little with them. He had to heal himself and get Clornamti out of here before they attempted to ransom her to her Grandfather. She likely wouldn't survive any exchange.

One of the smaller Harpies moved off to the balcony to send up a blazing signal of blue flame. His vision was starting to clear and his tenuous hold on consciousness began to firm. He could feel more of his magic pulsing from within his pool, almost as though it was calling to him to draw on it. With so many Harpies in the room, he didn't dare draw deeply, but he did cast the magic into the healing points throughout his body. The practice he had in healing himself had been hard won, but he was grateful for it. The slow trickle of power from his pool was frustratingly difficult to maintain, but anything more overt would signal to everyone who could see power within others that he was using magic. For now they didn't think him a threat, if he could keep up the ruse he may be able to do some good. If only he could mask his power completely like his former master, Waliyt, had done for most of his life.

He could see varying radiances within the Harpies around him, but some of them were truly odd. More than half of the bird-women had a strange black aura under the magic. Something within that aura was wrong, and he had seen it before. Barrah's magic was uncommon amongst the mortals, primarily because of his fall from grace. His original gift of magic was that of Justice, a magic that could find the truth within any statement and bring punishment to those that had earned it. That magic had vanished from the world when the other Arcana had banded together and banished Barrah from their realm. It had been replaced by a foul imitation of the magic that was primarily used to punish and enslave. Why the magic would be within the Harpies was a mystery to Charles, but it made their other gifts seem unnatural. Something about Barrah's magic had given them the ability to use Betala's magic. That was why there were just so many of them wielding magic, Barrah had given it to them with his powers.

A strong burst of air blew through the room from the balcony, shifting the wings of the other Harpies and sending the loose materials flying into the walls. A Harpy strolled into the room, her feathers a deep onyx rather than the chestnut brown of the others around her. A brilliant radiance surrounded her as she stood over the still form of Clornamti, a swirling fire interspersed with the depthless black of Barrah's gift. The power this Harpy could wield was immense, more akin to the magic Charles had fought against when he had fled Wylltraethel than anything he had faced from any lone magician.

"So this is the princess?" She made to kick the unconscious girl again but Charles' shout stopped her short. She turned slowly to level her wicked gaze upon him as he sat slumped against the wall. "And what is this creature?" She crossed the distance between them and bent low to stare into his eyes.

"It was with the princess, my queen," one of the other Harpies responded. "We thought it may help to draw out the ones we seek."

A taloned hand shot out faster than Charles could follow and closed about his neck. The queen lifted him from the floor and pinned him against the wall, his feet dangling. The Harpy was impossibly tall. "Why would they send a human to protect her? The Oberon hate humans, they hate everything that doesn't have their ridiculous bug wings. What makes you special?" A strange look passed over her face before a wicked grin split it. "I see," she cackled, turning to the subordinate who had spoken. "You've done well, child. This is the Chavox!" Every feathered head in the room spun to look upon Charles as he hung limply from the queen's grip. "Our lord will be pleased with us for this. Bind him, and set a guard over him. If half of the prophecy is to be believed, he is a potent mage."

She dashed him back to the floor, slamming his body into his legs and jamming his fingers as he tried to break the fall. Another Harpy broke from the crowd and pulled his arms roughly behind his back, eliciting another scream as he felt the muscles in his right shoulder tear from the strain. With dexterity that belied her taloned fingers, she bound his wrists tightly behind him before wrenching him up to a sitting position and repeating the process on his legs. The creature that bound him stopped to admire her work before spitting on him and kicking his legs savagely. "The great Chavox is a boy? You are the one we've been told to fear all these years? Ha!" She maliciously kicked him again, then wandered back to the crowd, laughing wickedly. Two smaller Harpies moved over to stand on either side of him, their magic a pale comparison to their queen.

He needed to do something, anything to get free of the vicious women and their horrid queen, but what could he do, bound and surrounded by nearly two dozen of them?

A low buzzing that vibrated the very air of the tower answered his thought. He craned his body so that he could see out through the balcony and hope rushed through him. A large force of Oberon, flying in a 'V' formation, were approaching from the distant crown tower. At their head flew the distinctive form of Driamati, his crown and cloth of gold robe shining brightly in the noon sun. Even from this distance, Charles could see a well of power swirling within the gathered Oberon, a great pool of Vielk's magic drawing into Driamati from the very air around him.

"Ezra!" His magically enhanced voice rattled through the tower, sending what objects had remained standing to the floor with a crash. "You will return my granddaughter, now, or I will kill every last one of you!"

The queen just smiled and lifted Clornamti from the floor with one hand. Moving to the balcony, she called up a blade of pure flame in her right hand while she held the unconscious girl against her with her left. "You will land alone, old man, or I will kill your heir here and now. I know there are no others from your line with even a fraction of the magic she has, think carefully about your next move." Her black wings lifted and beat against the air to emphasize her words, not strong enough to lift her into the air, just enough to crack a thump of air.

The two rulers just stared at each other, neither daring to make a move. Ezra had to know that Driamati would level the tower around her if she harmed Clornamti, but the king knew that his granddaughter was surely dead if he made the first move. Something had to give, something had to change the scales.

Charles drew from his pool quickly, throwing the magic in its raw form straight into his bindings. With a burst, he tore free from the rope and called forth two great lances of magic to impale the two guards before they ever had a chance to recognize what he was doing. Screaming, he threw Darl's hand at Ezra and set his will against hers. He pulled hard against the woman's body before she could react and nearly lost it when he saw Clornamti drop into the open air around the tower. Driamati acted as soon as he realized what was happening. He let go a spell he must have readied long before he had taken wing, shouting for his subordinates to rescue the princess. A storm roared into existence outside the tower, the result of Driamati's casting. Lightning flashed amongst the clouds and thunder boomed. The air hummed with the energy of the storm, creating conditions favorable to the magic of the Oberon. Rain fell in great drops all around the plain where Heimili álfa stretched, snuffing out some of the smaller fires and causing others to leap and dance in protest.

Ezra blasted free of Charles' spell by force, throwing him back into the wall as his own magic recoiled and struck him. Shrieking, she sent numerous lances of fire sailing directly toward him, but Charles managed to throw up a shield. The small trickle of power surged forward and forced the lances out wide. Two of them collided with the wall near him, sending flames rushing into the wood of the tower. The others struck the Harpies nearest him, killing two out right and wounding several others before the magic faded.

Driamati and the remaining escort burst into the tower, each of them sending a blast of air into a Harpy or at Ezra herself before drawing their swords and landing to engage them hand to hand. The bursts were enough to knock most of the Harpies from their feet, but Ezra merely crossed her wrists in front of her and ignored them. The blade of fire reappeared in her hand as she beat her wings downward and sailed directly for the Oberon king, just as he launched another assault with his magic. The air before her seemed to solidify into a great fist that slammed into her body and sent her careening back to the floor, but she was far from out. She shrieked to her assembled Harpies and flashed her empty hand before her, signaling them to attack. Bursts of flame erupted around the room, creating a great updraft of hot air. The Oberon who were still airborne found that their flight was suddenly easier, but the room didn't allow space for the surge in upward motion. No less than a dozen of the flying Oberon collided with the ceiling, hard, before crashing to the floor in heaps.

Ezra's sword flashed right and left as she killed the Oberon nearest her, moving too quickly for a creature of her size. More flames shot from her empty hand as she launched into the air toward Driamati. One of his guards attempted to intercept her, but the flames she released coalesced into a single blazing line, bifurcating the hapless Oberon and leaving clear the path to the king. There was a great showering of sparks as his steel blade began to heat and shift color, absorbing the heat of her sword of pure fire. Sweat beaded along the Oberon king's brow as his sword worked through the forms, each blow deepening the color of his blade to the cherry of superheated iron. His wings buzzed as they bobbed through the air on the erratic flight of two swordsmen dancing in their struggle. Ezra's great bird wings flapped a steady beat as she hovered, tucking close to her when she needed them and lashing out to force her body up with a near perfect rhythm.

His guards sought an opening in the flashing blades but the swords were moving in every direction, to blunder in there now would surely mean death for someone and it was just as likely to be Driamati as Ezra. Charles ducked under a pair of dueling warriors as he sought the relative safety of the balcony. He hoped to catch some glimpse of Clornamti, but he never dreamed he would see another battle raging around him. The Harpies had concentrated their forces about the tower and now waged a fierce aerial struggle with the Oberon who had escorted Driamati to the tower. Blasts of air from the Oberon met jets of flames. He could see no sign of Clornamti or her escort, he only hoped that they had cleared the conflict before it had escalated. Those hopes were dashed when a Harpy burst through the raging storm, bearing the still form of the Oberon girl. He could do nothing against the creature that wouldn't result in Clornamti tumbling to the earth far below. Two Oberon pursued the Harpy, but they were forced to dodge rapid blasts of fire that kept them from closing the gap between them.

The Harpy banked hard into the wind and dove for the balcony, tucking its wings close to its body to reduce its drag.

Charles readied himself and charted the progress of the dive as the great chestnut wings flashed open to slow its decent. The instant the creature was over the balcony, he let loose with an arc of raw magic that took the Harpy's head from its shoulders and dropped the body from the air. He dove beneath the creature just before it struck and wrapped himself around Clornamti to cushion her fall. The three of them crashed to the tiles of the balcony in a tangle of limbs and blood as the headless Harpy dropped onto the top of their pile. Charles wrenched himself and Clornamti free of the dead creature and pulled them both to the edge of the balcony.

    She didn't bear any new damage, but she was still unconscious. He had never attempted to heal another, but he prayed to all the Arcana that he could do so now. He reached into the pockets within his robe and drew out a thin oak branch to use as a focus. He channeled his power into a spell of healing, as a Druid would. With the limitation of the focus, the magic seemed thin and foreign to him. If he had carried something more firmly tied to Gelthar it would have been clearer, but it was not practical to walk about with a tree upon one's back.

    Her injuries were numerous, but nonlethal. Almost all her injuries were likely something she could ignore if given the power to do so, but the head injury practically sang with the pain of it. A great swelling within her skull pressed against her brain as the blood pulsated into the injury. He had to stop the leak of her life blood and reduce the swelling or it was likely she would never wake. His senses were foggy and he longed to have more magic to draw from, but it couldn't be helped. With the thin trickle of energy he had, he applied the healing to the small vein within her skull and allowed it to seal. The pocket of fluids pressing on her skull proved to be the real challenge. He couldn't wait for her body to absorb them on its own, the battle around them meant that he couldn't just leave her to sleep it off.

He withdrew from her, breaking his connection as he did so. He carefully drew directly from his pool and crafted a small lance of magic in the air before him. Gently, he applied the lance to the back of her skull where he knew the swelling to be and set it spinning. With a modicum of control, he bored a small hole into the base of her skull until the fluid began to leak out. He withdrew his drill and tore the sleeve from his undershirt to fashion a bandage of the cleanest cloth he had. Using his power once more, he healed the hole in her skull before dabbing the blood out of her hair.

He lay her head upon his lap and checked the pulse in her neck. It was slow, but she still lived. As he drew his hand away, her eyes fluttered open and began scanning the room before settling on his face. "Where are we?"

"In Vielk's chamber, your Grandfather is fighting Ezra. I have to go help, will you be alright?" He didn't want to leave her exposed on the balcony, but Ezra had to be stopped.

"Go," she told him, "Help Grandfather. End this!"

He lay her onto the tiles of the balcony as gently as he could and stood to face the raging battle within the tower.

Ezra and Driamati clashed in the air, dashing back and forth across the space with swords swirling magic in every direction. Driamati overcame the fire from Ezra's blade by summoning a whirlwind of his own magic to bleed the heat away. Each strike of their weapons sent a hot blast of air in the direction of their momentum. The room was heating up from the fire that licked its walls and the battle being waged over the heads of the Harpies and Oberon. Charles flung himself back into the battle, drawing on his magic and his training. His shield whorled around him, deflecting swords and blasts of fire alike while he shot thin lances of magic into the Harpies. The tiny shots took little from his pool, the conservation of his magic came naturally now. These smaller shots had to be carefully aimed, more so than the large lances he had used on his guards. He likened the practice to something like archery, each arrow of magic aimed like a shaft from a bow.

With Charles' help, the Oberon turned the tide of the battle within the tower in their favor. The bodies of Harpies were scattered all over the room, though they weren't alone. Many of the defenders lay with them, joined in death as they never would have in life. The battle above their heads grew fiercer as the two combatants sought some edge over the other. Charles had never seen a spectacle of swordplay such as this, with the limited exception of the sparring matches between Aurin and his master, Samuel Dorne but his friend never bore the mask of rage. Driamati turned one attack from his body, a bare fingertip from his chest before countering with a swipe of his cyclonic sword. Ezra fought with pure hate. Her blade slashed and cut viscously, slamming into Driamati's blade and driving him around the ceiling. She looked frustrated, much as Charles had when he tried to learn the sword from Aurin. She didn't seem to be able to defeat his guard, each of her attacks violently collided with his swirling weapon. In turn, his counterstrokes were reserved, never striking out far from his body. His face was dripping with sweat, but Charles couldn't say if it was the heat of the room or the exertion of the fight. Driamati's shoulders drooped and his blocks came slower and slower. Charles could see the man's radiance was quickly vanishing as his shield turned more and more of the attacks instead of his whirling sword.

The fires throughout the room had reached the ceiling's apex, quickly heating and cracking the glass of the mirrors that lined the sun shaft. With a great shutter, the mirrors shattered and split along the faults created by the heat. Taking advantage of the sudden distraction, Ezra launched into a series of attacks too fast for Charles to follow. Driamati was forced back until another clash of blades threw his arms wide. His eyes flashed open with shock as Ezra spun her blade within his guard and drove it straight through his shield. Hissing, the flaming sword burst from Driamati's back. Ezra shrieked with delight as she ripped the magical sword free of the Oberon's body, then spit into the old man's face as his arms dropped limply to his sides and his wings stopped buzzing. Grunting unceremoniously, Driamati, King of the Oberon nation, died. As the old king's body collided with the floor, millions of glimmering shards rained down from the ceiling of the room.

Aflame

Towers burned in the distance as Ardelle hugged Charles' sword to herself and dashed for the last place she had seen him. Aurin had entrusted his friend with her and so far, she hadn't been much of a protector. Winged figures darted through the air all about the city, the Oberon outnumbered their foes, but there were still many harpies flinging fire throughout the city.

An unnatural storm had briefly drenched the pavement around her, but the heat of the day had returned and the clouds were rapidly dissipating. She guessed Driamati had called the storm to aid his soldiers, but why had he stopped before the fires were out?

She broke into a run, pulling deeply on her magic to fuel her muscles. It was dangerous to use Betala's gift in such a way, the magic could burn through her energy reserves faster than her body could replenish it. If she pushed too hard, for too long, her muscles would simply burn away. She had little choice, it was her only hope of reaching the Charles in time to help. She knew that with Betala she could cover the distance in a heartbeat, but she couldn't bring herself to call out for her mistress now, not when she was this vulnerable. The thought of giving herself over to the Arcana now was abhorrent. The forest had been far more of a challenge and Betala never came to her there, why did she need the Arcana now? A sudden lance of fire brought her to attention. She fled from the cobblestone street and gathered herself to retaliate but it had just been a stray shot from a Harpy that had already moved on. The attackers weren't interested in a pitched battle, they were only sewing terror. Buildings burned around her, though most of the fires were small. The towers bore the brunt of the assault, one had even toppled from the hungry flames that licked its corpse. Charles' sword hummed against her as she pulled more on the flames from the buildings around her, drawing their energy into her body. She knew it had some kind of enchantment that enhanced the magic of the wielder, but without knowing the extent of its powers, she didn't dare risk using it.

"Ardelle?" A husky voice called from a nearby stall. Omesh was huddled with several other "land-bound," behind a large barrel filled with sooty water. The others with him were strangers, but the shop was familiar. She had passed it idly the day before, her eyes roaming over the trinkets of gold and silver. She guessed that the wizened Solterran with the deep black eyes was the goldsmith that operated this particular booth and the fresh faces of the others led her to believe they were his apprentices. "What are you doing here?"

"My friend is still in the city, I was trying to get back to him." She scanned the skies once more before stepping into the booth.

"Dyak, this is the woman I was telling you about, the one that helped me make the sword." The big smith stepped up to extend his hand in greeting, an odd action given the state of things around them. "I can't thank you enough for what you did, I've already gotten a commission from the guard for six dozen of their curved blades. That's enough to keep me fed for the next two years!"

"That's wonderful, but I can't stay Omesh. My friend is in the city and I need to get to him." She turned to leave, but Omesh quickly grabbed her hand.

"I understand, but I have something for you!" He reached under the table he had been hiding behind and pulled out a carefully wrapped bundle. The fabric binding his gift was exquisite, and its length and apparent weight gave it away as the sword she had helped him forge. "Dyak finished this just before the attacks started, he used his magic to cure the metal so that I could have it today."

"It was much too fine for me to just leave for another day." The old man admitted from his hiding place, a smile playing on his lips despite the fear in his eyes.

"I must confess that I haven't slept since you left my forge, I even dragged the poor man out of bed to finish it."

Her curiosity finally peaked, she drew the fabric away from the hilt and marveled at what she saw. Gold inlay chased around the hilt in the shape of a serpentine dragon winding its way to the blade, until its head crested the hilt and breathed a column of stylized fire onto the curved steel. The inlays were lined with runes, all in Solterran script depicting the very essence of fire, its consumptive nature and the life it brought to the world. The runes glowed at her touch and when she removed her hand, they had been infused with Betala's magic as well.

A ruby rested in the pommel, gleaming dully in the light of the sun. The stone must have been worth a fortune, it was not the common red stone that one would see about the neck of a noblewoman, but a blood ruby. Blood rubies were only mined from a single mountain deep within Gremen lands and only a handful ever left there. The stones were quite popular among the church of Betala, at least they had been in her time, due to their color and their properties concerning fire. Still, she had never seen one this large before.

"It's yours," Omesh told her. "I couldn't think of anyone more worthy of having it, and given that you put a piece of yourself into the crafting, it seems right that you should take it."

"I couldn't take this Omesh, the stone alone must be worth a fortune." She turned the blade over in her hands, losing herself in the facets of the flashing ruby.

"The stone is my gift to our Mistress' Avatar," the old Solterran stated solemnly. "It is my hope that you can bring sanity back to the church that has gone so far from the teachings of Betala."

She started to ask what he meant, but an explosion drove them all from their feet. An enormous ball of fire had struck the building next to them and rendered it to splinters. Shrapnel from the building struck the goldsmith's shop, with some striking those huddled inside. More explosions sounded around the city and a deep rumbling thundered out from the direction of the temple tower, the last place she had seen Charles. "I have to go, my friend was in there." She attempted to hand the sword back, but he shook his head.

"The sword is yours, and if you are going into that mess you are going to need it." He smiled at her once more, "Grandfather would insist you take it." He produced a scabbard from the table, its gold inlay matching that on the blade. With deft, experienced hands, he tied the new sword into the same baldric as Charles' sword, it was only then that she remembered her original mission.

"The sword!" she blurted, wrenching Charles' sword free of its scabbard. "This is the sword you were telling me about, isn't it? The sword that Omar made?"

Omesh scrambled to look at the base of the blade for a stylized flame moniker, Omar's smith's mark. "This is it! How do you have it?"

"It is a long story, but I promise someday I will tell you all about it. Right now I have to go, will you keep that sword safe for me? I can't use it and it will just be in the way."

"I will protect it with my life, to see my grandfather's work like this has been something I dreamed about my entire life." She couldn't be certain if the tear she saw streak his face was from the thought of a dream fulfilled, or the smoke from the shop next to them, but she was pretty sure she knew.

Quickly, she reached for the flames of the shop next to them and used it to fuel her muscles for another run. If she had concentrated on the fire, she could snuff out the flames altogether, but she didn't have time to do that. It pained her to leave the shop burning, but she had to get to Charles. The temple tower was shorn at the top by the last explosion, exposing what been the temple proper to the full light of the sun and displaying the carnage there for all to see. Where the altar had once rested, there was a single corpse staked to the wall, burning away under the magic of a pair of Harpies.

She pulled harder on the flames around her, pushing the magic out behind her with enough force to fling her dozens of strides at a time. With this push, she covered the distance between her and the cluster of towers that ringed the courtyard where she was supposed to meet Charles, but he wasn't in sight. She could see the litter that was to bear him away in the center of the practice field, but the majority of its escort was gone. Two lone Oberon fought to keep the harpies away from the parade grounds, but it was a losing battle. It dawned on her that Clornamti would likely have been in the temple's tower attending her studies. There was no way he would have left her there.

She drew heavily on the magic she had stored and leapt for the tower in one great burst of speed, but stumbled and struck the cobblestones. A pressure began at the back of her skull as she rolled to a stop and tried to leap back into her run. Betala was calling her, urgently now. The pull had been insistent before, but nothing like this. Her mistress was demanding attention and Ardelle could hardly keep her thoughts about her. If this continued she would go mad, she didn't know how long it would take for her mind to slip away, but the pressure was painful. She could barely keep a link to the magic she had left with the assault on her concentration.

She pulled more flames from the buildings around her, but couldn't hold it and dropped to her knees screaming wordlessly. She clutched at her head, but couldn't drive Betala out. She feared that the pressure would drive any semblance of sanity from her and forever strip what humanity she had reclaimed. She fought with everything she had to hold the Arcana back, but in the end she just didn't have the will to stop a being of Betala's strength. She finally surrendered and allowed the Arcana in, instantly washing away in a torrent of magic from her mistress. She had experienced this many times in the years before her banishment, but it had been different then. She had been more willing to submit to the will of her mistress. This time felt more like an invasion, an alien presence defiling her personality.

Why do you resist me, daughter? The thoughts pressed against Ardelle's consciousness. *Why have you ignored me?* Her body started to slip from her control as the Arcana took over. She lost the ability to move her legs first, then her arms. As the power washed over her, she had little choice but to slip into that disconnected place between asleep and awake.

You left me. Ardelle conveyed.

A wave of pity crashed about her. *I am sorry daughter, I could not undo what that monster did and without you, I could not intervene here.* She could feel the pain amongst the thoughts. *We will stop him, starting with the fallen ones here.*

Why did no one come for me? She begged of her mistress.

A deep sadness overwhelmed all other sensations. *Some did try, but in the end no one could breach the forest. There were those that felt it best that you were gone, those that believed Barrah's lies about me losing my power. Those voices were the loudest. I'm afraid I've little influence among the mortals any longer.*

Ardelle felt a rush of power and pulled her mind back to the world around them, her body expanding. Betala was pulling all of the heat and flames into their combined essence and using it to expand their energy into a giant flaming creature. Her flesh wasn't expanding, just the awareness of her body as her senses extended out into the fire about her. Soon she towered over the surrounding city in a body made almost entirely of flames.

The man you met is from the new church, an abomination of my teachings that puts the Harpies at the top of their hierarchy. Ezra has taken my place as the focus of their worship, guiding them on paths that take them closer to Barrah. We must stop her. I feel her close. That is why I forced myself upon you.

Betala stretched out her power, leeching strength from buildings farther away. She redirected this energy into balls of fire that she aimed at any Harpy she could see. Alerted to this new presence, Harpies darted at her, knowing who she was. They tried their own fire but it was useless to her new body and their talons couldn't pierce the flames. Some tried to pull the fire away from her, but Betala was master of fire and their wills paled in comparison. Everywhere a Harpy flew, a jet of flame shot from Betala and consumed the creatures so completely that no feathers lit upon the earth. Betala pulled at all of the largest flames within the city and channeled their heat and energy up into the sky. A great pillar of fire lit the area with such light that most turned their heads from it. It roared with such ferocity that Ardelle was left without any other sound. With the bulk of the flames gone, Betala began to release those that comprised her body. Ardelle's awareness shrank as she felt her feet returning to the earth.

The remaining Harpies fled, but a few still gathered about one tower, their center occupied by a single, black-winged Harpy that both Ardelle and Betala immediately recognized.

Bridge

Charles ducked another streak of fire and pulled Clornamti close behind him. They were still in the main tower but where, he didn't know. They left the mirror chamber as soon as the Driamati collapsed but were quickly turned around in the confusion. Even Clornamti, who had spent most of her life in this tower seemed lost, though her injuries were enough that confusion was a given. More Harpies flooded in to protect their queen the instant Driamati fell, driving the remaining members of his guard back into the air around the tower. Two particularly determined bird-women had chased them from the mirrored chamber throughout the halls of the tower. Though she still didn't know about her grandfather, Clornamti knew that something had changed the tide of the battle against them. He didn't dare stop and tell her what had happened, she would need to know soon enough, but getting Clornamti away from the creatures was the only thought driving him.

He could turn and fight the two that chased them, but he couldn't guarantee Clornamti would remain safe in the ensuing struggle. There was a risk she would be hit by a stray bolt of fire or get caught by the raking talons of a Harpy. He wished he had more courage, but his only thought was to run. If the Avatar of Vielk could be felled by one of these creatures, what chance did he stand against them? True, he had killed many in that room, but they had been distracted by the Oberon and it hadn't been a fair fight. There were no distractions out here, nothing to turn them away from their pursuit or allow him to strike from cover.

They were on the outer ring of the tower now, he could see the sunlight shining in through the multitude of windows that hadn't shattered. Broken glass littered the ramp as he ran, causing his shoes to slip and slide as he struggled for purchase. The Harpies appeared again, loping along behind them with the grace of an Oberon. More fire blasted forth and he knew he couldn't dodge this one.

He hurled Clornamti ahead of him on the ramp and threw a shield of magic between himself and the attackers. It was a larger shield than he had ever attempted before, and it was completely from raw magic. He had no focus with which he could direct a shield of this size, he could only rely on the training Clornamti had given him and sheer will.

The flames roared as they struck, but the shield held them back. The Harpies shrieked in unison, raising their hands to send more fire at him. Strengthening the shield as best he could, he lashed out with another stream of magic, striking the right Harpy with a solid bar of pure magic, the same spell he had used in the mirror chamber. The spell was difficult to deflect, harder still if you weren't already shielding yourself when it was cast. By keeping the magic pure, instead of attuning it to an element, you limited the ability of any elemental mage from stopping it. The Harpies' power was deeply rooted in fire, and as such offered little protection against his spell. The bar pierced the Harpy's chest and drove the beast from the tower, its tattered carcass fluttering out into the open air as it sailed to the ground.

Its partner shrieked at the loss of its comrade, but kept up its attack on Charles' shield. Fire poured from the creature as it slowly marched toward his shield. It was too late for the creature, though it didn't know it. Charles entrapped the thing in his shield, then collapsed the spell in on itself. His magic crushed the Harpy where it stood, snuffing out its magic as its body compressed under the weight of his spell. His training had paid off, he had used magic to kill, though he felt no joy in the outcome.

He turned to Clornamti and was pleased to see she remained whole. Shocked was etched on her face, but didn't deter her from grabbing his hand again and pulling him back along their path up the tower. They had tried to leave via the tunnels at the base of the spire, but the entirety of the ground floor was aflame. He feared that the tower would crumble at the loss of its foundation, but Clornamti had seemed sure that they were safe, for now. The tower had magical safeguards that fire couldn't break, at least not until the rest of the tower broke.

The brief fight left him winded, working in raw magic was a lot more difficult than attuning his spells to any single element. Raw magic was Ven's domain, but even his avatars always used a focus to change the magic into something more recognizable as a natural element. The Oberon schooled him in working the raw power, but they were shocked at how capable he was with it. Not one of his training partners could have held that shield while directing the bolt of energy. Most wouldn't have even been able to shield the entire hall. Truthfully before he had done it, he didn't think he could either.

"I know where we are now." Clornamti told him as she pulled him into an alcove off of the outer balcony. "We are about halfway up the tower. If I was alone I would just jump from here, but I can't leave you by yourself." She turned her brown eyes on him. "There is a landing about three stories up. There may be other Oberon there that could help me carry you down."

Charles had trouble listening, she was very close. They had to press against each other to fit into the alcove, it hadn't been made for people. Its previous occupant, an oversized statue of an Oberon warrior, was smashed onto the tiles next to them. He could feel her breath on his neck, and he could feel her racing heart against his chest through their thin Oberon clothing. She was very close, and very beautiful.

He shook his head. "If you can get out, you should go. I would feel better knowing you were safe at least." He tried to keep the subject on anything but their closeness. It was terrible that his mind had found that avenue, given the tragedy that she still didn't know about, but he couldn't help it. "I can go for the landing alone and find a way down from there."

She stared into his eyes again, the pools of hers told far more than her words. "I'm not leaving you alone. I know how easily you get lost in here. We go together, or we stay in this tiny hole until the Harpies leave."

It wasn't until then that he realized she had shielded the opening to the alcove. He had been too enamored with her to notice the spell. He was in trouble, he had to keep his wits but didn't know if he could with her so close. "Fine, we'll make for the landing together. On the condition that if we get into trouble, you escape."

"No," she stated fiercely. "We go together for the landing, no conditions."

"Alright," he sighed. Anything she asked of him, he would give her. He wanted her to be safe and the arrogant part of his mind insisted that the safest place was with him. His inner coward argued against it, but he really wasn't making the decision.

"Together then," she grabbed his hand and lowered her shield.

They rushed along the balcony, eyes trained to the sky where packs of Harpies burned with impunity and lone Oberon sought to stop them. The majority of the city's defenses had scattered after Driamati's fall and Ezra had taken advantage of their confusion. Charles could see masses of Oberon gathering in the distance, but it would take time for someone to assume leadership of the forces. Eventually, the warriors would drive the Harpies from the city, while any other able-bodied Oberon would help with the fires, but would it be soon enough to save them?

A sudden flare of brilliant light stopped them both cold. A huge creature was massing down in the city. Flames leapt from the buildings around the creature as it swelled to unbelievable proportions. As the flames pulled in, the fires within the buildings were blown out. It continued pulling in the fire until the mass of it was nearly as large as the guard towers that ringed the city. For a brief moment, the accumulation of flames just sat in a sphere within the grounds of the city, but soon it began to stretch out. Two flaming legs pushed the center of the inferno from the ground while two arms dropped loose. The conflagration stood from the courtyard, stretching out its mass until a torso and head were clearly visible. The humanoid fire tightened and firmed until it resembled a woman, one that sparked recognition within Charles. This was no foe, it was Ardelle.

The creature stretched out a huge, flaming hand to the nearest Harpy and snuffed it from existence. Other Harpies turned and winged toward the monster, but their magic was useless against it. Ardelle, still enlarged, marched toward the city center, pulling more fire with her as she went. More Harpies were incinerated as they vainly attempted to stop her. The battle, if one could call it that, was over quickly. The Harpies, seeing they had no chance against this creature, quickly flew from the scene. Those that weren't fast enough, Ardelle struck from the sky.

Slack-jawed, Charles turned to Clornamti who shared his expression. Most of the Harpies had fled, though a few still gathered about the farthest towers continued their attack, keeping their bodies behind the towers and out of sight of their attacker. The Ardelle creature roared and turned her hands skyward. A pillar of flame leapt from her hands, draining the fire away from her body and out of the city. She began to recede and vanished from Charles' sight, along with the pillar. As the light faded, a band of the bird women swooped from the tower below him, Ezra's black wings beating at the center of their pack. They moved in unison to where Ardelle had vanished between the buildings.

"What in the world?" Clornamti asked.

"I think that was Ardelle," Charles admitted and immediately regretted it.

"How could that possibly be your friend?" Clornamti pressed, "is she truly that powerful?"

"She could be…" he whispered, then let the thought drop. "We can't worry about it now, she didn't get rid of all the fire. We still need to get out of this tower!" A deep groan and a violent shaking stirred from deep within the tower. The Harpies had destroyed the magical wards holding the tower aloft before they had fled.

"Come on!" she shouted and grabbed at his hand again.

They ran up the balcony, the opposite direction his screaming instincts told him to run. His base desire was to run for the lowest floor of the tower, but his higher brain knew that was a mistake. There would be no exit down there, the Harpies had destroyed most of the bottom three floors to this tower. From the shaking, he guessed that even the structural supports had succumbed to their magic.

As they approached the landing, they weren't alone. Many of the Humans, Solterrans and even one big Tu'rokian stood about the landing, all sharing the same expression as they frantically tried to escape. There were no other Oberon here.

The big Tu'roki spoke first, in his deep, booming voice. "Where are the others, little girl?" The shell that covered the majority of his body was covered with tattoos in their alien language, a strange collection of symbols to represent word phrases and ideas. Charles knew enough Tu'rokian to know that this one was a priest of Ori, the Arcana of Life. The huge Tu'roki's stunted legs were covered by the stylized skirt that both genders of their race wore, though Charles was sure they didn't call it a skirt. His big, three-fingered hands were clenched at his sides, near the clan standard typical of their dress. "Well?"

"They should be here," Clornamti started. "The first step in our evacuation has always been to get the land-folk clear of the tower. I don't understand!" She was searching the sky around the landing, trying to spot any Oberon that could help. There was no way she could carry any of these people down on her own.

"Well us land-folk are trapped here!" a full-blooded Solterran spoke up. He was the first full-blood Charles had ever seen, but his lineage was clear. His hairless body was the color of wet granite. His eyes were simply black orbs, no pupil or iris as with human eyes. The robes he wore were of the order of Brokoom, the Arcana of Stone and patron to the Solterrans.

A thought struck Charles and was confirmed as he looked around the platform. Every person here was a priest, acolyte, or some other official of an Arcana. These were not simple land-folk who got trapped in a tower. They had been here for a specific purpose and likely were of great importance to their respective groups. Each Arcana had their mortal followers, and from the looks of those gathered, many were represented here. These were the coalition leaders he had heard of, the great priests and war leaders that meant to strike south and aid Aurin and the refugees.

The Tu'roki was a priest of Ori, the Solterran of Brokoom. A human man wore robes covered in the glyphs common amongst the priesthood of Mamrix, the Arcana of knowledge. A tall human woman with a thin face and nary a stitch on was a follower of Mormia, the Arcana of Light. Her priests were often unclothed so that their bodies could feel the light of Mormia everywhere, but when in the presence of the general population they typically wore thin white clothing that did little to hide their features, but was enough for modesty's sake.

Chelan, the Arcana of Water had his priest, a blue-green clad human. Sozenra, the Arcana of Valor, was represented by a grizzled old warrior in his battle-worn chain armor and a well-used sword at his hip.

Every person on the landing, with the exception of the warrior, also glowed in Charles' other sight. Their radiances were varied in color and strength, but each of them could use magic to some degree.

The more he stared at the others around the tower, the clearer it was that he had seen them all before. He was terrible with names, but he was sure the Tu'roki was the same that Ardelle had spoken with at the ball and the others had been there as well. This was the delegation from the new coalition force, all of them.

"It's not her fault we're trapped, Haldon. Driamati brought us up here, he should have seen to getting us down." The priest of Mamrix interjected. The sudden mention of the Oberon king sent a pang of guilt through Charles, but he still couldn't risk telling Clornamti. Another violent quake of the tower affirmed his need to keep the tragedy to himself for at least a little longer.

"Clornamti, you need to go," Charles told his companion. "There is no reason for you to stay and risk your life with the rest of us." She turned to look at him, tears filled her brown eyes. "Just go," he affirmed.

She shook her loose hair, "No! I will not leave you here. There has to be a way!" She turned back to the sky around the tower.

He pulled her back to him. "Go, before it is too late."

The tears ran freely down her smooth features, "I... I can't!"

He started to respond, but a pressure within his skull caused his hands to shoot up to his temples involuntarily. It was similar to the voice he had fought against in Hudcoeden, so he initially pushed against it, but it became clear that it wasn't the same voice. There were no words with this pressure, a presence yes, but no words. It was oddly calming, given that he was standing on the precipice of a falling tower with no hope of escape. He allowed the presence into his mind and felt something pulling at his memories.

Spells rolled through Charles' mind. He hadn't bid them to come to him, but they were there just the same. His spell from the first trial with the Druids flowed from his memories, a spell that moved a chair instantly from one place to another. Other spells accompanied it, the bridge he had raised to cross the river in the forest, the healing spell he had used on himself after the creature attacked him in Ven's cave, and more complex rituals he had read while staying there. They seemed random at first, but they began to coalesce into a tangible spell he could use to travel. The last image that appeared was the rune he had seen within Falderal, the one that had carried them here.

The pressure ceased and he was back on the balcony. Clornamti held his hands, staring into his eyes, shouting. "Charles! Are you alright?" In her panic, she had used his real name.

"I'm fine," he managed then turned to the assembled priests. "Everyone stand at the back of the hall!" He dropped to the floor, etching the rune he would need to complete the ritual. He had few foci with him, but he had a group of priests that could potentially serve the same role. The rune complete, he turned back to the group, just as the tower quaked again then lurched sideways. His time was running out.

"I think I can get us out of here," he shouted over the groaning of the tower, "but I'm going to need your help." He quickly laid out the plan and moved everyone into position. The tower had stopped its fall, but he had no way of knowing for how long.

Sighing, he delved into his pool of magic, pouring everything he had into the binding of the rune at his feet. Using small trickles of the massive energy, he connected each priest back to him as he moved through the phases of the ritual. First, he created the 'bridge,' though unlike the physical entity he had created in the forest, this was a bridge of power. He used Clornamti's attunement to Vielk, it wasn't perfect as she wasn't a dedicated priest, but it was enough. Through the magic of the ritual, he could see the rune in that small room down on the grounds of the old city. Next, he created the bond between those present, so that they could travel together using the link to Ori that the Tu'roki presented. The weave of this magic was based on his self-healing spell. He knew it wasn't perfect for this application, but it was the only one he had.

The final pieces of the first ritual came from the priestess of Mormia. Her power allowed him to tap into the sunlight shining down on them, offering a source to maintain the spell once he was in it. He finished off the last of the bridge spell with a sealing that would maintain the circle indefinitely, though if the tower came down it would be useless. The rune on the floor would have to remain intact to function.

Next, he moved into the traveling itself. It was one thing to bridge two places together, it was quite another to shift living things between them without them passing through the space between the points. He had done the spell once before, but that was a chair. If it didn't come through, you had a broken chair. These were living people.

There was no focus for this ritual, all of the power came from Ven and he was the best equipped to channel that energy. He reached out again, pulling in the loose magic not necessary to maintain the first ritual, gathering it about the grizzled warrior. It was a cruel decision, but the man had clearly lived far longer than any other here and Charles allowed his conscience to take solace in that.

He memorized the positions of the different pieces of the man's body, all the way to the very essence of his individual parts. The sparkling of dots that made up everything if you looked hard enough through the filter of magic. With this map, he built his ritual into the bridge. The connection between the places sang with the power he poured into it, the runes at either end glowing with anticipation. He gave the man one more look with his normal eyes and nodded to him. The old warrior understood what was behind that nod and returned it, the man knew what decision had been made.

Charles let the magic envelop him, and released the spell that swarmed about the warrior. The man's body vanished to the naked eye, but through his magic he could see the specks swirl into the bridge and shoot to the far side. They were small enough that they passed through everything between the balcony and the building at the other end. Nothing would impede him.

At the far end, the essence coalesced into the man and he was whole again. With a sigh of relief, Charles began his ritual again with the priest of Chelan. He continued until only he, Clornamti and the priest of Ori remained. With a sickening lurch, the tower supports gave out and the tower began to fall in earnest. From the corner of his eye, he could see the surrounding towers rushing to meet them.

He dove back into the magic and threw it at the priest just as they collided with the first tower. The bridge between the sites strained under the rapidly increasing distance and he could see the essence of the priest struggle to maintain its course. He wiped out his reserve of power for the second time in his life, forcing the bridge to maintain cohesion long enough for the priest to make the other end. His body began to crumble where he stood but Clornamti wrapped his thin frame in her arms and leapt from the balcony with all the muscle her legs could muster. Once free of the building, her diaphanous wings blurred into motion, buzzing as they fluttered faster than his eyes could follow. Their descent wasn't halted by her efforts, even though he was thin of frame, he was still too heavy for her to fly on her own. They maintained a downward motion, but she managed to slow them with her efforts.

He struggled to maintain his hold on reality as the ground rushed to meet them but it was no use, he had expended too much of his power. Just as in the forest, and again in the ruins of Falderal, his spent body needed to recover. He slipped from the waking world as he felt the first impact with the ground in his legs.

Justice

Crowlmer checked the blades in her scabbards again, they were as clear as they had been a moment ago when she had last checked them. Aurin smiled at her as mirrored her movements. She hadn't seen a true smile on his face since they first reached the camp, after his injuries and the ups and downs of his recovery he had been demure to a fault. It was good to see him hale and hearty again, but she worried what this battle would bring for him. The last one had left him comatose and in so much pain that she hadn't been able to bear being near him. This battle was on par with the last, with the added problem of their terrain. At the river, they at least believed the far side had been clear, here there was no such illusion. They were surrounded and penned into this tiny valley with the remaining wolves on one side and the Demon horde on the other.

Her men had rallied to clear their rear of the wolves, but there were still more than fifty of the creatures making hit and run attacks against their lines. They had no organizing force, but they kept the level of panic high enough to have the civilians ready to bolt if someone shouted 'boo.' She left the men to the work, feeling that her blades were better served here, especially after she learned that Aurin was to take the field after all.

She hadn't given herself over to any feelings of fondness to the young man, but he was the only one that didn't look at her with wide eyes. He treated her as he treated anyone else he encountered, with respect and kindness. Where others saw only her physical changes, Aurin seemed to only see her for who she had always been. Of course, he did this with everyone else so she shouldn't feel singled out, but it was hard not to feel special when someone like him called her a friend.

They stood on the crude northern rampart of the camp, near the center of the defenses. The ramparts themselves were only constructed this morning, thrown together from anything the refugees could find. To their credit, the craftsmen of Hudcoeden had given them solid footing to shoot bows from, but it wouldn't stand against the press of bodies for long.

The eastern ramparts were slightly better, having been constructed to guard their rear when they had settled into this area but they still weren't a stone wall.

Aurin insisted that they not participate in the command of the forces, claiming that he was better use here on the front line. With the power within him again, she knew that he could lay waste to vast swaths of the enemy but he refused to consider using his power that way. His face had fallen and his eyes had taken a haunted look when she even suggested the magic to him. He was going to face this battle as a warrior, on his feet with his sword in his hand, to prove to himself that the power hadn't corrupted him completely.

The Demons had arrayed themselves in standard battle lines just out of bow shot from the bulk of the army. Their primary force was made up of the violet skinned humanoid Demons and their taken handlers. Thousands of them stood in ranks before them, more than she had ever seen in a single place. Even during their campaigns with the Barric forces in the south, she had never seen more than a few hundred of the demons in the army. The primary troops in the southern forces had been Og'rai, the massive mountain dwellers who once held dominion over most of the world, and the reason Howlter joined with the army in the first place. There were no Og'rai visible today.

On the flanks of the demons stood a breed she had never encountered in any large force, only in passing. Large, dark skinned half-men, half-scorpions, the Karrekren, made up the skirmisher force. Karrekren were from the wastes of the east, somewhere beyond the great sea. They traveled in mercenary bands, serving whoever could afford their fees. In battle they were a nightmare, their upper torsos swinging great two-handed swords and maces while their lower bodies attacked with two huge claws. No standard cavalry had ever stood their ground against them, given their penchant for taking the legs from any horses they met. To have so many of the creatures on the field today spoke of an alliance of some kind with their nation, there were nearly a hundred of them present.

Above the force were a token escort of the bird-winged Harpies, enough to present a marginal defense if the refugees suddenly learned to fly. Crowlmer hated the Harpies, she never had much respect for creatures that never spoke the truth. Their long history of breaking their word didn't lend much credibility to them. It was said that they would sooner lie to your face than save another's life. Before she had met them personally, she had idealized them for their flight and the freedom it gave them but after serving with them, her opinion of them fell.

The human Guard from Hudcoeden made up the defensive line on the northern rampart, Samuel Dorne at their head. They had a little more than one thousand armed men and women with them, plus a few hundred on horse. Gremen irregulars backed their lines, not the well trained core of Howlter's forces, but still they were warriors. Behind the armies stood the militia. Formed just this morning, carpenters, smiths, farmers, and bakers all came together to throw their weight behind the defenses where they could. It was an admirable thought, but when faced with the Demons, most of those men would be cut down before they could even bring their spears to bear.

The Gremen core force defended the eastern flank with Howlter personally leading them. He had no cavalry with him, but he did have twice as many trained warriors. The Gremen would likely hold longer than the humans did.

"Eight hours," Aurin broke the silence, referring to the timeline given by the General from Krossfarin.

"Minutes will count on a field like this," she confirmed. "The wolves did their job well, we're trapped here."

He stared at the rank and file Demons. "If we could break the Demons they would have to flee. If only we could break the hold on those men out there."

"Big 'ifs'," she confirmed. "Any idea how to break them?"

Aurin sighed heavily before dropping his hand back to his sword, "no." He turned to face her, his blue eyes finding hers. "Short of killing them, I don't know how to release them." To a purely strategic mind, killing the enemy officers was logical, especially if the troops would break instantly, but these were not men that had made a choice to take the field. He had told her of the taken and what Dorne told him of

Caliban and his dark magic. Even now, the pain of those he had killed at the Balen still reflected in his eyes. Eyes that sparkled like ice melting in the spring.

"Your sword freed the wolves, couldn't it do the same here?"

His hand came away from the sword. "It couldn't save my father."

Cheers suddenly sprang up from the far end of the Guard line. Two figures had broken from the forest not far from the front lines. The lead was a grey-skinned man with a single stripe of hair running the length of his scalp, the other was a teenage boy wearing light armor under a tabard. It dawned on her that this was the disappeared Ryat and his apprentice, the last of the wizards that had left them shortly after the Balen to try to find a cure for the young man. The two were riding hard, they had been pursued initially, but after they neared the lines, the Guard bowmen turned their followers away.

Ryat reigned his horse at the center of the defensive line, "on your feet again Tor? We're going to need you." The half-Solterran climbed from his horse and handed the reins to a squire who had stepped up to assist. "The Demons have closed off most of the forest between here and Krossfarin, there are tens of thousands of them. Any word from the city?"

"Bjorn the Black promised he'd be here in half a day. Where have you been?"

"We were in the city, some of my old classmates and students have taken up there. We were trying to find a way to heal Dian's injury." Crowlmer had heard that the apprentice became crippled in their escape from the city, burning the magic out of himself by using too much power in a single day.

"Did you succeed?" Aurin could read the answer from the man's face, the same as she could, but it was polite to ask.

"No," Ryat started. "He still has the ability to use magic, just not the ability to generate it himself."

Dian hung his head, "I can direct the spells Master Ryat casts, but my pool is gone."

Horns tore their attention from the poor boy and back to the oncoming horde. Demonic weapons dropped along the front line of the force as they slowly marched forward. Drums beat cadence from the back of their lines, slowly increasing in tempo until the Demons broke into a run, just inside of bow range.

Aurin's sword leapt to his hand, "I guess it is time."

Crowlmer drew the twin swords from her hips and whispered the command to activate their magic. Her own magic pulsed within her, giving her an augmented view. Auras of light surrounded everyone around her, ranging in colors from Aurin's pure white to the deep obsidian of the Demons. She had seen the colors on occasion since her return from the forest, but never like this. Aurin's light was so pervasive that it seemed to leak into the men around him, overtaking their own meager colors and swelling them with his presence. Silently they watched as he slowly marched to the front of the line. No one challenged him as he moved through the ranks, some seemed to know he was coming before he raised his hand to touch their shoulders. Crowlmer followed in his wake, Ryat and Dian remained at the rear of the line. Ryat was already working his own magic into spells of destruction and sending them forth. To her new sight, they appeared as bright flares of crimson laced with greys and blues. The spells' effect was terrifying, rank upon rank of Demons, and the men leading them, incinerated instantly as the magic ripped through them. With her new sight, she could see the Demonic obsidian auras winking out as each of them died, but the humans were another matter.

    A leash of multihued light seemed to extend from their bodies and vanish into the air above them, almost like the strings of a puppet. She could feel things emanating from those threads. Whatever those threads connected to didn't want to be there and it was afraid.

Within the obsidian swirls, she could make out forms. Creatures moved through the magic, Demons in their own right, but without the physical form to act on this plane. These creatures occupied the flesh of the men, but not like a spirit occupying a dead body. The men still lived. What lurked at the other end of that leash? The creatures were hideous, twisted things that may once have been humanoid, but had long ago given up that guise. Their ethereal selves were marked by a single pair of pale, glowing eyes. The shadow of horns sprouted from what was once their heads and the trails of their arms ended in wisps of claws.

    Horrified, she watched as the creatures that possessed the dead and dying men hauled on those multihued threads, pulling the souls of the damned with them into a yawning black abyss that was slowly building above the battlefield. The Demons were taking the souls with them to whatever Hell they had spawned from.

She was so stunned by the apparitions that she nearly dropped her swords when Aurin screamed at her, "Not the time for daydreams, Crowlmer, wake up and get in the fight. Try to spare the men if you can." She watched Aurin cut his way into the ranks of Demons before them, his guardsmen on either of his flanks. His blade flashed through the Demons, but the edge never strayed to the humans among them. Rather than cutting them down, he left himself exposed to counters and additional blows from the Demons as he used the flat of his sword, or simply his fist, to incapacitate the humans.

She followed him into the fray, her enchanted swords cleaving through the Demons as if they were air. She avoided the men as best she could, especially considering what she had witnessed within her new sight. The fighting was terrible, men fell all around them as she and Aurin struggled to maintain their center. Bodies piled up, some still screaming for aid as the Demons poured over and around them. Inevitably, they lost ground, sacrificing their forward position for the smallest chance at defense. The Demons pushed them back behind the ramparts where fresh Guardsmen waited to spell them.

"How long do we have to hold?" One of the men asked as he slurped water from a proffered ladle.

"Too long," Aurin muttered loud enough for only her ears.

Crowlmer bent to drink from the ladle but stopped short, "Adla?"

Aurin's head snapped around at the mention of the small girl's name. "What are you doing here?"

"I wanted to help," she told them. "I know nothing about fighting and I'm too small to use one of those big bows, so I was sent out with water."

"You shouldn't be here Adla, it's going to get bad, real bad," Crowlmer admonished. "You should go back with the families waiting in their wagons."

"And wait to die like a lamb at slaughter?" Adla snapped harshly, "no, I should be right here, making sure the Captain doesn't murder innocents like he did at the Balen!"

Aurin's eyes dropped to the ground, this wasn't the first time he had heard that comment. Had it been Adla that had convinced him he was a murderer?

"Enough Adla!" Crowlmer shouted over the rising noise of battle, "Aurin did what he had to do that day. I was there, if he hadn't used his magic we would all have died then." A Guardsmen dropped from the ramparts above them, a Demon's spear standing erect from his chest. He was struggling for air, but it was no use, the spear had hit his heart.

Adla gasped and shrank back from the dying man. "How many have to die?" Tears leaked down her cheeks, smearing the dirt and grime that had built up there. It was only then that Crowlmer noticed the lack of an aura about the girl. Her new sight was still active, Aurin still shone like a noon sun but the small girl was completely devoid of any light. Even the Demons light offered its shine, to see Adla without left her unnerved.

"They're breaking through!" The Guards called from the ramparts above them.

Two men bearing signal flags set to passing the word to their small force of cavalry to charge forth, and break the Demons momentum. The men rushed out on their farm horses, swinging axes and throwing pitchforks instead of swords and spears. It would have been comical at any other time in her life, but today it was tragic. They were being slaughtered, even with the extra weight of their horses they just weren't a match for the well trained Demons.

Adla flopped in the dirt holding, her head in her hands as more empty than full saddles returned from the foray. The charge had worked, the Demons had pulled back but it was the last time the cavalry would be able to break them. One charge and their cavalry had been decimated.

You need to break them. A voice broke through to her mind. *Drive the demons out of their commanders and the others turn to a mindless mass of death. They'll tear themselves apart.*

Crowlmer looked for the source of the voice, but no one was near enough to be speaking to her in such hushed tones. "Who are you?" She spoke aloud, drawing a concerned look from Aurin.

I'm you, or I was one hundred and fifty years ago.

"Krelmer?" She asked aloud, turning even more heads from the Guards around her.

"Are you alright Crowlmer?" Aurin asked, looking more than a little confused.

They can't hear me, I'm not really here. Krelmer's voice told her. *We're all here, back to the beginning of the Just. Its time you learned.*

Crowlmer felt her spirit lift from her body and swirl away as it had in the tomb. She was whisked to a scene much like the last stand of the Just, only time wasn't moving.

In our time, Caliban sought to use men to control the Demons in a similar fashion, but his ritual had been poorer, less complete. We were able to break his hold over the men with our own, simply by reasserting the banishment of the Demons that sought to control them. Her focus turned to a single armored figure standing at the head of a column. With his great mallet, he launched a wave of ice blue energy into the ranks of demons before him. Those that had been taken crumpled under the power, their demonic possessors driven from their bodies, and the tether that kept their spirits tied to them pulled their souls back to the mortal world. As their commanders dropped, the Demons turned on one another, tearing their brethren limb from limb. The men facing them dropped behind their shields and waited as the slaughter worked itself out, killing any Demon that sought to break their line. The Demons farthest from the wave seemed to hold their discipline.

What of those? Crowlmer asked of the voice.

Barrah's generals, and Caliban, have the ability to control the Demons around them, but it is limited. Caliban sought to extend this by giving the power to others, but there were few volunteers. He was forced to take men against their will. Those closest to the generals will maintain their order.

The battle dissolved into a stark field of grey, like a swamp in the morning. A single figure stepped from the darkness, a female Gremen wearing the armor that Crowlmer now bore.

After our order failed, Caliban was free to perfect his magic. Barrah's banishment slowed him, but he still finished his ritual. The men here are his, taken by his dark magic, the magic of his true lord, Lookai. Now I fear that only you remain to disrupt his magic.

Krelmer held out her hands, *use this to drive the Demons from the taken.* A flash of light produced a Warhammer similar to the one the man in the vision had used. *Take heart young one, others will fear you for now but the time of the Just will come again.* The mist began to disappear and Crowlmer felt a strong pull from her navel.

With a lurch, she was back behind the ramparts, Warhammer in hand. Her body hadn't moved, but her swords were returned to the sheaths at her sides. "What just happened?" Aurin demanded, concern lining his features.

"Promise me you'll stay out of what comes next." Crowlmer begged the young man.

"What are you talking about? Where did the hammer come from?" Aurin reached for her, but she pushed his hand away.

"Keep the men behind the wall and keep their shields up."

Adla remained huddled where she had dropped, her face in her hands. Crowlmer reached down and placed a hand on the small girl's shoulder, smiling briefly as the girl looked at her. She released the girl and made for the defenses.

Men seemed to know what she intended. As they had with Aurin, they simply moved from her path as she stepped onto the ramparts and, without risking a backward glance, leapt into the mass of Demons below.

Queen

The fire welled within Ardelle, energy that she couldn't hope to hold on her own. Betala's presence swelled again as flames burst from her back. Two swan's wings stretched from her shoulder blades in direct mimicry of the Harpy's wings. With a twist of her arms that felt unnatural, the wings slammed downward, sending her into the air like an arrow from a bow.

Ezra has forgotten that it was I that gave them wings! The ferocity of Betala's presence was not something Ardelle was used to. The Harpies that had gathered at the crown tower scattered as Ardelle barreled into their formation, Ezra diving while those nearest her climbed. Betala reached back with Ardelle's arm and pulled the gleaming sword from over her shoulder. With a masterful stroke, two Harpies fell away, each missing a single wing. There was no resistance to the blade, the edge was so sharp that it passed straight through bone and sinew as if it were paper. Two more Harpies dove to meet them, but their weapons were no match for her sword. One blade simply shattered when Betala struck it, the other was split in twain as the Arcana pressed her attack into the Harpies body. With a simple release of will, deep blue flames leapt to wreath the blade.

This weapon is magnificent. The Arcana's compliment would have brought color to her cheeks had she been in control of her body. The weapon was truly remarkable, Omesh's skill with the steel and her magic had created a perfect instrument of death.

Ezra joined the battle with two more of her Harpies, sending fire at them in narrow beams. Betala let the power come, absorbing the energy into their growing pool just before it struck her flesh.

"Did you think you could turn my own power against me, traitor?" Ardelle's voice chided as she struck the two remaining Harpies from the air with bursts of power directed through the sword. "I should have striped you of your life when I took my boon from you."

Ezra dove into Betala with such fury that Ardelle feared they wouldn't be able to stay in the air. Their blades collided in a shock of magic-fueled energy that pulsed in every direction and threw the remaining two Harpies well clear of the conflict. Fire rippled in every direction as Ezra launched another barrage of magic, this time too fast for Betala to simply absorb. The sword served as a rudimentary shield, splitting the rays evenly as they struck its polished surface. Betala struck back with fire of her own, but a field of obsidian energy leapt into being around the Harpy and staved off the onslaught.

"My lord has not left me without gifts, false god." Ezra unfurled her wings from her body and snapped them down in one rapid motion, carrying her up and away from Betala's magic. "Would you like to see what a true god's power looks like?" Ribbons of that same obsidian energy shot from the core of Ezra's body and spun themselves into a single entity above her head. A dragon of pure black magic curled its way out from the coalescing energy, roaring furiously as it shot toward Betala and her flaming wings. Betala threw up a shield of flames, but the creature barreled straight through them. She dropped the magic that held them aloft just before the lightless fangs reached their shared body, dropping them from its reach, but removing any thought of a counter attack.

Betala called the wings back into being and sailed around the tower gaining altitude, flapping the flames frantically to stay ahead of the dragon that had barely paused in its pursuit of them. Black fire ripped from its gaping jaws, tearing hungrily at their heels as Betala struggled to maintain their dwindling lead on the creature. She sent more fire into the creature, but it had the same effect as the shield. Their magic would be of no use against this monstrosity.

They rounded the tower once more, spotting Ezra once again. The black lines of power still snaked their way from her body, as it hung transfixed in the air. Her head was back as if in the throes of passion, or perhaps immense pain. Betala turned their mage sight on the Harpy queen and discovered that all semblance of the pure fire was gone. Only the obsidian energy remained, rapidly being pulled into the creature that sought them. There was something else, something that shadowed the mad queen and gave a false light to her features. Something strained against the bounds of her mortal form, a creature of such magnitude that Ardelle could feel the weight of its presence in the air around her.

Barrah, her mistress whispered within their shared mind. *He seeks to cross over to this realm to escape the punishment we laid upon him, but our magic should prevent it.* Concern washed through their link. *He's too far into the world already, something is wrong.*

The shadow dragon chased them toward Ezra, but a sudden burst of magic sent them within striking distance of the petrified Harpy. Their sword arced forward to strike, but an errant blast of the obsidian energy struck their chest and sent them careening toward the earth. The world spun around them as Betala struggled to right their fall, stopping only a handbreadth from the ground. The dragon caught them as they tried to climb again, its black fire lancing pain up Ardelle's spine. The sudden blast interrupted the concentration from the linked Arcana and dropped them from the air. Their fiery wings evaporated as they slammed into the cool earth, their magic requiring too much concentration for their pain wracked body. Barrah's magic lanced through them, its power ripping through their shared body like a predator. Muscles contracted, bones creaked and Ardelle was confident she heard one of them break under the onslaught of the vile energy. Parts of her seemed to shear away as the magic ate into her being. Betala saved her from losing herself completely with a surge of fresh power from her domain, but the Arcana seemed to be flagging.

I can't continue to function at this level within your plane daughter. There are laws of nature that prevent overt interference from my kind, I can aid you where balance is a concern, but this is stretching my capabilities.

"What's the matter, false god?" Ezra cackled as she settled to the earth near them. The dragon had receded but the dark stain of Barrah's power still shone within the Harpy. "Have your powers given out?" The Harpy raised her hand and squeezed it into a fist.

The effects were instantaneous. The swirling tendrils of Barrah's magic slammed straight along her body's magical focal points, stopping her own magic from flowing freely within her. Her limbs refused to move and her hand cramped so hard that her sword fell away uselessly.

"Your powers pale in comparison to the true lord. Nothing you have ever done here will compare to what he can do. You are a worm before him. That is why he shunned you and took me as his wife. I gave him something you never could, a mortal son. How does it feel to have been useless in giving him the power he desired? How does it feel to be rejected in favor of a mortal?" Ezra's eyes lit upon Ardelle's presence within their shared body. "And you, false Avatar, how does it feel to be the second choice? I was always the more powerful, the better suited to carry the mantle. Harpies will always be the children of fire and our dominion will be complete once my lord has returned to his rightful place among the heavens."

Ardelle could feel Betala struggling to maintain the link between them, but the bonds were slipping. Her power was fading slowly and Ardelle could do nothing to aid her. The hateful magic still coursed through them, blocking all access to their own power. *Don't leave me!* She begged her mistress.

They are sapping my power, daughter. Through you they can steal magic directly from me! The link dimmed further. *That has been their plan, they never sought us directly, but our avatars!* The connection vanished from within her and pain exploded throughout her body at the sudden absence of Betala's magic. An involuntarily scream burst from her lips.

"She left you, didn't she?" Ezra purred as she stepped closer, relaxing her fist as she did so. "Such a coward, your mistress. My lord would never abandon me."

The pain subsided slightly. "Your lord abandoned his last Avatar when she needed him most. He left her to suffer for his decision."

"The Gremen bitch wasn't worthy of his gift!" Ezra snarled, "I was there when that mistake was ended, and the gift passed to a more suitable body." Her fist came up and the pain returned to Ardelle in spades, "but now is not the time to dwell on the past. The future is already written, pitiful creature. I will have Betala's power and I will rule alongside my lord. My son will inherit this plane and all will bow before him!" More magic rippled from her other hand, bands of obsidian wrapping Ardelle, lifting her from the ground. "But first, I will destroy one more barrier to my lord's return." She bent and retrieved Ardelle's sword from the dirt.

"Release her!" A voice boomed from behind Ardelle, familiar but stronger than she remembered.

A peel of laughter erupted out of Ezra, "and who are you to command me, cripple? You who can't even walk without a woman to support you."

"I," Charles shouted confidently, "am the Chavox." It was a desperate play that Ardelle only understood when Charles and Clornamti came into view. Charles' left leg was broken savagely below the knee, and his right arm hung uselessly from his shoulder. She couldn't use her mage sight, but given the extent of his injuries and his normal ability to heal, she guessed that he had no magic left to him.

Ezra's eyes widened slightly at the admission of his identity, then narrowed as she took in his pathetic state. "You think your name alone will stop me?"

The magic about Ardelle relaxed, but not enough to free her. She could feel the magic within her again, still heightened from Betala's presence and the magic they absorbed from the fires around them. It was nothing compared to the power that Barrah gave Ezra. She ran the scenarios over and over, but as long as Barrah walked with Ezra, she didn't have a chance.

"Release her, now, or you'll not live to regret it." Charles looked dangerous, even with his crippled arm and leg. Was it all bluster? What could he still have?

Ezra spat at Charles. "After I kill you, I will finish her. With you gone, my lord has nothing to fear from the mortal plane, prophecy or no." The bindings about Ardelle eased further and she could feel the poisonous magic fading. Ezra was drawing the magic back into herself for a strike.

She wanted to warn her friend, but she needed the distraction. The power within her was almost within her reach. She pulled with everything she had against Barrah's taint, but the magic was just out of her control. If she could just get a fraction of that power, she could strike.

Something about Charles had set the Harpy on edge, she feared him despite his physical handicap. The prophecy had been clear for them, this man was the only thing that could stop Barrah and if he could stop a fallen Arcana, what hope did Ezra have? Ardelle could almost see the internal argument within the Harpy queen.

"Enough!" The winged woman shouted finally, "You die, now!" The black fire leapt from her talons toward the hobbled young man, but it never struck.

An orb of crimson light leapt from Charles' throat and enveloped the incoming power, pulling it into him. Ezra screamed in shock, but the magic continued to flow from her, much as it had with her dragon earlier. Ardelle's bindings vanished completely, the poison within her receded until she could no longer feel its presence. She dropped to all fours and sucked in a glorious breath of air before turning her attention to the Harpy.

The black mass of Barrah's power rapidly vanished into the vortex created by Charles' power, soon Ezra dropped to her knees, tears in her eyes. "Don't go my lord! I need you!" Barrah had left her. Just as Betala had fled the power stealing energy, Barrah had retracted his connection to save his own magic. In her angst, Ezra let go of Ardelle's sword.

Ardelle gathered her power into her legs and launched herself at the Harpy, barreling into her back with enough force to send the queen sprawling. She snatched up her sword and rolled to her feet, swinging wildly at the other woman but catching only air. Ezra kept her body tight after the impact, rolling with the blow as Ardelle had done, but as the momentum lagged, she threw herself into the air. Sharply, she drew two flaming lines into the air that coalesced into a blade of fire. Ezra dove back toward Ardelle, a scream leaving her lips so full of rage and pain that it drove straight to the heart.

Ardelle snapped her sword up in a guard, adding her own power to the latent magic of the blade, summoning a solid shield of flames. The block intercepted the Harpy but her impact still drove Ardelle's back leg from beneath her. Instead of dropping to her knee, Ardelle leapt into another roll, slashing at Ezra's legs. She bounded to her feet and met another series of strikes from the Harpy, blow for blow. The Harpy wore a mask of rage, her attacks a chopping strike like she was attempting to split cord wood. The jarring blows kept coming, but Ardelle managed to turn them enough to keep from losing her blade. At several points she riposted, drawing lines in the flesh of the Harpy, but the queen ignored the injuries. Fire lashed from the queen's off-hand in a whip that would have scored the flesh from a bull, but Ardelle countered with her own magic and broke the enchantment before the Harpy could land a blow.

Lances of fire followed the lash, but these were easily deflected by a whirling shield of flames rapidly conjured from Ardelle's free hand. The attacks intensified, all thoughts of further magic driven from both combatants as they focused entirely on the swords in their hands. Blades whirled and danced as their wielders ducked and spun between them. A near miss seared a line in Ardelle's forearm, but her counter bit deep into Ezra's shoulder. More blows rained from the Harpy, but her body was flagging. Crimson blood ran from dozens of cuts over her arms and torso, each drop of the blood seemed to take something from the winged woman.

A wild swing left an opening within Ezra's guard and Ardelle capitalized with a thrust. Her blade erupted from the queen's back as the Harpy's limbs went limp around her. Ezra dropped to her knees once more, tears glistening on her cheeks as she sucked in one last breath. As the light left her eyes, her breath rattled out her last words, "I'm sorry."

The Harpy Queen's body fell to the side, pulling Ardelle's sword free as it did so. The fire within her blade blazed so hot that the blood burned away instantly. It was over, but what did that mean?

Epilogue: Reunions

Aurin walked the battlefield again, his eyes scanning for any sign of life among the tens of thousands that had perished on the field. Crowlmer's magic devastated the Demon ranks, that wave of icy blue energy dropped every man that had been with them to the ground before they even had a chance to register what was happening. The Demons began to tear themselves apart almost as quickly.

The defenders struggled to hold back the horde at first, but the Demon numbers quickly diminished. The Demons didn't want to come after the men on the walls, not when there were so many of their own kind so close. After several minutes of wanton destruction, he led a small force out of the walls to retrieve as many of the stunned men as he could. The Demons had gotten to some of them as well, but for the most part they escaped notice. Crowlmer hadn't fared as well.

Her initial leap into the Demons gave them ample time to tear at her, ripping rents in her armor as though it were sheaves of paper. She had barely survived long enough to call forth her magic. Aurin carried her to Castielle himself, refusing aid from the guards around him. She rested there now, among the handful of wounded that had been too badly injured to move on to Krossfarin. She had only opened her eyes once and seeing that it was he that carried her she had smiled slightly and dropped back into unconsciousness, without uttering a word, still clutching the hammer.

The refugees had moved on. Once the Demons had been set loose, the remaining forces under Barrah's generals fled the field. He still didn't know for certain if it had been

Caliban leading them personally, or if it had been some other general. He and Dorne had discussed it at length after the battle, both wishing they had a chance at the man.

The Demons that had assaulted their eastern defenses had been spared Crowlmer's magic, even her impressive display had its limits. Their commanders had fled with the rest, suddenly feeling outnumbered with the threat of Krossfarin so close.

Krossfarin had been true to their word, arriving at midday with a force that would have broken the bulk of the Demons had Crowlmer not done it for them. Bjorn the Black had led them personally. He had slapped Aurin on the back when he heard the tale of how the battle turned, claiming that he knew Aurin would come up with something just like at the Balen. He refused to give the credit to Crowlmer, despite Aurin's repeated insistence that it was her sacrifice. Eventually, Aurin could take no more of the man's misogyny and left him with Howlter to discuss the moving of the refugees.

The battle was won, he was still alive. Why did he feel so empty inside?

He turned back to face north once more, staring off into the sky. A small shape appeared there, a small carriage born by six smaller figures. A litter from the Oberon, their newly arrived allies from Heimili álfa, but why would it be this far out? There was nothing here but a makeshift hospital and the corpses of thousands of demons.

The litter descended slowly, landing not far from him, its gilded door swinging wide almost before it had finished its descent.

"Aurin!" A familiar voice called as two figures dashed from the litter and bowled him over.

Black fire swirled about her body as she rose from the pits. Her lover was there, standing with his arms crossed and eyeing her with suspicion. "How could you let that wench kill you?" he demanded.

She hung her head at his judgment. She had failed and with her failure she had lost him the edge he had held over Betala. With her death, the full powers of her former mistress had been returned. "I'm sorry master, that creature stole my powers and drove you from me. I wasn't strong enough to face the bitch alone."

"I was driven nowhere!" Barrah spat, "I felt you could handle things without me and left you to finish the deed. Now my former consort is back and I've still got nine Avatars to kill!" His pride had been hurt by the Chavox's spell. Barrah would never admit it, but she had felt the fear within him when he had fled.

Laughter drew her attention away from her master. A dark figure rose from the shadows near the entrance to the chamber. "It wasn't her fault that boy beat you Barrah." Lookai in all his dark glory chuckled as he settled near her. His serpentine smile sent a chill down her spine, "If you had listened to me and killed the boy when he was still swaddled then this would never have happened."

"You know I couldn't do that Lookai, the prophecy demands that I face the last Chavox and through him regain my seat as Lord of the Arcana. Without his lifeless corpse and his power to fuel the ritual, I'll be stuck in this hideous demon skin forever." Her master's violet flesh pulsed as he flexed. He was still beautiful, but it was true that he had lost something during his fall. That horned face wasn't the face of the man she had fallen in love with.

"No, the prophecy says that you must face *A Chavox*. It says nothing of it being the last, or even of Victor's line. You made him the last when you butchered his family and tortured those that survived until they were lifeless puppets." The Arcana of Death drifted closer to Barrah as he continued, "You had Stephen in your hands at the fall but you chose to make him one of your demons rather than leaving him for last. Sending him after the boy in his dreams was even more foolish. Thormane drove any sanity he had left from his skull when the boys beat him in the Druid's temple."

Stephen's mind had been destroyed in that attack. His body was intact and his powers were as strong as ever but he was little more than a tool now. He served as a magical storage vessel for Barrah's demon commanders on the mortal plane. Caliban kept him close and used him in his experiments. The plan had been to use Stephen to render Charles insane, given Barrah an easy victory but Stephen had sought to use the boy for his revenge against the Druids.

She had tried to clean up the mess with Drech by posing as Druids, but Waliyt had stopped them. Barrah nearly flayed the man for his arrogance, but Waliyt still held a great deal of her lord's power within him. Killing him would strip

Barrah of the magic he still needed if he was to retake his place among the Arcana.

"Your arrogance will be your end, Barrah." Lookai jabbed a finger at her lord's chest. "I told you to wait, consolidate your power among your fellow Aracana before you move against Betala, but you ignored me. You lusted for her Avatar, this feeble, powerless creature I've had to resurrect. You have nothing left of your former glory, not even the soul I tied to you when you fell. Your powers are out there now, former Lord of Justice, sitting in the body of some worthless human and yet you still ignore me."

"Enough!" Barrah boomed. "I've had enough of your scheming, Lookai. I will conquer the mortals, my way, and when I do I will use their power to kill the other Arcana. I will be lord of all and I will honor those that have served me faithfully."

The Lord of Death merely smiled his serpentine smile as he drifted away. "As you wish Barrah."

She knew it wouldn't be the last she heard from Lookai, something in that smile chilled her to the bone.

Made in the USA
Charleston, SC
22 December 2015